Contents

Volume 11 Issue 3

I0592948

Luxurious Sexualities: effeminacy, consumption, and the body politic in eighteenth-century representation
Edited by Mary Peace and Vincent Quinn

Articles

Contents

Contents

Contributions should be double spaced, and two copies should be sent. Address: Alan Sinfield, Textual Practice, Arts B, Sussex University, Brighton BN1 9QN, England.

Books for review should be addressed to Peter Nicholls, Arts B, Sussex University, Brighton BN1 9QN, England.

Advertisements. Enquiries to Routledge Journals, 2 Park Square, Milton Park, Abingdon, Oxon, OX14 4RN, UK; e-mail jadvertising@routledge.com

Subscription rates (calendar year only): UK full: £78.00; UK personal: £27.00; Rest of World full: £84.00; Rest of World personal: £27.00; USA full: $80.00; USA personal: $47.00. All rates include postage; airmail rates on application. Subscriptions to: Subscriptions Department, Routledge Journals, Cheriton House, North Way, Andover, Hants SP10 5BE.
Sample copy requests, e-mail sample.journals@routledge.com

ISSN 0950–236X
Typeset by Keystroke, Jacaranda Lodge, Wolverhampton
© Routledge 1997

Vincent Quinn and Mary Peace

Luxurious Sexualities

For many years, 'the eighteenth century' meant political corruption, Augustan satire and the rise of the novel – or, in the words of Sylvia Plath, 'all those smug men writing tight little couplets and being so dead keen on reason'.[1] Academic accounts of the period were restricted to discrete narratives with little interplay between the disciplines. Preoccupations such as the growth of the middle classes recurred in a variety of contexts, but there was rarely any sense that historians could learn from philosophers, or art historians from geographers. Fortunately this is no longer the case. Post-structuralist formations have encouraged a more sophisticated and interdisciplinary approach to period study and as a result we have a range of 'new' eighteenth centuries; not all of these are structured around 'theory' but few are wholly untouched by it.[2] Therefore, although some doyens of the period demonstrate a touchingly uncritical belief in a monolithic 'enlightenment', not many contemporary commentators are likely to represent satire or the novel as self-sufficient genres that can be detached from culture (in its widest sense) or from theories of readership and textual production.

However, despite fresh work from a range of critical perspectives, undergraduates still tend to perceive the eighteenth century in terms similar to those used by Plath to describe her 1950s education. One aim of the *Luxurious Sexualities* conference (which took place in Brighton on 7 December, 1996, under the aegis of the University of Sussex)[3] was that the event should reach beyond Plath's 'Whigs in wigs' view of the eighteenth century to explore some of the period's newer incarnations. By bringing together scholars from several disciplines, the conference aimed to demonstrate the eighteenth century's crucial position in late twentieth-century histories of sexuality, gender, ethnicity and class. Without indulging in a misguided search for mythical origins – and without pretending that 'modern' cultures and modern academic perspectives

Textual Practice 11(3), 1997, 405–416   © 1997 Routledge 0950–236X

are anything other than the latest in a series of historically contingent formations – it is possible to argue that scholars specializing in other fields might profit from paying closer attention to eighteenth-century studies. As it is, the period is still perceived as a poor relation, squeezed between Romanticism and the Renaissance.

If this is the general background from which the conference arose, a little more should be said about the terms that its title foregrounds. The next section of this introduction looks at the development of modern histories of eighteenth-century luxury and sexuality, and at how these concepts came to be united in our title. By bringing 'luxury' and 'sexuality' into a more explicit dialogue, the conference aimed to point to new possibilities in the formation, and re-formation, of eighteenth-century studies. The articles which follow are both a record of that dialogue and an extension of it.

Luxury and sexuality

John Sekora's *Luxury: The Concept in Western Thought, Eden to Smollett* (1977) was the first book to attempt a modern history of luxury. By using Foucault's notion of 'discourse' (a scholarly novelty at that time), Sekora was able to explore luxury's position within 'a network of fluctuating social, philosophic, and theological presuppositions'.[4] He examined the mutations that the concept has undergone and argued that the classical notion of luxury as a debilitating over-indulgence was replaced, in the late eighteenth century, by our contemporary understanding of luxury as a pleasant and relatively harmless affluence. In a way, Sekora's enormously wide-ranging text offers us the other side of the eighteenth-century progress poem – a genre that sought to validate Britain's claim on cultural and economic pre-eminence by following the travels of Liberty on her way from Roman corruption to a British safe haven.[5] By giving us the progress of Luxury, not Liberty, Sekora demonstrates the prominent role that luxury plays in early modern socio-political debate; and in doing so he also – almost incidentally – shows that notions of liberty and luxury are inextricably linked.[6]

Sekora's book is still extremely useful, not least because it demonstrates the frequency with which eighteenth-century commentators used the words of Cicero, Sallust and Seneca to warn their enlightenment contemporaries of the dangers of moral laxity in an age of empire: as the following articles demonstrate, classical accounts of luxurious decay echo constantly throughout the new Augustan age. However, the scope of the book and its frustratingly linear scheme lead Sekora in the direction of some dangerous generalizations, such as where he asserts that the 'classical' version of luxury 'extended from the rule of Moses to that of George III'.[7] This belief in a transhistorical tradition is confirmed when Sekora notes that the attack on luxury 'is the mode of Cato and Seneca, the *Republic* and the *City of God, Paradise Lost* and *Aureng-Zebe, Joseph Andrews* and *The Deserted Village;* of Swift and Bolingbroke, Davenant and John Brown'.[8] Luxury is certainly a preoccupation for these writers, but it seems unwise to argue that their texts are arranged wholly around it, or that their cultural contexts are sufficiently similar for them to share an identical understanding of the term. Sekora's justification of his position is that luxury is 'one of the very few traditional concepts in which aspects of change were inherent', and that it therefore 'accommodated change [and] absorbed it'.[9] But this is too easy – Sekora has elided enormous national and historical differences in his search for a seamlessly coherent version of 'classical' luxury.

Sekora derives much of his historical framework from J. G. A. Pocock's explorations of the relationship between political theory and political language; in particular, Sekora uses Pocock to sanction his argument that concepts of luxury are static before the eighteenth century but change decisively during the enlightenment.[10] It is possible to challenge this position (or to argue that Sekora is misinterpreting Pocock), but it is clear from the articles which follow that Pocock remains an important influence on eighteenth-century studies. His work does not emphasize luxury to the same extent that Sekora's does, but Pocock has investigated parallel issues, such as civic virtue and the health of the nation state. Moreover, he has insisted that 'notions of refinement and politeness . . . were crucial elements in the ideology of eighteenth-century commerce'.[11] This is significant given that politeness and refinement are recurring terms in the debate over effeminacy, as well as in the economic sphere with which Pocock is concerned. So although Pocock does not analyse effeminacy *per se*, his work none the less represents the beginnings of a fruitful overlap between social and economic history. In addition, by showing such an interest in the social frameworks that surround commerce, Pocock has made it possible to pursue a more fluidly 'cultural' approach to political history. Especially important in this area is his development of the concepts of civic humanism and classical republicanism, both of which are invoked elsewhere in this volume.[12]

John Sekora's book provoked much new interest in luxury but the next full-length account of the topic only came in 1994, when Christopher Berry published *The Idea of Luxury: A Conceptual and Historical Investigation.* This followed a less chronological scheme than Sekora's book and adopted a more explicitly political agenda. Berry shared Sekora's sense that the discourse on luxury was conditioned by, and helped to structure, a broad variety of modern social phenomena, including the language of advertising and consumption. Like Sekora, Berry stressed the importance of the eighteenth century in bringing these phenomena to birth; he also argued, rightly, that the topic of luxury 'straddles various academic disciplines, bringing together issues of philosophy, history, anthropology, theology and economics as well as politics'.[13] However Berry's list of disciplines omits the field that was most important in Sekora's book, namely literary studies. So while Berry's book usefully foregrounds social politics, it sidelines the questions of textuality that Sekora was keen to uncover in his culminating re-evaluation of Smollett. That said, both Berry and Sekora follow agendas that take them away from key aspects of social history – especially questions of gender and sexuality. Given that classical and eighteenth-century anti-luxury writers dwell at length on eunuchs, mannish women and the effeminate, it is a shame that neither Sekora nor Berry address the different ways in which these categories have been represented through history. Nor do they fully consider the part that sexual politics might have played in maintaining the visibility of the luxury debate.

At around the same time that Sekora was using Foucauldian notions of discourse to delineate luxury, some social historians and literary scholars were beginning to exploit another element of Foucault's thought, namely his emerging work on sexuality. Mary McIntosh had anticipated aspects of this project in her 1968 essay, 'The Homosexual Role'; in *Coming Out: Homosexual Politics in Britain* (1977), Jeffrey Weeks used Macintosh's work, plus the first volume of *The History of Sexuality*, to explore the emergence of the modern sex-gender system.[14] The first chapter of *Coming Out* concentrated on the nineteenth century, so Weeks (who is both an academic and a gay activist) was able to avoid the anachronistic assumption that pre-nineteenth-century sexual deviants could be appropriated as the direct forebears of twentieth-century homosexuality. By contrast, writers who turned their attention to the eighteenth century were in danger of eliding cultural differences in their understandable search for a linear history of sexual behaviour.

Nevertheless, the attention that lesbian and gay writers were paying to the eighteenth century meant that the categories ignored by Sekora and Berry were at last being addressed, albeit by historians who were generally less interested in the matter of luxury. The last chapter of Alan Bray's *Homosexuality in Renaissance England* (1982) tentatively suggested that the eighteenth century was the period in which homosexual subcultures began to develop in London; in particular, he looked at the 'mollies' who often appear in eighteenth-century anti-luxury and anti-sodomy tracts.[15] In the same year Paul-Gabriel Boucé edited the influential *Sexuality in Eighteenth-Century Britain*. Two of the contributors to this volume noted subsequently that Lawrence Stone had described the book as 'almost entirely unhelpful' because most of the contributors were literary scholars;[16] it was to counter such accusations from mainstream historians that Roy Porter and G. S. Rousseau produced *Sexual Underworlds of the Enlightenment* (1987), which used a multi-disciplinary approach to develop an alternative social history of the eighteenth century – one that could explore cross-dressing, prostitution and homosexual behaviour, as well as divorce and inheritance laws. From this point on, there was an increasing flow of material dealing with gender and sexuality in the eighteenth century. The attention of gay scholars put masculinity – in its most general sense – under the microscope so that figures such as fops, dandies and libertines began to be considered alongside sodomites and sapphists. Although still controversial, gender issues were no longer seen as a ghetto for lesbian and gay activists, while overall there was a growing sense that eighteenth-century gender roles were more complex than had previously been thought. One key development was that effeminacy could no longer be directly equated with same-sex desire. Susan Sontag may have located the origins of camp in the late seventeenth century, but writers such as Alan Bray have argued that Restoration effeminacy cannot be identified with twentieth-century notions of effeminacy-as-campness, let alone with specifically homosexual acts.[17] (In a similar way, it became problematic to appropriate all cross-dressing women as proto-lesbians.) Indeed the range of roles that seemed to be available in the eighteenth century for men, women and various forms of 'third sex' meant that it was becoming increasingly difficult for scholars to recover a simplistically linear history of either homosexuality or heterosexuality.

It would take too long to examine all the interventions that have been made in this area from the late 1980s to the present day. Besides Bray, Boucé, Rousseau and Porter, one thinks of Randolph Trumbach, Rictor Norton and Emma Donoghue,[18] but there are many others, including a number of European academics who have written on equivalent themes in Dutch and Scandinavian history.[19] Generally, though, most of the writers in this tradition have emphasized the importance of the written word, and have approached their subject matter from broadly empirical perspectives.

From the late 1970s through the early 1980s, therefore, there are two critical histories beginning to emerge one revolving around luxury as an economic or political discourse, and the other revolving around gender and sexuality. As our title suggests, this volume is intended to bring these threads together: to wed the sexual discourse to the economic one, and to show the interplay between the two. However, there is an additional dimension that tends to be absent from both the economic tradition and the sexual tradition. For example, Christopher Berry's list of the disciplines on which luxury impinges ('philosophy, history, anthropology, theology and economics as well as politics') implies a series of entirely verbal formations. The same has also been true of histories of sexual dissidence and gender dysfunction; although non-literary materials such as trial documents and anti-effeminacy tracts have frequently been used, many commentators tend not to address visual culture, or theories of representation. Therefore another aim of *Luxurious Sexualities* was to bring discursive theories of luxury and effeminacy into dialogue with work (such as Terry Castle's and Kristina Straub's) that has focused on representation and notions of spectatorship.

Terry Castle's *Masquerade and Civilisation* (1986) used a Bahktinian framework to investigate bodily identity and disguise in eighteenth-century fiction and society: besides interpreting canonical texts via visual culture, Castle's book re-invented public spaces as sites for exploring the relationship between public and private in eighteenth-century England. (A similar line was taken in the same year by Peter Stallybrass and Allon White in *The Politics and Poetics of Transgression*.)[20] Castle's subsequent work has demonstrated her continuing interest in the relationship between perception and the body, a field that has also been explored by Kristina Straub in *Sexual Suspects* (1992). Straub's analysis of eighteenth-century theatre examines (among other things) the gendering of eighteenth-century actors and theatre-goers; she explores the feminizing effects of the gaze, and the thrills of both spectatorship and exhibitionism. Straub's wide-ranging account of the politics of spectatorship is a cultural reconstruction that partly arises out of the empirical researches of Trumbach, Bray and others; indeed she acknowledges a debt to Trumbach on more than one occasion, even though they approach the eighteenth century from very different disciplinary backgrounds.[21] Without relying excessively on psychoanalytic notions of the gaze, Straub produced a text that was both epistemologically sophisticated and historically specific – for instance, in her detailed use of theatrical memoirs and her sensitivity to eighteenth-century philosophy.

Terry Castle's work on the masquerade and Straub's work on acting represent further stages in the coming together of the visual and verbal commentaries that were most pertinent to the *Luxurious Sexualities* conference. Historians of luxury confront us with an analysis of social and economic forces that necessarily involves an account of 'the body politic'. By contrast, historians of sexuality have explored issues such as transvestism and effeminacy so as to advance a different set of concerns – not so much 'the body politic' as 'body politics'. Such interests have been further supplemented by approaches that analyse visual culture and the objectification of gender roles; besides investigating verbal formations, it is therefore possible to turn one's gaze (literally and metaphorically) on to visual representations of some of the luxurious bodies of eighteenth-century culture. It was for this reason that we used the conference poster to showcase an image in which so many of these luxurious themes converge – namely plate IV of Hogarth's *Marriage-à-la-Mode*, with its references to *castrati*, adultery, the masquerade, national stereotyping and conspicuous consumption. Here typologies are rendered concrete for, as Lamb remarked, Hogarth's graphic works are 'books' which contain 'the teeming, fruitful, suggestive meaning of *words*. Other pictures we look at – his prints we read'.[22] Our hope is that the articles in this volume will form a body of their own in which different intellectual traditions come together in an equivalent melding of the graphic and the verbal, and of the luxurious and the sexual. To facilitate this, we have grouped the articles under titles indicating shared interests or complementary approaches; such categorizations are necessarily provisional – readers will doubtless construct alternative narratives in the light of their own disciplines and preoccupations.

Effeminacy reconsidered

The contributors in the first section of this collection – Cath Sharrock in 'Reviewing "the Spirit of Man-hood,"' and Philip Carter in 'An "effeminate" or "efficient" nation?' – share a wish to reconsider, in the light of recent historical work on eighteenth-century discourses of luxury, the simple equation of effeminacy with sodomy; an equation which the work of critics such as Trumbach has tended to promote.

Cath Sharrock argues that in ecclesiastical law effeminacy was understood to mean masturbation, and that sodomy and effeminacy had thus historically been coupled together as non-procreative, and were therefore sinful practices. This common identity, she suggests, was maintained through the secularization of sexual regulation which occurred in the sixteenth century. Medical texts, for example, tended to treat both acts as unhealthy modes of sexual practice on precisely the grounds of their non-procreativity. Focusing on an anti-sodomy pamphlet from 1728, Sharrock argues that, with the growth of empire in the eighteenth century, and the tendency to read contemporary history through classical paradigms, the non-procreative emphasis of the medical/Christian discourses on effeminacy was overlayered with narratives about the dangers of luxury. The sinful and unhealthy body of the effeminate, masturbating individual was increasingly read as an indication of the corrupt body of an effeminate, because luxurious, polity. Effeminacy in this discourse, she suggests, is associated with an idle aristocracy and is seen to pose a threat not just to their individual productivity, but to the productivity of the state as a whole. In such writing, Sharrock argues, sodomy is identified as just one of various non-procreative symptoms associated with effeminacy.

Philip Carter's critique of the simple equation of effeminacy with sodomy moves the argument further into the eighteenth century. Carter identifies two contrasting, but to some extent symbiotic, discourses on effeminacy: a civic humanist discourse, and a progressive discourse. Carter's civic-humanist discourse has much in common with the one Sharrock has described: he argues that this discourse represents effeminacy as the product of increased luxury and commerce, and that it implies a weakening of the individual body and a corruption of the body politic. Carter also, however, identifies the emergence of a progressive discourse which is concerned to transform the luxury associated with commerce from a social evil into a social stimulant. This progressive discourse is consequently concerned to redefine the idea of effeminacy so that it can accommodate the positive attributes of sensitivity, refinement, politeness and sentimentality; attributes which, it was argued, were essential to the health of commercial society. Carter, like Sharrock, argues that by automatically equating effeminacy with sodomy, we miss the broader cultural implications of the term. He also warns that by not taking on board the positive re-evaluation of effeminacy which takes place in the progressive discourse, the modern reader is liable to interpret the refined masculinity which it promotes, anachronistically, as a negative, 'unmanly' model.

Sites of pleasure and crisis

The second section of this collection moves us into the 1770s, and its contributors, Miles Ogborn in 'Locating the Macaroni' and Robert Jones in 'Notes on *The Camp*' are both exercised by the anxieties about sexual identity and gender roles which had been generated by the new public spaces of commodity culture: the pleasure gardens and the camp.

Miles Ogborn, from the perspective of new geography, takes as his text an incident which occurred at Vauxhall Pleasure Gardens in 1773, when Henry Bate, an Essex parson, was provoked into a fight after his female companion was disconcertingly ogled by a member of the notoriously fashionable, upper-class group of young men known as the Macaronis. Ogborn, while not questioning Carter's assertion that effeminacy in the later eighteenth century has to some extent been incorporated into a positive model of productive masculinity, identifies in the Macaroni a version of effeminacy which proves unrecuperable for narratives of commercial virtue. The Macaroni, he suggests, is a figure who, in uniting self-conscious posturing with conspicuous consumption, triggers anxieties about the systems of 'credit' on which a capitalist society depends; anxieties which are exacerbated by encountering such a figure in the illusory grandeur of Vauxhall Pleasure Gardens. In particular, Ogborn argues, the Macaroni's notorious inversion of the heterosexual rules of spectatorship – whereby women were 'stared out of countenance' and looks of admiration were reserved for the self – effectively 'outed' manhood as a commodity which like any other was subject to the fluctuations of market confidence.

Robert Jones's article ostensibly leads us away from the frippery of the urban pleasure gardens to the austerity of the military encampments which were established throughout the country in the summer of 1778 in order to reassure the populace in the face of possible invasion. Yet his readings of literary treatments of these camps suggest that they proved anything but reassuring to a significant proportion of the population. The camps were represented as military pleasure gardens to which the men and particularly the women of the fashionable world flocked in their hundreds, and whose resident soldiers were perceived to have more in common with the effeminate Macaronis of Vauxhall than with the disciplined, manly heroes who peopled old England in the civic-humanist imagination. Jones examines in detail two contemporary texts: an anonymous novel entitled *The Coxheath Camp*, and Richard Sheridan's play, *The Camp, a Musical Entertainment*. Both of these texts, Jones suggests, are troubled by the idea that the camps promote a promiscuous and public intermingling of the sexes, and an erosion of strict gender roles. Both, he argues, trace such anarchy to the luxurious aristocratic mores which they imagine govern the encampments. These texts are, Jones argues, in different ways concerned to assert that the virtuous mores of the commercial, yet self-regulating middle classes will be required to re-establish the natural sexual order of things.

Women and the iconography of luxury

The two articles in the third section, Sue Wiseman's 'From the luxurious breast to the virtuous breast' and Marcia Pointon's 'Intriguing jewellery' again share many common features both in terms of approach and subject matter. Both are concerned to tease out the tangled network of discourses – particularly discourses around luxury – which contributed to the iconography of particular historical women in the 1790s. In the case of Wiseman's article, the historical subject is the slave mistress of John Gabriel Stedman, a picture of whom appeared in his *Narrative of a Five Years Expedition Against the Revolted Negroes of Surinam*, published in the 1790s. Pointon's historical subject is Queen Charlotte, consort to George III.

Sue Wiseman's immediate concern is to understand how the luxurious and avaricious breasts of early modern iconography are transformed
through discursive reconfiguration in the eighteenth century into the
virtuous political icons of the French revolutionary period. Wiseman's
genealogy takes her back to seventeenth-century texts on pap fashions, to
Rousseau's advocacy of breast-feeding in *Emile*, and to eighteenth-century
rereadings of classical texts on aesthetics and luxury. Wiseman argues that
the female breast can be read as a symptom of the changing relations
of the female body to the political sphere as the early modern period
became the Enlightenment. She concludes with a sophisticated reading of
the picture of Stedman's slave mistress, Joanna, in which she argues that
the viewer is typically invited both to read the breast as virtuous and to
experience the breast as an object of, albeit submerged, desire.

Marcia Pointon's article also contains an image of a virtuous and
arguably political breast; in this case the implicitly nurturing breast of
Queen Charlotte, depicted sitting in a chair with a baby asleep on her
knee. Pointon is not directly concerned here with the iconography of the
breast, rather she is concerned with the textuality of the jewellery which
adorns it; however, in the light of Wiseman's conclusions, her discussion
of this picture seems significant. For Pointon's article looks both at
attempts to establish the virtue, authority and fecundity of the Queen
through the depiction of her jewellery, and at the great potential for such
depictions to unleash traditionally damaging narratives of luxurious
corruption and physical decay, unless carefully contained. The depiction
of Charlotte as nursing mother, Pointon argues, represents precisely such
a strategy of containment, for it, like many other pictures of Charlotte,
invokes the story of Cornelia who, on being asked to produce her jewels,
produced her sons: it suggests, in other words, that the possible excesses
of luxurious femininity have been replaced by the virtuous devotions of
maternity.

A coda on Rome

The collection concludes with Brian Young's discussion of the treatment
of sexuality and luxury in the personal and political writings of Edward
Gibbon. Young argues that though there has been much discussion of
Gibbon's prurience in *The Decline and Fall*, and of the contrastingly
puritanical nature of his personal writings, there has been little discussion
of the ways in which his treatment of lust relates to his treatment of luxury,
and this despite the indissoluble coupling of the two terms in the discourse
of civic-humanism by which Gibbon is so evidently informed. Young
argues, however, that Gibbon evinces a far more nuanced and ambivalent

attitude to sexuality and luxury than could be accommodated on the Spartan benches of civic-humanist discourse. These ambivalences and nuances, he suggests, are to be located in Gibbon's refusal to commit himself fully to any one part of the dynamic tripartite structure of European history which he identifies, namely a structure in which pagan virtue activates creative luxury but is overwhelmed in its turn by the sterilities of Christian virtue.

The complexities that Brian Young uncovers in *The Decline and Fall* provide an appropriate conclusion to this volume, not least because the eunuchs, silks and empresses of Gibbon's Rome are the ultimate touchstones of luxury in eighteenth-century discourse. But Young's account also reminds us that a language of scholarship can simultaneously be a language of evasion – as, for example, in Gibbon's use of Latin and Greek when describing sexual impropriety. Although the critical idioms of our own day are notorious for a less elegant form of obscurity, we hope that this present volume remains accessible to a variety of scholars, irrespective of any period affiliation they may feel; we also hope that they will continue the dialogues started here between empirical history, intellectual history, literary studies, art history, human geography and the history of medicine.

Vincent Quinn, University of Sussex, UK

Mary Peace, University of Nottingham, UK

Notes

1 Sylvia Plath, *The Bell Jar* (London: Faber and Faber, 1963), p. 131.
2 As a term, 'theory' suggests a number of disparate and often contradictory approaches; here it is used to note any body of work that is produced from a set of explicit methodological principles.
3 Particular thanks are due to the English Subject Group and the School of English and American Studies for their joint sponsorship of the conference.
4 John Sekora, *Luxury: The Concept in Western Thought, Eden to Smollett* (Baltimore and London: Johns Hopkins University Press, 1977), p. 4.
5 For notable examples of the form, see James Thomson, *Liberty* (1735–6) and William Collins, 'Ode to Liberty' in *Odes on Several Descriptive and Allegorical Subjects* (1746).
6 The relationship between liberty and luxury is explored more fully by Sue Wiseman elsewhere in this volume.
7 Sekora, p. 68.
8 Sekora, p. 216.
9 Sekora, p. 68.
10 Sekora, pp. 67 ff. and p. 309.
11 J. G. A. Pocock, 'The mobility of property and the rise of eighteenth-century sociology' in *Virtue, Commerce, History: Essays on Political Thought and*

History, Chiefly in the Eighteenth Century (Cambridge: CUP, 1983), pp. 103–23, p. 115.

12 See the articles by Philip Carter, Robert Jones and Brian Young (this volume). Also see J. G. A. Pocock, 'Civic humanism and its role in Anglo-American thought', and 'Machiavelli, Harrington and English political ideologies in the eighteenth century', both from *Politics, Language and Time: Essays on Political Thought and History* (London: Methuen, 1972), pp. 80–103 and pp. 104–47 respectively, and *The Machiavellian Moment: Florentine Political Thought and the Atlantic Republican Tradition* (Princeton: Princeton University Press, 1975).

13 Christopher Berry, *The Idea of Luxury: A Conceptual and Historical Investigation* (Cambridge: CUP, 1994), p. xi.

14 See Mary McIntosh, 'The homosexual role', *Social Problems*, 16(2), Fall 1968, and Jeffrey Weeks, *Coming Out: Homosexual Politics in Britain from the Nineteenth Century to the Present* (London: Quartet, 1977).

15 See Alan Bray, *Homosexuality in Renaissance England* (London: GMP, 1982), pp. 81–114.

16 G. S. Rousseau and Roy Porter, *Sexual Underworlds of the Enlightenment* (Manchester: MUP, 1987), p. vii. See also Paul-Gabriel Boucé, *Sexuality in Eighteenth-Century Britain* (Manchester: MUP, 1982).

17 See Bray, pp. 130, 131. See also Susan Sontag, 'Notes on camp' (1964) in *A Susan Sontag Reader* (New York: Vintage Books, 1983), pp. 105–19.

18 See Rictor Norton, *Mother Clap's Molly House, The Gay Subculture in England 1700–1830* (London: GMP, 1992), and Emma Donoghue, *Passions Between Women: British Lesbian Culture 1668–1801* (London: Scarlet Press, 1993). Trumbach's role in generating debate has been enormous, but his interventions have been scattered over a variety of publications. For a cross-section of his work, see 'Sodomitical assaults, gender role, and sexual development in eighteenth-century London' in *The Pursuit of Sodomy: Male Homosexuality in Renaissance and Enlightenment England*, ed. Kent Gerard and Gert Hekma (New York and London: Harrington Park Press, 1989), pp. 407–29; 'London's Sapphists: from three sexes to four genders in the making of modern culture' in *Body Guards: The Cultural Politics of Gender Ambiguity*, ed. Julia Epstein and Kristina Straub (New York and London: Routledge, 1991), pp. 112–141; 'Modern prostitution and gender in *Fanny Hill*: libertine and domestic fantasy' in *Sexual Underworlds of the Enlightenment* (see n. 16 above), pp. 69–85, and 'Sodomitical subcultures, sodomitical roles, and the gender revolution of the eighteenth century: the recent historiography' in *'Tis Nature's Fault: Unauthorized Sexuality during the Enlightenment*, ed. Robert Purks Maccubin (Cambridge: CUP, 1987), pp. 109–121.

19 For articles dealing with continental Europe, see *The Pursuit of Sodomy*. Rudolf M. Dekker and Lotte C. van de Pol's *The Tradition of Female Transvestism in Early Modern Europe* (Basingstoke: Macmillan, 1989) is also useful.

20 See Terry Castle, *Masquerade and Civilisation: the Carnivalesque in Eighteenth-Century Culture and Fiction* (London: Methuen, 1986) and Peter Stallybrass and Allon White, *The Politics and Poetics of Transgression* (London: Methuen, 1986).

21 For example, see Chapters 1 and 2 of *Sexual Suspects: Eighteenth-Century Players and Sexual Ideology* (Princeton: Princeton University Press, 1992).

22 Charles Lamb, 'On the genius and character of Hogarth' (1811; revised 1818), pp. 81–101 of Vol. I of *The Works of Charles and Mary Lamb*, ed. E. V. Lucas, 6 vols (London: Methuen, 1912), p. 82.

Cath Sharrock

Reviewing 'the Spirit of Man-hood': sodomy, masturbation and
the body (politic) in eighteenth-century England

Julia Epstein credits Ambroise Paré with having begun 'the process of
naturalizing and medicalizing gender disorders and other anomalies' in
his book, *On Monsters and Marvels* (1573). She also attributes to him the
conceptual shift of stressing that 'cultural ideas about gender appropriate
behavior have equal importance with genitalia' when determining, for
example, whether an hermaphrodite be reclassified as male or female and
cites the following criteria from Paré's text: 'whether the whole disposition
of the body is robust or effeminate; whether they are bold or fearful, and
other actions like those of males or females.'[1] Such a gendered pattern of
teratological analysis does lend itself most readily to interpretations of
hermaphroditism. As both I and Emma Donoghue have argued elsewhere,
this kind of methodology was used within eighteenth-century paramedical
treatises to try to explain away female homosexuality, for example, as
a physiological anomaly: a perverse desire was thus discreetly redesigned
as bodily malfunctioning.[2] Randolph Trumbach's readings of hermaphroditism in the seventeenth and early eighteenth centuries present both
the female and the male homosexual as subjects who were, when their
particular sexual practice contravened the patriarchal code, classified as
hermaphrodites.[3] However, I want here to explore the ways in which
the ideas of 'gender appropriate behavior' that we find articulated by Paré
were mobilized in eighteenth-century writings against both sodomy and
masturbation in texts other than those which use hermaphroditism to
pathologize sexually deviant practices. Within the discursive contexts of
this article the effeminacy that Paré had diagnostically employed to detect
the 'real' sex of an hermaphroditic person becomes symptomatic of an
'unhealthy' mode of sexual practice. In particular, I want to emphasize
the discursive frame within which this 'unhealthy' effeminacy encodes
fears that exceed the literal boundaries of the sexual body. Paramedical
condemnations of sodomy and masturbation will be seen to register

Textual Practice 11(3), 1997, 417–428

an anxiety about the emasculation of the nation state by its sexually degenerate subjects.

The historical linking of sodomy and masturbation has been identified most recently by Paula Bennett and Vernon A. Rosario. In their introduction to the first collection of literary-cultural essays to be produced solely about masturbation, *Solitary Pleasures*, they offer the following commentary:

> The Roman Catholic condemnation of the mortal sin of 'pollution' or '*mollites*' (softness or effeminacy) was elaborated in the Middle Ages. Self-pollution was considered a 'sin against nature' and its biblical condemnation was traced back to God's condemnation of Onan for having spilt his seed on the ground rather than conceiving an heir by his widowed sister-in-law Tamar as Levirate law demanded. . . . Theologians . . . consistently condemned such voluntary emissions along with fornication, adultery, mollites . . . sodomy, and bestiality – all classified as forms of unlawful sex.[4]

It is revealing to reflect here upon the etymological links between masturbation and effeminacy, as *mollites* signified both masturbation and effeminacy; an identification that was to resonate in the term 'mollies', given to effeminate homosexuals in the eighteenth century.[5] We can also see how masturbation, effeminacy and sodomy were incorporated within the ecclesiastical catch-all category of 'unlawful sex' and that they were included within this category by dint of being condemned by the specifically theological coda of sinfulness. If we move on to Henry VIII's 1533 statute a significant shift in interpretation occurs, as deeply anti-Catholic state legislation wrests the power away from the ecclesiastical court and translates a previously theological into a secular issue. Here I am indebted to Ed Cohen's reading in his book, *Talk on the Wilde Side*. Cohen writes that this statute 'made "the detestable and abominable vice of buggery committed with man or beast" a felony' and that 'it transformed the broader implications of the religious offense into a specific legal injunction against a set of non-procreative sexual practices.'[6] This secular transition did not, of course, have the effect of making the rhetoric of sinfulness entirely anachronistic in relation to specific sexual acts, but it did register a redistribution of ethical authority and introduce an alternative way of framing the political and cultural significance of the sexual acts themselves. It is this secularized and secularizing redefinition of 'buggery' as an illegal, because non-procreative, act that I want now to consider. I am going to trace the continuing effect of this redefinition within the eighteenth century in terms of an interplay between paramedical treatments of non-procreative sexual practices and the secular issue of nation state politics. My discursive territory is that which is constructed by the interlinking categories of masturbation, effeminacy and sodomy.

The 'anti-onanistic crusade' in the eighteenth century, to borrow Bennett and Rosario's phrase, is thought to have been initiated by an anonymous treatise, *Onania*, which was first published in 1708/9 and is attributed to a quack clergyman, Balthazar Beckers. The enormous popularity of this piece, which swelled in size with the addition of *The Supplement to the Onania* in about 1710, is evident in the fact that it went through at least nineteen editions and sold nearly 38,000 copies.[7] A key example of the moralistic anxiety about masturbation within the eighteenth century, which it did so much to generate, it also displays the secular preoccupation with non-procreativity that I have outlined above:

> For whether we commit Abomination with those of our own Sex, as the Scripture says, '*Men with Men*, or with Beasts, or that we defile our own Bodies ourselves with this shameful Action, the Consequences are the same to the Society and our Species. . . . It destroys conjugal Affection, perverts natural Inclination, and tends to extinguish the Hopes of Posterity.[8]

The expanse of its destructive range is later further elaborated as 'SELF-POLLUTION' (so melodramatically presented) is said to lead to '*Lying, Forswearing*, perhaps *Murder*, and what not . . . '.[9] The reader is left to imagine the ludicrously euphemistic catastrophe of 'what not'! However, it is the allegedly unproductive sweep of masturbatory activity that concerns me here. Along with bestiality, sodomy and masturbation are found to arrive symptomatically at the same end – non-procreativity – and sodomy is textually refigured as a form of masturbation. Although the writer of this piece frequently gestures, as here, to biblical authority to endorse his own ethical position, he also opens his text out into the specifi-cally secular framing of this sexually deviant behaviour. Such onanistic activity is not simply condemned as non-procreative, it is also forced to carry the enormous potential guilt of social dissolution: the 'extinguish[ing of] the hopes of Posterity' concomitant also with the destruction of the productive, heterosexual coupling – 'conjugal Affection'.

With these extracts from the *Onania* we have witnessed the discursive transformation of an 'unlawful' into a specifically antisocial practice. More generally, the treatise encapsulates within itself the translation of the religious sin of masturbation into what Bennet and Rosario describe as 'a uniquely pernicious personal and social disease'.[10] The delineation of mas-turbation as a disease is apposite, because the text, as Robert MacDonald has noted, can be thought of as 'the first to preach that masturbation caused disease', and in this way popularized ideas that MacDonald traces back to the late seventeenth century.[11] His phraseology here is helpful. A text that 'preaches' about medical issues is potentially also a text that adapts quasi-medical phenomena to fit an admonitory and religious goal. Although I am understanding the religious inflexion of the text to be less resonant than its secular connotations, the idea that the text manipulates its supposedly medical material for admonitory effect remains pertinent. A later eighteenth-century medical writer upon masturbation, S.A.A.D. Tissot (to whom I shall be returning later) was not merely trying to discredit an old rival when he wrote: 'The English *Onania* is a real chaos; it is one of the most unconnected productions that has appeared for a long time . . . all the author's reflections are nothing but theological and moral puerilities.'[12] 'Puerilities' they may be, but the significance of these 'reflections' is more culturally telling than Tissot was concerned to acknowledge. Arguably, its capacity to assume cultural significance can be located in the very discursive 'chaos' that Tissot deplores. The textual slippage between theological and moral 'reflections' and the paramedical representation of masturbation as a disease opens out the religious and ethical debate into the terrain of secular anxiety. It is only if the preventative remedies and cures that the text recommends with such religious fervour are adopted that the social dissolution it so generously itemizes will not be realized. Through its very cautionary 'reflections' the treatise implicitly expresses a fear that a personal might become a social malaise.

The *Onania* also implicitly conflates masturbation and sodomy through the physiological symptoms produced by onanism. If the disease-ridden, insatiable masturbator manages to escape the claws of death, he has still to face the death of his own masculinity: 'In others . . . whom it has not killed, it has produced nightly and excessive Seminal Emissions, a Weakness in the *Penis*, and a Loss of Erection, as if they had been castrated.'[13] The unmanly state of this 'as if . . . castrated' figure inserts effeminacy into the pathologically emasculating practice of both masturbation and sodomy. This melodramatic collapse is drawing upon the perception, still dominant within this period, that semen was a vital fluid and that its loss inevitably sapped the strength of the body. Tissot was to encapsulate this view: 'the loss of an ounce of this humour [semen] would weaken more than that of forty ounces of blood.'[14] Hence the popular conception of onanism as a wasting disease. The *Onania*, however, by so emphasizing the demise of sexual virility, foregrounds the symbolic sexual-social nature of its subjects.

Many critics and cultural historians have stressed the politically symbolic nature of eighteenth-century treatises on masturbation. Tissot's anti-masturbation, *Onanism* (first translated into English in 1760) has been read in this way. Like the *Onania*, its huge impact upon popular conceptions in the eighteenth century is evident in the numerous translations of it in the eighteenth century alone. Ludmilla Jordonava's reading of *Onanism* stresses, as I have done with the *Onania*, the complex inter-weaving of religious coda and medical opinion. She also sees its very 'inclusiveness' as being culturally significant: 'Notions of sin, evil, crime and punishment are all incorporated into a larger vision, which sets improper sexual activity in the context of class relations, family dynamics, responsibility and dependency, allowing [Tissot] to move effortlessly between individual and social identity.' Hence her insistence that the distinction between procreativity and non-procreativity within this text needs to be reinterpreted within the socio-political frame offered by productivity versus non-productivity.[15] Ed Cohen's analysis of the pedagogical function of anti-masturbation writing specifically aligns notions of productivity – the subject saved from the non-productive wasting of its own reproductive potential – with the cultural construction of the middle classes.[16] He also quotes R. P. Newman's complementary reading:

> [The] anxiety about masturbation after 1700 was primarily characteristic of middle-class doctors and educators, who provided their clients (parents, pupils, patients) with an anti-masturbatory theory which reinforced and gave medical support to a cluster of social and sexual attitudes inextricably bound to the bourgeois Trinity of work, family and paternal authority.[17]

My own reading of the *Onania* concurs with these analyses, rendering its fear of non-procreativity a specifically bourgeois anxiety. In this way, the wasting disease of masturbation is found symptomatically to figure both the non-productive practice of sodomy and the laying waste to the productive potential of the (bourgeois) nation.

I want now to think a little more about the ways in which perceived sexually deviant behaviour is represented as a socio-political threat by turning to a later anti-sodomy text *Plain Reasons for the Growth of Sodomy in England* (1728? or 1730?).[18] This pamphlet specifically directs itself to 'fine Gentlemen'. It is concerned exclusively with the aristocracy and is addressing only the sexual behaviour which it deems to be indicative of the aristocratic lifestyle. The anonymous author begins by lamenting the mal-effects of contemporary education upon the sensibilities of boys. He nostalgically yearns for a conveniently non-specific historical past when boys learned the art of being boys, when their schooling gave them 'a Thirst after Honour, and a Proneness to warlike Exercises'. Tutored in the 'old-fashioned' way, the boy's 'abilities of Mind and Body, render[ed] him capable of serving his King, his Country, and his Family'.[19] The state could then rest secure, as the boys were always there to defend it. The contemporary system of education, on the other hand, is said to be teaching young men the fine art of losing their manhood. In short, this 'enervated effeminate Animal' is fit for nothing. Again we find that effeminacy rewrites sexual as socio-political impotence:

> Thus, unfit to serve his King, his Country, or his Family, this Man of *Clouts* dwindles into nothing, and leaves a Race as effeminate as himself; who, unable to please the Women, chuse rather to run into unnatural Vices one with another, than to attempt what they are but too sensible they cannot perform.[20]

The delicious illogicality of this conclusion, in which Eunuchs can only do with men what they can no longer do with women, assumes a semblance of logic only if one equates 'real' sex with procreativity. Significantly, the health or disease of the body and body politic is seen to be dependent upon the man's being able to 'perform' his part well. With its stress upon the need for good tutoring, the text, in fact, gestures towards the fragility of its manly ideal. It presents the boy as one who needs to be taught to behave like a man and so renders vulnerable the militaristic defence of the body politic to the invasion of an effeminate impotence.

Alan Sinfield, Ed Cohen and Rictor Norton have all interpreted this 'image' of the effeminate man as one which has, to borrow Sinfield's words, 'precious little to do with mollies'.[21] In so doing they are drawing attention to the text's specifically aristocratic delineation of effeminacy: 'mollies', as Rictor Norton's *Mother Clap's Molly House* substantially documents, were not members of the aristocracy, but artisans. With this in mind, are we to read the effeminate male of *Plain Reasons* as revealing more about a specifically bourgeois construction of the aristocracy in eighteenth-century England than it does about any homosexual identity? Sinfield quotes from Eve Kosofsky Sedgwick's representation of the aristocracy in this period in which she writes of 'the feminization of the aristocracy as a whole' whereby 'the abstract image of the entire class, came to be seen as etherial, decorative, and otiose in relation to the vigorous and productive values of the middle class'.[22] From this angle, the effeminacy within *Plain Reasons* functions more as a register of class conflict than as an encoding of anxieties about the security or insecurity of the state. Ed Cohen interprets the same passage from *Plain Reasons* as an example of the powerful impact of emergent bourgeois values: 'rather than being seen as the cause of social decay . . . "sodomy" here is merely the rhetorical designation for an extreme form of social dissolution predicated on the negation of the "manly" ideal' of the middle classes. The text, he argues, 'addresses "sodomy" only as a symptom of behavioural deviations', as its author goes on to worry about such indiscretions as 'The Effeminacy of Men's dress and Manners'. Because of this Cohen contends that 'the specific sexual/sinful significance formerly attributed to the charge [of sodomy] has been (re)articulated in the legitimation of an emerging masculine norm'.[23] This is his version of the secularization of the issue of sodomy, in which he represents the bourgeoisie as identifying itself through a model of manliness, against which effeminate deviations were seen as failures to realize the bourgeois dream of productivity.

Nancy Armstrong's understanding of the '"feminization" of values' in the eighteenth century as being expressive of a developing sense of self-identity for the middle classes might seem to be rather at odds with the kind of readings that I have just discussed.[24] Similarly, Armstrong seems, though only at first, to be opposed to Sedgwick's understanding of the 'feminization of the aristocracy' in this period. But Sedgwick's aristocratic 'feminization' is non-productive and so leaves at play a productive notion of the feminine against which the 'effeminacy' of the aristocracy can be viewed as a bad (non-productive) kind of femininity. It is the bourgeois feminine gone perverted. In fact, one could also read the nostalgia of *Plain Reasons* as a desire to disrupt the identification of the aristocracy with a degenerate effeminacy. From this perspective, one might also suggest that the pamphlet is not necessarily invoking the '"manly" ideal' of the bourgeoisie against which the aristocracy are seen to fail, as Cohen seems to be arguing that it is, nor, as Rictor Norton suggests, as expressing 'the lower-class prejudice against the "soft" aristocracy'.[25] Instead the pamphlet is, I think, open to a reading of an aristocracy divided within itself, and in this way could even be seen to encode the ideological opposition of the Country faction to that of the Court.[26] I offer this only as a suggestion and as a possible way of thinking about the pamphlet's patriotic zeal, which I will be discussing later, in terms of the values that were character-istic of Country propaganda at the time that *Plain Reasons* was published. Whichever way it is read, the pamphlet mobilizes ideals of manliness, against which effeminacy is made to figure both cultural and political malaise.

I want now to expand the boundaries of this debate by reviewing the socio-political resonance of *Plain Reasons* in terms, not of sexually inflected class conflicts, but of the impact of a sodomitical effeminacy upon the self-identification of the nation state. The author, with a disarming capacity to reorientate himself seemingly at whim, goes on to offer the following observation. The habit of 'men's kissing each other', which has produced an effeminate and so both biologically and militaristically impotent 'race', has historically had yet further consequences:

> *Rome* likewise sank in Honour and Success, as it rose in *Luxury* and *Effeminacy*; they had Women Singers and Eunuch's from Asia, at a vast Price: which so softened their Youth, they quite lost the Spirit of Man-hood, and with it their Empire.[27]

Effeminacy no longer merely lays waste to the internal body politic; it is now deemed responsible for the loss of the Roman Empire. Given that by 1728/30, when this text was written, England was busily establishing itself as the dominant colonial power in Europe, it is difficult not to read this passage as an encoded expression of anxiety about the possible collapse of English colonial strength into the weakness of its effeminate subjects. Sodomy is here succinctly burdened with the guilt of sapping the strength of the colonialist nation. Non-productivity is refigured as England's impotent inability to produce for itself a colonial inheritance.

Michèle Cohen has recently cautioned against what she perceives to be a reductive reading of effeminacy in the eighteenth century. In *Fashioning Masculinity* she specifically criticizes cultural historians of homosexuality, such as G. S. Rousseau and Randolph Trumbach, who understand 'effeminacy' to be unambiguously associated with homosexuality; she makes a bid, instead, 'to resist the attempts to make "effeminacy" coherent and unitary by reducing it to gender, to sex or to politics'.[28] I hope that my reading of effeminacy in this article is not falling into this reductive trap, but delineating, instead, the complex cultural matrix which imbricates issues of gender, sex and politics. Michèle Cohen's exploration of effeminacy relocates the anxieties associated with it in terms, in part, of a fear of Englishness losing itself to the seductiveness of the French. Such an emphasis on the impact of the French upon the English self-identity both complements and contributes to historical readings of English nationalism in the period. Gerald Newman and Linda Colley stress the embattled nature of English–French relations and its impact upon what Newman calls 'the critical years in the launching of English nationalism': the mid-1740s to the mid-1780s.[29] Recently, Kathleen Wilson has added a specifically colonialist inflection to this English–French combativeness by identifying patriotic nationalism as an aspect of the intense imperial rivalry between these two countries from the mid-1730s to the early 1760s.[30] I would be pushing it, to say the least, if I were to insist that the colonial anxiety of *Plain Reasons* needs to be read specifically in terms of an earlier articulation of the English–French imperial rivalry that Wilson discusses. The anonymous author, after all, had the bad grace pointedly to condemn Italy, rather than France, as 'the *Mother* and *Nurse* of *Sodomy*'. However, he did make a rather circuitous concession to the needs of my article by conceding that France 'copies from [the Italians], the *Contagion*' of homosexuality.[31] Thus he allows me adeptly to gesture towards such a reading, while preferring to emphasize a general sense of English colonial vulnerability; a vulnerability which produces the textual displacement of blaming England's effeminate and sodomitical subjects for importing a foreign '*Contagion*' through their sexual practice.

Although the first publication of *Plain Reasons* predates the decades upon which Wilson focuses, it is, I think, significant that it was reprinted as an appendix to another anonymous volume, *Satan's Harvest Home* in 1749 – a historical juncture which falls into the midst of the period specified by Wilson. The timing of this reprinting very much opens up the possibility of a rereading in 1749 that was alert to the need of England's 'manly' subjects both patriotically to ensure the continuing strength of the nation and to maintain the country's colonial power. Kathleen Wilson's reading of the mood of the country by the end of the 1740s, however, would question the extent to which such confidence in the virile and refor-mative powers of patriotism to overcome the anti-patriotic weakness of effeminacy might have been current in 1749:

> The confidence that, given patriotic leadership, Britain could attain national imperial greatness had been replaced with widespread anxiety that the nation's patriotic verve had been sapped, the victim of a creeping effeminate supineness that had corroded martial spirit and courage to the point where British imperial decline and defeat were all but inevitable.[32]

The 'effeminate' subject of *Plain Reasons* who, as we have already seen, is 'unfit to serve his King [or] his Country', reverberates here. If we were to read the 1728/30 *Plain Reasons* as an admonitory text that seeks to rescue the country from its threatened collapse into impotence and degeneracy, then Wilson's representation of the 1740s invites a reading of the 1749 republication of it as a rather despairing and condemnatory text: the degenerate aristocracy are to blame for the country's having been robbed of its manly and imperial vigour.

In this article I have been understanding a 'masculine norm' as being operative not only in terms of a conflict between the bourgeoisie and the aristocracy and possibly within the aristocracy itself, but also as the register against which England was trying to legitimate itself as both a national and colonial power. The strategies of cultural displacement, which have been at play in both the anti-masturbation and anti-sodomy texts discussed are, of course, not peculiar to them. Indeed, we can find such patterns often repeated in writings against sodomy as attempts to locate the origin of sodomy as always somehow outside of the (cultural) self.[33] The designated origin of sodomy can be found to change, in fact, according to historical contingency. For example, Rictor Norton shows how the 1376 laws against homosexuality in England identified 'foreign artisans and traders, particularly "Jews and Saracens"' as those who had introduced '"the too horrible vice which is not to be named" [i.e. sodomy] which would destroy the realm'.[34] This sense of the sodomite as being culturally 'other' to the English, Anglican self – the Jews and Saracens – was also, in the medieval period, attributed to the dissenting and invasive

Lollards; an attribution that continued to be defensively active even in the nineteenth century.[35] My own reading of such defensive strategies has emphasized how 'effeminacy', symptomatic of both the masturbating and sodomitical male, is textually condemned as that which is 'other' to a 'healthy', because productive model of manliness. However, as the texts take as their starting point the corruption of the (re)productive health of the British subjects and nation by 'effeminacy', they register also an anxiety about a continuing slippage between these two modes of being. As the 'Spirit of Man-hood' hangs rather limply between an idealized image of itself and the threat of its own emasculation, the male, British subject is discursively constructed as one who is capable of either patriotically sustaining or robbing the nation of its virility. Effeminacy is figured as both cause and symptom of national malaise.

School of English and American Studies, University of East Anglia, UK

Notes

1 Julia Epstein, 'Either/or – neither/both: sexual ambiguity and the ideology of gender', *Genders*, 7 (Spring 1990), pp. 107, 108.

2 Emma Donoghue, *Passions Between Women. British Lesbian Culture 1668–1801* (London: Scarlet Press, 1993), pp. 25–58; Cath Sharrock, 'Hermaphroditism; or, "the erection of a new doctrine": theories of female sexuality in eighteenth-century England', *Paragraph*, 17:1 (March 1994), pp. 38–48.

3 Randolph Trumbach, 'London's Sapphists: from three sexes to four genders in the making of modern culture', in Julia Epstein and Kristina Straub, eds, *Body Guards. The Cultural Politics of Gender Ambiguity* (New York and London: Routledge, 1991), pp. 112–41.

4 Paula Bennett and Vernon A. Rosario II, eds, *Solitary Pleasures. The Historical, Literary, and Artistic Discourses of Autoeroticism* (New York and London: Routledge, 1995), p. 3.

5 For studies of 'mollies' in the eighteenth century, see Rictor Norton, *Mother Clap's Molly House. The Gay Subculture in England 1700–1830* (London: Gay Men's Press, 1992); Randolph Trumbach, 'Sex, gender, and sexual identity in modern culture: male sodomy and female prostitution in enlightenment London', in John C. Fout, ed., *Forbidden History. The State, Society, and the Regulation of Sexuality in Modern Europe* (Chicago and London: University of Chicago Press, 1992), pp. 89–106; Trumbach, 'London's Sapphists', pp. 112–41; Alan Sinfield, *The Wilde Century. Effeminacy, Oscar Wilde and the Queer Moment* (London: Cassell, 1994), pp. 37–42.

6 Ed Cohen, *Talk on the Wilde Side. Toward a Genealogy of a Discourse on Male Sexualities* (New York and London: Routledge, 1993), p. 104.

7 The first date of publication of the *Onania* is sometimes thought to be 1710; see Robert H. MacDonald, 'The frightful consequences of onanism: notes on the history of a delusion', *Journal of the History of Ideas*, 28 (1967), p. 424. I

am, however, relying upon Peter Wagner for the publication history of the *Onania*; see his *Eros Revived. Erotica of the Enlightenment in England and America* (London: Paladin Grafton Books, 1988), p.17.

8 *Onania: Or, The Heinous Sin of Self-Pollution, and all its frightful consequences (in Both Sexes) considered* (17th edn, 1752), p. 7.

9 *Onania*, p. 18.

10 Bennett and Rosario, eds, *Solitary Pleasures*, p. 5.

11 MacDonald, 'The frightful consequences', p. 424.

12 S.A.A.D. Tissot, *Onanism: Or, A Treatise Upon the Disorders produced by MASTURBATION: Or, The Dangerous EFFECTS of Secret and Excessive Venery* (1766), trans A. Hume, p. 21.

13 *Onania*, p. 13.

14 Tissot, *Onanism*, p. 2.

15 Ludmilla Jordanova, 'The popularization of medicine: Tissot on onanism', *Textual Practice*, 1 (1987), pp. 76, 77. An alternative and, I think, less persuasive reading of *Onanism* is offered by Antoinette Emch-Dériaz, who argues that Tissot, in secularizing the issue of masturbation, is 'taking it away from clerical influences and turning it over to lay professionals'. See her *Tissot. Physician of the Enlightenment* (New York: Peter Lang, 1992), p. 44. Although a medic, Tissot was also inclined to dabble in the kind of moral and theological theorizing for which he condemns the *Onania*.

16 Cohen, *Talk*, p. 45. See also pp. 35–68.

17 Quoted in Cohen, *Talk*, p. 229.

18 The exact date of publication of *Plain Reasons* is unclear and is given in relation to different copies of it as 1728? or, according to the British Library *Eighteenth-Century Short Title* Catalogue, as 1730? and even 1740?. The earlier two dates, however, occur most regularly.

19 *Plain Reasons for the Growth of Sodomy in England* (1728?), pp. 4, 5.

20 *Plain Reasons*, pp. 9, 9–10.

21 Sinfield, *Wilde Century*, pp. 39–40; Cohen, *Talk*, pp. 113–14; Rictor Norton, *Mother Clap*, pp. 126–7.

22 Quoted in Sinfield, *Wilde Century*, p. 40.

23 Cohen, *Talk*, p. 114.

24 Nancy Armstrong, *Desire and Domestic Fiction. A Political History of the Novel* (New York and London: Oxford University Press, 1989), pp. 3–27. I am taking the phrase, the '"feminization" of values', from Terry Eagleton's discussion of this subject in his *The Rape of Clarissa. Writing, Sexuality and Class Struggle in Samuel Richardson* (Oxford: Basil Blackwell, 1982), p. 14.

25 Norton, *Mother Clap*, p. 127.

26 I am indebted to Mary Peace for suggesting this reading of *Plain Reasons* as articulating a tension within the aristocracy.

27 *Plain Reasons*, p. 18.

28 Michèle Cohen, *Fashioning Masculinity: National Identity and Language in the Eighteenth Century* (London and New York: Routledge, 1996), p. 6. For her bibliographical references to G. S. Rousseau, Randolph Trumbach and Kristina Straub, see. p. 114.

29 Gerald Newman, *The Rise of English Nationalism. A Cultural History 1740–1830* (London: Weidenfeld & Nicolson, 1987), p. 67; see also pp. 63–84; Linda Colley, *Britons. Forging the Nation 1707–1837* (New Haven and London: Yale University Press, 1992).

30 Kathleen Wilson, *The Sense of the People. Politics, Culture and Imperialism*

in England, 1715–1785 (Cambridge: Cambridge University Press, 1995), pp. 137–205.

31 *Plain Reasons*, p. 12. For a reading of the representation of male and female homosexuality as contagion in eighteenth-century paramedical discourses, see Cath Sharrock, 'Pathologising sexual bodies', in Andy Medhurst and Sally Munt, eds, *Lesbian & Gay Studies: A Critical Introduction* (London: Cassell, 1997), pp. 356–67.

32 Wilson, *Sense*, p. 165.

33 Rudi C. Bleys discusses the representation and construction of male homosexual identity as cultural 'other' to the European in the pre-Enlightenment and Enlightenment periods in *The Geography of Perversion. Male-to-male Sexual Behaviour outside the West and the Ethnographic Imagination 1750–1918* (London: Cassell, 1996), pp. 17–109.

34 Norton, *Mother Clap*, p. 15.

35 Robert Holloway, *The Phoenix of Sodom, or the Vere Street Coterie* (1813), pp. 26–7.

Philip Carter

An 'effeminate' or 'efficient' nation? Masculinity and
eighteenth-century social documentary

Scholars looking to capture mid-eighteenth-century concerns over a
deteriorating national condition can do little better than to reach for a copy
of John Brown's two-volume *Estimate of the Manners and Principles of the
Times* (1757/8). Few authors rival this minister and political commentator
in his protestations of gloom and doom. Brown's survey offered up an
ignoble recent history, a parlous present and a bleak future for a once
vigorous country. The nation, wrote Brown, had reached 'a Crisis so
important and alarming' by which we 'are rolling to the Brink of a Precipice
that must destroy us'.[1] Brown's message chimed with a significant proportion of the population who in recent years had experienced rising prices,
Jacobite invasion and shocking military setbacks in the opening campaign
of the Seven Years War. Within a year of its publication, the first volume
of *The Estimate* had run to seven editions, with sizeable extracts being
reprinted in, amongst others, *The Gentleman's Magazine* and *London
Magazine*. The book shot its author to fame, earning him the nickname of
John 'Estimate' Brown; a man popularly associated with an unpalatable
story unnervingly told.

Brown's fame has also had an impact on recent eighteenth-century
historiography. *The Estimate* reveals the attitudes of many mid-century
readers and writers alarmed at what they believed to be a rising tide of
luxury. A dominant theme in Brown's work, luxury has found a number
of its historians in recent years. These scholars have explained luxury's
importance to the eighteenth-century mind, and its dramatic shift from
social evil to social stimulant following the rise of political economic
theories. But luxury is not the only theme which is raised time and again
in *The Estimate*. With luxury comes 'effeminacy', a condition which
Brown believed to be closely intertwined with injudicious consumption.
Society had, in Brown's opinion, reached a state of 'vain, luxurious and
selfish EFFEMINACY', an assertion made on a number of occasions in

Textual Practice 11(3), 1997, 429–443

the work.[2] Nor was this interest in effeminacy a feature of *The Estimate* alone. According to Brown's contemporary, John Shebbeare, modern Britons were a 'Race of soft, effeminate Dastards', while an anonymous *Tryal of Lady Luxury* (1757) spoke of its subject's ability to 'soften and effeminate the bravest, roughest and honestest of mankind'.[3] The prominence of such references has not gone unnoticed. Writing in 1985, J.G.A. Pocock reminded us that there was among classical republican writers a real concern that luxury would 'render societies effeminate', a term which 'ought not to be neglected'.[4]

However, since this date relatively little attention has been paid to examining the meaning of the state of 'effeminacy'. This shortcoming has recently been commented on by Michèle Cohen who points out that unlike luxury effeminacy is still not treated as a serious subject for scholarly analysis. In contrast to luxury which is correctly viewed as historical, 'effeminacy tends to be treated with the casualness usually bred from familiarity. Its present meanings are assimilated to those of the past. . . . We all "know" what effeminacy means and what it has always meant. But do we?'[5]

Cohen's question is timely. Until recently, historians of eighteenth-century politics and society have tended to work in isolation from scholars of gender identity and gender relations. However, the current lack of insight lies not only in a failure to acknowledge the subject's existence, but also with an over-reliance on the work that has been done in this field, notably by historians of male sexuality such as Randolph Trumbach. Trumbach's work charts the emergence of a new homosexual type, the 'molly', in the principal cities of early eighteenth-century Western Europe.[6] The molly served as a barrier between men and women: men could not be 'manly' if they behaved like the molly. Contemporaries equated non-heterosexual individuals with effeminacy and effeminacy with sodomy. In turn, eighteenth-century definitions of masculinity rested on men's participation in heterosexual sex. Trumbach's thesis has received widespread support over the last decade. However, this equation of manliness with sexual activity does not help us to understand the numerous references to 'effeminacy' in the work of John Brown, John Shebbeare or other civic commentators. A reading of *The Estimate*, for example, reveals that its author was not primarily concerned with discussing men's sexual behaviour but with men's social conduct; their pursuit of trivial entertainments and luxuries and their search for a reputation for delicacy in polite society.

This article does not intend to question the contribution of historians such as Trumbach to our knowledge of early eighteenth-century representations of sexual deviance. However, we must acknowledge that this discussion of the molly, and related meanings given to effeminacy, is based on a study of a specific set of texts: what may be termed less respectable publications, such as newspaper articles or verse pamphlets discussing sexuality, or commentaries on the urban 'underworld'. In contrast, references to mollies and indeed to male sexuality in general rarely appeared in eighteenth-century social documentaries or behavioural studies, which were published either in book form or in the more 'polite' and increasingly popular formats of the essay periodical and, later, the magazine.

It is the meaning of 'effeminacy' in these latter genres that I wish to focus on here. In looking more closely at the understanding of 'effeminacy' this article will be divided into two parts. To begin with, I want to offer a few possible answers to Michèle Cohen's question by thinking about 'effeminacy', first in civic humanist writing, and second in a small selection of 'enlightened' or 'progressive' texts which questioned the former's pessimistic assessment. We see from these studies that effeminacy was a condition which contemporaries believed to refer not just to the individual, but also to specific social groups and to the nation at large. Effeminacy was a subject for intellectual debate; emerging as a cornerstone of civic ideology and rhetoric, and as an important target for enlightened writers of both documentary and conduct literature who were keen to dismantle the old orthodoxies in what became a vigorous eighteenth-century contest between social conservatives and modernizers.

In thinking about the historical meaning of 'effeminacy' we are led to ask another question about which eighteenth-century scholars also have limited knowledge. Effeminacy, as Alan Sinfield has argued, is best understood as a 'male falling away from the purposeful reasonableness that is supposed to constitute manliness, into the laxity and weakness conventionally attributed to women'.[7] The question 'What was meant by 'manliness' in the eighteenth century?' duly arises.

I will examine this problem in the second part of the article. It is argued that effeminacy's importance must be explained not just because it acted as a profound critique of modern manners and consumption patterns but also because it served as an exhortation to more 'manly' forms of conduct. What emerges is a debate over the acceptable standards of male conduct in a society experiencing considerable social, economic and cultural change. Competing standards of masculinity took the form of what I term 'classical' and 'refined' manliness, closely mirroring civic and 'progressive' interpretations of national character.

Effeminacy and the national condition

Civic criticisms

Among civic writers it would appear that effeminacy was predominantly used to label forms of social deviance, with the effeminate individual often being connected to the foibles of polite urban culture. Occasionally, references did draw attention to men's sexual misconduct. *The Tryal of Lady Luxury*, for example, included 'Pathics' – that is, sodomites – in a list of personalities thought to prosper in an age of unregulated commercial activity; other deviants who thrived in an 'effeminate' Britain included cruel fathers, highwaymen and murderers.[8] However, such references were rare. When sexual conduct was considered it was more common for effeminacy to imply instances of asexuality, with debilitating luxuries rendering men incapable of rearing healthy children. As Jonathan Swift argued in a 1728 essay on elite manners, 'weak and effeminate' men 'enervated their Breed through every Succession, producing gradually a more effeminate race, wholly unfit for Propagation'.[9] Others picked up on this theme but chose to concentrate on declining standards of physical health rather than sexual impotence. Concern over men's physicality was most clearly stated in discussions on the condition of the army. For many, the extent of the nation's physical degeneration had been borne out by military defeat at the beginning of the Seven Years War. But for civic writers who identified and delineated the characteristics of the effeminate nation, the current catalogue of failings extended far beyond the army. Rather, writers like Brown maintained that it was the army's participation in a polite civilian society which had initiated this decline in the nation's martial spirit; reminding us that within eighteenth-century civic discourse, definitions of effeminacy and manliness extended far beyond the classical equation with the warrior. Thus, physical weakness was also identified in the civilian population's vulnerability to disease. John Gregory was one of a number of physicians who believed that the 'current softness and effeminacy of manners' weakened the constitution and 'undermined our natural defences against the diseases most incident to our own climate'.[10]

Effeminacy was, however, always more than a parlous physical condition. Effeminate mid-century Britons were also often described as lacking the traditionally manly attributes of reason or sense. Deficiencies of this kind could prompt effeminate men into unexpected courses of action. One example of this is found in *The Gentleman's Magazine*'s 1761 essay 'On duelling' which asked how an undoubtedly 'effeminate aristocracy' was able to participate in this violent and dangerous practice. Such actions, it was argued, contradicted the classical connection between effeminacy, weakness and cowardice. The answer lay in the fact that modern effeminacy had eroded men's ability to think in a consistently rational manner, prompting individuals to engage in violent and potentially fatal acts such as duelling. An examination of 'corrupt ages' like this provided 'but too many examples that effeminacy and outrage are by no means incompatible. . . . An enervated mind is by its very weakness subjected to every excess', prompting men to be 'often harrowed by sallies from langour to brutality'.[11]

For many civic writers, it was this weakness of mind which underpinned different manifestations of effeminacy in modern society. Mental weakness meant an unwillingness or inability to engage in traditionally disciplining activities such as scholarship, forcing modern males to turn to ready-made diversions which, given men's lack of sense, they were unable to evaluate and dismiss as worthless. For those suffering from what John Brown described as a 'vain and empty Mind', the result was a struggle to avoid 'the Tedium of Solitude and Self-Converse' through the pursuit of fashionable 'Parties of Pleasures'.[12] The 'effeminate nation' was above all a society in which such 'parties' proliferated, taking a variety of forms: gaming, attendance at the new imported Italian opera, participation in feminine activities such as tea-drinking, or the purchasing of comfortable, and hence enervating, household objects ranging from upholstered chairs and carpets to properly fitting doors and windows.[13] At the heart of these concerns was a fear that the nation was becoming fixated with all things fashionable. Attachment to the fashionable world denoted an unacceptable dependence in individual men who collectively as citizens sacrificed their nation's political independence to absolutism. *The London Magazine* carried an essay on 'Profligacy and Effeminacy become Universal', which informed readers of the current 'plague of effeminacy' that had led to a shift 'from the simplicity and customs which alone keep us from slavery'; 'effeminacy' being, as was noted in the following year, 'above all . . . passive in its obedience'.[14]

Enlightened responses

To many eighteenth-century readers, civic pronouncements on the rise of effeminacy provided a credible interpretation of a deteriorating national condition. None the less, these claims did not go unquestioned. Two lines of argument emerged in reaction to the judgement of authors such as Brown. The first was proposed by those who, while working within a civic humanist paradigm, questioned the extent of current physical and moral corrosion. For these writers, 'effeminacy' carried similar connotations to those just described. Charles Hanbury-Williams, for example, praised recent studies on the national condition, acknowledging that 'effeminacy' had indeed become 'a great Foible' of the population. At the same time, Hanbury-Williams questioned whether effeminacy was as yet the 'Characteristick of the English Nation'. Swithin Swing, author of a series of *Letters to the Estimator* (1758), similarly denied that effeminacy was rife, pointing instead to the continued domination of the 'sour, severe, laborious, spirited and masculine Briton'.[15]

Proponents of a second line of argument were not so much concerned with questioning the details of civic assessments as the underlying theories on which these judgements were based. These 'progressive' or 'enlightened' commentators provided a more intellectually ambitious critique which struck at the civic equation of luxury and social decline, luxury and effeminacy. As the mid-century historian James Ralph maintained, claims of 'National Effeminacy' were the preoccupation of 'Gentlemen of the Old Stamp'. Such writers failed to realize that commercial activity was a source not of effeminacy but of what Ralph termed 'National Efficiency'.[16] To end this first section I want to look at discussions of the 'effeminate' nation in a few examples of what might be termed 'progressive' social documentaries. Writers of such accounts reduced the state of effeminacy from an absolute truth to a point of view. This said, critics of the civic assessment varied considerably in their treatment of 'effeminacy'.

In the writings of Bernard Mandeville, for example, there are a number of echoes of the traditional civic reading of luxurious consumption. Certainly Mandeville's thesis was a clear attack on those holding what he called 'such dismal Apprehensions of Luxury's enervating and effeminating [of] People'.[17] However, in arguing his case, Mandeville did not deny the links between luxury and effeminacy in the individual. Rather, he questioned the civic equation between the effeminate individual and the effeminate nation. Mandeville believed that the division of labour would prevent individual weaknesses contributing to societal decline, a point made clear in his discussion of the military. A successful army required only that the infantry remained uncorrupted by consumption. Mandeville argued that such fortitude was inevitable, given that the majority of common soldiers were drawn from 'the working slaving People'; working and slaving, as Mandeville added, to produce luxury goods for the rich.

But what of those affluent members of society who made up the army's officer class? It was, after all, the effeminacy of these groups that caused most anxiety among civic writers. Mandeville offered two arguments intended to prove officers' ability to serve the national cause. First, the conditions of modern warfare did not demand hardiness from its leaders who were simply required to give orders, and who could choose to 'destroy Cities a-bed, and ruin whole Countries while they are at

Dinner'. Mandeville's second argument emerged from observations drawn from recent British history. Events during the War of the Spanish Succession had proved that an officer class of 'embroider'd Beaux with fine lac'd Shirts and powder'd Wigs' were, at times, just as fearless as 'the most stinking Slovens'. How was such martiality possible? Mandeville dealt with this problem in a manner which to his many critics summed up the author's amorality. Such actions were neither classical displays of courage nor virtuous acts of public spiritedness but episodes of selfishness as officers, emboldened by self-interest, sought personal glory through one-off acts of heroism.[18]

For all its distastefulness, Mandeville's iconoclastic message of 'private vices and public benefits' had an important influence on later redefinitions of luxury. Two points stand out. First, while luxury continued to have a deleterious effect on the minority who consumed to excess, luxury's impact on society at large was quite different. Indeed, for the majority luxury stimulated hard work, not physical or mental enervation. Second, Mandeville stated that luxury was not an absolute category but a social construct open to interpretation, and variable over time. Thus if definitions of luxury were relative, so, it could be argued, were states of 'effeminacy'. Just as one man's luxury was another's source of industriousness, so civic concepts of effeminacy were later reinterpreted by Scottish enlightenment writers as examples of superior refinement in a civilized world. As Adam Smith demonstrated, the 'Spartan' North American Indians considered simple displays of social affection to be signs of the 'most unpardonable effeminacy'. Such displays, Smith noted, had long been considered acceptable in the more advanced socio-economic environment of Western Europe.[19]

Scottish writers were equally keen to challenge the claims of those proponents of the Spartan lifestyle found closer to home. To David Hume, the modern world was not only a more civilized and prosperous place but also more disciplined, and even more martial. Hume focused specifically on the nation's ability to participate successfully in war, one of the key sources of national strength, or weakness, as identified by civic authors. For Hume, the English remained a people whose 'bravery is uncontestable'. The nation's active participation in commerce did not result in men losing 'their martial spirit' or becoming 'less undaunted and vigorous in defence of their country and their liberty', the refined arts having 'no such effect in enervating either the mind or the body.' Indeed, Hume argued that the new modes of behaviour which developed in a commercial society actually improved the nation's martiality. To begin with there was 'industry' which was stimulated by a desire to gain material wealth and which added 'new force to both' men's physical and mental capacities. Industry was compounded by 'politeness and refinement' which accompanied innocent forms of luxury and which replaced impetuousity and anger with a more measured form of courage based on 'a sense of honour which is a stronger, more constant and more governable principle'.[20]

Constructions of manliness

Hume's statement was, of course, more than a refutation of the civic equation of luxury and effeminacy. In reworking the impact of luxury, Hume reinterpreted the luxurious man and the luxurious society as a manly individual and a vigorous nation. Moreover, it was Hume's belief that men within a luxurious society were not just as good as the classical warrior but were, in fact, superior. Still able to remain physically hardy and still able to pursue the public good, the refined male was also more controlled, honourable and civilized. With eighteenth-century discussions of 'effeminacy' therefore came references to 'manliness' or 'manly' conduct. The contest between traditional and modern evaluations of the national condition provided an important ideological framework within which notions of male conduct were constructed. It is the argument of this article that the majority of eighteenth-century readers would have understood references to 'manliness' as relating to various modes of social behaviour centred around themes including courage, self-command, independence, and conduct both in the home and in public. However, the relative merits of these themes did not go unquestioned. Just as there was debate over the meaning and reach of 'effeminacy', so definitions of manliness became an important subject in some social documentary studies, as well as in an increasingly vibrant genre of behavioural literature, comprising courtesy books, conduct literature, and specific guides offering instructions on subjects including men's education and health.

'Classical' manliness

For all his alarm at levels of national effeminacy, John Brown had surprisingly little to say about the characteristics of normative masculinity and the routes to individual and societal well-being. However, other civic writers were more forthcoming in delineating aspects of a suitably 'classical manliness'. It is not surprising, given civic concerns over men's physical debility, that the male physique was a prominent subject in many of these discussions. Commentators deemed a healthy, 'firm' constitution to be necessary if men were to fulfil public responsibilities and remain sufficiently disciplined to maintain moral and physical independence.

Regular exercise was a key part of any healthy regime, and calls to participate in vigorous sports took a number of forms, which were not without controversy. An example of a more colourful request was that from John Broughton, a self-styled 'Professor of Athletics' and author of *Proposals for Erecting an Amphitheatre for the Manly Exercise of BOXING* (1742). Broughton contrasted the torpor of modern men with the vigour of the ancient Spartans for whom athletics had been a way of life. Links between sport and national character allowed Broughton to claim that the discipline required for boxing would serve both to perfect the body and strengthen the nation as men regained their 'natural Fortitude'. Broughton's call met with a mixed response. *The Connoisseur* periodical commended Broughton and praised boxing as a 'truly British exercise' and a 'manly practice'. Others, while keen to promote physical hardiness, condemned the brutality of a sport which in their opinion bred a false notion of courage divorced from virtues such as humanity.[21]

Writers ambivalent towards the merits of boxing promoted alternative activities. Many of those who discussed the subject of male physicality owed much to the contribution of John Locke's *Some Thoughts Concerning Education* (1693). Locke believed that care of the body was fundamental for young men to achieve what he called a 'Happy State'. For Locke, efforts to achieve physical well-being began in infancy. Cold baths and frequent exposure to the elements were top of his list for the early years. Failure to make a boy follow this programme was, he believed, 'a good way to make him a *Beau*, but not a Man of Business'. Lessons continued as part of the young man's formal education. One of the most beneficial activities for these years was horse-riding which Locke thought 'such vigorous Exercise'. Reluctant to have young men taught fencing in case it encouraged duelling, Locke suggested that riding be supplemented with tuition in wrestling.[22] But constructing the hardy individual was only part of the process leading to manliness since physique and fortitude could be lost through an indulgence in luxuries. For Locke, exercise contributed to the development of mental rigorousness, the 'happy state' consisting of both a 'sound body' and a 'sound mind'.[23]

Such were the temptations of the modern world that many later writers considered it necessary to restate Lockeian strictures on personal discipline. Self-control, it was argued, facilitated moderation and, crucially, ensured that all-important quality of classical manliness: independence. Discussions of moderation took many forms but were particularly prominent when instructing men on the consumption of food and drink. Readers were encouraged to pursue a middle ground between abstemious-ness and excess, and were provided with role models to emulate in search of the 'golden mean'. Those who refused to follow this advice were in danger of losing their masculine identity. Richard Peers's *Companion for Youth*

(1738), for example, chastised the drunkard for 'unmanning' himself, and for then repeating an action which, over time, 'renounces Manhood'.[24]

Refined manliness

In an age of increasing material temptation, moderation distanced men from the vagaries of fashion, and stimulated a lifestyle that was healthy, wise and, above all, independent. However, it was becoming equally important that independence did not isolate men from the rest of their community. For many, it was no longer satisfactory to refer, as did Swithin Swing, to a British manliness founded on sourness and severity. The bullying soldier, the bluff squire and the pedantic academic were taken to task by proponents of a new spirit of refined masculinity which urged men to display a capacity for social refinement. Proponents of refinement sought, in effect, to redefine the traditional association between masculinity and public life; requiring gentlemen defenders of public liberty to combine civic responsibilities with a willingness to participate in the new public world of polite spaces located within a developing urban culture.

How was the eighteenth-century male to achieve a reputation for refinement? The answer to this question varied over time, and may be said to broadly follow the shift from an early century culture of politeness to a mid- to late-century culture of sensibility. Common to both models of refined masculinity were calls for greater participation in respectable female company. Women were thought to be more receptive to the refined male and, on account of their innate civilities, capable of stimulating higher standards of interpersonal conduct. David Hume was one of many who spoke of the benefits of mixed company where 'both sexes meet in an easy and sociable manner; and the tempers of men, as well as their behaviour, refine apace'.[25] In a clear redefinition of civic concepts of manliness, Hume stated that involvement in mixed society led not to effeminacy but to new forms of masculinity whereby manliness was measured, not lost, by men's ability to narrow the gap between the sexes through displays of social refinement. It was Hume's belief that 'the male sex, among a polite people, discover their authority in more generous, though not a less evident manner; by civility, by respect, and in a word by gallantry'.[26]

It needs to be pointed out that Hume's refined manliness was not unproblematic. He, like other proponents of polite masculinity, remained aware of the damaging effects of excessive refinement. In the same essay, Hume warned that 'modern politeness ... runs often into affectation and foppery'.[27] In so doing, Hume's argument showed similarities to the concerns of contemporary civic writers for whom false manners and trivial male recreations had done so much to stimulate national effeminacy. The difference between Hume and civic authors was found in the definition and location of excess on a male gender spectrum ranging from, on one side manliness, to effeminacy on the other. Keeping men on the correct side of excess demanded the setting up of boundaries, beyond which deviant behaviour was located. For Hume, as for other civic and modernizing writers, it was the insincere, delicate and tiresome fop which indicated this point to the careful male reader. In guiding men to manly politeness rather than to foppery, polite theorists stressed that complaisance should not degenerate into an uncontrolled show of social affection.[28] Such displays indicated a lack of self-control and proved embarrassing to one's companions and antisocial to observers. In order to avoid such situations, conduct writers characterized polite masculinity not only in terms of polish and social affection but also as carefully regulated behaviour, as much concerned with not causing offence as with promoting goodwill.

Over the course of the century the importance of control as an integral part of polite masculinity began to give way to more expressive forms of social interaction, embodying sensibility. By the mid-century, commentators were establishing a notion of refined manliness in which social ties were formed through virtuous and refined displays of mutual sympathy, sentiment or sensibility, expressed through less regulated, more emotional actions.

There has to date been relatively little written on the impact of sensibility on notions of eighteenth-century manliness. Typically, the archetypal sentimental male, or 'man of feeling', has been viewed as a distinctly feminine figure existing in an age prepared to accept such transgressions in male manners. However, this interpretation is in danger of misreading Georgian notions of refined masculinity through the lens of nineteenth- and twentieth-century standards of a more overtly stoical manliness.

To many late eighteenth-century conduct writers, supposedly 'feminine' acts such as weeping were less signs of womanliness than an indication of new standards of manliness compatible with the current vogue for sentimental display. Moreover, men's tears were valorized as signs of a manliness superior to the now seemingly hard-hearted behaviour promoted by many civic commentators. The man who refused to weep was no longer a courageous public servant but a self-interested individual unconcerned with the condition of his neighbours. As the mid-century essayist and editor Peter Shaw put it, when interest in one's fellow men had been lost it was impossible 'to drag such men out of that mine of unmanly vice and . . . stoical insensibility'. Such were the links between insensibility and inhumanity that 'it may be questioned whether those are properly men, who never weep upon any occasion'.[29] Further confirmation that tears were a positive expression of a new style of masculinity was later provided by Vicesimus Knox. Knox, like Shaw, believed that men's refusal to cry was symptomatic of an unacceptable insensitivity, concealed under 'the appellation of a manly fortitude'. Knox attributed this erroneous understanding of manliness to a misreading of classical texts, and cited the weeping of the Trojan hero, Hector, as a counter to the enduring fashion among some men for emotional indifference. The 'manly' Hector also featured prominently in Knox's discussion of benevolent and compassionate fatherhood. For Knox, Hector's true virtue was found not in his martiality but in his treatment of children: when we 'see him taking off his helmet, that he may not frighten his little boy with its nodding plumes'.[30]

Conclusion

This article began with a brief examination of some of the meanings of 'effeminacy' within mid-century social documentary literature. The frequency with which civic authors drew attention to the condition of 'effeminacy', and the attempts by modernizing authors to engage with such claims highlights the centrality of gender to this genre. Within civic discourse, references suggested physical weakness, loose thinking, and an absence of self-determination resulting in dependence. It was, for some writers, an all too apparent feature of daily life. For others, the state of effeminacy, if not yet a reality, was a spectre that haunted a nation preoccupied by self-interest. Others questioned this interpretation. Mandeville saw effeminacy as an inevitable feature of a vicious world but denied that this threatened national security. Progressive writers chose to strike at its root source, rendering luxury harmless. In doing so, they transformed the state of effeminacy from a reality to a perspective and, with this, many of its previous manifestations into industriousness and social refinement. Enlightened writers also expressed this inversion with reference to gender identities. The luxurious individual who in civic discourse was rendered effeminate, now became manly. This, moreover, was a new style of manliness which not only squared vice with virtue but improved on now outmoded notions of male conduct. Here I have suggested that the ensuing eighteenth-century debate over normative manliness took the form, broadly speaking, of a contest between two rival interpretations – one 'classical', the other 'refined' – both of which defined their subject in terms of a series of social, not sexual, acts.

This said, it is important to note that these discussions also featured many points of convergence; reminding us that the true picture of manliness in this or in other periods is more of a synthesis of opinions than a simple contest between authors extolling rival concepts of manly virtue. Points of convergence appear at a number of stages. By the mid-century, definitions of courage, once the cornerstone of the civic idea of manliness, were being redefined to incorporate a capacity for refinement, sensibility and private interest. Obituaries of General James Wolfe, the commander of the British campaign to capture Quebec in 1759, for example, depicted his heroism both in terms of his public spirit and his capacity for feeling, not on outdated displays of Spartan aggression which were condemned as barbaric. Through his first biographer, Wolfe emerged as a man who was 'polite, affable, free . . . truly brave, truly noble, friendly and candid, gentle and benificient'.[31]

We see a similar synthesis between classical and modern manliness in the writings of Adam Smith. For Smith, self-command was an integral part of a manliness dependent on a capacity for sensibility. Smith's theory of the impartial spectator stated that an observer could never fully appreciate another person's feelings unless these were regulated to what he called 'a certain mediocrity'.[32] Emphasis on the place of self-command should also remind us that the history of eighteenth-century male conduct is not the history of the emergence of a single victorious concept of refined manliness, a sort of cultural equivalent of the highly influential theories of political economy. The eighteenth century does not see the invention of a 'modern' definition of a manliness configured in terms of social civility.

Late Victorian strictures on Spartan living clearly have their roots in a more complex eighteenth-century understanding of manliness in which Stoicism remained a vital component. Nor does the condition of effeminacy die out in our period. Rather, as Smith reveals in his delineation of the limits of sentimental masculinity, 'effeminacy' in enlightenment discourse is redefined to indicate a personal, rather than a societal, fall from manliness, though in time this latter association also re-emerged. This last point has suggested the problems of seeing the eighteenth-century challenge to civic concepts of effeminacy and masculinity as necessarily creating an alternative 'modern' definition of normative manliness. In some ways, however, the reach of the enlightenment into the modern world is all too apparent in histories of eighteenth-century gender. For the majority of writers today, gender still implies 'women', a taxonomy that can be traced back to the enlightenment identification of women as natural, particular and gendered, defined in opposition to the general, that is, 'male'. It is perhaps our failure, until recently, to break free of this dichotomy that has obscured the fact that enlightened writers were also interested in manliness and its antithesis, effeminacy; two historical subjects we neglect to our disadvantage.

Wolfson College, Oxford, UK

Notes

1 John Brown, *An Estimate of the Manners and Principles of the Times* (2 vols, London, 1757/8), i, pp. 15–16.

2 Ibid., i, p. 67.

3 John Shebbeare, *A Second Letter to the People of England* (London, 1755), p. 51; *The Tryal of Lady Allurea Luxury* (London, 1757), p. 75.

4 J. G. A. Pocock, *Virtue Commerce and History* (Cambridge: Cambridge University Press, 1985), p. 114.

5 Michèle Cohen, *Fashioning Masculinity. National Identity and Language in the Eighteenth Century* (London: Routledge, 1996), p. 5. A notable exception to this lack of scholarly attention is Kathleen Wilson, *The Sense of the People. Politics, Culture and Imperialism in England, 1715–1785* (Cambridge: Cambridge University Press, 1995).

6 Randolph Trumbach, 'The birth of the queen: sodomy and the emergence of gender equality in modern culture, 1660–1750', in Martin B. Duberman *et al.* (eds), *Hidden From History. Reclaiming the Gay and Lesbian Past* (London: Penguin Books, 1991).

7 Alan Sinfield, *The Wilde Century. Effeminacy, Oscar Wilde and the Queer Moment* (London: Cassell, 1994), p. 26.

8 *Tryal,* p. 77.

9 Jonathan Swift, *The Intelligencer,* no. 9 (6–9 July 1728), ed. James Woolley (Oxford: Oxford University Press, 1992), pp. 123–4.

10 John Gregory, *A Comparative View of the State and Faculties of Man* (London, 1765), p. 34.

11 *The Gentleman's Magazine,* xxxi (February 1761), p. 59.

12 Brown, *Estimate,* i, p. 50.

13 Ibid., i, pp. 36–7, 125. Kathleen Wilson's study of Brown, although not primarily intended to examine contemporary definitions of 'effeminacy', highlights a similar collection of failings: the effeminate individual/nation emerging as childish, injudicious, ignorant and cowardly. *Sense of the People,* pp. 185–8.

14 *London Magazine,* xlii (July 1773), p. 332; *Universal Magazine,* xliv (February 1774), p. 83.

15 Charles Hanbury-Williams, *The Real Character of the Age* (London, 1757), p. 2; Swithin Swing, *Letters to the Estimator* (London 1758), p. 33.

16 James Ralph, *The Case of the Authors* (London, 1758), pp. 11–13.

17 Bernard Mandeville, *The Fable of the Bees* (1714, 1732 edn); F. B. Kaye (2 vols, 1924, rpt Indianapolis: Liberty Press, 1988), i, pp. 120–2.

18 Ibid., i, pp. 122–3.

19 Adam Smith, *The Theory of Moral Sentiments* (1759), eds D. D. Raphael and A. L. Macfie (Oxford: Oxford University Press, 1976), p. 205.

20 David Hume, 'Of refinement in the arts and sciences', in *Essays Moral, Political and Literary* (Parts I and II, 1742/1752, 1777 edn), ed. Eugene F. Miller (Indianapolis: Liberty Press, 1985), pp. 274–5.

21 John Broughton, *Proposals for Erecting an Amphitheatre for the Manly Exercise of BOXING* (London, 1742), p. 2; *Connoisseur,* no. 30 (22 August 1754), ed. Alexander Chalmers (3 vols, London, 1808), i, pp. 158–9. For criticisms of boxing as intemperate, willfully aggressive and hence unmanly, see Vicesimus Knox, 'On the art which has lately been heard with the name of pugilism', in *Winter Evenings* (2 vols, London, 1788).

22 John Locke, *Some Thoughts Concerning Education* (1693), in *The Educational Writings of John Locke*, ed. James L. Axtell (Cambridge: Cambridge University Press, 1968), pp. 121–2.
23 Ibid., p. 114.
24 Richard Peers, *A Companion for Youth* (London, 1738), p. 84.
25 'Of refinement in the arts', in *Essays*, p. 271.
26 'Of the rise and progress of the arts and sciences' (1752), in *Essays*, p. 133.
27 Ibid., p. 130.
28 For the fop's place in this learning process see my 'Men about town: representations of foppery and masculinity in early eighteenth-century urban society', in Hannah Barker and Elaine Chalus eds, *Gender in Eighteenth-Century England. Roles, Representations and Responsibilities* (Longman: London, 1997).
29 *Man, A Paper*, no. 43 (22 October 1755), pp. 2–5.
30 Knox, 'On the unmanliness of shedding tears', in *Winter Evenings*, ii, pp. 182–3.
31 John Pringle, *The Life of General James Wolfe* (London, 1760), pp. 5, 17.
32 Smith, *Theory*, pp. 27, 238.

Miles Ogborn

Locating the Macaroni: luxury, sexuality and vision in Vauxhall Gardens*

The Vauxhall affray

In the summer of 1773, Henry Bate – an Essex parson, editor of *The Morning Post*, and a man with a love of boxing and self-publicity – visited Vauxhall Gardens with the actress Elizabeth Hartley and her husband. During the evening Mrs Hartley was somewhat distressed by being stared at by a group of fashionable young men, later identified as Captain Croftes, Thomas Lyttelton and George Robert Fitzgerald. Lyttelton was the son of a well-respected politician who had been a staunch opponent of Robert Walpole. He was a product of Eton, Oxford and the Grand Tour and, unlike his father, was known for his loose and prodigal lifestyle. Fitzgerald had been born into a well-connected Irish Protestant family and educated at Eton. He was a soldier, gambler and duellist who had fought for his honour twenty-five times by the mid-1770s. 'Fighting Fitzgerald' carried a limp from a duel in Paris and a cracked skull from being shot in the head in Galway. He was a quarrelsome and dangerous man whose final act was to be hanged for arranging the cold-blooded murder of an Irish neighbour.[1] Collectively, these men were known as 'the Macaronis' in the newspaper debate and gossip that the incident provoked.[2]

In order to protect Mrs Hartley, Bate moved to a position which blocked the men's view. He stared and made faces at them. They stared and grimaced back. When his party left their table Bate traded insults with Croftes. Later that evening they re-encountered each other and the spat was resumed. Fitzgerald's arrival on the scene prompted a heated exchange on the rights and wrongs of men looking at women and another flurry of strong words. Fitzgerald lambasted the incompatibility of Bate's profession and his love of boxing. Bate attacked Fitzgerald's clothing and his appearance: 'The dress, hat and feather, – miniature picture [of himself], pendant at his snow-white bosom, and a variety of other

Textual Practice 11(3), 1997, 445–461   © 1997 Routledge 0950–236X

delicate appendages to this *man of fashion*. . . . '[3] A crowd gathered but the battle was postponed. At two o'clock that morning Bate and Croftes met at a coffee house in town and arranged to duel in Richmond Park. As they prepared to leave, Fitzgerald arrived to tell Bate that there was a gentleman outside – a Captain Miles – who wanted to box him then and there. Bate was unwilling to fight but eventually made things up with Croftes and fought Captain Miles in the front dining room of the Spread Eagle Tavern, beating him easily (Plate 1 represents Bate's victory as the sacrifice of the Macaronis to 'revive degraded MANHOOD'). Strangely, however, the supposed Captain turned out to be Fitzgerald's footman and not a gentleman at all.

This incident is becoming increasingly well known. Kristina Straub has used it to explore the sexual politics of looking within eighteenth-

Plate 1 The Maccaroni Sacrifice, 1773. (By permission of the British Library from *The Vauxhall Affray*, 1414.e.28)

century theatre. Peter de Bolla has provided an account of it within a Lacanian reading of the eighteenth century's economy of vision. Both agree that it is a contest over the gaze: a struggle between different masculinities over rights to the visual, and particularly the right to look at women.[4] This, however, raises the question of why a contest between masculinities should be structured in terms of the visual. It also demands close attention to the nature of the masculinities involved, particularly the troublesome character of the Macaroni. Put simply, my argument is that by exploring the meanings of the Macaroni – paying attention to the significance of identifying Croftes, Lyttelton and Fitzgerald in this way – this contest over looking can be interpreted as structured by the relationships between masculinity and commodity consumption. Interpreting it in this way enables an understanding of several parts of the 'affray'. First, the sources of the conflict: Why was it that these men looking at Mrs Hartley was so problematic? Second, the nature of the insults: Why was 'Macaroni' a term of abuse, and what were the meanings it carried which made sense of miniature portraits, feathered hats and Herculean clubs? Finally, the conflict's resolution: What (mis)understandings of masculinity and virtue can be attached to a footman fighting a parson while dressed as a gentleman? In addressing these questions I will also argue that *where* the incident happened is a key to interpreting it; that the connections and tensions within the 'affray' – between masculinity, commodification and illusion – also structured and troubled the meanings of Vauxhall Gardens and, beyond that, the wider landscape of eighteenth-century cultural production. Doing this means 'locating' the Macaronis within two contexts. First, the new geographies of the eighteenth-century consumer revolution, what has been called the 'world of goods'.[5] Second, a key site within that landscape of consumption, the pleasure gardens at Vauxhall.

The Macaroni in the world of goods

From the mid-1760s 'Macaroni' designated a particular sort of fashionable man. The term originated with a group of rich, young associates of Almack's Club who, having returned from European Grand Tours enamoured of continental style, had set up, as a punning rejection of the robust anglophilia of roast beef, the Macaroni Club – 'composed of all the travelled young men who wear long curls and spying-glasses'.[6] From being an amusement for a small coterie the term became, via the popular periodicals and the prints of Matthew and Mary Darly, the primary vehicle for satire in 1772 and 1773. These caricaturists produced an extensive series of engravings – including *The Clerical Macaroni, The*

Macaroni Haberdasher and *A Mungo Macaroni* – which satirized both social types and individuals.[7] Joseph Banks appeared as the *Fly-Catching Macaroni* and Charles Fox was *The Original Macaroni*. Elsewhere, William Dodd, the ill-fated Chaplain of the Magdalen Hospital, was 'The Macaroni Parson'.[8] These prints were 'a guide to the celebrities of the day', but they were also political attacks on the young nobles of St James's, and on Fox in particular, which questioned the legitimacy of an aristocratic political system by connecting a mode of luxurious consumption to a lack of patriotism, and therefore to a failure of cultural and political leadership. Macaroni satire became widespread. Robert Hitchcock's play *The Macaroni* was performed in York; *The Town and Country Magazine* which vigorously attacked Macaroni fashions was read by both urban merchants and country gentry; and it even went transatlantic as Yankee-Doodle-Dandy put a feather in his cap and called it Macaroni.[9]

Macaronis were defined from the outset in terms of what they consumed, and particularly what they wore. While being a Macaroni was still a matter of elite play, Frederick St John, second Viscount Bolingbroke, wrote to George Selwyn in Paris seeking a new look:

> As Lord B much admires the taste and elegance of Colonel St. John's [his younger brother] Parisian clothes, he wishes Mr Selwyn would order Le Duc to make him a suit of plain velvet. By plain, is meant without gold and silver; as to the colours, pattern, and design of it, he relies upon Mr Selwyn's taste. A small pattern seems to be the reigning taste amongst the Macaronis at Almack's, and is, therefore what Lord B chooses. . . . As to the smallness of the sleeves, and the length of the waist, Lord B desires them to be outré, that he may exceed any Macaronis now about town, and become the object of their envy.[10]

Dressing as a Macaroni was a matter of masculine fashion and display; a competitive and European world of men turning themselves into spectacles to impress other men. In the newly fashion-conscious eighteenth century these styles soon spread. *The Town and Country Magazine* told its readers that 'The infection at St. James's was soon caught in the city, and we have now Macaronies of every denomination, from the colonel of the Train'd Bands down to the errand boy.'[11] As it spread, Bolingbroke's self-conscious humour turned to satire. The Darly prints worked by simply dressing up people like Banks and Fox as Macaronis. The clothes carried the satirical meanings. In this process the Macaroni followed the path described by Neil McKendrick for eighteenth-century fashion in general. It went from being something that was 'expensive, exclusive and Paris-based' to being something 'cheap, popular and London-based'. To go further, like the dolls which carried new fashions to England, and which McKendrick took as his way into explaining the 'consumer revolution', Macaronis went from being something life-sized, extravagantly decked out and at court to being something small, made of paper and widely distributed.[12]

The periodicals' satires depended upon characterizing the Macaroni as an entirely modern figure, a man driven by the dictates of fashion's novelties – 'In short he must be a *museum* of everything that has not yet been imagined or worn before the year 1772'.[13] They then mocked this figure through exhaustive and lovingly detailed descriptions of the new styles, cuts and materials of the clothes, hairstyles, hats, shoes and accessories which would guarantee that a fashionable man 'cuts a Figure – A-la-mode de Macaroni'.[14] They also located this figure in the world of goods by situating him on the streets of a commercial city tied into the global relations of fashionable consumption:

> Walking in the Streets of London is the true orthodox Tread upon Fairy Ground – You have the Spells of Pick-pockets, the enchantments of Beauty, the Incantations of Pleasure, and the Lures of Vice, around you. You may have Intoxication in a Tavern – Love in an Alley – Musick in the Market-place – Coffee in every street – and Ox-cheek and Oysters in every Cellar. . . . London is the grand Mart of the World. . . . It is more religious and more profligate – more rich and more admired than all the Cities of the World for its modern Excellencies. . . . A man who has money, may have at once every delicate, every dainty, and every ornamental Beauty of the four Quarters of the World. Asia, Europe, Africa, and America, are cultivated and ransacked to indulge the Inhabitants in every luxury; and when this Island shall be conquered and depopulated, how will the rising World wonder at the luxurious Lives which English Peasants led, when they are informed, that their common Drink was composed of a Plant which grew in China, drawn with hot Water, and mixed with the Juice of the West India Sugar-cane made into a hard Consistence; and that Liquor was called *Tea*!
>
> It is this luxury, that will prove the ruin of this island.[15]

This discourse on luxury situated the Macaroni within a global snow-storm of commodities which threatened to dissolve the connections between Englishness and the martial masculinities that had shaped and shored up an imperial geography of power and goods. Thus the first Macaroni appeared on stage in George Colman's comedy *Man and Wife* and, through a comparison of masculinities at Garrick's theatre of Englishness, the Shakespeare Jubilee of 1769, dramatized the notion that 'modern Italy is no more to be compared to Old England than a sirloin of beef to a spoonful of macaroni'.[16] This also turned on the effeminacy which luxury threatened. A Macaroni, it was said, 'renders his sex dubious by the extravagance of his appearance'.[17] Moreover, Macaroni effeminacy was understood as rendering a proud martial nation unsafe with only such men to fight for it. In this vein *The Matrimonial Magazine* described 'One of the modern mysteries of St James's' as follows:

> Our modern monkey of manhood, is by name a soldier; but never felt any ball, but a wash ball; nor ever smelt any powder, but hair-powder; who never saw any service but that of the table and the toilet; who never had any wounds but from minikin pins and Cupid's darts; who never marched further than the gay parade.[18]

To attack the Macaronis was to attack an aristocratic form of government through notions of luxurious consumption and the effeminate masculinity associated with it. Through the codes of cultural nationalism and the polemical debates over luxury they were presented as unpatriotic, undemocratic and un-English; offering a dangerous relationship between masculinity, empire and global commodity consumption. As such they stood in clear contrast to the representations of a powerful but merciful imperial masculinity like those which Francis Hayman rendered in his pictures of General Amherst and Lord Clive's victories in the Seven Years War.[19] That these images hung in the salon at Vauxhall brings me back to the pleasure gardens.

The Macaroni in the garden

Vauxhall (Plate 2) was a key site in the geography of eighteenth-century cultural production.[20] After it had been redesigned and reopened by Jonathan Tyers in 1732 it became London's most popular pleasure garden. It was one of the nurseries of English song.[21] It was also the first place where new artistic genres were displayed to a paying public on any scale. In and among its twelve acres of tree-lined walks, brightly lit groves, carefully designed buildings and eye-catching decoration it staged a new polite sociability marked by the 'elegant pleasures enabled by commercial wealth' – dining, conversation, music and art.[22] Its significance is as one of the locations where this cultural production was being newly commodified. The weakness of court and church in England meant that the polite pleasures of places like Vauxhall were produced as fashionable commodities by 'the new capitalists of cultural enterprise' who aimed at accumulation through titillation and commercial success through hedonistic consumption.[23] Pleasures in and around the gardens – the summer entertainments, but also puffs, prints, fans, songsheets and dancing lessons – were sold as commodities by Tyers and others willing to profit from his investment.[24] Again, the discourse of luxury was used to understand and undermine these diversions.

Plate 2 A general prospect of Vaux Hall Gardens, c. 1751. (© British Museum)

Even if Vauxhall's pleasures were refined ones, this always involved a *frisson* of sexual intrigue for both men and women. Vauxhall was a site for flirtation and assignation: 'Gentlemen who come alone are open to the overtures of any amiable companion, and Ladies who venture without a masculine guide, are not, generally speaking, averse to the company of a polite protector.'[25] That Vauxhall's walks and shades were heavy with sexual tension made it a place for 'intrigue, "play" and experimenting with social roles'.[26] This malleability of identity in the gardens – a flirtatious manipulation of illusion – connects the pleasures they offered to concerns over commodification and luxury. Henry Fielding, in two essays masquerading as letters from a Frenchman in London, denounced England as a place where 'Money is the universal Idol of all Ranks and Degrees of People', and ended with an account of Vauxhall:

> I must avow, I found my whole Soul, as it were, dissolv'd in Pleasure; not only you, but even *Paris* itself was forgot – My whole Discourse, while there was a Rhapsody of Joy and Wonder. Assure yourself such an Assemblage of Beauties never, but in the Dreams of the Poets, ever met before – and I scarce yet believe the bewitching Scene was real –
> See here the Taste of *Britain!* And reason like a Philosopher and a Politician upon the Consequences! – I add no more, but am now awake, and very sincerely, *Yours etc*[27]

Presenting the gardens as an enchanting dream world does not deny its pleasures. Indeed, similar descriptions were used by Tyers to sell Vauxhall.[28] However, by differentiating between the bewitching enticements of a fantasy world and what should be thought about the love of money and pleasure when the philosopher or politician is 'awake', Fielding presents the dangers of luxury as working through the powers of illusion. These commodified pleasures hide their 'real' social relations and, as for Karl Marx, commodification becomes 'a visual problem in perception'.[29] This discourse on luxury stages the gardens as the haunt of illusions and mysterious enchantments; the site of misperceptions and dreams; and the place of the pleasures and dangers of the dissolution of the self. It is a concentration on the reveries of consumption which effectively foreshadows recent re-evaluations of eighteenth-century consumption as the creation of new identities through a 'peculiar, daydream-like fusion of the pleasures of fantasy and reality'.[30] Therefore, in Vauxhall, questions of masculinity and vision intersected in the presentation of imperial heroes as spectacles and in the connections between luxury and sexual pleasure. They also intersected in the causes of the Vauxhall affray.

As it was later retold, the cause of the conflict was when 'Fitzgerald, evidently for the purpose of reckless insult, put up his glass and peered into the lady's face'.[31] Bate certainly reported that Fitzgerald had asked him

'Whether any man had not a right to look at a fine woman?', and that he had replied, 'Most certainly, and that I despised the man that did not look at a fine woman; However, I begged leave to observe, that there were two distinct ways of looking at her – with *admiration*, and with *unauthorized contempt* – that the conduct I censured was strongly of the latter kind'.[32] Looking was both differentiated and problematic when it came to what passed between men and women. The subsequent newspaper debate revealed Mrs Hartley – an actress but not on stage, and a woman defended in public by a man who was not her husband – as a complex visual problem.[33] As the author of 'The Macaroniad' had it:

Many ills doth him environ,
Who madly meddles with a siren;
And such *Fitzgiggio's* case was partly,
For gazing upon Madam *Hartley*.
To Gaze! – Or not to gaze! In Fun
Fops, fools, and fiddlers are Undone.[34]

A key part of the problem lay in the Macaronis' relationship to the visual. *The London Magazine* argued that they were devoted to the refined pleasures of the eye rather than the grosser pleasures of the belly:

The eye is the paunch of *a virtuoso Maccaroni*, as the stomach of the glutton. The *devouring Maccaroni* does not derive the appellation from an immoderate indulgence in animal food; the idea would be too coarse and sensual; nor is it intended to convey a carnivorous or vinibibous meaning.[35]

This hungry gaze was constructed as dangerously self-regarding, and was interpreted as creating men who wanted to be looked at by women but only pretended that they enjoyed looking back. It was also a gaze that was used to terrorize women. Macaronis were said to go to church only 'to ogle the Women, and put the Parson out of Countenance'.[36] *The Macaroni Magazine* warned that 'If you see him at the theatre, he will scarcely wink without his opera-glass, which he will thrust into a lady's face, and then simper, and be "pruddigishly entertenn'd" with her confusion'.[37] Fitzgerald's reported act was certainly the act of a Macaroni, and his gaze can be located within a rich culture of vision by taking seriously Parson Bate's insistence that there were different ways of looking and understanding how they were present in Vauxhall Gardens.[38]

The pleasure gardens take their place among the shows of London: an array of tableaux, illusions, panoramas, phantasmagoria and automated pictures.[39] Vauxhall was made of spectacles. The walks were vistas which framed views with trees and buildings. There were paintings and pictures in all their variety; statues of Aurora, Handel and Milton; fashionably decorated rooms; the illuminated moon, sun and stars on the gothic temples; the painted backdrops and alcoves which terminated the cross-walks; and, if one looked out of the gardens, contrasting views of country and city. Visual pleasures predominated, and were staged for the spectators. Tyers used devices from the baroque theatre and elaborate lighting to heighten the effects. John Lockman's publicity also concentrated on guiding vision. He instructed his readers on how to view the composition of the buildings, on where to stand so that 'the whole may appear to him a magical Scene', and on ways of looking at the gardens so as to continually see them anew. As he concluded: 'In short, when the Night is warm and serene; the Gardens fill'd with fine Company, and different Parts of them are illuminated, the Imagination cannot frame a more enchanting Spectacle.'[40]

The audience itself was very much part of this spectacle. Lockman said of the Grove that 'Here the Splendour is so great, as well as in the *Temple of Pleasure*, that the juvenile Part of both Sexes may enjoy their darling Passion:- the seeing others, and being seen by them.'[41] Everyone was on stage, and if these forms of observation of others can be understood as techniques for disciplining refinement in the public sphere, they were also sexually charged.[42] The pleasures of looking at others were emphasized, particularly of men looking at women. For example, 'Toupee' suggested that men might cast their eyes over the women in the supper boxes while pretending to examine the pictures. However, there was assumed to be pleasure in being looked at too.[43] As an intersection of these gazes the spectator became intensely self-conscious and self-regarding. Again, the gardens presented this act of looking as a pleasurable one. Lockman encouraged his readers to stand in the Rotunda of the 'Temple of Pleasure' surrounded by its sixteen mirrors, where 'In all these glasses the spectator, when standing under the balls of the Grand *Chandelier*, might see himself reflected at once, to his pleasing wonder'.[44] Here the solitary, self-observing subject is involved in the pleasurable consumption of 'his' own image.

Finally, Vauxhall's visual pleasures were the pleasures of illusion. The three separate triumphal arches which punctuated one of the walks were to be viewed so 'that the whole has the Appearance of a noble *Edifice*'. The moving picture and the painted backdrops that terminated the cross-walks were pleasing visual tricks, making it look as if they really ended in classical ruins or mythical alcoves. The gardens and the elements within them were arranged so that they would 'sometimes deceive the Eye very agreeably'.[45] More generally, the appeal of Vauxhall was to the imagination. Its architects manipulated the visual to create an aura of 'enchantment', a blurring of the real and the represented, of fantasy and reality, in the name of pleasure.[46] Visitors could be led to these pleasures through Lockman's positioning of their gaze:

> A Spectator, who, in the Night, should stand at that *Obelisk*, and look down the *Garden*, would perceive at the Extremity of this View, a glimmering Light, (that in the opposite *Alcove*) which might image to him an *Anchoret's* Cave; for instance, that of the imaginary *Robinson Crusoe*.[47]

In a world where the Enlightenment's clarity of vision structured many gazes these illusions were pleasurable diversions. When it was said in 1755 that the paintings were 'damaged last season by the fingering of those curious Connoisseurs, who could not be satisfied without *feeling* whether the figures were alive', the appeal was to the enchantments of the visual imagination rather than to fact.[48]

All this was brought together in the obelisk which, from the 1760s, was framed by buildings and trees at the end of the grand walk's long vista. On closer inspection it was revealed to be, like most Vauxhall spectacles, only painted canvas and boards. It was modern not ancient, and it had been made for money. Alongside Hayman's paintings of chained slaves it bore the legend '*Spectator fastidiosus sibi molestus*' – 'the fastidious spectator troubles himself'. This mild rebuke reminded the spectators of their active part in the maintenance of the fictions required to establish the pleasure of the illusion and, at the same time, made them aware of their position as spectators. It turned their gaze back upon themselves once more.[49] As Peter de Bolla has argued, what was made visible at Vauxhall was visuality, the act of looking itself.[50]

These visual pleasures were, however, troubled ones when the connections between masculinity, commodification and illusion came into view. The Macaronis served to demonstrate these tensions. They created problems by turning men's bodies into the wrong sorts of spectacles. They disrupted the heterosexual structuring of gazes expected of Vauxhall flirtations – with men gazing and women being gazed upon – by 'aim[ing] only to be looked at and admired' by both men and women and, at the same time, 'drawing up their *brazen artillery* to attack a *woman*, and *stare* her out of countenance'.[51] They also created themselves as spectacles of commodities rather than, for example, spectacles of heroic and sympathetic imperial masculinity. Like actors 'who make spectacles of themselves for a living', the Macaronis 'muddy the distinction between sexual object and sexual subject, spectacle and spectator, commodity and consumer'.[52] As the *Macaroni Jester* more succinctly put it, 'manhood is a thing unbought'.[53]

Macaroni spectacles were illusions just as Vauxhall's were, but they were problematic rather than pleasurable deceptions. It mattered that there was nothing behind their painted boards. Macaronis were described as 'Puffs of Wind', 'hollow Animals', or a '*perfect nothingness*'.[54] Fitzgerald was described as 'A thing so meagre and so thin,/ So full of *emptiness* – and sin'.[55] They were represented as nothing but their modish clothes. This was part of a critique of fashion as an empty illusion, but it also ran deeper than that.[56] As Barbara Maria Stafford argues:

> What was new to the eighteenth-century experience – as codes of polite behaviour spread to broader and lower strata of society – was the frightening possibility that nothing stood behind decorum. No gold standard guaranteed inflated or deflated currency; no original preexisted the copy; no durable skeleton shored up the frail anatomy. Fashion, masquerade, theater, cross-dressing emphasised the total disagreement between seeming and being, the deliberately fabricated incongruity between exterior and interior.[57]

Or, as an attack on the Macaronis had it, 'For shame, for shame, shake off this apish whim / and be without as you should be within.'[58] Macaronis were dangerous fakes whose world of refined appearances and ambiguous spectacles threatened to undermine gender and class boundaries and the systems of credit and value which depended upon them. Vauxhall's pleasures had always been about experimenting with social roles, and this had always held the excitements of transgression. However, Fitzgerald's dressing up of his servant as the fictitious Captain Miles to fight Parson Bate was an act of class cross-dressing which provoked outrage at the erosion of boundaries that it represented.[59] The disruption caused by these transgressions was only partially restored by Bate's rather late decoding of the fraud's visual signs; that 'His most amazingly confused address, the manner in which his friends treated him, and his new awkward vestments, all conspired to convince us he was a *made-up gentleman* for the business'.[60] The concern arose because 'social "transvestism"' was a crucial part of the extensive and fragile networks of credit upon which England's economy depended in the eighteenth century. Credit depended upon reputation which, in turn, depended upon self-presentation within the market place and, more importantly, within tight and sociable networks of similarly placed traders. These gendered performances involved a simulation of solidity, respectability and gentility in the interests of stability. Those seeking credit sought to create a spectacle of gentility – often one which crossed class boundaries – and a fiction which *would* provide the otherwise absent gold standard.[61] In the credit crisis of the 1770s the Macaronis threatened to show that the modern self was an illusion made of commodities and fantasies with no real, knowable substance.[62] Because their illusions were ones of masculinity, class and commodification they threatened to erode boundaries and destroy realities that others sought to protect.

Finally, the pleasures of Vauxhall's self-regarding spectator became, with the Macaronis, an illegitimate narcissism. This, as reflected in Fitzgerald's miniature portrait of himself, was a key part of the charges of effeminacy:

> When *Britain* calls her valiant sons to arms,
> Their milky souls no martial ardour warms,
> For all their *courage* lodges in the heel,
> And *fear's* the only passion they can feel;
> Save that, in which they every hour employ,
> (Narcissus-like) – *the self-admiring joy.*
> Haste – seize the *dear insipids* – bravely dare
> To wage with Folly and with fashion war.[63]

The pleasures of self-observation threatened military defeat and imperial decline. They also threatened decline through a failure to marry and reproduce. The Macaroni 'loves nobody but himself; and by nobody, except himself; is he beloved.'[64] He prefers the pleasures of the mirror to those of the marriage bed. In all these ways Macaroni masculinity disturbed the gardens' economy of vision and pleasure.

Conclusion

My purpose has been to show that examining the meanings and locations of the Macaroni reveals how luxurious commodity consumption shaped the Vauxhall affray, the pleasure gardens and the wider landscape of eighteenth-century cultural production through problematic constructions of masculinity, vision and pleasure. It was the Macaronis' position in the world of goods as men composed of commodities which meant that various signs and symbols were made meaningful and deployed as Bate had Croftes, Lyttelton and Fitzgerald burnt outside the Temple of Virtue. The Herculean club – a symbol of a rugged, moralizing masculinity – was counterposed to Fitzgerald's miniature portrait – a symbol of an effeminate and foreign self-love. The Macaronis' feathered hats – symbols of private, venal and luxurious consumption – were juxtaposed to Bate's quill pen, a symbol of the power of a supposedly virtuous public sphere. Moreover, their positionings within the field of vision – as spectacles, illegitimate spectators, narcissists and dangerous illusions – can also be understood, at least in part, in terms of the commodity as 'a visual problem in perception', and therefore through the political dangers of Vauxhall's luxuries. Their luxurious effeminacy made looking at Mrs Hartley such a problem, and explained the appearance of Captain Miles both in terms of cowardice and the peddling of yet another illusion. This contest over male vision was also a matter of commodification.

The Macaronis were, I have argued, very much creatures of Vauxhall and its modern modes of consumption as well as destabilizing them. Commodified pleasures and the new identities that came with them were part of a world of illusion which brought both the enchantments of the gardens and the fear of a hollow luxurious excess. As well as presenting new pleasures and new possibilities, these modes of consumption also posed the dangers of the fluidity of identities rooted in fashion and commodification. Masculinity would, under these conditions, be an illusion without solidity. However, if the Macaronis can be read as a disruption of the idealized relations between commodification, masculinity and vision which Vauxhall sought to put in place and to profit from – symbolized perhaps by the refined viewing of spectacles of imperial masculinity – it was not that they overturned the polite pleasures that Vauxhall presented. The pleasures of commercialized leisure, the pleasures of looking at men, and the pleasures of illusion were always both refined and luxurious. They were always underpinned by sexual desire and venality. What the Macaronis did was to push them to excess, revealing the tensions and contradictions upon which the gardens and the wider landscapes of eighteenth-century consumption were built. Bate rushed to shore up the breach. Yet even this could be packaged and sold. The pages of *The Vauxhall Affray* show the affair to have been both a pleasurable and a profitable disturbance.

Department of Geography, Queen Mary and Westfield College, UK

Notes

* This article forms part of a fuller discussion of the gardens in the author's forthcoming book *Spaces of Modernity* (New York: Guilford Press).
   I would like to thank David Solkin and Catherine Nash for comments on an earlier version.
1 *Dictionary of National Biography*; Mary MacCarthy, *Fighting Fitzgerald and Other Papers* (London: Martin Secker, 1930) and *The Life of George Robert Fitzgerald, Esq* (London, 1786).
2 *The Vauxhall Affray; or, the Macaronies Defeated*, 2nd edn (London, 1773).
3 Ibid., p. 14.
4 Kristina Straub, *Sexual Suspects: Eighteenth-Century Players and Sexual Ideology* (Princeton: Princeton University Press, 1992) and Peter de Bolla, 'The visibility of visuality', in Teresa Brennan and Martin Jay (eds) *Vision in Context: Historical and Contemporary Perspective on Sight* (London: Routledge, 1996), pp. 63–81.
5 John Brewer and Roy Porter (eds), *Consumption and the World of Goods* (London: Routledge, 1993).
6 Horace Walpole to Lord Hertford, 6th February 1764 in W. S. Lewis (ed.)

Horace Walpole's Correspondence (New Haven: Yale University Press, 1974), Vol. 38, p. 306.

7 M. D. George, *Catalogue of Political and Personal Satires. Volume V: 1771–1783* (London: British Museum, 1935) and Diana Donald, *The Age of Caricature: Satirical Prints in the Age of George III* (New Haven: Yale University Press, 1996).

8 John Gascoigne, *Joseph Banks and the English Enlightenment: Useful Knowledge and Polite Culture* (Cambridge: Cambridge University Press, 1994); Valerie Steele, 'The social and political significance of Macaroni fashion', *Costume*, 19 (1985), pp. 94–109; and Gerald Howson, *The Macaroni Parson: A Life of the Unfortunate Dr Dodd* (London: Hutchinson, 1973).

9 George, *Catalogue*, p. xxix; Steele, 'Macaroni fashion'; and Robert Hitchcock, *The Macaroni: A Comedy* (York, 1773).

10 John H. Jesse, *George Selwyn and His Contemporaries* (London: Richard Bentley, 1843), pp. 44 and 113. This undated letter is from *c.* 1766.

11 *Town and Country Magazine*, IV (1772): 243.

12 Neil McKendrick, 'The consumer revolution of eighteenth-century England', in Neil McKendrick, John Brewer and J. H. Plumb (eds) *The Birth of a Consumer Society: The Commercialisation of Eighteenth-Century England* (London: Hutchinson, 1982), p. 43.

13 *The London Magazine*, 41 (1772): 194.

14 *The Macaroni Jester, and Pantheon of Wit* (London, 1773?), p. 6.

15 *Macaroni Jester*, pp. 26–7.

16 George Colman, *Man and Wife: Or, The Shakespeare Jubilee* (London, 1770), p. 17.

17 *Town and Country Magazine*, IV (1772): 243.

18 *The Matrimonial Magazine*, 1 (1775): 59.

19 David H. Solkin, *Painting for Money: The Visual Arts and the Public Sphere in Eighteenth-Century England* (New Haven: Yale University Press, 1993).

20 Roy Porter and Mary Mulvey Roberts (eds) *Pleasure in the Eighteenth Century* (London: Macmillan, 1996).

21 Mollie Sands, *Invitation to Ranelagh, 1742–1803* (London: John Westhouse, 1946).

22 Solkin, *Painting for Money*, p. 106.

23 John Brewer, '"The most polite age and the most vicious": Attitudes towards culture as a commodity, 1660–1800', in Ann Bermingham and John Brewer (eds) *The Consumption of Culture 1600–1800: Image, Object, Text* (London: Routledge, 1995), p. 347.

24 Engravings from Caneletto's views of Vauxhall were sold for a shilling with *A Sketch of the Spring-Gardens, Vaux-Hall, in a Letter to a Noble Lord* (London, 1752) – attributed to John Lockman. The 'Vauxhall fan' is in *Duchy of Cornwall Archives. Folder 4: Vauxhall* with an advertisement (29 July 1739) for another version. See also *A Collection of Tickets, Bills of Performance, Pamphlets, Ms. Notes, Engravings and Extracts and Cuttings from Books and Periodicals relating to Vauxhall Gardens* (British Library), ff. 182, 187, 204, 209 and 325.

25 S. Toupee, 'An evening at Vaux-Hall', *The Scots Magazine*, 1 (1739): 364.

26 John Dixon Hunt, *Vauxhall and London's Garden Theatres* (Cambridge: Chadwyck Healey, 1985), p. 17.

27 *The Gentleman's Magazine*, 12 (1742): 315 and 420.

28 *Sketch of the Spring-Gardens* and *The Gentleman's Magazine*, 13 (1743): 439.

29 Ann Bermingman, 'Introduction', in Bermingham and Brewer (eds) *The Consumption of Culture*, p. 8.

30 John-Christophe Agnew, 'Coming up for air: consumer culture in historical perspective', in Brewer and Porter (eds) *Consumption and the World of Goods*, p. 25.

31 *The Life and Times of George Robert Fitzgerald* (Dublin, 1852), p. 68.

32 *Vauxhall Affray*, p. 13.

33 Ibid., pp. 54 and 112. See Straub, *Sexual Suspects* and Christina H. Kiaer, 'Professional femininity in Hogarth's *Strolling Actresses Dressing in a Barn*', *Art History*, 16 (1993): 239–65.

34 *Vauxhall Affray*, n.p.

35 *The London Magazine*, 41 (1772): 194.

36 *Macaroni Jester*, p. 51.

37 *The Macaroni, Scavoir Vivre, and Theatrical Magazine* (1774), p. 242.

38 See Peter de Bolla, 'The visibility of visuality: Vauxhall Gardens and the siting of the viewer', in Stephen Melville and Bill Readings (eds) *Vision and Textuality* (London: Macmillan, 1995), pp. 282–95.

39 Richard D. Altick, *The Shows of London: A Panoramic History of Exhibitions* (Cambridge: Harvard University Press, 1978).

40 *Sketch of the Spring-Gardens*, pp. 7 and 15. See also *A Description of Vaux-Hall Gardens. Being a Proper Companion and Guide for all who Visit that Place* (London, 1762).

41 *Sketch of the Spring-Gardens*, p. 13.

42 Scott Paul Gordon, 'Voyeuristic dreams: Mr Spectator and the power of the spectacle', *The Eighteenth Century: Theory and Interpretation*, 36 (1995): 3–23. A cutting (1738) in *Vauxhall Gardens Archive, Borough of Lambeth. Press Cuttings 1732–1823* reports on a 'masculine' woman at Vauxhall and that 'the Company, out of Respect to themselves, had the Pleasure to stare her and her Attendants out of the Gardens'.

43 Toupee, 'An evening at Vaux-Hall', pp. 323 and 363.

44 *Sketch of the Spring-Gardens*, p. 10.

45 Ibid., pp. 7 and 19.

46 *Description of Vaux-Hall Gardens*, p. 48.

47 *Sketch of the Spring-Gardens*, p. 5.

48 *The Connoisseur*, I (1755), p. 404.

49 *Description of Vaux-Hall Gardens*, pp. 6–7.

50 de Bolla, 'The visibility of visuality'.

51 *Vauxhall Affray*, pp. 65 and 100.

52 Straub, *Sexual Suspects*, pp. 10 and 57.

53 *Macaroni Jester*, p. 108.

54 Ibid., pp. 14 and 108.

55 *The Vauxhall Affray*, n.p.

56 *Fashion. A Poem* (Bath, 1775), p. 7.

57 Barbara Maria Stafford, *Body Criticism: Imaging the Unseen in Enlightenment Art and Medicine* (Cambridge: MIT Press, 1991) p. 86.

58 'Ferdinand Twigem', *The Macaroni. A Satire* (London, 1773) p. 11.

59 *Vauxhall Affray*, pp. 67 and 75.

60 Ibid., p. 24.

61 Lawrence E. Klein, 'Politeness for plebes: consumption and social identity in early eighteenth-century England', in Bermingham and Brewer (eds) *The Consumption of Culture*, p. 374 and John Brewer, 'Commercialisation and

politics', in McKendrick, Brewer and Plumb (eds) *The Birth of a Consumer Society*, pp. 197–262.

62 John Money, 'The masonic moment; or, ritual, replica, and credit: John Wilkes, the Macaroni Parson, and the making of the middle-class mind', *Journal of British Studies*, 32 (1993): 358–95.

63 Hitchcock, *The Macaroni*, n.p.

64 *The Macaroni Magazine* (1774), p. 242.

Robert W. Jones

Notes on *The Camp*: women, effeminacy and the military in late eighteenth-century literature

I

In the summer of 1778, amidst fears of impending French invasion, Lord North's already beleaguered government established a series of military encampments across Britain.[1] Located at strategic vantage points and with the army's ranks swelled by the incorporation of militia companies, the camps were intended to frustrate the advance of any invading force, while giving reassurance to a concerned populace.[2] Given the role expected of them, the camps at Coxheath, Bury St Edmonds and Warley Common could be praised lavishly within the stirring verse offered to the public by the Reverend William Tasker.

> Genius of Britain! to thy office true,
> On yonder heath the warring banners view;
> Where Maidstone's antient fabric stands,
> And Midway's streams refresh the thirsty lands;
> > British spirit never droops:
> > Where late the foreign hireling troops,
> > A servile, mercenary band!
> Disgrac'd the state, and sham'd the land;
> > Now behold a native race
> With freer step, and bolder grace![3]

The poem was well received, *The Gentleman's Magazine* noting that 'it is well-calculated to rouse the martial spirit of the nation'. Furthermore, *The Gentleman's Magazine* recognised that the main purpose of the poem was to 'celebrate our . . . encampments'.[4] By underlining this connection the reviewer was returning his readers to what was already a well-documented theme within the magazine's pages; namely, the fashionable enthusiasm

Textual Practice 11(3), 1997, 463–476   © 1997 Routledge 0950–236X

for martial display and for military camps in particular. In its number for October 1778 the magazine had reviewed Lewis Lochée's *An Essay on Castrametation*, a dry little book describing the design of fortified camps. Despite the technical nature of Lochée's work, the reviewer opined that 'there never was a Treatise more seasonably introduced, nor, perhaps, better accommodated to the prevailing Endemia'. Lochée's timeliness came from the fact that 'the whole kingdom seems, for several months past, to have been seized with what we may call a CASTAMANIA, of which few of the better sort, either gentlemen or ladies, have escaped the infection.'[5]

The concerns expressed by *The Gentleman's Magazine* were not without foundation, the habit of frequenting the army's encampments being newly fashionable in the summer months of 1778. The most forceful complaint made against the practice of visiting the camps was that such visits endorsed a mixing of genders and classes within the uncertain environment of the camp site. This concern is implicit within *The Gentleman's Magazine*'s dismay that people of quality, and women in particular, should exhibit such a ludicrous and unseemly attraction to military affairs. For many commentators, the spectacle of fashionable ladies conversing with either splendidly dressed regimental fops or rough troopers was not something to be encouraged. Indeed in a variety of texts the camps came to signify a particularly acute concern with the nature of gender difference. For while the camps could be seen as indicative of the modernity of the Hanoverian age in terms of its military power and organization, the encampments also revealed the unsettling mutability of identity which was thought to characterize contemporary culture. Parading in their highly coloured uniforms or lounging in their well-appointed tents and pavilions, army officers appeared to falter on the brink of effeminacy, while the women who languished after them appeared brazen, even mannish. Accordingly, satires on the questionable habit of camp visiting abounded, with many texts representing camp life as either lascivious or absurd.

In the majority of texts which represented visits to military camps during the late eighteenth century it is possible to detect questions of masculine and feminine propriety figured through appeals for self-restraint or critiques of self-display. However, by far the most prominent complaint levelled at the camps and their visitors was that of 'effeminacy'.[6] The condemnation of effeminacy is made broadly, almost haphazardly, in most treatments of the camps. The conjunction of a concern about masculinity with a satire on the military repeats a connection found in a wide variety of eighteenth-century texts where members of the armed forces are represented as luxurious or foolish. Not infrequently, this critique emerged from within the discourse of civic humanism which regarded the existence of a professional soldiery as in itself luxuriant and hence effète.[7] However, while there is an echo of this attitude in Tasker's reference to the 'servile mercenary band', the camps were more often seen as a social rather than directly a political issue; as such commentators referred to questions of social and sexual propriety and to the regulation of consumption. This account retained the camps as a luxurious or effeminate space, but did so with less regard to the presentation of civic masculinity. Indeed the most pressing problem during the 1770s was the way in which the site and spectacle of the camps provided society ladies with an opportunity for brazen affectation while presenting men with a space for foppish dalliance.

II

I want to examine representations of the camps and the 'luxurious sexualities' found within their precincts via a close reading of a sermon given by James Fordyce in 1776. Preaching to an audience of young men, Fordyce claimed that they could improve their morals as well as their manners by entering more readily into the society of women. Women, because they combine 'easy comprehension, natural taste [with] sprightly imagination', are able to offer young men 'some of the sweetest pleasures which the soul can taste'.[8] Furthermore, Fordyce was enthusiastic about the polishing effect which social intercourse with women might have on the emerging sociability of adolescent males. It was, he suggested, precisely the desire to please women which rendered men sociable (pp. 4–8). Given this connection it was important that women were not too closely confined or wholly separated from contact with men; predictably, he added the rider that women who entered too readily into the 'gaze of the glittering throng' were incapable of virtue. For Fordyce therefore, while women could embody the private virtues which he believed had a role in reforming young men, it was equally clear that women could not continue to possess these virtues if they themselves moved from the private to the public arena (pp. 17–20, 23, 49–54, 88–101).

Significantly, Fordyce's concern with the dangers of 'modern impertinence' and the inequities of 'places of gay resort', coincided with his sense that a culture which excludes or rejects the society of women is bound to be effeminate (pp. 27–9). Fordyce's claim that a lack of association with women leads men to degenerate was a claim he felt necessary to support through an appeal to ancient precedent. However, the reference reflects a more ambivalent attitude, both to the state of contemporary Britain and to the role of women in a well-regulated society, than Fordyce was aware:

In Rome matters were conducted with, what many of the sex would esteem, a more flattering indulgence: they were not only admitted to convivial intercourse with the men, but to public festivals, theatrical entertainments, and even military games; where young virgins appeared openly with a freedom of attire, an exposition of beauty, and a boldness of manner, but ill consistent with the just standard of female decency and attraction; though by these means they would, no doubt, acquire uncommon vigour and resolution, become more strongly interested in the achievements and honours of a warlike race, and be qualified in due time for giving birth to conquerors and heroes.

(pp. 25–6)

It is striking that the formation of male identity through the medium of women's participation in masculine pursuits is imagined to take place at what Fordyce terms 'theatrical entertainments, and even military games'. These terms denote the area of public life which ought to be exclusively masculine and opposed to 'the just standard of female decency'; and yet Fordyce does not wholly deny the benefit of women's involvement. Continuing his partial defence of such practices, Fordyce suggests that:

the fair sex in those days being, on many occasions, respected as the judges and rewarders of manly enterprises . . . would naturally kindle, in the youth of their country, an emulation and ardour peculiarly conducive to the exalted flights of spirit and patriotism that marked the purest ages of antiquity.

(pp. 26–7)

Fordyce's text implies that because women have become more feminine, in the sense that they no longer exhibit themselves publicly or seek to imitate men, they have relinquished the capacity to render or to fashion masculinity, at least in its heroic form. The logic of Fordyce's argument is to suggest that the extension of the difference between men and women envisioned by the greater femininity of women has led to the effeminization of men. To a degree this was Fordyce's project – to render men more feminine and hence more social – and yet he is never fully reconciled to the pliant manners his position required, remaining a critic of what he sees as the 'enervating luxury' of modern society.

Fordyce's delineation of the rude health of ancient societies should have sounded incongruously in the ears of his audience as it was simply not true that women had stopped frequenting 'public festivals, theatrical entertainments . . . even military games'. If the satires the 1770s produced are to be believed, it was a decade in which it proved increasingly difficult to keep women away from theatres and harder still to wrest them from the pleasures of military games. In the novel *The Coxheath Camp*, for example, the heroine, Eleanora Rivers, writes enthusiastically about the pleasures of the camp:

> I should first tell you, we had dined . . . *en militaire* in that gentlemen's marquee. Our table was covered, at the sounding of martial music; every toast was received with martial plaudits; and we constituted a very pretty spectacle for metropolitan curiosity; whole troops of gapers passing and repassing the door, and envying us our festive interval, our momentary relaxation from the toils of the field.

Here the camp is represented as a self-consciously superficial arena with an emphasis upon giddy pleasure. Later Eleanora adds: 'we have the prospect of eating from one end of the camp to the other.'[9] If Fordyce looked back to an era of ancient integrity, *The Coxheath Camp* imagines a future of dissipation and intrigue in which women were far from acting the part of republican mothers and in which 'military games' were unlikely to produce 'conquerors and heroes'. For, while the camp contained stockades which demonstrated the severity of an army life, the concurrent display of fine uniforms and high living suggested that the officers were more concerned with luxuriant consumption than the rigours of campaigning. As a result, the space of the 'holiday camps', as they are termed in *The Coxheath Camp*, was an ambivalent one characterized by fashionable and dissipated living (II: 95, 271–2).

The image of the officers and men offered by *The Coxheath Camp* was not uncommon; satirical pamphlets often represented soldiers as the consumers of male corsetry, cosmetics and other emblems of an effeminate personality. The supposed degeneracy of such figures points to the ambiguities of male identity in the Hanoverian period, with many commentators identifying the soldier as the sign of a weakened national character.[10] Indeed, it appeared that the very guardians of the nation offered, not civic virtue and self-denial, but foppish and excessive eccentricities. The satirical verse-epistle *The Camp-Guide* makes the accusation emphatically: much of the text is taken up with the laments of Ensign Tommy Toothpick, who bemoans the hardships of the camp in a series of letters to his mother. Toothpick's grievances range from his commanding officer's disregard for his new boots to the loss of his chest, which included 'thousands of nick-nacks' and sundry toiletries.[11] The poem represents Toothpick as the archetypal modern young gentleman, unwilling to adapt himself to a soldier's life and unable to comprehend the role expected of him. Also published as part of *The Camp-Guide* were the similarly affected epistles of Nelly Brisk. Nelly writes to her correspondent Miss Gadabout, recording everything which is new and exciting about the camp:

> The Dutchess of D_____, Beauty's fair queen,
> At the head of our mess, is constantly seen.
> She's the life of our pleasure, the queen of our Camp,
> And for our amusement, Her Grace we may thank!
> So gallant our heroes, at Beauty's fair shrine,
> Their pass-words are sonnets – their billet all rhime![12]

As this extract makes clear, Nelly's letters took their reference from the recent visit of the Duchess of Devonshire (*The Camp-Guide* was dedicated to her) to the great camp at Coxheath, near Maidstone in Kent. In a direct reversal of Dr Fordyce's pious expectation, Nelly's pleasure comes from the inversion of military and masculine authority brought about by the commanding presence of fashionable women.

III

The idea that women of fashion were peculiarly disposed to view the encampment at Coxheath can also be found in both *The Coxheath Camp* and Richard Brinsley Sheridan's afterpiece, *The Camp, A Musical Entertainment*. Accordingly, each text contains many sidelong glances at the inhabitants of the camp and the women who visit them. The intention throughout is to suggest that, like Tommy Toothpick, the soldiers are unable to achieve the hardening of character required for military service and that the women have forgotten the softness appropriate to their sex. An early scene in Sheridan's play established that the officers are not only 'mighty delicate looking Gentlemen' but also followers of peculiar fashions: 'they wear a sort of a Pettycoat as it were, with a great Hat and Feathers, and a Mortal sight of hair – I suppose they be of some of your outlandish Troops, your Foreign Hessians, or such like.'[13] For the most part the comedy is simple, imaging the camp as a site of affected pleasure and shady dealing, yet connects its specific concerns with the larger issue of sexuality and consumption (II: 731–2, 742–4).

However, during the final scene Sheridan extended and complicated the depiction of the army as luxurious through a representation of effeminacy which is both elaborate and ambiguous. The scene begins with the arrival on stage of Lady Plume, Lady Sarah Sash and Miss Gorget. It is significant here that Gorget, Sash and Plume constitute the more flamboyant parts of an officer's uniform, a mode of dress or identity which the women seem at once to constitute and to dissemble; this impression would have been underlined in performance by the *en militaire* costumes worn by the actresses. The incongruity of their appearance is taken further when the ladies are joined by Lady Plume's brother, Sir Harry Bouquet.

The ladies discuss their residence in camp and lament that Sir Harry has declined to enter the military life and thinks nothing of ridiculing the camp. This attitude has not pleased the party, and Lady Sash in particular has been caustic in her response, much to the chagrin of Bouquet: 'all I said was that he look'd so French, and so finical that he ran the risk of being mistaken for another female Chevalier' (II: 744). Continuing her complaint, Lady Sash states that:

> LA. SASH: . . . He vows there is an Eternal Confusion between our Lords' Camp Equipage, and our dressing Apparatus – between Stores Military and Millinery – such a description he gives – on the same Shelf Carti[d]ges and Cosmetics, Pouches and Patches – here Stands of Arms, and there a file of Black Pins.
>
> (II: 744–45)

The speech contains more than an echo of Pope's description of Belinda's dressing-table in *The Rape of the Lock*. Significantly, the allusion serves to install not only a shared reference point but a position from which critique, rather than merely comedy, may be reached. The confusion of fabrics and cosmetics represented by Pope and reworked by Sheriden suggests not only the dangerous intermixing of masculine and feminine pursuits, but also indicates something of the dangers of both an overly refined femininity while also indicating an uneasiness about contemporary masculinity.[14]

Despite this connection, a simple reading of the scene is frustrated because the attack on the camp has been made by an evidently luxurious, even effeminate, character. Most problematically, it is unclear, given that the line is spoken by Lady Sash, whether Bouquet is the object of the satire or (by proxy) its mouthpiece. In the dialogue which succeeds Lady Sash's speech, the satiric focus is similarly uncertain:

> LA. PLUME: Now . . . Brother, what can make you Judge so differently of the Camp from everybody else.
> SIR H.B.: Why then Seriously I do think it, the very worst plann'd thing I ever beheld, for instance now the Tents are all ranged in a Strait Line. Now Miss Gorget, can anything be worse than a Strait Line? Isn't there a horrid uniformity in this infinite Vista of Canvas? No curve no break – and the Avenue of Marquees – abominable!
>
> (II: 745)

The comedy cuts two ways in this exchange. Bouquet is clearly the object of ridicule, his sense of the camp's tastelessness at a time of national emergency being both affected and ludicrous. His inability to distinguish between the requirements of necessity and discipline (exemplified by the straight lines of the tents) and the niceties of aesthetics (he suggests later that Capability Brown might be employed to improve the camp) is plainly connected with his ambiguous appearance, partially male, potentially feminine, apparently French. Yet it is perhaps equally clear that the presence of the ladies at Coxheath is at least as tasteless and as indiscriminate. Throughout the scene Bouquet insists that both the camp and the women lack refinement; the point is perhaps that the camp is rather unpleasant and the women are foolish in their credulous acceptance of it as a place of fashionable resort. The message is underlined when Bouquet condemns the confusion of place and social class wrought by the arrival of camp.

> SIR H.B.: . . . the Ridicule of it is to see how this Madness has infected the whole Road – from travelling to Maidstone. The Camp jargon is as Current all the way as bad Silver. The very Postil[l]ions that drove me, talk of their Cavalry [which] refuses to charge on a trot uphill, the turnpikes seem'd converted into Redoubts, and the Dogs demand the Counter Sign from my Servants instead of their tickets – then when I got to Maidstone I found the very Waiters had a smattering of Tactics, for enquiring what I could have for Dinner.
> (II: 746)

Bouquet may be being affected here – as when he laments that 'the Officers' tents [are] all close to the Common Soldiers' – but in commenting on the folly of others he is occupying an unexpectedly normative position. His sense of the bad currency infecting the Kent countryside confirms his belief (reported by Lady Sash) that the encampment disturbs the proper constitution of both feminine and military identity.

Bouquet's critique serves to remind the audience that the ladies are not truly martial; their appearance, he suggests, is merely costume. To emphasize his point, Bouquet tells the ladies that 'on the first bad Weather you'll give orders to Strike your Toilets, and each Secure a Retreat to Tunbridge' (II: 749). Given that Bouquet is represented as both foppish and effeminate, the critique of the camp has taken an unexpected turn. Although Bouquet has argued for the social and sexual distinctions which define the discourse on luxury central to eighteenth-century critiques of modernity, he himself is the probable target of such a critique.[15] The ambiguities of Bouquet's character were underlined by the diverse reviews the play received in October 1778. A review appearing in the *Public Advertiser*, for example, recorded that a 'Macaroni connoisseur rallies the Ladies on their Military Appearance, and by several well timed Witticisms, enlivened this pleasing entertainment', while the *London Evening Post* described Bouquet as a 'Macaroni officer'; other reviewers suggested that he was fop or a wit. That Bouquet could be mistaken for an officer is understandable, given that foppishness functioned as the sign of the effeminized military. However, the easy slide between 'officer' and 'connoisseur' is significant, for it is as a connoisseur, as a feminized man of fashion, that Bouquet attacks Sash, Plume and Gorget. It is difficult to imagine the effect being the same if Bouquet was a soldier, the very figure the ladies covet and imitate.

However, Bouquet's distance from the self-promoting, sexually available officer might be the grounds upon which his peculiar and rather fragile authority is based. As Susan Staves has suggested, the stage comedy of the late eighteenth century is characterized by a softening of attitudes towards foppish characters.[16] Of the theatrical fop she writes:

> Though fops are in various ways effeminate, they are rarely repre-sented as homosexual. On the contrary, they are asexuals who like to spend time with the ladies. As connoisseurs of fashion, they have interests in common with women. . . . Such a lack of sexual appetite was itself, in the increasingly polite mind of the eighteenth century female or effeminate.[17]

Although Staves is hasty in her alignment of the 'asexual' and the 'effemi-nate', her suggestion that 'effeminacy' is not automatically a pejorative term (or at least not simply so) is intriguing.[18] More strikingly, effeminacy is deployed in the late eighteenth century rather vaguely, and is often used to offset mannish qualities in women. This is arguably the intention behind Bouquet, his character working to highlight the dangers of destabilizing gender categories and roles. In this sense Sheridan's representation of the camp may have functioned as a reminder of the stability of gender distinctions rather than their contravention. This point is indicated by *The Camp*'s main plot, in which the romantic Nancy (played by Miss Walpole) masquerades as a soldier in order to retrieve her lover from the army. As one reviewer commented:

> Miss Walpole had great merit in her disguised character of a recruit; she was one of the prettiest breeches figures that a painter could wish for, she went through her exercise with an ease and exactness very extraordinary for a lady.

In this account, cross-dressing functions as a resumption of stable gender difference; a resolution achieved because Nancy's transgression is more apparent than real. If the camp and its diverse inhabitants threatened confusion, the self-evident heterosexuality of Nancy and her lover offered some compensation. This recuperative manœuvre is significant as, although the representation of Tommy Toothpick and Sir Harry Bouquet is homophobic in its condemnation of deficient masculinities, the charge is not made with reference to a normative model of civic or public man. As such, the camps do not represent a problem because they disclose the unseemly potential in terms of a perceived threat to political liberties, but because they offer a space for affected or ridiculous behaviour.

IV

It does not follow however, that all the texts depicting the camp at Coxheath were devoid of political or social critique. Most strikingly, *The Coxheath Camp* exhibits a moral discourse about the army unconcerned with the pieties of civic humanism; indeed the novel illustrates how a middle-class cultural politics could be figured within a discussion of the camp at Coxheath. Like many sentimental novels of the late eighteenth century, *The Coxheath Camp* makes plain its class concerns by detailing the circumstances of its heroine. In this case Eleanora is the exuberant yet virtuous daughter of an indigent subaltern serving in the militia. Like many of her *ton* acquaintance, Eleanora is much taken with the splendour of the officers, their tents and entertainments. The arrival of the camp she says will be the 'era of our animation' (I: 4). In this excited spirit Eleanora writes to a friend describing how a soldier might appeal to women of fashion:

> A Soldier, if he be a pretty fellow, has a thousand advantages over the rest of the sex. He is a gentleman, which is the infallible passport for him into the best company. He is a hero; – a hero who, perhaps, will so be called upon to take the field in defense of the very circle he so agreeably entertains with his chit-chat: he is therefore beheld with a mixture of approbation and gratitude by all his acquaintance.

The stress falls here upon the soldiers' prettiness, their rather specious gentility and their capacity for 'chit-chat'. As Eleanora concedes, Coxheath is a place of 'martial encampments, if not martial prowess' (I: 7–8). Despite these misgivings, Eleanora values extravagant display and defends the camp against the insinuations of her correspondent who suggests that it is a den of vice (II: 29–31). However, the narrative is keen to indicate that Eleanora is mistaken in her admiration of army life. Critically, she has confused magnificence with value, a connection rejected and devalued by the emerging culture of the middle class.

As the novel progresses, the incongruity and impropriety of a military life becomes increasingly obvious. Indeed Eleanora is shown to be foolish, even manly, in her defence of the camp's pleasures (II: 38–42). This suggestion first emerges when the arrival of fashionable ladies from London leads to a visit to the marquee of Lord Brazen:

> To his Marquee we went, where the air of the pretty fellow made us quite forget the Soldier. Everything was so fine and so finikin, so

dainty and so studied, so bedecked and so befringed, that there was no end to the marvellings and the applaudings of the ladies; and we were obliged to sacrifice our truth to the altar of his vanity, and close in at every favourable pause with 'very pretty! very pretty, indeed!'.

But with all this *petit-maitreship* about him, he was no degenerate son of the Brazens. He ogled me with a confidence that startled me, and chatted away without fear or wit.

(I: 101–2)

Brazen's sexuality, if not his status as a soldier, is all too clear. However, it is interesting that the charge of sexual deviance can only be countered by the revelation of a crude heterosexuality: he is 'without fear or wit'. The insinuation will appear again, when, as a signal of her changed attitude, Eleanora describes a moment of 'bustle and confusion' in the camp during which 'the Bobadils strut, the Drawcansirs stare, and the Fribbles trip' (II: 137).

However, the encounter with the variously degenerate Brazen also discloses a middle-class attitude towards the military which regarded the camp not only as sexually suspect but also as unpleasantly upper class. Following his initial encounter with Eleanora, Brazen is keen to make his addresses to a woman whose poverty, he believes, will ensure the success of his design. To a degree Brazen judges shrewdly, as Eleanora's widower father, Lieutenant Rivers, is unable to offset the force of Brazen's superior social and military rank, and is obliged to allow his commanding officer access to his daughter (I: 120–1). Brazen's pursuit of Eleanora underlines an already existing opposition between the privacy and contentment of the family in which gender positions and roles are firmly established and the world of the camp where scheming officers are able to exploit their social and sexual privileges. Fortunately, Eleanora is not totally abandoned, as her rich middle-class benefactress Mrs Mildmay intervenes to protect her from the brutish officer (I: 107–21). Possessed of a massive West Indian fortune, Mrs Mildmay has no need of Lieutenant Rivers's caution; indeed she actively shields Eleanora from Brazen's advances. Naturally, this leads to conflict between them: in a key confrontation, Brazen rejects Mrs Mildmay's involvement in the affair precisely because she is a woman of merely commercial wealth. Throughout the scene Brazen's insouciant posturing and foppish arrogance is readily apparent (II: 140–3).

In contradistinction to the effrontery and effeminacy of Lord Brazen, Mrs Mildmay's function in the novel is as the good mother of Coxheath, assisting the needy, saving the threatened; throughout *The Coxheath Camp*, Mrs Mildmay repairs marriages and rescues the weaker recruits from the cruelties of military discipline (I: 240–50; II: 2–14). Combining money with manners and morals, Mrs Mildmay's benevolent conduct

offers an alternative to the follies and excesses of the camp. Most importantly, her efforts to ensure that, at least amidst her protégés, valiant,
industrious men marry virtuous, monied women offers the possibility of
more stable gender identities than the camp alone is able to provide.
Throughout her later stages of the novel, Mrs Mildmay counsels her
young friends, urging prudence and restraint while quietly constructing a
sentimental community within the camp (II: 138–40). In effect, the camp
becomes virtuous to the degree to which it is incorporated within Mrs
Mildmay's personal domain, becoming in Eleanora's phrase a 'kind of
larger household'. Having transformed the public world of the military
into the private world of the home, *The Coxheath Camp* indicates that
an army camp can become an acceptable place only if virtuous women
participate in order to regulate male practice. Mrs Mildmay's marriage to
Lieutenant Rivers completes this ideological resolution, endorsing an
image of the family in opposition to the army (II: 226–8, 250–2). This is
to argue not, as Fordyce suggested, that women are needed to produce
heroic masculinity, rather that the account of sexual difference embodied
by the novel's sentimental discourse requires virtuous women to prevent
the evolution of sexual sameness: in this instance brazen, mannish women
and foppish, effeminate soldiers.

V

In these terms the camp satires seem to lack the political edge of, for
example, Mary Wollstonecraft's attack on soldiery later in the century. In
a crucial passage in her *Vindication of the Rights of Woman*, Wollstonecraft
compared soldiers to fashionable women, indicating that both had degen-
erated into affected gallantries characterized by an effeminate desire to
please. Soldiers, she argued, were like women in that they possessed only
a fashionable manner and a tawdry 'knowledge of the world'. Indeed,
for Wollstonecraft a comparison between soldiers and women revealed
the superficiality of a distinction between the sexes, in that soldiers, like
women, practised 'the minor virtues with punctilious politeness'.[19] The
Vindication is a reminder that the hostility to the army is most marked in
texts which in seeking to critique commerce, endorse a civic humanist
emphasis on restraint and probity. Wollstonecraft, in a rather complicated
way would be one such; a more straightforward example might be John
Brown, author of *An Estimate of the Manners and Opinions of Our Times*.[20]

For diverse reasons this was not the attitude adopted by those who
wrote about the camp in the summer and autumn of 1778. By contrast, the
texts discussed in this article are largely unconcerned with the ideological
focus offered by civic humanism's condemnations of the standing army.

Certainly, texts such as *The Camp* and *The Camp-Guide* do not deploy that discourse's sense of the responsibilities and requirements of military service. Indeed the assumptions of civic critique of luxury appear to be mocked – as when they are spoken by Bouquet. Satires on the camps were not without ideological purpose, however; for example, *The Coxheath Camp* is a rather complicated tale into which is woven an affirmation of middle-class values, most conspicuously charity, privacy and benevolence. In contrast to these virtues the camp is divided between foppish affectation and brutish disregard. Despite these concerns military men, and army officers in particular, have a necessary as well as ambiguous place in the heterosocial and heterosexual world of late eighteenth-century society. In literary texts they represent the dangerous excesses into which masculinity could be drawn and provide a limit against which other characters can be tested; a vital task in a culture in which the norms of social life were under-going rapid transition. More forcefully, texts such as *The Coxheath Camp* critique a culture of display in which identity is seen to be performative rather than essential. Texts such as *The Camp-Guide* and *The Coxheath Camp* are clearly the products of a culture wary of its own excesses, yet one that is willing to evade the most severe implications of its own critique by pressing the case more fully against an aristocracy deemed to be already dissolute: Lord Brazen, Ladies Sash and Plume and the almost upper-class Tommy Toothpick.

Dept of English, University of Wales, Aberystwyth

Notes

1 This article is taken from a much larger project on the military and the culture of war during the late eighteenth century. In a longer version of this study I am more careful to explain the political cross-currents underlying the invasion scare of 1778 and its relation to Admiral Keppel's court martial; Sheridan, in particular, is treated more copiously than space permitted on this occasion. I would like to thank Shaun Regan for providing a careful reading of an early draft of this article.

2 For an account of the invasion scare of 1778–79 see A. Temple Patterson, *The Other Armada: The Franco-Spanish Attempt to Invade Britain in 1779* (Manchester: Manchester University Press, 1960).

3 Revd William Tasker, 'An ode to the warlike genius of Great Britain', *Poems* (London: Dodsley, Bew *et al.*, 1779), pp. 7–8.

4 *The Gentleman's Magazine; or Monthly Intelligenser*, vol. 49 (London: F. Newberry, 1779), pp. 357–8.

5 Ibid., pp. 480–2.

6 Throughout this article I use the term 'effeminacy' in the 'constructionist' sense outlined by Alan Sinfield. See *The Wilde Century: Effeminacy, Oscar Wilde and the Queer Moment* (London: Cassell, 1994), pp. 3–4, 11–17.

7 For a discussion of this issue see Lois F. Schwoerer, 'The literature of the Standing Army Debate', *Huntingdon Library Quarterly*, 28(3) (1964–65), pp. 187–212; J. G. A. Pocock, *The Machiavellian Moment: Florentine Political Thought and The Atlantic Republican Tradition* (Princeton: Princeton University Press, 1975), pp. 401–22; see also E.J. Cleary, 'The pleasure of terror: paradox in Edmund Burke's theory of the sublime', in Roy Porter and Marie Mulvey Roberts, *Pleasure in the Eighteenth Century* (London: Macmillan, 1996), pp. 164–81.

8 James Fordyce, *The Character and Conduct of the Female Sex, and the Advantages to be derived by Young Men from the Society of Virtuous Women* (London: T. Cadell, 1776), pp. 72, 81. Fordyce's discourse was first delivered on 1 January 1776 at the Monkwell Street Chapel, London. All subsequent citations are given parenthetically in the text.

9 *The Coxheath Camp. A Novel in a Series of Letters. By a Lady*, 2 vols (London: Fielding and Walker, 1779), vol. I, pp. 70–1, 214–15. All subsequent citations are given parenthetically in the text.

10 See, for example, George Coleman, Bonnell Thornton *et al.*, *The Connoisseur*, no. x (4 April 1754), *The Connoisseur. By Mr. Town, Critic and Censor-General*, 4th edn, 4 vols (London: R. Baldwin, 1761), vol. I, p. 81.

11 *The Camp Guide in a series of letters from Ensign Tommy Toothpick to Lady Sarah Toothpick and from Miss Nelly Brisk to Miss Gadabout* (London: Fielding and Walker, 1778), pp. 2–3.

12 Ibid., p. 12. Satires on the Duchess's behaviour and her reputed influence on male affairs were quite commonplace. See William Coombes, *An Interesting Letter to the Dutchess of Devonshire* (London: J. Bew, 1778).

13 Richard Brinsley Sheridan, *The Camp. A Musical Entertainment*, in *The Dramatic Works of Richard Brinsley Sheridan*, ed. Cecil Price, 2 vols (Oxford: Clarendon Press, 1973), vol. II, p. 732. All subsequent citations are given parenthetically in the text.

14 For a discussion of this theme in Pope's writing see Laura Brown, *Alexander Pope* (Oxford: Basil Blackwell, 1985), pp. 6–45, and Susan Staves, 'Pope's refinement', *Eighteenth Century: Theory and Interpretation*, vol. 29 (1988), pp. 145–64.

15 John Sekora, *Luxury: The Concept in Western Thought, Eden to Smollett* (Baltimore: Johns Hopkins University Press, 1977), pp. 23–62.

16 Susan Staves, 'A few kind words for the fop', *Studies in English Literature*, vol. 22 (1982), p. 421.

17 Ibid., pp. 414, 415.

18 A more theoretical account of fops, fribbles and their relation to the construction of homosexuality has been provided by Thomas A. King; see his 'performing "Akimbo": queer pride and epistemological prejudice', in Moe Meyer (ed.) *The Politics and Poetics of Camp* (London: Routledge, 1994), pp. 23–50.

19 Mary Wollstonecraft, *Vindication of the Rights of Women*, ed. and intro. Miriam Brody (Harmondsworth: Penguin, 1985), pp. 105, 106.

20 John Brown, *An Estimate of the Manners and Opinions of Our Times* (London: L. Davis & C. Reymers, 1757), see esp. pp. 73–84.

Sue Wiseman

From the luxurious breast to the virtuous breast: the body
politic transformed

The iconography of liberty, as one critic has observed, operates by a 'series
of inversions'. That which is opposite to, or other than, 'liberty' comes to
stand as a sign of that very quality; and (conversely) figures for liberty
incorporate meanings which undermine them.[1] This article offers a brief,
and therefore inevitably fragmentary genealogy of the relationship of
apparent opposites, 'luxury' (an invitation to lust and through chains
of association an index of political degeneracy), and 'liberty' (implying
political virtue, enfranchisement), as they are focused in the gradually
naturalized iconography of the female breast during the seventeenth and
eighteenth centuries.

I will argue that the breast begins as an icon and index of luxury but
comes to signify political freedom and, as Marina Warner puts it, acts as
a sign of 'that utopian condition, lawful liberation'. Besides the place of
the breast and breast-feeding in the ideologies of domesticity (illuminated
by the work of Mary Jacobus and Ruth Perry) another genealogy can be
traced, in part derived from the Amazonian warrior women of the ancient
world, in which the luxurious sexual and even pornographic breast is
rearticulated as virtuous.[2] Evidently the virtuous breast as political icon
derives its power, at least in part, from the internalization of the pleasurable
allurements of the luxurious breast, but how did that gradual internalization mark discourses of political virtue and luxury, and how can it be
traced? What follows is an attempt to analyse some of the iconographic and
political changes that made this 'internalization' possible.

Luxurious breasts

The breast had a long history as an indicator of luxury. In the *Republic*
Plato describes 'a State at fever-heat' where 'we shall be more likely to see
how justice and injustice originate':

Textual Practice 11(3), 1997, 477–492

we must enlarge our borders; for the original healthy State is no longer sufficient. Now will the city have to fill and swell with a multitude of callings which are not required by any natural want . . . makers of divers kinds of articles, including women's dresses. And we shall want more servants. Will not tutors be in request, and nurses wet and dry.[3]

Plato's *Republic* reads the breast as a sign of luxury. The misuse, or lack of use of the breast, signifies social excess and consequent collapse. The wetnurse, like the tutor, is needed to care for the children produced as byproducts of this state. The breast in the *Republic* has a literal connection to the luxurious state, imbricated with questions of proper and improper production and reproduction which counterpose the appropriately useful and the luxurious use of the body. Here it is but a short and very literal step from the organization of breast-feeding to sociopolitical structures: one is the sign of the other.[4]

Political theory and training of the individual were both areas that took up the question of luxury for which, in Plato's description of 'the State at fever-heat', the breast had acted as an index.[5] Early modern Christian interpretation builds figurative structures on the 'practical' or evidentiary use of the breast as sign. For example, Renaissance images of avarice situate the breast in an ethical-political sphere, linking femininity and luxury through a dynamic of disgustingness uncovered, youth transformed into age, and so on. In Durer's image of an aged woman, possibly an allegory of 'Avarice', the old woman's long hair and sexual grin indicate the chaste, youthful virgin she is not – and in a double move call into question the very chastity of such a virgin whose youthful image always harbours the possibility of deceit.[6] The much circulated early modern icon of avarice as an old woman with hardened and hanging breasts contrasted with the image of charity, suckling either mother or father in prison: these paired images indicate the breast's ethical valency and ability to signify both chastity and lasciviousness.[7]

One example, although it does not focus explicitly on the breast, is Spenser's *Faerie Queene* where the dynamic between a desirable surface and a disgusting 'truth' always ready to appear is an important narrative dynamo. The dynamics of discovery of foul beneath fair dominate much of *The Faerie Queene* – in the usurping of true by false, in the imprisonment of men and women by luxurious old women, and in the repeated 'revelations' of Duessa – 'a filthy foule old woman', a 'divelish hag' (Fradubio, Bk I, Canto II).[8] The aged female bodies which in Spenser stand for the absence of virtue are enmeshed in a narrative in which the body, though it usually has an 'undertruth' to be revealed, is poised between allegorical and evidentiary status; the hanging breasts, forensic evidence that the woman is past childbearing age, are simultaneously a naturalized sign of her lustful propensities.[9]

What, then, is the status of the 'truth' revealed? The awful disclosures – 'partes misshapen, monstrous' (Fradubio, I, II, 40) – can be read as uncovering allegorical or verisimilar truth and the two are not mutually exclusive. Thus the aged woman's breast, allegorical of avarice, can simultaneously be 'naturalized' as improper (unproductive) female desire. Such naturalization of the breast-as-sign through an 'internalization' of symbolic qualities is, as we shall see, a key to the potential of the breast to become a political symbol.

The tension between allegory and naturalization, or the 'internalization' of ethical qualities within a naturalistic order of representation can be seen in John Bulwer's *Anthropometamorphoses*. Writing in the 1650s of fashions in bodily rearrangement as an index of the world's revolutions, Bulwer tends to read bodies forensically and ethnographically as signs of social circumstance, offering his analysis of 'our *Vox Corporis*, or *Moral Anatomy of the Body*'.[10] Fashions of the breast, like the rest of the body, for him indicate good or bad social organization. His discussion of 'pap-fashions' reserves for the Irish special abuse connecting them with the long-breasted symbol of avarice. Irish women's breasts are described as 'fit to be made Money-bags for East or West-Indian Merchants, being more than half a yard long, and as well wrought as any Tanner in the like charges could ever mollifie such leather.'[11]

Such animus against the colonized contrasts with his description of the development of a breast during adolescence – as though his audience did not know it:

> There being good reason in Nature, why women should have a modest regard of them, and not so openly expose them; because the consent between the Breasts and Wombe is very great as the onely contrectation provoketh lust. These Breasts, the store-houses of Milk, resemble half a Bowl, they rise the breadth of two fingers high, when Maids begin to have their courses, and when they are full ripe and grown marriageable, they swel so that they may be covered with the hand; which *Aristophanes* calls . . . the goodly Apple of the Breast.

(p. 177)

As Schiebinger argues, ideas of 'nature' found in forensic and ethnographic discourse are 'infused with sexuality and gender'.[12] Bulwer's discussion, mixing ethical prohibitions, forensic detail and lascivious description suggests the multiple significances of the breast, signifying purity but also through 'consent between the Breasts and Wombe' linked to the generative organs.

Written as pornography was coming to have wider circulation in England, Bulwer's account of the breast corroborates Lyn Hunt's assertion that pornographic or eroticized description in the mid-seventeenth century was habitually at the service of a purpose other than or exceeding that of pornographic reading.[13] Contemporary recognition of the pornographic potential of forensic writing is evident in the prosecution for obscenity of John Martin (or Marten) in 1709 on the basis of the sixth appendix to a quasi-medical work, *A treatise of all the degrees and symptoms of the Venereal Disease.*[14]

A similar intertwining of distinct discourses and generic purposes, linking the ethical, sexual and potentially political into a close discursive network, can be seen in *The Complete Midwife's Practice Enlarged* (1680), a compendium of several midwives' manuals including a dissection of the breast which foregrounds its connection to the sexual organs, but also suggests its contrasting cultural position.[15] It is connected to the reproductive apparatus by a tube that goes 'behind the scenes' in this theatre of the body, but is presented in a slightly different representational order from the folded back flesh and skin of the anatomy. It is as if the skin has dissolved away to give a blurred and soft-focus image of the breast beneath. In this illustration the breast occupies its own order of representation between diagrammatic and verisimilar, a status which, arguably, replicates its ambiguous, even dualistic status as index of purity and of procreation.[16]

The shifting status of much discourse on the body is something to which both Lacqueur and Sawday call attention: as Lacqueur argues, 'nothing in this cultural system is *just* metaphor – but not just corporeal either'.[17] The flexibility in the different discourses enunciating the body, specifically the breast, facilitated the breast's emergence as a relatively popular political icon; as the political valency of luxury began to change during the eighteenth century, so did that of the breast.

Moralized understandings of the breast fed with equal ease into justifications of medical practices and into politicized uses of the body, including figural uses. Luxury itself, by the end of the seventeenth century, figured as vice and corruption but also more equivocally suggested the potential of a new society in which commercial rather than landed interests had undesirable but increasing purchase, if not on the political establishment then on trade and social relations.[18] Condemnation continued, yet the increasingly complex political, or national-political, implications of luxury are clear.[19] Dennis, writing on the relationship between luxury and the state in *An Essay Upon Publick Spirit* (1711), associated a potentially benign version of luxury with the Venetian republic:

> 'Tis morally impossible that Liberty and Luxury should live any where so long in strict a Confederacy as they have done in Venice;

which is secure from faction by the Harmony of its Orders, and from Invasion by its Scituation. But in a mix'd Monarchy like ours, where we are neither secure from Division by our Constitution . . . nor from Invasion by our Scituation, both which are too evident from History and Experience, Luxury that nourishes our Passions and augments our Wants, must of Necessity inflame our Factions, and augments our Divisions, and cannot be with too much Care repress'd.[20]

Dennis's distinction between Britain and Venice nevertheless instantiates a displaced association between luxury and republican virtue. Once political virtue and luxury can be linked, albeit in a disavowed way, the ground is prepared for pleasure and liberty to coincide and the breast, already as this section has shown, a signifier of virtue and vice in several closely related discourses, is aptly positioned to internalize the pleasurable qualities of luxury while standing for virtue.[21]

Plato, Rousseau and the luxurious-virtuous breast

Thus, in the seventeenth century it appears that the breast enters political discourse and iconography as an index to liberty because of the changing relationships among the discursive networks into which it was bound – dominantly the erotic, ethical-political and forensic-evidentiary. This section discusses two factors in the emergence of the virtuous breast as political symbol; first, the emphasis on the breast's relationship to the nation, and second, a renewed emphasis on the importance of the antique world.

In the *Republic* Plato signalled improper uses of the breast as a sign of the state in luxury. In his reinterpretation of the *Republic* Rousseau put breast-feeding and the state together in a different way, involving a reconfiguration of the place of the breast as a signifier of luxury and virtue. In the 1760s Jean Jacques Rousseau claimed the *Republic* as the definitive educational-political tract:

> If you wish to know what is meant by public education, read Plato's *Republic*. Those who merely judge books by their titles take this for a treatise on politics, but it is the finest treatise on education ever written.[22]

The relationship of private and public virtue has its own complicated life in the thought of Rousseau. However, in this particular instance education and political virtue are interlocking and, it turns out, political virtue is founded on a correct relation to the breast. Rousseau writes, 'Would you restore all men to their primal duties, begin with their mothers . . . every

evil follows in the train of this first sin.' Thus, the highly politicized place
of breast-feeding in Rousseau's envisioned restoration of mothers and men
to 'primal duties' connects filial affection, sexuality and public duty.
Although elsewhere Rousseau is at pains to separate political and domestic
economy, published in the same year as the *Social Contract*, *Émile* covers
some similar ground within the two overlapping discourses of political
theory and civic virtue or education.[23]

As Ruth Perry notes, the descriptions of breast-feeding in *Emile*
combine voyeurism and sentiment (and a sexual element in breast-feeding
as a spectacle foregrounded, for example, by de Sade and the satirist James
Gillray).[24] Breast-feeding is also proposed by him as foundational to a
true commonwealth. At the moment of breastfeeding, though within a
problematic frame that chastises women as mothers and as wetnurses, the
more familiar Rousseauian image of the woman as hyper-civil (dedicated
to the elaboration of 'the moral part of love . . . a factitious feeling born
of social usage') is subsumed in the male child's encounter with the breast
as a moment of foundational political importance.[25] Rousseau underwrites
the child's entitlement to the fount of political virtue by reallocating to the
father the breast's long-standing association with avarice: 'Ambition,
avarice, tyranny, the mistaken foresight of fathers, their neglect, their
harshness, are a hundredfold more harmful to the child than the blind
affection of the mother.'[26] In contrast, crimes against the breast amount
to rebellion against all proper orders and invite a death by intimately
maternal means:

> if a child could be so unnatural as to fail in respect for the mother
> who bore him and nursed him at her breast, who for so many years
> devoted herself to his care, such a monstrous wretch should be
> smothered at once as unworthy to live.[27]

Rousseau's influential conversion of the breast into the foundation of
a political order involves its temporary alignment with virtue (rather than
with the artificial pleasures of luxury delineated in the *Discourse of
Inequality*). But Rousseau does not relinquish the sexual charge associated
with the breast in its luxurious rather than its virtuous aspect. Admission
of the sexual-sentimental into the discourse on political education
combines with the elision of education – private virtue – and politics such
that the political sphere is not, in *Emile* (or in *The Discourse on Inequality*),
either isolated from the psychic development of the individual or at a
distance from the passions which drive states and individuals equally to
regard luxuries as necessities and to be dominated by sexual drives.[28]

A second factor in the emergence of the breast as political icon was
the rediscovery of the antique world, especially Greece. This contributed
to the fusion of images of political virtue and luxury as it renewed and

changed the circulation of images of the Greek male body as the essence of an ideal.[29] For Winckelmann, Alex Potts argues, the Greek male body represented both subjective and political freedom, associated with the realm of aesthetic appreciation.[30] The political potential of the classical aesthetic had a powerful and arguably motivating place in his work.

If the antique male body could easily come to stand for republican liberty, the female body as represented in classical statuary provoked extended discussion. In its desirable manifestations like that of the Venus de Medici, this body was tangential to the political ideal and problematic because of its culturally recognized potential to evoke desire. The female classical body had a complex relation to political and subjective freedom, as femininity both compromised its use in the symbolization of political freedom (through its temptation to masculine desire and linked potential to drain the energies of civic virtue) and facilitated it (through its status as a cultural cipher). Thus, as John Barrell has argued, in the early years of the eighteenth century, for a man to gaze on the Venus de Medici involved a test in aesthetic self-mastery, but during the later years of the century masculine self-mastery in aesthetic engagement as proof of the political worth of the viewer faded as a test of civic virtue.[31]

The discourse on beauty, linked to the rediscovery of the ancients by Wincklemann and others, fused contemporary and classical, sexual and aesthetic. It also tended to naturalize aspects of female beauty and femininity which had been understood in allegorical terms.[32] Female beauty at different points signified the goal of masculine desire, the seat of female sexuality, or a model imbued with political associations of form and costume. Thus in Dandre Bardon's *Costume des Anciens Peuples*, where female statues are contrasted in terms of modesty, desirability and political orientation.[33] In *Lysias: or, a Dialogue Concerning Beauty and Virtue* (1762), the speaker Lysias draws repeatedly on classical precedent as well as contemporary aesthetic theory (such as Hogarth) to describe absolute – perhaps transhistorical – standards of beauty, epitomized in the circling lines of the female form.[34] For Lysias, the

> female form is an assemblage of . . . elegant lines; they are seen in the lips, the eye-lids and eye-brows, they flow from the head to the shoulders, and run in all directions over the breasts, winding down the whole body, and twining to the last extremity of the foot.[35]

The classical and natural are here fused in an image of beauty and virtue, but again without relinquishing the pleasurable – sexual – implications of the breast and of female beauty. In this example the female body is classicized – bringing political implications of freedom – and sexualized. Generalized personification of virtue enables the naturalization of fetishistic emphasis on the breasts and the body's insertion into a representational order in which it becomes, as it were, a 'natural symbol of freedom'. The body, and therefore the breast, here are apparently freed from the taints of luxury and, through such a disavowal of symbolic power, internalized without acknowledging the desirous qualities of the luxurious breast.

The idea of beauty was articulated through particular (though shifting) codification of what is required of the beautiful body, focused sharply by attention to the breasts.[36] As Klaus Theweleit indicates, the fantasy of women comparing their bodies, particularly breasts, implied 'the putative goal is voluptuous pleasure with the right man', and he cites the *furor uterens* as an instance of the power of the female imagination to call up perfect men.[37] Yet, the discourse on beauty at some points introduces disavowal of sexual pleasure as its object. Indeed, a precondition of the discourse on beauty could be said to consist in that disavowal, or perhaps the sublimation of the erotic charge into principles of organization and codification. The luxurious and the virtuous, therefore, can coincide within the naturalizing frame of beauty.[38] Understandings of female beauty can be seen to both efface and rest upon the contradictoriness of the breast's associations as virtuous and yet sexual and luxurious. The breast as political symbol resolves, or sublimates, these tensions through a political – and therefore ostensibly 'virtuous' – harnessing of the breast's contradictory associations.

Thus, in both Rousseau's concentration on breast-feeding and the uses to which the antique was put, the 'luxurious' breast, transformed from its allegorical-naturalistic status and more fully absorbed in a rhetoric of naturalism, comes to inhabit the virtuous political breast. The emphasis of Winckelmann and others on the Greek ideal, and its particular relation to political freedom and sexual desirability, is a final piece in the cultural-political jigsaw that transformed the ethical-forensic-allegorical early modern breast into the breast as political symbol. The breast as a political symbol is connected to the way the sexual-pleasurable and the political came to coexist in associations with the female form; the pleasurable qualities of the sexual breast were absorbed into rather than excluded by the breast as political symbol.

To summarize: the confounding and mixing of discourses, combined with a disavowal or attenuation of the connection between the breast and the sexual organs (as in the cult of beauty) permitted the internalization of the pleasures of the luxurious breast into the political symbol of the virtuous breast which, in order to act as a powerful symbol, requires precisely the sexual reading it invites and disavows. In the light of this changing relationship between 'luxury' and 'liberty', the next section examines an image of a slave girl, Joanna, circulated in the mid-1790s as an illustration to 'Captain' John Stedman's *Narrative*. This image both illuminates the sexualized valency of the breast as a symbol of political liberty and, as an image of slavery, provides a different and complicated enunciation of the relationship between luxury and liberty.

'Some account of a beautiful female slave': liberty and luxury reconfigured

Stedman's *Narrative of a five years expedition against the revolted Negroes of Surinam* narrates his time in Surinam where he went as a volunteer from Holland, prepared to fight the escaped slaves who were making depradations on the troops of the Dutch States General.[39] Stedman went to Surinam in 1773, the narrative was completed in 1790, and the first edition was published, heavily edited, in 1796. The 1790 text excised or reworked diary entries in which Stedman had sex with slaves to produce a romance narrative which created Joanna the slave as a virtuous and senti- mental object.[40] Stedman's relation to Joanna is explained as a 'Suriname marriage' involving payment, cohabitation and, in the case of married European men, a kind of polygamy for the extent of their stay in the colony.[41] The text is in part supported but in part undermined by engravings of Stedman's drawings and watercolours – of which Stedman produced 106 and of which the first publisher, Johnson, published 104. T. Holloway engraved the image of Joanna in a style, as Price notes, 'reminiscent of William Blake's work on the project'.[42] This plate was engraved in 1793.

Stedman offers to 'diversify the mind of the reader after the preced- ing scenes of horror by giving a description of the beautiful Mulatto maid Joanna':[43]

> Rather more than middle-sized, she was perfectly straight with the most elegant shape that can be viewed in nature, moving her well-formed limbs as when a goddess walked. Her face was full of native modesty and the most distinguished sweetness. Her eyes, as black as ebony, were large and full of expression, bespeaking the goodness of her heart. With cheeks which glowed (in spite of her olive complexion) a beautiful tinge of vermilion when gazed upon, her nose was perfectly well-formed and rather small, her lips a little prominent which, when she spoke, discovered two regular rows of pearls as white as mountain snow. Her hair was dark brown, next to black, forming a beauteous globe of small ringlets, ornamented with flowers and gold spangles. Round her neck, her arms, and her ankles she wore gold chains, rings, and medals, while a shawl of the finest Indian muslin, the end of which was negligently thrown over her polished shoulder, gracefully covered part of her lovely bosom.

Plate 1 *Joanna* from John Gabriel Stedman, *Narrative of five years expedition against the revolted Negroes of Surinam* (1796) Reproduced by permission of the British Library

Herself a luxury item, blushing cheeks and speaking eyes nevertheless disclose Joanna as a subject similar to the European reader, even as her colour and chains distinguish her as a slave. Though, like Oroonoko in Behn's *Oroonoko or The Royal Slave* and Friday in *Robinson Crusoe*, Joanna is described in the terms of colonial blazon, unlike them she is a sentimentalized subject, an example of the freedom of female movement afforded by the absence of corsets, and, as the illustration implies, a paradoxical image of slavery as liberty – physical, sexual and potentially political. The description of her body differs from those of the earlier narratives in its emphasis on the accoutrements of slavery reworked as jewels (the narrative describes them as heirlooms) and, in the illustration, emphasis on the breast suggests *simultaneously* virtue and desirability.

These contradictory qualities repeated in the image make the illustration of Joanna a meditation on liberty. This is especially focused in the image by the use of breast and jewels as signifiers of liberty and enslavement. As Yalom notes, the breasts of female slaves were part of their value. But maternity, or reproductive potential, though implicit in the image is not its central valency.[44] How is the European viewer invited to read the image? Is 'he' to take pleasure in the 'freedom' of Joanna's figure or engage with the ethics of slavery? I would suggest that the image is coded in such a way that the reader is not forced to choose between modes of interpretation or to use the image as a text of aesthetic self-mastery. Sexualization, and signifiers of Joanna's slavery – the bracelets, even her status as a 'mulatto' – licence the viewer to take pleasure in the spectacle. The exposure of her upper body, partially naked, sexualized and yet also signifying her slave status – a signification only emphasized by the draping of the bodice as if in reference to the French sash of liberty – produces the exposed breast as epitomizing viewing relations which condense a politicized and sexualized understanding of the figure. Her status as a slave gestures towards liberty (underwritten by sash, virtuous breast, by 1796 at least signifiers of freedom and liberty) and *simultaneously* binds the figure into a sexualized chain of associations to do with femininity, sexual desirability, slavery.

Thus, the figure of Joanna presents a complex reworking of questions of luxury and liberty, using signifiers which simultaneously evoke and deny the chains of slavery, partially naturalizing them as decoration and an index of desirability. Indeed, her pose seems to be what gives Stedman's editor, Price, the idea of the link between the engraver Holloway and Blake's designs for this book, and it seems that this is because both modelled their illustrations on Greek and Roman statuary – a detail which ties this representation of a slave woman to the European politics of liberty in its iconographic manifestation.

The image's contradictory power comes in part from the way in which the things which make her figure speak 'liberty' simultaneously tie it to an iconography of slavery which, though understated, coexist with and are insistently placed in the iconography. The liberty of Joanna's figure is founded upon the contradictory information, derived from the narrative but also from the iconography: Joanna is always in a complex relation to liberty through the eroticization of her own lack of it. In this image, then, the erotic cathexis of the breast's relationship to a politics of liberty is visible because the opposite of liberty, slavery, is represented simultaneously in the same sign as liberty – the breast. As Marina Warner puts it, 'the galley slaves' headgear becomes a cap of freedom; the capitulating barbarian's cap becomes a sign of Liberty.'[45]

Arguably, because of its situation as a colonial-virtuous Venus, this engraving presents the luxurious pleasures incorporated in the breast of liberty very clearly. It permits the overt mixture of the excess of the luxurious desire for the slave's body and the virtuous implication of the political breast of freedom in a way that echoes the contradictions of Stedman's text and, in a wider context, suggests the luxurious desires of revolution also expressed while simultaneously effaced. The representation of Joanna, subject and in chains, as an icon of pleasure and liberty, luxury and freedom, is a problematic instance of the power of the fused symbolic charge of virtue and luxury by the end of the eighteenth century.

Coda

In tracing the relationship of luxury and liberty and the factors which, ultimately, made the breast of liberty desirable as a political symbol, this article has also touched on the shifting connections between desire and disgust, politics and virtue, which produced the female body as a newly desirable sign when the political sphere changed from the seventeenth into the eighteenth centuries.

As this study has begun to suggest, the place of the female body as part of the dynamic of the English political imaginary at a time when the early modern period is being reshaped by the Enlightenment is not solely within the frame of domesticity. Historians of the growth of domestic ideology have interpreted eighteenth-century emphasis on breast-feeding as an aspect of domestic ideology used to circumscribe female sexuality and labour; Felicity Nussbaum and Ruth Perry have rightly argued for the centrality of the breast in an ideological nexus in which the domestic and the colonial are run together in such a way as maternity and domesticity both distinguish British women and dominate and place them in the home.[46] However, as suggested here, this emphasis on the domestic is in tension with a different set of discourses running contrary to any definitive separation of sexual and domestic, political and erotic. In this discursive network the breast has a central symbolic place, one which produces the breast's existence as political symbol of liberty and in Rousseau of breast-feeding as the foundation of the citizen. The two strands of thought might be held in tension but, as the place of luxury in the moral and political economy changed, the sexual, sentimental and political were not necessarily always contradictory.

As this implies, the political symbol is hybrid, compounded as in a Freudian dream-work of a narrative genealogy which 'makes sense' of it and gives it a 'why' – ('We wear red bonnets because of their republican associations') – and arbitrariness suggesting the excess of desire over purpose in producing such a symbol. Because of their simultaneously conscious and unconscious operations, political symbols are available both for stylization and for naturalization, or for a process whereby their political implications can be diffused within an apparently non-symbolic discourse, so that a political iconography can come to inhabit apparently naturalistic representational orders in a way which renders the signifier a bearer of covert knowledge and meanings. The naturalization of the breast as political symbol in *post-hoc* representations of the French revolution – and Delacroix's *Raft* and the representation of the 1830 uprising *Liberty on the Barricades* (1830) are only the best known – testifies to the genealogy I have been tracing. These images make clear that an iconography of the female body as a *symbol* of liberty coexisted with and emerged from the forensic-ethical-pornographic-sentimental discourses enunciating the breast at the beginning of the eighteenth century and that, in the virtuous freedom of Delacroix's female body, epitomized by the release of the breast from even the most casual revolutionary drapery, offers a pleasurable political symbol precisely because the iconography of political freedom is inhabited by the desirability of the luxurious breast.

Acknowledgements

Thanks are due to Tim Armstrong, Vincent Quinn, Mary Peace and Catherine Sharrock for their critical comments.

Notes

1 Marina Warner, *Monuments and Maidens* (London: Weidenfeld & Nicolson, 1985), p. 277.
2 Ibid., p. 293; Mary Jacobus, 'Incorruptible milk: breast-feeding and the French Revolution', in *First Things: The Maternal Imaginary in Literature, Art, and Psychoanalysis* (New York and London: Routledge, 1995), pp. 207–30;

Ruth Perry, 'Colonizing the breast: sexuality and maternity in eighteenth-century England', *Eighteenth-Century Life* 16 (February 1992): 185–213, esp. 195. See also Marilyn Yalom, *A History of the Breast* (London: HarperCollins, 1997), pp. 115–17.

3 Plato, *The Republic*, 8.555b.ff, quoted in John Sekora, *Luxury, the Concept in Western Thought, Eden to Smollett* (Baltimore and London: Johns Hopkins University Press, 1977), pp. 30–1.

4 *The Anthropology of Breast-Feeding*, ed. Vanessa Maher (Providence RI & Oxford: Berg, 1992), pp. 10–11.

5 Sekora, p. 39.

6 Durer's image of Avarice (1507); in *The Political Works of Edmund Spenser*, ed. E. De Selincowe (London: Oxford University Press, 1952).

7 See Yalom, p. 26.

8 Edmund Spenser, *The Faerie Queene*. For an illuminating discussion of Spenser's use of femininity in this way see Richelle Munkoff, forthcoming.

9 See Anthony Pagden, *The Fall of Natural Man* (Cambridge: Cambridge University Press, 1982).

10 John Bulwer, *Anthropometamorphoses* (London, 1650), p. 179.

11 Ibid., scene xviii, p.178; see also pp. 176–80. I am grateful to Dr Dominic Monserratt for conversations on Bulwer.

12 Londa Schiebinger, *Nature's Body: Sexual Politics and the Making of Modern Science* (London: Pandora, 1993), p. 1.

13 '[P]ornography was almost always an adjunct to something else until the middle or end of the eighteenth century. In early modern Europe . . . pornography was most often a vehicle for using the shock of sex to criticize religious and political authorities' (Lyn Hunt, *The Invention of Pornography* (New York: Zone 1993), p. 10).

14 *A treatise of all the degrees and symptoms of the Venereal Disease* (1708), David Foxon, *Libertine Literature in England 1660–1745* (repr. from The Book Collector, 1964), p 13. See also Peter Wagner, *Eros Revived: Erotica of the Enlightenment in England and America* (London: Secker & Warburg, 1988), p. 101.

15 Louise de Bourgeois, *The Complete Midwives Practice Enlarged*, 4th edn (London, 1680).

16 The practical aspects of the relationship between fertility and lactation are analysed by Dorothy McLaren, 'Marital fertility and lactation 1570–1720', in Mary Prior(ed.) *Women in English Society* (Methuen: London, 1985), pp. 22–53.

17 Thomas Lacqueur, *Making Sex, Body and Gender from the Greeks to Freud* (Cambridge, MA and London: Harvard University Press, 1990), p. 109; Jonathan Sawday, *The Body Emblazoned* (London: Routledge, 1995), pp. 5, 16–22.

18 Shelley Burtt, *Virtue Transformed, Political Argument in England 1688–1740* (Cambridge: Cambridge University Press, 1992); on corruption and luxury in the 1750s see Sekora, pp. 63–71. See also *Letter on the Spirit of Patriotism* or *Idea of a Patriot King, Englands Vanity or the Voice of God Against the Monstrous Sin of Pride in Dress and Apparel* (1683) (see especially frontispiece); *The Friendly Monitor, Laying open the crying sins of cursing, swearing, drinking, gaming, detraction, and luxury or immodesty* (London, 1692), p. 69.

19 Sekora, p. 78; Christopher Berry, *The Idea of Luxury* (Cambridge: Cambridge University Press, 1994), pp. 126–77.

20 Dennis, *An Essay Upon Publick Spirit, Being a Satyr in Prose Upon the manners and Luxury of the Times,* iv–v.

21 Berry, p. 135.

22 Rousseau, *Emile,* trans. Barbara Foxley (London: Dent, 1969), p. 8. For a discussion of Rousseau's relationship to *The Republic* and to Sparta, see Joel Schwartz, *The Sexual Politics of Jean-Jacques Rousseau* (Chicago and London: University of Chicago Press, 1984), pp. 48–61. As Schwartz notes, certain configurations of the family and affective relations between the sexes can, in Rousseau, be seen as impediments to engagement with the polis. Schwartz notes that Rousseau prefers Lycurgus's Sparta to Plato's *Republic* for its recognition of the interrelationship of family and state (p. 50).

23 *Émile,* p. 13. Compare the discussion of first ownership and the bean plant in *Émile* with Chapter 9 of *The Social Contract* on 'real property' and the establishment of the right of the owner when 'the right of property' has been established. In *A Dissertation on Political Economy* Rousseau distinguishes political and domestic economy.

24 Louise de Bourgeois, *The Complete Midwife's Practice Enlarged;* Roger Thompson, *Unfit for Modest Ears* (London: Macmillan, 1979); Perry, p. 193. de Sade (who also attacked Rousseau) makes explicit sexualized breast-feeding in the sixth of the 'passions' narrated by the whore: a young man suckles the wetnurse/prostitute/(mother), ejaculating on her thighs. de Sade, *120 Days of Sodom,* trans Austryn Wainhouse and Richard Sever (London: Arrow, 1989), p. 306. For a reading of these scenes see also Jane Gallop, *Thinking Through the Body* (New York: Columbia University Press, 1988), pp. 56–65. The satirist James Gillray also foregrounds the connection of the sexual and the maternal in his use of voyeurism in *The Fashionable Mama* (1796).

25 *A Discourse on the Origins of Inequality,* trans. G. D. H. Cole (London: Dent, 1913, repr. 1947), p. 186.

26 Rousseau, *Emile,* p. 5.

27 Ibid., p. 5.

28 Rousseau, *Discourse on Inequality,* trans. G. D. H. Cole (London: Dent, 1913, repr. 1947), pp. 186–8, 199–208.

29 Alex Potts, *Flesh and the Ideal* (New Haven and London: Yale University Press, 1994), p. 249; see also pp. 1–6.

30 Ibid., p. 215.

31 John Barrell, 'The dangerous goddess', in *The Birth of Pandora* (Basingstoke: Macmillan, 1992), pp. 63–87, esp. pp. 76–8.

32 This naturalization by the next century came to be associated with the freed female body of the life–drawing class – also important in naturalizing the symbolic associations of the female form. I am grateful to Professor Poynton for this point. See Ilaria Bignamini and Martin Postle, *The Artists' Model* (University of Nottingham, 1986).

33 Michel François Dandré Bardon, *Costume des Anciens Peuples* (Paris, 1784–86), p. 174.

34 *Lysias: or a Dialogue Concerning Beauty and Virtue* (Dublin, 1762), e.g. p. 39. Lysias as in Plato's *Phaedrus.*

35 Ibid., p. 29.

36 Klaus Theweleit, *Male Fantasies* (1987), trans. Stephen Conway in collaboration with Erica Carter and Chris Turner (Cambridge: Polity Press, 1993), p. 336.

37 Ibid., p. 341.

38 See Dorinda Outram on Mme Roland in *The Body in the French Revolution: Sex, Class, and Political Culture* (New Haven and London: Yale University Press, 1989).
39 John Gabriel Stedman, *Narrative of a five years expedition against the revolted Negroes of Surinam* (London, 1796); Richard Price and Sally Price (eds) *Stedman's Surinam* (Baltimore and London: Johns Hopkins University Press, 1992).
40 Ibid., p. xxx–xxxii.
41 Ibid., p. xxxii.
42 Ibid., p. xxxvi.
43 Ibid., p. 40.
44 Yalom, pp. 123–5.
45 Warner, p. 277.
46 See Nancy Armstrong, *Desire and Domestic Fiction, A Political History of the Novel* (Oxford: Oxford University Press, 1987).

Marcia Pointon

Intriguing jewellery: royal bodies and luxurious consumption[1]

The idea of royal femininity and that of jewellery appear to be inseparable. A queen stripped of her jewels is no longer identifiable as separate and different from a common mortal. Therein lies one of the factors contributing to the troubles of royalty in late twentieth-century Britain: we all know in our heart of hearts that those who would be queens wear jewels, not tracksuits. Jewels worn about the body have traditionally constituted the most spectacular way of displaying extraordinary wealth while simultaneously disguising capital as artistry. Confronted with someone wearing a diamond *parure*, notions of aesthetic value fuse with speculations of financial worth. Jewellery signifies, however, in much more complex ways than this simple equation might suggest. Jewels raise issues of the Law, for court societies in Europe have, since earliest times, depended upon gifts of valuable jewellery as the medium of national and international diplomacy. Whereas money changing hands is understood to be a tithe, a levy or a bribe, jewellery made up of precious stones and metals compresses into one object that can be displayed upon an individual body, marks of wealth, of esteem, and of symbolic possession. In the Tudor period, for example, presents given on special occasions and, under Queen Elizabeth I, particularly at the New Year festivities, were a well-established form of levy in anticipation of favours to come. Gifts included clothes and furniture but also notable jewels.[2]

Chief among the occasions upon which jewellery changes hands are marriages and births. These are temporal events pertaining to the body, events that are both juridical and individual. While the bodies of the subjects involved in such exchanges are consumed by the passage of time, gem stones, virtually indestructible, and gold, outlive their owners and stand, whether in old settings or in new, as markers of fleshly frailty and the relative permanence of the mineral world. For these reasons, jewellery is a key European cultural component in symbolic and economic exchange

Textual Practice 11(3), 1997, 493–516

rituals[3] and as a textual field is heavily invested in ideological significance relative to bodies, and by extension also to colonialism, gender and sexuality. Indeed jewellery not only stands as a symbol of the special occasions it commemorates (its economic worth translated by the act of giving into transcendent value), but may actually represent those occasions by acting as a place for inscribing texts which literally act as mnemonics (as artifices to aid the memory). Thus, for example, heart-shaped brooches are known to have been popular as engagement or marriage tokens since the fourteenth century and surviving examples date from the seventeenth. In shape they stand for the idea of love but they were also inscribed with words: one example reads 'I fancie non but the[e] alone.'[4] In such instances jewellery designed to be worn on the body becomes a field for inscription that interprets the body which, in interactive relationship, both frames and supports it. Posy rings (rings inscribed with rhymes or exhortations) and mourning rings (inscribed with the names of deceased individuals) work to bridge time, linking bodies through the epigrammatic inscription of a sentiment. 'Divinely knit by grace are we, / Late two, now one, ye pledge here see' written inside a ring linguistically glosses the form of the jewellery – a ring whose circularity symbolizes eternity.[5]

In these introductory paragraphs I have indicated something of the complexity of jewellery as material artefact. But jewellery, made up of gem stones and settings, is also a site of cosmological myth and symbol. This is not the place for an exploration of the linguistic richness of gemmology, but it is none the less worth drawing attention to ancient traditions (whether religious and deriving from the *Book of Revelations*, or Pagan and related to medicine) through which gem stones are highly invested in systems of belief.[6] My topic is the discourse of jewels and of jewellery within the practice of court politics in late eighteenth-century England; none the less the traditions of gemmology have a bearing on this study since, if we are to understand formulaic similes like 'teeth white as pearls', we need to recognize that within any invocation of jewels or gems is implied an allusion to cosmological order.[7] My concern is, however, to examine the connection between the evaluation of jewellery as part of the process of luxurious consumption and the construction of the feminine as royal. I shall focus on Queen Charlotte, consort of George III.

Scholarship on kingship has established the now widely recognized actual and conceptual split between the king's two bodies (the natural and the political) and the importance of this concept for our understanding of the function of representation.[8] Of the ways in which the symbolic body of a queen consort may have functioned we know much less.[9] Charlotte arrived in England from the German principality of Mecklenburg Strelitz on 8 September 1761 and, at the age of 18, married that same evening the as yet uncrowned George III.[10] Charlotte knew no English and set eyes on her husband to be for the first time as she descended from the coach that had brought her from Gravesend via Colchester through the City of London to St James's Palace. However, she arrived with an impressive array of jewellery with which she had been equipped through the efforts of General David Graeme, who had spent the previous weeks in Charlotte's home territory commissioning elaborate personal ornaments from local jewellers as well as from craftsmen in Berlin and Hamburg.[11] Meanwhile in England, George III had been purchasing even more jewellery with which Charlotte was presented upon her arrival in episodes represented and re-represented across a range of media.[12] Thus, as a historical subject she was in years to come described as a prisoner, albeit a well-ornamented one who was frequently in receipt of gifts of diamonds.[13] Access to the historical subject is, of course, through texts. In the case of Queen Charlotte, the question I wish to ask is how the textuality of jewellery informs and shapes an understanding of the royal consort.

The jewellery worn by the Queen when she appears either at court or in public functions both as a personal attribute and as a measure of the status and significance of the event, enters into discourse as exemplary and unique on the one hand and, on the other, as typical and indicative. In addition to regalia (as with the crown which was one of George III's gifts)[14] which does not belong to the wearer, Charlotte was widely represented in word and in image wearing personal jewellery. The composition of jewellery, its dimensions, and the parts of the body to which it is attached are foregrounded in a network of descriptive prose that crisscrosses private correspondence, journalism and court circulars. Thus, as part of her bridal attire, Charlotte wore a diamond stomacher, an elaborate and expensive item that dominated the wedding images in the popular press at home and abroad (Plate 1):

> The Fond [ground] is a Network as fine as Cat Gut of Small Diamonds & the rest is a large pattern of Natural Flowers, composed of very large Diamonds, one of which is 18, another 16 & a third 10 Thousand pounds price.[15]

Charlotte was the first English queen since the early seventeenth century to possess jewels rivalling those of continental royalty.[16] In addition to her wedding ring, the King had had made, we are told, a diamond hoop ring 'of a size not to stand higher than the wedding ring, to which it was to serve as guard'.[17] A third new ring, which she was to wear on the little finger of her right hand at the marriage ceremony, 'bore a likeness of the king in miniature, done exquisitely beautiful' by Jeremiah Meyer.[18] At the coronation on 22 September, the Queen is described as wearing a:

CHARLOTTA.

Plate 1 *Portrait of Queen Charlotte* by John Elias Nilson, engraving, Augsburg, 1761. Plate size 22 × 16 cm. The young queen, surrounded by amorini, and accompanied by Apollo (to whom she is pleasing), is portrayed in an oval framed in flowers and superimposed on a rococo cartouche inscribed with the initials of the royal couple. She is represented wearing the famous stomacher. Copyright © The British Museum (1895–6–17–187)

stiffen body'd Robe silver embroidered [with gold] Tissue Petticoat, Diamond Stomacher, Purple Velvet Sleeves Diamds, Pearls as big as Cherrys, Girdle, Petticoats Diamds, Purple Velvet Surcoat and Mantle with Ermine and Lace, Purple Velvet Cap, only one string of Diamds & Crown Aigrette, Fan Mother of Pearl, Emerald, Rubys & Diamds.[19]

The spectacle of the Queen's jewels ultimately finds its watershed in the itemized sale catalogue of Queen Charlotte's possessions. Occasioned by the Queen's death, the sale catalogue with its technical minutiae – each object described and numbered – is the apogee of the narrative that commences in Mecklenburg Strelitz, and its moment of authentication, the moment when history and text converge. For the performance occasioned by the Queen's death, and predicated upon the very absence of her body, manifests the plenitude of jewellery which gave that body its visible worth; the imaginary body of the Queen therefore has its finest and most complete showing once the historical and biological body has disintegrated (literally so, since she left instructions in her will that her corpse should not be embalmed). In a series of sales Charlotte's personal effects, including her jewels, carvings, trinkets, plate, drawings and paintings, and her distinguished library passed under Christie's hammer between May and July 1819.[20] By far the greatest number of objects are those that had continued to adorn her person into old age (Plate 2). The pearls which, when viewed on the Queen's body were 'big as cherries' are in the sale catalogue defined in the language of the market:

39 A pair of large single-drop pearl ear-rings with brilliant rosette tops
42 A row of two hundred and eighteen pearls
43 A row of two hundred and twenty ditto
44 A pair of three loop ear-rings of pearls, a 2 parts of a pearl bow
45 A pair of <Scotch> pearls tops, and a pair of ditto <Pearl> drops
46 Fifty-eight large pearls, and a quantity of seed ditto
47 A pair of pearl link bracelets, and pearl purse
48 An enamel frame for a locket, set round with large pearls, and a turquoise broach set with pearls
52 A necklace of sixty-eight pearls, chiefly large and fine
60 A necklace, consisting of eighty-five large pearls
61 A pair of buckles composed of large pearls
74 A necklace or row, consisting of seventy-one round and white pear
75 A ditto of seventy-six ditto
76 A gold buckle, bordered with twenty large pearls, and a broach of pearls as a serpent, with large drop pearl suspended from its mouth
77 Three oblong and three oval ditto square pearl broaches
84 A small water-colour drawing, set round with thirty-seven very large and fine pearls and pearl loop[21]

Plate 2 *Portrait of Queen Charlotte*, engraving after W. M. Craig's 1815 portrait, published in 1820, two years after her death. 18 × 12 cm. Copyright © The British Museum (1861–3–8–79)

The Queen consort's function is to breed heirs to the throne; this Charlotte accomplished magnificently (Plate 3), bearing fifteen children of whom thirteen survived. Indeed, her fecundity was a source not only of public interest but also of ribaldry: she was regularly shown as visibly pregnant in caricatures (see Plate 9).[22] Moreover the forms of her jewellery symbolically reiterated the notion of fecundity. The famous stomacher of diamonds served to draw attention to the queen's materiality, to her role as mater for the nation; it was a dazzling ornament and also one that confirmed Charlotte's reputation as a lover of diamonds.[23] The elaborate series of rings given to her by George III – one of which bore a portrait of the monarch and another of which served to protect the wedding ring while standing no higher than it – evokes the martial art of defending the citadel by the erection of concentric circles of fortification. Furthermore, jewellery events in Queen Charlotte's biographies are narrated interactively with pregnancies, thus ritually inscribing the connection between economic and generative roles.[24]

Plate 3 *The Royal Dozen; or the King and Queen of Great Britain with the 10 Royal Children*, anon engraving, 17 × 10 cm. Copyright © The British Museum (1877–10–13–1185)

Rings are symbols of eternity, their circularity an emblem of continuity, but they also possess well-established associations with female genitals. Allusions to sexual acts articulated in terms of ring and finger narratives are widespread in English seventeenth- and eighteenth-century literatures.[25] However, Queen Charlotte is also widely represented wearing pearls; one set of pearls was said to have descended from Mary Queen of Scots, through George I's mother, the Electress Sophia. Charlotte had them re-strung and added the pearl drop she had brought with her from Germany with her pearl ear-rings framed in diamond chains.[26] Thus Bartolozzi's engraving of 1799 based on Sir William Beechy's portrait (and affixed to R. J. Thornton's *Temple of Flora* of 1807) shows the Queen, as patroness of botany and the fine arts, in a frame of clouds surrounded by cosmic rays of light and being adorned with flowers and pearls by putti, one of which holds her crown. On her head, she wears a jewelled tiara in the shape of a sickle moon, suggestive of the goddess Diana, while pinned to her breast is a portrait of George III in Roman profile surrounded by pearls (Plate 4). The familiarity of this kind of display through subsequent

Plate 4 *Portrait of Her Majesty, Patroness of Botany, and of the Fine Arts*, published by Dr Thornton, London, 1799. 45 × 30 cm. Copyright © The British Museum (M.M. 15–20)

representation in descriptive accounts as well as through popular prints situates the queen's body within an honorific narrative of Protestant victory over the Jacobite threat, and the triumph of the House of Hanover. The failure of those earlier queens – both Elizabeth and Mary, as well as Anne – to produce adequate heirs for the nation is finally (and, so it seems) conclusively compensated by the prolific womb of Charlotte.

The efficacy of female jewellery in endorsing a monarchy that was widely viewed as lack-lustre needs little explanation; the King and Queen established elaborate court rituals in their early years; on the King's birthday the Queen appeared in the most sumptuous costume and ornaments but on her own birthday she dressed down. Thus, on 18 January 1782, Charlotte's official birthday, 'Her Majesty, as usual, was plainly dressed, without her jewels, in a boue de Paris satin, trimmed with gold, crape, &c.'. The King, on the other hand, 'wore a rich suit of black velvet, decorated with a brilliant [i.e. diamond] star and garter loop', while the Princess Royal 'had a white and gold, with a green spot, the beautiful manufacture of England, superbly ornamented with a profusion of jewels'. On the King's official birthday, by contrast, he was as usual 'rather plainly attired' while the Queen was 'most splendidly ornamented with jewels'.[27] But these rituals, and their repeated representation, suggest also the profound unease with which these all-too-necessary sumptuary practices were accompanied. If commerce was necessary for the good of the nation but luxury was inevitably a dreaded consequence,[28] a similarly precarious balance was maintained between the requirement that a queen be bejewelled and the provocative associations that the relationship between female bodies and jewellery invoked.

The Queen's identity rapidly came to rest upon the jewelled artefacts in which she was represented. Thus, for example, she is readily identifiable in caricatures by the large cross of rose and brilliant cut diamonds on a diamond chain which she wears, one of the King's wedding gifts.[29] Moreover, we may remark that, as the plates for some of the many popular portrait prints gradually wore out and were retouched in order to lengthen the print-runs, it is not the face or hands that are re-worked, but the jewellery which is given added definition by the engraver. The process – whereby a coronation portrait drawn *ad vivum* and engraved (reproduced) in mezzotint by Thomas Frye (1710–62) as a plate capable of producing multiple copies (Plate 5)[30] is then re-engraved selectively at a later date by Boydell, literally highlighting the jewellery and making it more prominent (Plate 6) – points up both the nature of popularizing prints as palimpsests and the function of popular visual imagery in mythologization. The text is the Queen's body, structured and shown forth in the officially sanctioned portrait, the engravings are 'authorized' copies for her subjects, the overwriting by subsequent engravers marks the appropriation

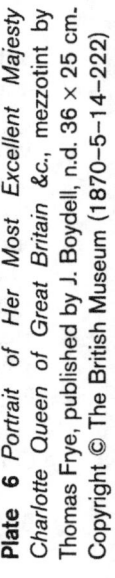

Plate 5 *Portrait of Her Most Excellent Majesty Charlotte Queen of Great Britain &c.*, mezzotint (first state) by Thomas Frye, 24 May 1762. 32 × 25 cm. Copyright © The British Museum (1902–10–11–8143)

Plate 6 *Portrait of Her Most Excellent Majesty Charlotte Queen of Great Britain &c.*, mezzotint by Thomas Frye, published by J. Boydell, n.d. 36 × 25 cm. Copyright © The British Museum (1870–5–14–222)

of the text leading to fragmentation and reformulation. Ultimately therefore the 'body' of the Queen is merely a 'fond' or base on which the engraver writes jewellery, just as the ground of her stomacher is the support for the diamonds which speak to the beholders at her coronation. In the semiotics of luxury, the signs that denote superfluity and ornament (those things that should at a literal level be understood as inessential, in contrast with the actual or political body of the Queen) become, through the historical practice of restoring a printer's plate in order to extend the life of an image, the very guarantee of permanence. The mechanics of publishing thus instantiates the very process of subversion through which luxury works to invert humanistic values, and through which that which is additional to the body is made to stand in the body's stead.

Historical narrative and textuality therefore work to position Charlotte in relation to her subjects as an image field upon which are inscribed marks that figure financial worth and imperial power. For diamonds are mined beyond Europe's borders, and in late eighteenth-century England they formed an important part of the East India Company's trade. George III and Queen Charlotte achieved some considerable notoriety in the 1780s as a consequence of accepting gifts from Nawabs, brought into the country by East India Company officials under suspicion of corruption.[31] The process whereby colonial trade transforms the meanings of what is imported and, by extension, constructs a colonial subject is established by Adam Smith in *The Wealth of Nations* with specific reference to jewellery and toys.[32] Eighteenth-century London was in no doubt as to the origins of diamonds.[33] The process of substitution and reversal which I have identified in the engraving process is also to be seen in the colonialist discourses of diamond importing. In the thematization of the corruption of colonial rule (Plate 7), diamonds signify through a process of inversion: in these explicitly critical discourses European depradation of the East Indies and, simultaneously, the superfluity of the 'other', of India, are formulated in images of diamonds. The conceptualized body of the nation (that is, of India) is, like the body of Queen Charlotte, discursively constituted by what is supplementary – and therefore by what is also disposable.[34]

Diamonds have a very overt presence in eighteenth-century representation; they are hard to cut but, once the stone has been turned into a 'brilliant', they are the most spectacular of ornaments. References to individuals 'covered in diamonds' are commonplace in eighteenth-century discourse where diamonds are virtually synonymous with ostentation.[35] Pearls, on the other hand (for which, as we have seen, Charlotte also possessed a penchant), have a distinct and more nuanced discursive function. In English cultural history pearls are associated with Queen Elizabeth I and with tactics for negotiating, and turning to political

Plate 7 *The Diamond Eaters, Horrid Monsters!*, anon engraving, May 1788, showing Warren Hastings, impeached Governor of Bengal, pouring diamonds into the open mouths of Thurlow, Queen Charlotte and King George III. 19 × 15.8 cm. Copyright © The British Museum (7288)

account, the Queen's virginity.[36] As we have seen (Plate 4), pearls are part of the *mise-en-scène* that associates the Queen with the natural world through her adornment by putti (who can be understood both as amorini and as babies, in both cases suggestive of generative powers). Moreover, in Francis Cotes's portrait of Queen Charlotte nursing the Princess Royal (Plate 8), diamonds have been completely displaced by pearls, while the crown is laid aside in the interests of a maternal authority as the Queen warns viewers not to wake the baby. But the more general association of pearls with Venus and profane love opens up a set of ambiguities that pertain to the situating of a royal female subject within debates about luxury. By considering also the origins of pearls, in mythology rather than topography, and not around the neck of a queen but in the ocean, as told in Pliny's classic account, we may begin to understand the discourses of

Plate 8 *Portrait of Charlotte Queen of Great Britain and the Princess Royal,* engraved by W. Wynne Ryland after Francis Cotes RA, 31 July 1770. 59 × 39 cm. Copyright © The British Museum (Q 2–4)

jewellery as they pertain to the queenly body and to representation of that body. In his *Natural History*, Book IX, Pliny introduces a discussion of pearls within the context of a diatribe against luxury. An examination of the biological processes through which a pearl is produced enables Pliny to draw a series of connections between the human body (*totum corpus anima hominis*) and the desire for luxury which endangers not merely the individual but, most importantly, the nation. The generative powers of oysters and the capacity of pearls to mirror natural changes in the universe are described in a passage through which Pliny also establishes a female underwater economy:

> Oyster shells . . . when stimulated by the generative season of the year gape open as it were and are filled with dewy pregnancy, and subsequently when heavy are delivered, and the offspring of the shells are pearls that correspond to the quality of the dew received. . . . If the sky was lowering (they say) the pearl is pale in colour: for it is certain it was conceived from the sky, and that pearls have more connexion with the sky than with the sea, and derive from it a cloudy hue, or a clear one corresponding with a brilliant morning.[37]

In this account the production of the pearl is part of the organic world of female parturition; the product, on the other hand, receives its determining character from the universal and temporal conditions of the natural world. If it thunders, Pliny tells us, 'wind pearls' are produced. These are 'only inflated with an empty, unsubstantial show: these are the pearls' miscarriages'.[38] When a shell sees a hand, it shuts itself up and conceals its treasures. Moreover, it is found in deep water and has sea dogs in attendance. But – and here Pliny changes tack to link manifestations of parturition and protection of progeny with the (seemingly contradictory) idea of woman as predator and perpetrator of luxury – nevertheless these 'do not protect it against women's ears!'; it is a brilliant move that enables a construction of femininity as simultaneously universal and biological, *and* controlled and wasteful, greedy and implicitly dangerous to the male subject and the masculine republic. 'Dewy pregnancy' as a female process is, through the universalizing phenomenalization of meteorological and marine data, split off from femininity, which can then be construed as grasping, destructive and luxurious. From this disjuncture, Pliny can then move easily into a discussion of Roman luxury in general and to the paradigmatic case of the 'abandoned extravagance' of women who, whether rich or poor, covet pearls while treating them with scandalous disregard for their natural properties. The text thus effectively separates the discourse of universal knowledge (Pliny's terrain) from that of gross consumption of artefacts (the feminine domain):

There is no doubt that pearls are worn away by use, and that lack of care makes them change their colour. . . . The highest praise given to their colour is for them to be called alum-coloured. The longer ones also have a charm of their own. Those that end in a wider circle, tapering lengthwise in the shape of perfume-caskets, are termed 'probes.' Women glory in hanging these on their fingers and using two or three for a single earring, and foreign names for this luxury occur, names invented by abandoned extravagance, inasmuch as when they have done this they call them 'castanets', as if they enjoyed even the sound and the mere rattling together of the pearls; and now-a-days even poor people covet them – it is a common saying that a pearl is as good as a lackey for a lady when she walks abroad! And they even use them on their feet, and fix them not only to the laces of their sandals but all over their slippers. In fact, by this time they are not content with wearing pearls unless they tread on them, and actually walk on these unique gems![39]

From such general censure – the female subject guilty of debasing the oyster's offspring by walking on it – it is a short step to the story of Lollia Paulina who appeared not at a grand ceremony but at an 'ordinary bethrothal banquet' covered 'with emeralds and pearls interlaced alternately and shining all over her head, hair, neck and fingers'. Lollia Paulina, according to Pliny, carried around with her the documentary proof of her entitlement to these jewels which were not a present to her but 'ancestal possessions, acquired in fact with the spoil of the provinces'. This, as Pliny declares, 'is the final outcome of plunder':

> Now let some one reckon on up on one side of the account how much Curius or Fabricius carried in their triumphs, and picture to himself the spoils they displayed, and on the other side Lollia, a single little lady reclining at the Emperor's side – and would he not think it better that they should have been dragged from their chariots than have won their victories with this result? Nor are these the topmost instances of luxury. There have been two pearls that were the largest in the whole of history; both were owned by Cleopatra.[40]

From this point, Pliny can move into his finale with the story of Cleopatra's destruction not only of one of the largest pearls ever found, but also of one of the greatest men ever known. This completes the loop that connects woman as producer (of offspring) with woman as consumer of male vitality: the produce of the female body (like the pregnancies and miscarriages of oysters) may be a necessary part of nature but the female subject's claim to status through her reproductive organs is cancelled out by her key role in the processes of depradation and excess.

To sum up so far, we may observe that the historical relationship between Queen Charlotte and the jewellery she is represented as wearing, a relationship that both defines her physical body and transcends it, is linked to ideas and principles of generation that are both economic (colonial) and physiological. At the level of myth and theory, while female fertility is – as in the case of oysters producing pearls – a beneficent part of the natural world – female consumption is unnatural (literally cannibalistic) and destructive. Women transform the beauty of the natural world into luxury and excess, exposing as futile the martial exploits of the male subject. In the case of a queen these linked questions of fertility and excess are also questions of nationalism. Luxuria, as she appears in iconographic traditions, signals both sexual excess and economic consumption and is personified by a female figure.[41] So, underlying the connection between the benign universe where pearls are generated and the dangerous feminization of a society predicated upon consumption, is a fear of uncontrolled female sexuality. What is acceptable in oysters is not permissible in humans, or such is the implication.

Eighteenth-century texts offer ample evidence of the widespread identification with jewellery as a signifying system understood to be universal – and timeless. As Rouquet puts it in 1755:

> we would fain attract the attention of others, as we do our own; we use all sorts of means to encompass this end: we cover ourselves with little thin plates of gold and silver . . . we try everything that is capable of procuring a little homage to our dear individual, even if it be extorted. The brilliancy and value of jewels is one of the surest means of adding something to the importance of our being.[42]

On the other hand, not only were the associations of jewels with excess (of the kind established in Pliny's account) commonplace; jewellery also staged through metonymy the disjuncture between the timeless perpetuity of gem stones and the frailty of human flesh. Jewellery as an artefact made of gem stones endeavours, in a manifestly futile project, to disguise this raw truth. Women are positioned within jewel narratives as key elements in a world of disintegration and instability from which (by implication) masculine subjects with their more contained habits of jewel-bearing (hilts of swords, buttons and shoe buckles) might have been thought to be immune. One example, recounted by Mrs Delany, will suffice:

> Lady Bute [?] and her daughter, lady Weymouth, *most splendid* in jewels, but in came Mrs. Montagu, who *rivall'd her* in sparkling gems. I could not help calling to mind (on seeing her so beset with jewells) Lady Clarendon's answer to Lady Granville when she ask'd her 'what was become of her jewells?' They are in my cabinet. When

my eyes outshone my *diamonds* I wore them; now *they* outshine my eyes I lock them up', and I thought if Mrs. M's *coronet* of *brilliants* which crown'd her *topee* had been in her cabinet it would have been their proper place.[43]

If women are defined by jewellery – in their fundamental roles of producers (of children) and as excessive consumers (of men's wealth both economic and sexual) – how is the bejewelled female body situated on the axis of the temporal? The apparent disjuncture between flesh and ornament unsettled observers of ageing women; Walpole remarks of a woman visiting an elderly female friend in Italy, a country renowned for its antiquities, 'whose ruins she has not discovered; but with few teeth, few hairs, sore eyes and wrinkles, goes bare necked and crowned with jewels!'[44] Jewellery worn by a young woman signals the position she occupies at the nexus of the reproductive cycles, economic on the one hand and biological on the other. Jewellery could be understood as a continuation of the body since it melded with female flesh, as with the piercing of ears, for example. While men have, at certain times in history, worn ear-rings, forms of jewellery as systematically functioning to regulate the social body are particular to women. I will cite, as an example, the case of Grace Boyle, who wrote of her arrival in London:

> Many things have happened to me since I came here viz: the borring of my Ears, Papa's giving me a pair of £100 Earrings, a pink Diamond ring, & a pair of gold buckles . . . with 4 guineas for my pocket. Mama is giving me a pair of star Errings, a set of stay buckles, & an Ermine muff. So I think I came to town to some purpose.[45]

Here jewellery points up the equivalence between the young female body and marriage as an economic act; but what of jewellery on the aged or ageing body, the post-menopausal and no longer (re)productive body? The practice of comparing female physical attributes with gem stones is commonplace; it is a mode of flattery that derives from the long traditions of attributing properties to gem stones. In Delany's account of Mrs Montagu, however, an account written from a woman's point of view, the body is in competition with the stones; what enhances the presence in youth, threatens it in age. The hypothesized continuity between body and ornament in the case of a young woman broke down at a certain point, producing a hiatus that threatens the social organization of the female body. Thus, in the case of the ageing Mrs Montagu, jewels that outshine the eyes should be locked up in a woman's cabinet. In other words, they should cease to be seen in public on her body.

I shall now return to Queen Charlotte to ask, in the case of a queen known to have loved and owned jewellery and, arguably, publicly identified with jewels and excessive consumption, what strategies were devised to secure her royal personage (as opposed to her individual body which, as we saw from a reading of her will was ineluctably linked to ornament) from the contaminating effects of jewellery narratives? These narratives commenced, as I have established, with Charlotte's arrival in England but they reached a climax in 1787 with accusations of bribery implicating the royal pair in events that led to the impeachment of Warren Hastings at the same time as the scandal of the diamond necklace was unravelling in France and threatening the very survival of the French monarchy.[46] One of the many caricatures from this period shows George III, a bulse of diamonds under his arm, standing by Charlotte whose pregnant belly matches the bulse, gazing in consternation as Warren Hastings is hauled on to a gibbet by Major Scott, his agent (Plate 9).[47] It is perhaps ironic that the connection of precious jewels and pregnancies that is unravelled in Pliny's account, and which is satirized by Gillray, should be re-inflected as a containing device within the textual narrative of Charlotte, Queen of England. But it is surely not accidental: the replay of classical narratives lent much-needed gravitas to the institution of the English monarchy and wrapped up the repeated images of excess in an alternative trope of maternity. When Charlotte gave birth to the Prince of Wales on 12 August 1762 'all was joy, merriment, and gladness in London'.[48] But the gladness related not only to the birth of a royal heir but also, we are told, to the arrival in London of the immense riches taken in a Spanish galleon. While Queen Charlotte lay at St James's, the carriages carrying the treasure passed under her windows on the way to the Bank.[49] This much-repeated story offers not only a satisfying coincidence – and an omen of good fortune for the future of the state on two levels – but it also reinterprets the connection between artefacts of precious materials and the Queen's fertility.

The most daring and successful device of this kind was the casting of Charlotte as Cornelia, an identification that served to erase the unpleasant narratives of excess and disintegration raised by Pliny and contemporary writers on luxury, and reinscribed in satirical discourse, while reaffirming the link between jewellery and femininity.

The story of Cornelia, Mother of the Gracchi, is one of the great jewellery narratives (along with Pliny's account of Cleopatra swallowing the pearl, John Donne's poem *The Relique*, Bizet's opera *The Pearl Fishers*, Anita Loos's *Gentlemen Prefer Blondes*, and Ian Fleming's *Diamonds are Forever*). Cornelia was a model Roman matron, mother of the social reformers Caius and Tiberius Gracchus (2000 BC). When a visitor asked to see her jewels, she had her two boys brought in and said: 'These are my jewels!' The story was well known and was used by Angelica Kauffmann for a painting exhibited at the Royal Academy in 1785.[50] In a poem by Stephen Egleton published on Queen Charlotte's birthday in 1780, an

Plate 9 James Gillray, *The Friendly Agent*, 9 June 1787, published by S. W. Fores. 21.5 × 17.l cm. Copyright © The British Museum (7169)

analogy is made between the Queen and Cornelia;[51] it is reiterated in the *Memoirs* of the Queen published in 1819 in a way clearly designed to counteract the popular view of a queen 'whose virtues make the soul of Envy sick, / Strong as her snuff, and as her di'monds thick':[52]

> . . . the Queen of England did not affect splendour in her apparel . . . she seldom wore jewels except on public ceremonies; and . . . so far

from devoting hours to her dress, she studied neatness and simplicity. Her conduct exactly resembled that of Cornelia, who, being asked by a Roman lady of rank for a sight of her toilet, waved the subject till her children came from school, and then said: 'These, Madam, are my ornaments.' In like manner did Her Majesty look upon the progeny which surrounded her, as a circle more valuable than diamonds.[53]

Cornelia's jewels are displaced on to her children. They may therefore be understood as the ostensive evidence of her gender in de-sexualized form. The existence of the children renders not only invisible, but also uneccessary, the notion of the queen as possessing jewels, and as possessing sexuality. If Cornelia possessed jewels she kept them hidden, as women *d'un certain age* were being exhorted to do in eighteenth-century England. Queen Charlotte was the owner of an exceptionally beautiful jewel cabinet, purpose-built in 1761 to contain the large number of jewels she possessed including all the wedding and coronation gifts from the King.[54] This was known to be kept in the Queen's bedroom where an observer commented on the twenty-five watches all adorned with jewels as well as the gilt plate and innumerable knick-knacks.[55] Women were provided with jewel cabinets, secure containers wherein their precious possessions – their jewels and by extension their sexuality – could be secured.[56] So what might this mean? How might we explain these connections between material culture and sexual politics? As Irigaray points out, the articulation of female sex is impossible in discourse 'and for a structural, eidetic reason'. She proposes that the enunciation of female sexuality involves mimicking what does not correspond to woman's own model.[57] The mimetic role, argues Irigaray, is complex, 'for it presupposes that one can lend oneself to everything, if not to everyone. That one can copy anything at all, any one at all, can receive all impressions, *without appropriating them to oneself,* and *without adding any.*'[58] I wish to suggest that the jewelled female body is a receptive form of the kind Irigaray suggests, capable of bearing impressions; insofar as ornament produces an illusory surface for the body, the body in turn mimics through its exotic discourses a universalizing other. That surface is legible within the social contexts of court culture, matrimony, generation and genealogy. The problem is first, how the female body can be wrested from its impressions, its supplements, when it is no longer needed for those social functions, and second, how this mimicry can be contained, can be prevented from being taken for the real, held back from appearing to be a substitution for the universal phallic. The case of Queen Charlotte demonstrates how narrative devices mobilize artefacts in the interests of this process. Locking up jewels in cabinets is one stage towards reasserting phallic authority. The next is the transposition, through myth, of jewels into children, a move that produces the queen as arbiter of her own moral position in her rejection of luxury (both sexual and economic) but also as, again, engaged in mimicry of a pre-ordained, elegant and well-orchestrated script sanctioned by Antiquity.

Dept of Art History and Archaeology, University of Manchester

Notes

1 I would like to thank Lucy Peltz for her assistance in locating material for this article, and Lindsay Smith for generously finding time to read and comment upon a first draft.

2 See J. L. Nevinson, 'New Year's gifts to Queen Elizabeth I, 1584', *Costume*, vol. 9 (1975), pp. 27–31.

3 I draw here on J. Baudrillard, 'For a critique of the political economy of the sign' in M. Poster (ed.) *Jean Baudrillard: Selected Writings* (Cambridge and Oxford: Polity, 1990), but see also M. Mauss, *The Gift* (1950), trans. W. D. Halls (London: Routledge, 1990) and J. Derrida, *Given Time: Counterfeit Money* (Chicago: Chicago UP, 1992).

4 R. K. Marshall and G. R. Dalgleish, *The Art of Jewellery in Scotland* (Edinburgh: HMSO, Scottish National Portrait Gallery, 1991), p. 41.

5 For a range of such inscriptions, see J. Evans, *English Posies and Posy Rings* (London: OUP/Humphrey Milford, 1931) (this quote on p. xix).

6 For a fascinating exploration of jewellery as literary imagery, see Kurt Tetzli von Rosador, 'Gems and jewellery in Victorian fiction', *R.E.A.L.*, vol. 2, 1984. I am grateful to Judy Rudoe for drawing my attention to this important article. See also W. Jones, *Finger-ring Lore* (London: Chatto, 1877).

7 There is a large literature of ancient origins on this topic. See J. Evans and M. S. Serjeantson, *English Medieval Lapidaries* (Oxford: OUP, 1933, repr. 1960).

8 See, especially, E. H. Kantorowicz, *The King's Two Bodies: A Study in Medieval Political Theology* (Princeton: Princeton UP, 1957).

9 This is, at least, true of eighteenth-century Europe. There is, however, a significant and growing body of work on Marie-Antoinette. See, in particular, S. Maza, *Private Lives and Public Affairs. The Causes Célèbres of Prerevolutionary France* (Berkeley and Los Angeles: UC Press, 1993), and C. Thomas, *La Reine scélérate: Marie-Antoinette et les pamphlets* (Paris: Editions du Seuil, 1989).

10 Accounts of the life of Queen Charlotte date from the period immediately following her death and include W. C. Oulton, *The Memoirs of Her Late Majesty Queen Charlotte* (London: J. Robinson & Co., 1819); J. Watkins, *Memoirs of Her Most Excellent Majesty Sophia-Charlotte Queen of Great Britain, from authentic documents* (London: Henry Colburn, 1819); O. Hedley, *Queen Charlotte* (London: John Murray, 1975). All are dependent upon the memoirs of Delany, Papendiek and Walpole (see below, nn. 17, 32, 43).

11 Invoices for some of the jewellery purchased thus are in the British Library, Add.MSS. 38333, ff. 126–37.

12 For example, *The Diaries of a Duchess. Extracts from the Diaries of the first Duchess of Northumberland*, ed. J. Greig (London, 1926), p. 28, quoted in Hedley, p. 42.

13 H. Walpole, *Memoirs of the Reign of King George the Third*, ed. G. F. Russell Barker (London and New York: Lawrence & Bullen / Putnams, 1894), pp. i, 56–7.

14 E. F. Twining, *A History of the Crown Jewels of Europe* (London: Batsford, 1960), p. 159.

15 *The Diaries of a Duchess* . . . , quoted in Hedley, p. 43. See also *Gentleman's Magazine*, 78, part 2 (1808), p. 1069, quoting a letter of 1761: 'The lustre of her stomacher was inconceivable, being one of the presents she received whilst Princess of Mecklenburg, on which was represented, by the vast profusion of diamonds placed on it, the magnificence attending so great a king. . . . '

16 D. Scarisbrick, *Jewellery in Britain 1066–1837* (Norwich: Michael Russell, 1994), p. 227.

17 *Court and Private Life in the Time of Queen Charlotte, being the journals of Mrs. Papandiek, assistant keeper of the wardrobe and reader to Her Majesty*, ed. Mrs Vernon Delves Broughton (London: privately printed, 1887) (hereafter Papandiek), i. p. 12, quoted in Hedley, p. 43 with details. It was common practice to protect the wedding ring in this way.

18 Ibid.

19 Northumberland, quoted in Hedley, p. 51.

20 The jewels appeared in the sales at Christie's 17–19 May, and 24–26 May 1819.

21 Ibid., Monday 17 May 1819.

22 Caricatures on the Warren Hastings affair are discussed in M. Pointon, 'Intrigue, jewellery and economics: court culture and display in England and France in the 1780s' (forthcoming).

23 Many caricatures allude to this attribute. See, for example, *The Queen of Hearts covere'd with Diamonds*, c. 1786, anonymous caricature (British Museum, London, 6978).

24 This is evident, for example, in W. C. Oulton, where each jewellery gift episode is counteracted with the pregnancy episode following it.

25 See, for example, Middleton's and Rowley's play, *The Changeling* (1623) in which notions of female sexuality are articulated through the exchange of jewellery, and in particular of rings. In one exchange, the jealous doctor Albius worries about his young wife's fidelity, saying: 'I would wear my ring on my own finger; / whilst it is borrowed it is none of mine, / But his that useth it', to which his servant replies: 'You must keep it on then; if it but lie by, one or / Other will be thrusting into it' (T. Middleton and T. Rowley, *The Changeling*, ed. N. Bawcutt (Manchester: MUP, 1958), II, iv, i). I am grateful to Jonathan Dollimore for drawing my attention to this text.

26 Scarisbrick. p. 227.

27 Oulton, p. 141; she is described as wearing 'a beautiful crown of brilliants, with eleven large diamonds stuck in her hair; her stomacher, bouquet, and sleeve-bows were also immensely rich'.

28 On the political and moral discourses of luxury in eighteenth-century England, see J. Sekora, *Luxury. The Concept in Western Thought, Eden to Smollett* (Baltimore and London: Johns Hopkins UP, 1977), and C. Berry, *The Idea of Luxury* (Cambridge: CUP, 1994).

29 Diamond crosses were extremely fashionable during the early Georgian period and were more high-fashion items than a sign of religious devoutness. Queen Victoria, *Statement on behalf of Her Majesty in Answer to the Claims made on behalf of His Majesty the King of Hanover to Certain Jewels* (1844, p. 39),

quoted in D. Scarisbrick, *Jewellery in Britain 1066–1837* (Norwich: Michael Russell, 1994), p. 260.

30 Frye is recorded as having produced his mezzotint in three different sizes at, presumably, three different prices (H. Bromley, *A Catalogue of Engraved British Portraits* (London: T. Payne *et al.*, 1793)). Boydell must have reworked the plates that had worn out after the death of Frye which occurred in the same year as he issued his print.

31 The question of royal involvement in the Warren Hastings affair is the subject of work in progress. My research on all these questions is part of an ongoing project for a book on the display culture of jewels and jewellery.

32 A. Smith, *The Wealth of Nations* (1776), Book 1, Ch. XI (Harmondsworth: Penguin, 1986), pp. 277–8; in *Lectures on Justice, Police, Revenue and Arms* (*c.* 1763–4), ed. E. Cannan (Oxford: Clarendon, 1896) ('Of the natural wants of mankind', Div. ii, part ii, p. 159); Smith states that: 'Variety of objects also renders them agreeable. What we are every day accustomed to does but very indifferently affect us. Gems and diamonds are on this account much esteemed by us. In like manner our pinchbeck and many of our toys were so much valued by the Indians, that in bartering their *jewels* and diamonds for them they thought they had made by much the better bargain.' See also many references in Horace Walpole's correspondence to diamonds and India (e.g. to Mary Berry on 22 October 1790 on goods from Peru and Mexico, 'though we should come by them a little more honestly than we did the diamonds of Bengal' (*The Yale Edition of Horace Walpole's Correspondence*, ed. W. S. Lewis, 48 vols (London: OUP and New Haven: Yale University Press, 1937–80), vol. 11 (1944), pp. 122–5).

33 Popular print and doggerel, especially at the time of the impeachment of Warren Hastings in 1786, places great emphasis on the Indian origins of the brilliants that contributed so much to the London scene.

34 It is appropriate here to recall the long tradition for visualizing the nation state as a human body, even though England was not a single nation.

35 As, for example, in Walpole's *Correspondence*, where observations such as 'Lady Betty Montagu's jewels are very pretty; she had better have non. Mrs. Donaldson's daughter [Anna Maria Montagu] is covered with them *en nabob*' (Letter from George Montagu, 7 March 1766, vol. 10 (1941), pp. 203–5).

36 On Queen Elizabeth I and the symbolism of her depictions see F. A. Yates, *Astraea. The Imperial Theme in the Sixteenth Century* (London and Boston: Routledge, 1975).

37 Pliny, *Natural History*, Book IX (LIV), trans. H. Rackham, 10 vols (London and Cambridge: The Loeb Classical Library), 1938–57, iii (1940).

38 Ibid.

39 Ibid. (LVI).

40 Ibid. (LVIII).

41 Luxury is represented as a woman with a mirror in the rose window of Notre Dame, Paris, and locked in lascivious embrace in a relief which pairs her with Chastity, at Amiens.

42 J. Rouquet, *The Present State of the Arts in England* (London, 1755), pp. 89–90.

43 R. Brimley Johnson (ed.) *Mrs. Delany at Court and Among the Wits* (London: Stanley Paul & Co., 1925), pp. 229–30, Mrs Delany to Mrs Port, 2 January 1773.

44 H. Walpole to T. Mann, 22 December 1750, *Correspondence*, vol. 20 (1960), pp. 221–6.

45 Strafford Papers, 18 September 1735, BM Add.MS 22, 256 (36). I am grateful to Karen Stanworth for drawing my attention to this correspondence.

46 I will address this in my forthcoming study of jewellery and display culture in eighteenth-century England.

47 Scott's detailed testimony was widely expected to lead to Hastings' indictment.

48 Papandiek, i, p. 27.

49 Walpole is just one who reports on these simultaneous events of 12 August when the Queen was delivered of the Prince of Wales and 'the same morning the treasure of that capital prize, the Hermione, arrived in town in many waggons and passed through the City to the Tower. The sum taken amounted to near eight hundred thousand pounds' (H. Walpole, *Memoirs*, i, p. 150).

50 *Cornelia, the Mother of the Gracchi, Pointing to her Children as her Treasures* is one of a group of paintings executed by Kauffman for George Bowles in 1785 and shown at the Royal Academy in 1786; it was engraved in November 1788 by Bartolozzi and published by Ryland. See W. W. Roworth, *Angelica Kauffman. A Continental Artist in Georgian England* (London, 1992), pp. 91, 187. The subject was repeated for Her Majesty the Queen of Naples in 1785 and for Prince Poniatowsky in 1788; see Lady V. Manners and Dr. G. C. Williamson, *Angelica Kauffmann, R. A. Her Life and Works* (London: John Lane & the Bodley Head, 1924), p. 149. Lucy Peltz has kindly drawn my attention to a copy of Lucan's *Pharsalia* published at Strawberry Hill in 1760 and bound with a very expensive decorative vellum binding by Edwards of Halifax, the back board of which contains a grisaille representation of the Cornelia subject. Clarissa Campbell-Orr has drawn attention to the inclusion of this story in Mme de la Fite's *Questions to be resolved or, a new method of exercising the attention of young people* (London, 1790) dedicated to Queen Charlotte.

51 S. Egleton, *A Poem for Queen Charlotte's BIRTH-DAY; Which for the Good of TRADE, is Appointed to be Kept on the Eighteenth of JANUARY: But is Originally on the Nineteenth of May* (London: Printed by the Author for the Relief of Himself, an infirm Wife, and Six small Children, who will gratefully acknowledge the smallest Favour, n.d. (1780 ?)).

52 *The Works of Peter Pindar, Esq.* (London: F. C. & J. Rivington, J. Nunn et al., 1816), ii, p. 120.

53 Watkins, p. 280.

54 Made by William Vile and John Cobb, it is still in the royal collection. See M. Snodin (ed.) *Rococo Art and Design in Hogarth's England* (London: Victoria and Albert Museum, 1984, catalogue, London: Trefoil, 1984), no. L60.

55 Mrs. L. Powys, quoted in Hedley, p. 102.

56 The imagery of jewel boxes and female sexuality is widespread; in the literary field one thinks immediately of the division of jewels from Dorothea's and Celia's mother's jewel box in *Middlemarch* and the significance of Dora's mother's jewel case in Freud's case history of Dora (see Penguin Freud Library vol. 8, Case Histories, 1, 'Dora' and 'Little Hans').

57 L. Irigaray, *This Sex which is not one* (1977), trans. C. Porter (Ithaca: Cornell UP, 1985), p. 149.

58 Ibid., p. 151, author's italics.

Brian Young

Gibbon and sex

> A crowd of disgraceful passages will force themselves on the memory of the classic reader.[1]

Sex is all-pervasive in the writings of Edward Gibbon, while sex in his personal life, at least as mirrored in his letters and memoirs, is marked by a cultivated absence. Fertility and abundance characterize both his style and his subject matter, especially in *The Decline and Fall of the Roman Empire*; sterility and a marmoreal anxiety mark his personal existence. He begins his *Autobiographies* with a family history replete with excursions into cadet branches and an extended cousinage, and he closes them as a bachelor only child whose nearest relatives had long been a widowed step-mother and two maiden aunts. Sex is also deeply entangled with history in Gibbon's writings, as opulent cultures of display are richly delineated in an empire of the senses as much as of men and of nations.

Explicit sexual self-disclosure is not something one should expect of an eighteenth-century memoir, and in this respect Gibbon's *Autobiographies* were typically as far removed from the proto-Romantic example of the compulsively confessional Rousseau as it was possible for them to be. It may be possible to make the occasional inference concerning Gibbon's broader views on sexual *mores* from the argument of *The Decline and Fall*, but again this can be achieved only with great caution. Gibbon devoted his life to becoming 'the historian of the Roman Empire', and that is the persona one can be most sure of recovering from his writings, including the *Autobiographies*. Sacrifices may well have been entailed in achieving this ambition, but it is not the place of the historian to assume what cannot be known. An examination of certain of the preoccupations and themes developed in the argument of *The Decline and Fall* serves to demonstrate the centrality of sex to Gibbon's understanding of the past, but it cannot be made to substantiate the inferences regarding his own sexuality which modern critics might otherwise want to make of an eighteenth-century text as richly suggestive as Gibbon's history.

Textual Practice 11(3), 1997, 517–537   © 1997 Routledge 0950–236X

'Of lust and luxury'

The theme of Gibbon and sex is surprisingly underexplored in secondary
writing, and this despite his lurid reputation for excessive prurience in *The
Decline and Fall*.[2] The theme of luxury, however, is one which historians
and literary scholars have identified and commented on at some length in
writings concerned with Gibbon's work. It is one of the primary purposes
of this article to demonstrate the essential *melding* of sexuality and luxury,
both positive and negative, in Gibbon's work. This fusion maintains a
central dynamic in the argument of *The Decline and Fall*: pagan virtue
activating a creative luxury which is overwhelmed in its turn by the sterilities of Christian virtue. This tripartite structure, which informs much of
the argument at least of the first two volumes of the work, is announced
in the opening chapter of Volume 1 in an economically evocative image
of the Roman landscape: 'On that celebrated ground the first consuls
deserved triumphs; their successors adorned villas, and *their* posterity have
erected convents' (p. 50).[3]

The ambivalent relationships between luxury, power and sexuality are
a source of tension throughout the work. Writing of the excesses of the
emperor Elagabalus, Gibbon refers to his 'sovereign privilege of lust and
luxury' (p. 168), an alliteration that becomes an animated elision for many
of the more decadent Romans who people the opening volumes. In a footnote concerned with homosexuality among Rome's precursors, Gibbon
likewise lamented the 'luxury and lust of the Etruscans' (Vol. II, p. 837,
n. 191). This identification of intimately connected vices is something of
a commonplace in the language of virtue which informs much of Gibbon's
analysis, an extension of such long-held views as those put into the mouth
of Musidorus in Sidney's *The Countess of Pembroke's Arcadia*, where the
somewhat priggish warrior early denounces love as an effeminate fusion
'engendered betwixt lust and idleness'.[4]

As befits an autobiographer (albeit a reticent one), the private
fascinated Gibbon as much as the public, although he was less confident
of reconstructing the reality of *l'histoire de la vie privée* than are modern
historians. This realm of the private was potentially ever-present in the
public world, as Gibbon intimates with typically pregnant reticence:

> but though we may suspect, it is not in our power to relate, the secret
> intrigues of the palace, the private views and resentments, the
> jealousy of women or eunuchs, and all those trifling but decisive
> causes which so often influence the fate of empires, and the counsels
> of the wisest monarchs.
>
> (Vol. I, p. 563)

Thus, for Gibbon, sex is at least as much a means of explaining other issues as it is an end in itself, a lesson which historians have seemed constantly to need to relearn since.

Discussion of sex was a peculiarly powerful means of demonstrating this link between the private and the public, and therefore marriage was an institution of some moment in *The Decline and Fall*. This was especially marked in relation to the growth of Christianity, since as Gibbon presciently noted, the faith 'has acknowledged its important obligations to female devotion' (Vol. I, p. 558). Following Tacitus, Gibbon rather conventionally praised the 'conjugal faith and chastity' of the ancient Germans, who would come to restore a 'manly spirit of freedom' to a decadent empire. The greatest enemies to such chastity were 'softness of mind' and 'sentimental passion', and its strongest proponents were therefore those women who were prepared to 'emulate the stern virtues of *man*' at the unfortunate cost of 'the charm and weakness of *woman*'. Such masculinized women were, Gibbon assured his readers, neither 'lovely, nor very susceptible to love' (Vol. I, pp. 84, 243–4). In the classically binary moral universe, virtue is not always as immediately attractive as vice, and the supposed virtues of the barbarians were clearly more to Tacitus's taste than to those of many eighteenth-century minds, especially to those as subtle and innately ambivalent as that of Gibbon. Nor yet, however, was primitive Roman marriage any more attractive to minds affected by the cult of sentiment, as Gibbon noted that they had usually 'married without love, or loved without delicacy and respect' (Vol. I, pp. 170–1). Not that modern marriage was always so much to be preferred: Gibbon slyly noticed that, while modern susceptibilities might be adversely affected by the old tradition of the forced removal of the bride from her parental home on the day of her wedding (one preserved among the primitive Christians), 'Our form of marriage requires, with less delicacy, the express and public consent of a virgin' (Vol. II, p. 105). Similarly, he implicitly posits that the relationship between property and marriage was less egregious under the subsequently much-condemned laws of the Germanic tribes than it was in eighteenth-century society. The Visigoths were praised for legally restraining the size of such nuptial gifts, described as 'the prodigality of conjugal love'. Even more controversially, in his discussion of 'the famous, and often fabulous, right, *de cuissage, de marquette*' Gibbon considerably underplayed the offence it otherwise might have given to sentimental readers by a ready deployment of civilized irony: 'With the consent of her husband, an handsome bride might commute the payment in the arms of a young landlord, and the mutual favour might afford a precedent of local rather than legal tyranny' (Vol. III, pp. 215, 878 and n. 74). Gibbon's own anxieties at his father's remarriage and the costs that this entailed inform both his letters and, to a lesser degree, his memoirs: the frequently fraught relationship between property, marriage and children was one with which the historian was all too familiar, and self-disclosure seems to make its way in this manner into *The Decline and Fall* at least as much as into the *Autobiographies*.

'Monkish virtues'

However ambivalently, Gibbon preferred the idea of marriage to the chilly perfections of celibacy, whether enforced or otherwise: hence his intense distaste for the Priscillianists and their opposition to the use of the marriage-bed (Vol. II, p. 39). Accordingly, the Zoroastrians were praised for their abhorrence of fasting and celibacy; theirs were productively benefical virtues:

> The saint in the Magian religion, is obliged to beget children, to plant useful trees, to destroy noxious animals, to convey water to the dry lands of Persia, and to work out his salvation by pursuing the labours of agriculture.
>
> (Vol. I, p. 218)

Sex provides a healthily productive dynamic to societies which celibacy denies. Gibbon early set himself firmly against the 'monkish virtues' which Hume had identified and condemned in the *Enquiries*. Hume had argued that it was the 'delusive glosses of superstition and false religion' which had turned the antisocial vices of celibacy, fasting, penance, mortification, self-denial, humility, silence and solitude into virtues, concluding that 'A gloomy, hairbrained enthusiast, after his death, may have a place in the calendar; but will scarcely ever be admitted, when alive, into intimacy and society, except by those as delirious and dismal as himself.'[5] Aside from the Church calendar, long fallen into desuetude in Protestant England, only history could wish to disinter such fanatics, and then only as a warning to the uniquely sociable modern reader. The many fanatics who wander through the pages of *The Decline and Fall* are plainly part of this dangerously antisocial 'other' world of late antiquity and early medievalism.

Gibbon's dispraise for female chastity was conventionally less vehement than that which he meted out to male celibacy. It was, after all, an Eastern princess, Zenobia, who (somewhat unsurprisingly) 'far surpassed' her ancestor Cleopatra 'in chastity and valour' (Vol. I, p. 313). Likewise, there was deeply ambiguous praise for Sophronia, an early Christian martyr, who 'preserved her chastity by a voluntary death' – a case of suicide the seemingly anomalous justification of which by Catholic casuists clearly entertained the historian (Vol. I, pp. 418–19 and n. 45).[6] He was quite simply appalled by nuns, typified by 'the credulous maid' who was all too readily 'betrayed by vanity to violate the laws of nature';

and he utterly lamented the condition of 'the useless multitude of both sexes who could only plead the merits of abstinence and chastity' (Vol. II, pp. 417, 511).

Monks, nuns and priests were in every sense sexless. Speech and example were literally their only means of reproduction, as 'The popular monks, whose reputation was connected with the fame and success of the order, assiduously laboured to multiply the number of their fellow-captives' (Vol. II, p. 417). Opposing the peculiar tales which emanated from the 'lazy gloom of their convents' to the active and usually healthy life of the citizenry, Gibbon made hay with the sexual temptations and preoccupations of the celibate caste (Vol. I, p. 505). In his short excursus on homosexuality, he observed, in a manner common to English critics of celibacy, that 'every vice was fomented by the celibacy of the monks and clergy' (Vol. II, p. 838). Much to Gibbon's mordant taste was a 'strange story' taken from Jerome, an arch-celibate, which concerned 'a young man, who was chained naked on a bed of flowers, and assaulted by a beautiful and wanton courtezan. He quelled the rising temptation by biting off his tongue' (Vol. I, p. 539, n. 65). Gibbon was plainly at least as interested in Jerome's desire to pass on this tale as he was in the tale itself; as he noted elsewhere in *The Decline and Fall*, 'The devils were most formidable in a female shape' (Vol. II, p. 425, n. 64).[7] A similarly potentially compromising instance is given when the heroically orthodox Athanasius, in flight from his Arian persecutors, was left in an 'extra-ordinary asylum, the house of a virgin, only twenty years of age, and who was celebrated in the whole city for her beauty'. Gibbon's final detailing of the story is yet more studiedly ambiguous, and its deeply sensual elements are by no means cancelled out by its conventional closure:

> As long as the danger continued, she regularly supplied him with books and provisions, washed his feet, managed his correspondence, and dexterously concealed from the eye of suspicion this familiar and solitary intercourse between a saint whose character required the most unblemished chastity, and a female whose charms might excite the most dangerous emotions.
>
> (Vol. I, p. 813)

The self-control of an orthodox idol contrasts with the self-indulgence of a heterodox bishop, Paul of Samosata, who had 'received into the episcopal palace two young and beautiful women, as the constant companions of his leisure moments' (Vol. I, p. 557). Orthodox readers might have settled for these two accounts, but the hint that something is amiss with Athanasius that is not amiss with Paul recurs in another passage where Gibbon refers to the case of Synesius, a briefly and reluc-tantly co-opted bishop, in terms of implicit approval: 'He loved profane studies and profane sports; he was incapable of supporting a life of celibacy; he disbelieved the resurrection: and he refused to preach *fables* to the people, unless he be permitted to *philosophize* at home' (Vol. I, pp. 754–5, 761 and n. 118). Gibbon insisted, in terms not unfamiliar to Anglican critics of that state, that celibacy was not the same as chastity, a belief he voiced in one of his most mordantly satirical footnotes:

> I have somewhere heard or read of the frank confession of a Benedictine abbot: 'My vow of poverty has given me an hundred thousand crowns a year; my vow of obedience has raised me to the mark of a sovereign prince.' – I forget the consequences of his vow of chastity.
>
> (Vol. II, p. 424, n. 57)[8]

Not that the orthodox alone were celibate or chaste. Gibbon noted that Athanasius's opponent, the arch-heresiarch Arius, 'reckoned among his immediate followers two bishops of Egypt, seven presbyters, twelve deacons, and (what may appear almost incredible) seven hundred virgins' (Vol. I, p. 779). Indeed, Julian the Apostate was himself a model of chastity – 'the chaste Julian never shared his bed with a female companion' – a state of affairs which was 'voluntary' and, in his own opinion, 'meritorious' (Vol. I, pp. 851, 929, n. 59). In this important respect, Julian provided a strong contrast with Jovian, who yet survived the comparison with Christians since, despite a noted 'taste for wine and women', he 'supported with credit, the character of a Christian and a soldier' (Vol. I, p. 947). Similarly, the emperor Constans, who indulged 'unlawful pleasures', had still managed to profess a 'lively regard for the orthodox faith' (Vol. I, p. 802). It was of the essence of Gibbon's decision to provide a chrono-logically driven narrative history that such blatant and inevitable, if telling, anomalies in public and private morals should make their way into the consideration of a knowing posterity.

Equally paradoxical was Gibbon's insistence that chastity was, poten-tially at least, not without the possibility of sensual or even luxurious rewards. While nuns admittedly 'sacrificed the pleasures of dress and luxury; and renounced, for the praise of chastity, the soft endearments of conjugal society', monks were, potentially at least, rather better rewarded for their pains:

> By their contempt of the world, they insensibly acquired its most desirable advantages; the lively attachment, perhaps, of a young and beautiful woman, the delicate plenty of an opulent household, and the respectful homage of the slaves, the freedmen, and the clients of a senatorial family.
>
> (Vol. I, pp. 985–6)

A more contemporary insinuation may well lurk in a similar reference to another ascetic ideal of the primitive Church, where Gibbon undermined the community of goods mentioned in Acts by stating that 'The community of women, and that of temporal goods, may be considered as inseparable parts of the same system' (Vol. I, p. 490, n. 128). The community of goods was a declared standard of the faith in the thought of John Wesley (which he later abandoned), and Gibbon would not have been by any means the first of his critics to associate Wesleyanism with sexual promiscuity.[9] The same sentiments regarding the implicit ambivalences of asceticism dictated Gibbon's suspicion of allied questions, as when he declared that 'The chaste severity of the fathers in whatever related to the commerce of the two sexes, flowed from the same principle, the abhorrence of every enjoyment, which might gratify the sensual, and degrade the spiritual, nature of man' (Vol. I, p. 479). An implied preference for the older religions shone through when Gibbon mischievously adverted to the fact that 'It was with the utmost difficulty that ancient Rome could support the institution of six vestals; but the primitive church was filled with a great number of persons of either sex, who had devoted themselves to the profession of perpetual chastity' (Vol. I, p. 480).

'The decency of modern language'

It was, then, an ironic act of charity for Gibbon to claim that 'It is a very honourable circumstance for the morals of the primitive Christians, that even their faults, or rather errors, were derived from an excess of virtue'. A contemporary note reappears in an allusion to those moral reform societies which worked, with varying degrees of success, throughout the eighteenth century, as Gibbon adverted to 'the reformation of manners which was introduced into the world by the preaching of the gospel' (Vol. I, pp. 477, 475).[10] Despite the ironic tone his sentiment is undoubtedly not without sincerity, as his concomitant censure of Roman sensuality makes abundantly clear. He condemned Hadrian's passion for Antinous, albeit allowing that 'of the first fifteen emperors, Claudius was the only one whose taste in love was entirely correct' (Vol. I, p. 101, n. 40). Faustina, Marcus Aurelius's notoriously promiscuous wife, was introduced in suitably euphemistic terms: 'The Cupid of the ancients was, in general, a very sensual deity, and the amours of an empress, as they exact in her the plainest advances, are seldom susceptible of much sentimental delicacy' (Vol. I, p. 108). Similar tones betray the faults of a later empress: 'if we may credit the scandal of ancient history, chastity was very far from being the most conspicuous virtue of the empress Julia' (Vol. I, p. 150). Reverting to the Latin of his sources, Gibbon declared of Commodus that he gave way to 'abandoned scenes of prostitution, which scorned every restraint of nature or modesty; but it would not be easy to translate their too faithful description into the decency of modern language' (Vol. I, p. 116 and n. 29).

This last claim was famously affirmed in his remarks relating to the pious Empress Theodora, an ex-entertainer whose most notorious act involved a swan and corn hidden about her person: 'but her murmurs, her pleasures, and her arts, must be veiled in the obscurity of a learned language.' His note then goes on to lay out a lurid quotation in Greek, a passage which, he mischievously informs his readers, 'a learned prelate, now deceased, was fond of quoting . . . in conversation' (Vol. II, p. 565 and n. 24). There is something odd about this declaration, the historian quoting a passage at least as much to reveal the prurience of a bishop – identified by some as William Warburton, Pope's editor – as to mask his own. Similarly, Gibbon only declared that 'it must not be forgot, that the bishop of Cremona was a lover of scandal' after he himself had quoted a good deal of that scandal (Vol. III, p. 402). The double standards he imputes to his clerical coadjutors could equally be levelled against him at this point and, as the poem in the Appendix to this article makes clear, they sometimes were. Again, the resort to Greek in writing about Theodora reminds one of the obvious distaste that John Aubrey felt in accusing his hero Francis Bacon of pederasty, an accusation he could only make, for whatever now obscure reason, by using the original Greek characters to signify his alleged vice.[11] Just how many schoolboys (or undergraduates) were encouraged to improve their classical learning in order to appreciate the racier elements of *The Decline and Fall* is surely one of the great imponderables in the history of English education.[12] For Gibbon the sexual is intimately linked with the textual, and constant quotation of classical improprieties, in a variation of the rhetorical figure of *occupatio*, allowed him a licence which the English language could not afford him.

The question of language insinuates itself into much of his discussion of sex. His readers are reminded that the Emperor Elagabalus promoted three ministers, who 'were all recommended, *enormitate membrorum*' (Vol. I, p. 167). He wonders with some deliberation if πορνεια really is best translated as fornication, speculating in turn whether Christ spoke either the Rabbinical or the Syriac tongue in order to wonder about the true nature of certain sexual injunctions in the New Testament, leaving the historian to remark suggestively 'How variously is that Greek word translated in the versions ancient and modern!' (Vol. II, p. 816). The apotheosis of such linguistic playfulness is reached in his retelling of Origen's disarming of the 'tempter' through a mistaken reading of castration for circumcision, elaborating this point in a more than usually satirical footnote: 'As it was his general practice to allegorize scripture; it seems unfortunate that, in this instance only, he should have adopted the literal sense' (Vol. I, p. 480 and n. 96).

'The effeminate luxury of Oriental despotism'

Origen, an accidental eunuch, is by no means the only representative in *The Decline and Fall* of what Gibbon called 'that imperfect species' (Vol. I, p. 685). Monks, rendered sexless by their vocation, are curiously interchangeable with eunuchs in Gibbon's text: pitied as 'unhappy exiles from social life', he claimed that 'all the manly virtues were oppressed by the servile and pusillanimous reign of the monks' (Vol. II, p. 416, 429). Parallels with the eunuchs are not hard to find, and their corruptions compromised the despotism of Imperial rule as certainly as the ascetic dominance of the monks compromised the sway of the Church. So it was that Justinian II's favourite ministers were decried as 'two beings the least susceptible of human sympathy, an eunuch and a monk' (Vol. III, p. 32). The masculine virtues of Rome were mirrored by the literal emasculation of a cadre of eunuchs in its political and social decline, as 'the use and value of those effeminate slaves gradually rose with the decline of the empire'. Eunuchs were a final luxuriant import from the reign of Elagabalus, when Rome 'was at length humbled beneath the effeminate luxury of Oriental despotism'; their very rise in numbers was 'the most infallible symptom of the progress of despotism' (Vol. I, pp. 182, 166, 389). Castigating Elagabalus's Syrian effeminacy, Gibbon similarly placed the Eunuchs 'as that pernicious vermin of the East, who, since the days of Elagabalus, had infested the Roman palace'. They were 'the ancient production of Oriental jealousy and despotism . . . introduced into Greece and Rome by Asiatic luxury' (Vol. I, pp. 177, 208, 684). Their power comprised a 'jealous vigilance'; the Emperor Constantius was 'a prince who was the slave of his own passions, and of those of his eunuchs' (Vol. I, pp. 389, 820). One is reminded of the closing pages of Montesquieu's *Lettres Persanes*, in which eunuchs exact a terrible vengeance in harems at the distant behest of their masters, the ambivalently civilized Persian travellers; and there is more than a little of *l'esprit des lois* in Gibbon's contention that 'if we examine the general history of Persia, India, and China, we shall find the power of the eunuchs has uniformly marked the decline and fall of every dynasty' (Vol. I, p. 685, n. 7).[13] A shocking instance of the collusion of despotism and emasculation is given in the story of the Praefect Plautianus's castration of a hundred free Romans, some of whom were married and the fathers of families, 'merely that his daughter, on her marriage with the young emperor, might be attended by a train of eunuchs worthy of an Eastern queen' (Vol. I, p. 146, n. 68). Not all eunuchs were merely presented in order to be routinely condemned, and the often sickly, noticeably short Member of Parliament and former militia officer may have made some sort of tacit identification with Narses, whom he ranked 'among the few who have rescued that unhappy name from the contempt and hatred of mankind. A feeble diminutive body concealed the soul of a statesman and a warrior' (Vol. II, p. 751).

It was not, however, merely eunuchs which Elagabalus introduced at the cost of the well-being of the Empire, and his proclivities were opportunely delineated in terms suggestive of Gibbon's own ambivalent attitudes towards luxury and excess:

> A rational voluptuary adheres with invariable respect to the temperate dictates of nature, and improves the gratifications of sense by social intercourse, endearing connections, and the soft colouring of taste and the imagination. But Elagablus . . . corrupted by his youth, his country, and his fortune, abandoned himself to the grossest pleasures with ungoverned fury, and soon found disgust and satiety in the midst of his enjoyments.
>
> (Vol. I, p. 167)

It was Elagabalus who played his part in promoting that most luxurious of commodities, silk, whose importance in the sociopolitical dynamics of *The Decline and Fall* cannot be over-emphasized: the silk road is one of the major routes through the historical geography of which Gibbon was a supreme master. A paean to the silkworm, 'a valuable insect, the first artificer of the luxury of nations' is quickly followed by a condemnation of its effects:

> Two hundred years after the age of Pliny, the use of pure or even of mixed silks was confined to the female sex, till the opulent citizens and the provinces were insensibly familiarised with the example of Elagabalus, the first who, by this effeminate habit, had sullied the dignity of an emperor and a man.
>
> (Vol. II, pp. 579–80)

Once again, however, one should not read this as an isolated instance of easily derided excess, although it was one which Gibbon's fellow-historian William Robertson would emphasize in his study of relations between the ancients and the East which he published in 1791.[14] While Elagabalus was derided by Gibbon for what amounted to cross-dressing, the great Constantine himself, a supreme example of a warrior-emperor, stood condemned for the vice of over-dressing in eloquently contemporary terms, as Gibbon denounced the claim that this was done for the public and not for himself: 'Were this admitted, the vainest coxcomb could never want an excuse' (Vol. I, p. 646, n. 6). That vanity should compromise the first Christian emperor was plainly to Gibbon's mocking taste, and is a natural corollary to his claim that 'For the credit of human nature, I am always pleased to discover some good qualities in those men whom party has represented as tyrants and monsters' (Vol. I, p. 801, n. 111). It is this attempt at balance which informs so much of his discussion both of luxury and of sex.

Balance sometimes requires near silence, and it is notable how the issue of homosexuality is often broached from the most oblique of angles. This is apparent even in that section in Chapter 54 which is directly concerned with 'a more odious vice, of which modesty rejects the name, and nature abominates the idea.' This does not prevent Gibbon from making a typically learned and alarming observation which, equally typically, peters out in apparently self-censoring Latin:

> A curious dissertation might be formed on the introduction of paederasty after the time of Homer, its progress among the Greeks of Asia and Europe, the vehemence of their passions, and the thin device of virtue and friendship which amused the philosophers of Athens. But, scelera ostendi oportet dum puniuntur, abscondi flagitia.
>
> (Vol. II, p. 837, and n. 192)

Gibbon quietly noted how tolerant opinion in the ancient world had tended to be on the matter, while expressing his wish to believe 'that at Rome, as in Athens, the voluntary and effeminate deserter of his sex was degraded from the honours and rights of a citizen'. A shift in opinion in the early Christian era was deftly delineated, as Gibbon portrayed something very like a double standard with sympathy for heterosexual adulterers being denied to 'lovers of their own sex', who were instead 'pursued by general and pious indignation'. Similarly, the legal reforms of Justinian revealed a sinister element when he 'declared himself the implacable enemy of unmanly lust, and the cruelty of his persecution can scarcely be excused by the purity of the motives'. Justinian's rigour was followed through in a description of the particularly hideous punishments facing those found guilty of this crime, and the cases of two bishops, who may well have been innocent of the crime imputed to them. Again, a suggestive invocation of a conspiracy of silence and moral panic informs Gibbon's discussion of homosexuality when he writes:

> A sentence of death and infamy was often founded on the slight and suspicious evidence of a child or a servant: the guilt of the green faction, of the rich, and of the enemies of Theodora, was presumed by the judges, and paederasty became the crime of those to whom no crime could be imputed.
>
> (Vol. II, pp. 838–9)

Sympathy for the plight of the homosexual is clearly discernible beneath the conventional language of distaste, but it is at least as much sympathy for the victims of Christian puritanism as it is anything as intangible as fellow-feeling which Gibbon voices in these pages. The elusive and often dangerous skill of reading between the lines is obviously necessary in reading as consciously and persistently ironic a writer as Gibbon, but the interpretation of silence, particularly in so personal a domain as sexual identity, is yet more fraught with peril.

'The meaner passions'

There is a fascination with the varieties of human experience in Gibbon, and this clearly includes the sexual and the gendered in a way that was still fairly unusual even among the consciously enlightened scholars of late eighteenth-century England. Strong women, for example, are occasionally presented as a necessary counterpart to effeminate or merely weak men. The empress Pulcheria, whose Christian devotion Gibbon gladly punctures, is none the less praised, since she, 'alone, among the descendants of the great Theodosius, appears to have inherited any share of his manly spirit and abilities'. What a contrast she provides with Theodosius the younger, who was damagingly 'condemned to pass his perpetual infancy, encompassed only by a servile train of women and eunuchs' (Vol. II, pp. 264, 265). Luxury is likewise usually announced as a vice, but it is one which often has the effects of a virtue:

> in the present imperfect condition of society, luxury, though it may proceed from vice or folly, seems to be the only means that may correct the unequal distribution of property. The diligent mechanic, and the skilful artist, who have obtained no share in the division of the earth, receive a voluntary tax from the possessors of land; and the latter are prompted by a sense of interest, to improve those estates, with whose produce they may purchase additional pleasures. This operation, the particular effects of which are felt in every society, acted with much more diffusive energy in the Roman world.
>
> (Vol. I, p. 80)

Such realism allowed for a cynically effective comment on the nature of faith and iconoclasm: 'Even the reverses of the Greek and Roman coins were frequently of an idolatrous nature. Here indeed the scruples of the Christian were suspended by a stronger passion' (Vol. I, p. 461, n. 47).

It is clear that Gibbon's real enmities were reserved for the more ascetic Christians. His frequently favourable account of the origins of the Islamic faith demonstrate this with great clearness, as when he notes of the

Islamic heaven that the 'image of a carnal paradise has provoked the indignation, perhaps the envy, of the monks', and when he compares Mohammed's uxoriousness favourably with that of a figure more conventionally acceptable to Christians: 'If we remember the seven hundred wives and the three hundred concubines of the wise Solomon, we shall applaud the modesty of the Arabian who espoused no more than seventeen or fifteen wives' (Vol. III, p. 189, 215).[15] Certainly, by the time he comes to write of a Europe in which the Western Roman Empire is effectively dead, Gibbon is less keen to identify private with public vices, and altogether less happy to continue to chart a decline from pagan virtue to Christian denial, as when he characterizes Charlemagne in terms far removed from those with which he vehemently criticized the later Roman emperors:

> Of his moral virtues, chastity is not the most conspicuous: but the public happiness could not be materially injured by his nine wives or concubines, the various indulgence of meaner or more transient amours, the multitude of his bastards whom he bestowed on the church, and the long celibacy and licentious manners of his daughters, whom the father was suspected of loving with too fond a passion.
>
> (Vol. II, pp. 124–5)

For Gibbon, narrating the increasingly erratic course of European and Byzantine history between 800 and 1453, Charlemagne and his ilk were but aggrandized barbarians, ignorant, avaricious, and, above all, superstitious.[16] Even luxury had contracted itself to an inglorious shadow of its former lustre, so that the ambition of the Avignon popes could be seen as having 'subsided in the meaner passions of avarice and luxury', while the celebrated condemnation of one of their number, John XXIII, has about it an air of world-weary lassitude: 'the most scandalous charges were suppressed; the vicar of Christ was only accused of piracy, murder, rape, sodomy, and incest' (Vol. III, p. 380, 1050).

'The standard of modern times'

It would take the deeply compromised age of Augustus fully to engage its eighteenth-century analogue: each were societies in which issues of luxury and sexuality preoccupied a great many moralists, both public and private.[17] It is very much as if Tacitus's concerns that the Romans had effeminized the ancient Britons by 'civilizing' them were being critically reconsidered by modern Britons.[18] This was Gibbon's more sceptical point of entry, and the moralists he condemned and praised as occasion demanded were to be found in both cultures, a point that was also made, albeit in a more firmly moralizing manner by Adam Ferguson, whose own work on Roman history implied a more self-congratulatory perspective than that allowed his readers by Gibbon:

> The manners of the Imperial court, and the conduct of succeeding emperors, will scarcely gain credit with those who estimate possibilities from the standard of modern times. But the Romans were capable of much greater extremes than we are acquainted with.[19]

It was greatly to Gibbon's credit that he estimated the extremes of the Romans a little more charitably than his severely judgemental contemporary. Gibbon's ambivalence and subtlety in approaching sex clearly demarcates his work from the firmly masculine inclinations of 'civic humanism',[20] as well as from the style of conjectural history developed by Ferguson and other representatives of the Scottish Enlightenment. Allied with the suspicion of his religious views entertained by Christian contemporaries, the legacy of his laconically tolerant approach to the history of sex was something which served to separate him from such occasionally solemn representatives of nineteenth-century proprieties as Macaulay, who famously declared that 'I have always thought the indelicacy of Gibbon's great work a more serious blemish than even his uncandid hostility to the Christian religion'.[21] Macaulay here echoed the tones of Thomas Bowdler, who introduced his expurgated edition of *The Decline and Fall* by claiming to 'have endeavoured to avoid the insertion of any thing which might be thought objectionable, on account of irreligious tendency or indecent expression. From defects of this nature, it is extremely desirable that historical composition should be as strictly guarded as possible'.[22] As Norman Vance has recently shown, Bowdler actually retained a great deal of sexual material, including the notorious sections regarding the Empress Theodora: it was Gibbon's animadversions directly concerning Christianity which Bowdler most severely pruned.[23] For Macaulay, then, it was Gibbon's innuendo which most offended a sensibility nurtured in Evangelicalism, while for Bowdler his critique of Christianity was the historian's major fault. For Gibbon himself, the serious playfulness of sexual innuendo was very much part of his criticism of Christianity, a strategy which was clear to most of his contemporaries, not least the anonymous poet whose address to Gibbon supplies the Appendix to this article. No easy separation could be made either for Gibbon or for his contemporaries between the frequent indulgence of compromisingly sexual imagery and an implied, and occasionally more explicit criticism of Christian morality.

School of English and American Studies, University of Sussex

Notes

1 Edward Gibbon, *The Decline and Fall of the Roman Empire*, ed. David Womersley, 3 vols (London, 1994), Vol. II, p. 838, n. 195. Citations to this edition will henceforth be made in the body of the text, citing volume and page number. I am grateful to Mishtooni Bose, Heather Montgomery, Karen O'Brien, John Robertson and David Womersley for their comments on an earlier draft of this article.

2 For some discussion see W. B. Carnochan, *Gibbon's Solitude: The Inward World of the Historian* (Stanford University Press, 1987), and Lionel Gossman, *The Empire Unpossess'd: An Essay on Gibbon's Decline and Fall* (Cambridge University Press, 1981).

3 For a valuable discussion of the structure of the first volume of the text, see David Womersley, *The Transformation of The Decline and Fall of the Roman Empire* (Cambridge University Press, 1988).

4 Philip Sidney, *The Countess of Pembroke's Arcadia*, ed. Maurice Evans (Harmondsworth: Penguin, 1977), p. 133; *The Old Arcadia*, ed. Katherine Duncan-Jones (Oxford: Oxford University Press 1985), pp. 17–19. For an invaluable discussion of the intellectual context of this text and its concerns, see Blair Worden, *The Sound of Virtue: Philip Sidney's Arcadia and Elizabethan Politics* (New Haven and London: Yale University Press, 1996).

5 David Hume, *Enquiries Concerning Human Understanding and Concerning the Principles of Morals*, ed. L. H. Selby-Bigge, 3rd rev. edn, ed. P. H. Nidditch (Oxford: Oxford University Press, 1975), X.i.219, p. 170.

6 A stray comment in Augustine's *de Civitate Dei* likewise exercised Gibbon's occasionally and conveniently literalist imagination, as he noted the saint's 'curious distinction between moral and physical virginity' (Vol. II, p. 203, n. 103). For a parallel case with that of Sophronia, see Brent D. Shaw, 'The passion of Perpetua', *Past and Present* 139 (1993): 3–45.

7 On Jerome, see Peter Brown, *The Body and Society: men, women and sexual renunciation in early Christianity* (London, Faber and Faber, 1988), pp. 366–86; Elaine Pagels, *Adam, Eve, and the Serpent* (London, Penguin, 1988), pp. 89–96. For a more sympathetic reading, see John Oppel, 'Saint Jerome and the history of sex', *Viator* 24 (1993): 1–22.

8 For the wider apologetic context of Gibbon's views, see B. W. Young, 'The Anglican origins of Newman's celibacy', *Church History* 65 (1996): 15–27.

9 John Walsh, 'Methodism and the mob', *Studies in Church History* 8 (1972): 213–27; Walsh, 'John Wesley and the community of goods', in Keith Robbins (ed.) *Protestant Evangelicalism: Britain, Ireland, Germany, and America c. 1750– c. 1950: Essays in Honour of W. R. Ward* (Oxford: Blackwell, 1990), pp. 25–50; Henry Abelove, 'The sexual politics of early Wesleyan Methodism' in Jim Obelkevich *et al.* (eds) *Disciplines of Faith: Studies in Origins, Politics and Patriarchy* (London, Routledge, 1987), pp. 86–99; Abelove, *The Evangelist of Desire: John Wesley and the Methodists* (Stanford: Stanford University Press, 1990).

10 Tina Isaacs, 'The Anglican hierarchy and the reformation of manners movement, 1688–1738', *Journal of Ecclesiastical History* 33 (1982): 391–411; Joanna Innes, 'Politics and morals: the reformation of manners movement in late eighteenth-century England', in Eckhard Hellmuth (ed.) *The Transformation of Political Culture: England and Germany in the Late*

Eighteenth Century (Oxford: Oxford University Press, 1990), pp. 57–118; Shelley Burtt, 'The societies for the reformation of manners: between John Locke and the devil in Augustan England', in Roger D. Lund (ed.) *The Margins of Orthodoxy: Heterodox Writing and Cultural Response* (Cambridge: Cambridge University Press, 1995), pp. 149–69.

11 Aubrey writes of Bacon, 'He was a παιδεραστης' ('Francis Bacon', in *Brief Lives*, ed. Andrew Clark, 2 vols (Oxford, 1898), Vol. 1, p. 71).

12 For an earlier instance of the relationship between the classical education of boys and tales of sexual excess, see Marjorie Curry Woods, 'Rape and the pedagogical rhetoric of sexual violence', in Rita Copeland (ed.) *Criticism and Dissent in the Middle Ages* (Cambridge: Cambridge University Press, 1996), pp. 56–86.

13 The shocking denouement of Montesquieu's *Lettres Persanes* is aided by the apparent spirit of tolerance of his main protagonists, especially as this is rather conventionally illustrated in their general suspicion of clerical authority: Montesquieu, *Oeuvres complètes*, 2 vols (Paris, Pléiade, 1949–51), Vol. 1, Lettres CXLVII–CLXI, pp. 362–73. They are both puzzled and amused by clerical celibacy, especially as represented by what are satirically referred to as 'Le grand nombre d'eunuques. . . . Je parle des prêtres et des dervis de l'un et de l'autre sexe, qui se vouent à une continence eternelle: c'est chez les Chrétiens la vertu par excellence; en quoi je ne les comprends pas, ne sachant ce que c'est qu'une vertu dont il ne résulte rien' (Lettre CXVII, pp. 305–7). Gibbon also noted, in an interesting association of ideas, that the military campaigns of the Persians 'were impeded by a useless train of women, eunuchs, horses, and camels' (Vol. I, p. 228).

14 William Robertson, *An Historical Disquisition Concerning the Knowledge which the Ancients Had of India* (London, 1791), pp. 54–5.

15 On Solomon's standing in Christian culture, see Mishtooni Bose, 'From exegesis to appropriation: the medieval Solomon,' *Medium Aevum* 65 (1996): 189–210.

16 On the changing nature of the later volumes, see Peter Ghosh, 'The conception of Gibbon's *History*', in Rosamond McKitterick and Roland Quinault (eds) *Edward Gibbon and Empire* (Cambridge: Cambridge University Press, 1997), pp. 271–316.

17 On the critical identification of ancient Rome by eighteenth-century writers, see Howard A. Weinbrot, *Augustus Caesar in 'Augustan' England: The Decline of a Classical Norm* (Princeton: Princeton University Press, 1978).

18 Tacitus, *Agricola*, ed. R. M. Ogilvie and Sir Ian Richmond (Oxford: Oxford University Press, 1967), especially the conclusion of section 21, at pp. 106–7: 'inde etiam habitus nostri honor et frequens toga; paulatimque discessum ad delenimenta vitiorum porticus et balineas et conviviorum elegantiam. idque apud imperitos humanitas vocabatur, cum pars servitutis esset.' Note how Tactitus, like Gibbon, makes much of clothing as an indication of moral and social change.

19 Adam Ferguson, *The History of the Progress and Termination of the Roman Republic*, 3 vols (London, 1783), Vol. 3, p. 563.

20 J. G. A. Pocock, 'Between Machiavelli and Hume: Gibbon as civic humanist and philosophic historian', in G. W. Bowersock *et al.* (eds) *Edward Gibbon and the Decline and Fall of the Roman Empire* (Cambridge, MA: Harvard University Press, 1977), pp. 103–19.

21 Macaulay, letter to an unknown recipient (31 March 1849), in Thomas

Pinney (ed.) *The Letters of Thomas Babington Macaulay*, 6 vols (Cambridge: Cambridge University Press, 1974–81), Vol. 5, pp. 41–2.

22 Thomas Bowdler, (ed.) *Gibbon's History of the Decline and Fall of the Roman Empire: For the use of families and young persons. Reprinted from the original text, with the careful omission of all passages of an irreligious or immoral tendency*, 5 vols (London, 1826), Vol. 1, p. ix.

23 Norman Vance, *The Victorians and Ancient Rome* (Oxford: Oxford University Press, 1997), p. 203.

Appendix

Anon, *A Poetical Address to Edward Gibbon. Esq. Occasioned by His History of the Decline and Fall of the Roman Empire* (London: R. Falder, 1786). *Illa, quis & me, inquit, miseram te perdidit? – Virgil.*

> Whether reclin'd, secure, 'mid Alpine snows,
> Thou courtest liberty and learn'd repose,
> Or steer'st thy course across the fretful main,
> Eager thy Country's gale to breathe again;
> GIBBON, no more thy potent pen employ,
> Thus to embitter a fond Father's joy.
> Alas, my Daughter! dear lamented name!
> Once my sole pride, now source of grief and shame!
> Why did I listen to that tuneful tongue,
> Attracted, GIBBON, by thy Syren Song?
> Thy thoughts magnificent, thy diction bold,
> Through my full soul, like Roman TYBER, roll'd.

> Thy principles, I'll own, I disapprov'd;
> But who e'er scann'd the faults of those he lov'd?
> Not so my Daughter; she, poor heedless maid!
> Caught by thy style, was, by thy sense betray'd.
> Her Mother, long ago to death consign'd,
> To piety had formed her infant mind;
> And easy elegance, and polish'd taste,
> Her brilliant wit and vivid fancy grac'd.
> One blemish e'en my fondness could descry,
> The sweet deceiver, learned vanity.
> She lov'd to speculate; nor thought it wrong,
> In reas'ning high, to leave the vulgar throng:
> Nor strange, if, thus prepar'd, thy specious page
> Should in vain doubts her spirit soft engage,
> Till faith relaxing gently sunk away,

And rising vapours hid the face of day.
Perplex'd, bewilder'd, with a sceptic sight
She follows, step by step, thy glimm'ring light.
Thus some belated hind the wand'ring fire
Misleads, and plunges in th'unfathomable mire.

Meantime, a Youth, won by my Daughter's charms,
With soft attention woo'd her to his arms.
His mien was noble, lively was his mind,
And Fortune had her gifts to Nature join'd:
But underneath a frank and gen'rous face,
A soul he cover'd, profligate and base.
Alarm'd I saw the danger of my child,
And wrought by reason on her temper mild.
Obedient, to my Villa soon she went,
In silent solitude to live content:
There under gloomy shades she oft would rove,
While studious thought supply'd the face of love.
But how shall I the sequel dare disclose,
And publish to the world my secret woes?

Among my Servants, one, EUGENIO nam'd,
Was for his elegance of manners fam'd.
With graceful air he touch'd the lute, and sung,
With soft persuasion smooth'd his flatt'ring tongue.
His strains melodious sooth'd my Daughter's ear,
And plaintive oft beguil'd her of a tear.
Too conscious of his power, the wretch survey'd
With eyes of wantonness the blooming Maid;
Treac'rous he tried the weaken'd citadel,
Till in some fatal hour subdued it fell.
Her guilt and shame, betray'd by symptoms clear,
To me a busy friend was prompt to bear.
Appall'd I heard the news; and, prone to ire,
In vain I stifled the collected fire.
Indignant through the house aloud I rave,
'What, is my Daughter strumpet to a slave?'
Then rushing enter'd, where she sat reclin'd
In her lov'd room, with fav'rite volumes lin'd.

'Abandon'd Prostitute! – Stop, Sir!' she cry'd;
'Condemn me not till I am duly try'd.
'Where,' she continued, 'where am I to blame?

'How do I merit that opprobrious name?
I've Nature follow'd, our unerring guide:
'Her dictates who shall rashly dare deride?
'See my authority; 'tis GIBBON sage,
'GIBBON, *the glory of th'historic page.*
'Such was your eulogy – Following this I read,
'By words sublime and beauteous, captive led.
'From him I learn'd, that to indulge my sense
'(By Priests and Churchmen styl'd Concupiscence)
'Is venial, nay, is spotless innocence:
'From him I learn'd to scorn imperious man,
'By diff'rent rules. – GIBBON, more just and kind
'To the weak texture of the female mind,
'Pities HONORIA'S undeserved pain,
'Who sought the arms of her lov'd Chamberlain.
'GIBBON with lenient eye HONORIA saw,
'Because obsequious to kind Nature's law,
'Though vengeful she to marriage-rites could urge
'E'en ATTILA the Hun, her Country's scourge.
'My arguments, I see, have had their weight;
'That show relaxing is no counterfeit;
'That glist'ning eye – ' She paus'd. Her troubled soul,
Contending passions could no more controul.
Sighs, sobs, and shrieks, come rushing on amain,
While from her eyes descends the briny rain.
Her speech returning – 'Father, kindest Friend,
'And canst thou pity to a wretch extend;
'A wretch like me,' she cry'd, 'who've brought disgrace
'On thee and all the honours of thy race?
'Think not, a real part I undertook,
'When fix'd and firm I met thy dread rebuke:
'That moment keen remorse congeal'd my blood,
'And self-condemn'd, before thy face I stood.
'Ill-fated day, when, emulous and vain,
'And proud to deviate from the vulgar train,
'GIBBON'S seducing pages I perus'd,
'And on his system philosophic mus'd.
'I reverenc'd no more Religion's laws,
'For which th'Historian finds a human cause.
'That antidote remov'd, my soul sank deep
'The luscious potion, drugg'd with deadly sleep.
'Lull'd and deluded, I to Nature gave
'The reins, from principle vile Passion's slave.

'Alas, my Father! I have both destroy'd;
'Render'd thy life one dismal, dreary void;
'Myself degraded; so that all around
'From tattling tongues my infamy shall sound,
'While prudent matrons bid their daughters shrug
'Infectious converse with a wretch undone.'
She paus'd. The red her trembling lips forsook,
And every limb a death-like horror shook.

Such are thy trophies :- but time draws near
When for these trophies thou shalt pay full dear.
Yet why, alas? GIBBON, that heart of thine
Was never dug from th'adamantine mine:
'Twas kind Religion's soil, most kindly given,
Meet to receive the genuine plant of Heaven,
True Charity; which, if thou cultivate
(Hark! Something whispers – 'Tis not yet too late.')
Shall bloom eternal in a better state.
'Tis that, forbidding vengeful thoughts to rise,
Makes me regard thee, for they own and others' welfare, wise.
The meagre, famish'd wretch, wouldst thou deprive
Of the poor crumbs that bid his soul revive?
Far hence the thought! – Thy mind benevolent
Is, as my own, on acts of mercy bent.
Why then from him who sinks oppress'd with grief,
Why wouldst thou snatch his spirit's sole relief;
Leave him to comfortless despair a prey,
Till, sick of life, he throws the gift away?
Let cavil cease:- such is the consequence,
When the sight is dimm'd by evidence
On which Religion stands; when doubts succeed,
And into air dissolves th'unsettled creed.
Ah! how could I this torture undergo,
This poignant anguish of a Daughter know,
But that another life of endless bliss,
And promis'd succours through the pain of this,
Renew my force? Though waves on waves assail
My shatter'd bark, I will not dread the gale,
That to the wish'd-for port directs my swelling sail.
Return then, GIBBON, dare to be a Man,
A Martyr: dare reverse thy former plan.
Awake a sleeping world; assume the rod,
The rod of eloquence, and cause of God:

Thy witness doubly strong, when all shall know
That thou'rt a Friend, who once wert thought a Foe.
The hand which dealt the blow with hostile hate,
Shall pour the balm, the pain to mitigate;
Shall mitigate the pain, shall health restore,
Nay, vigour to the limb, not felt before.
Lo! future volumes Albion's land adorn,
With wisdom fraught for ages yet unborn.
And, as the tide historic rolls along,
Purg'd and refin'd, Earth's various tribes among,
Th'admiring Nations shall behold imprest
Heav'n's sacred image on thy lucid breast.
Pursue then, GIBBON, thy well-chosen theme,
Till dawning Silence dissipate the dream
Of Superstition's night, and brightest rays
Of meek Religion gild th'improving days.
Illustrious task with radiant eloquence
To trace the wondrous ways of Providence,
And blazon Truth, despight of Sceptic Insolence
Nor let the jest oblique, the scornful sneer,
Nor of loquacious tongues th'unmanly fear,
Arrest thy course; but still push boldly on,
(The steady eye fix'd on th'immortal Crown)
And midst the mock of fools thy Saviour dare to own.

Reviews

Ania Loomba

David Johnson, *Shakespeare and South Africa* (Oxford: Clarendon Press, 1996), 276 pp., £30.00 (hardback)

Scholarship in the last fifteen years or so has analysed the global spread of English studies and its most popular export, William Shakespeare, as a measure of the imperial will to power rather than as a marker of the universal humanism of English high culture. Or rather, humanism itself, with its claim to speak fluently across cultural and temporal divides, has been shown to be the ideological glove for racism and other ugly realities of colonialist regimes. Said's *Orientalism* inspired such studies of the work of European cultural products in their colonies, but somewhat paradoxically, these studies may have also ensured a new lease of life for such cultural products. In the process of being demystified and re-examined, Western cultural icons have continued to occupy the attention of literary critics both within and outside the Anglo-American academy, even (or especially) those who are critical of the Eurocentric parameters of their discipline. Whose interests does it serve for academics to reinterpret, reteach, re-circulate these texts, and to show that they mean, or can be made to signify, something entirely different from their received meanings? Do such rewritings and appropriations lock us forever into the dominance of European culture and disable the project of creating truly postcolonial cultures?

David Johnson's book, *Shakespeare and South Africa*, intervenes in such debates by examining, in painstaking detail, the 'political mission' of English studies in South Africa over the last two hundred years. It does so

    © 1997 Routledge 0950–236X

TP

by placing the relationship between British and South African literary criticism (especially as it relates to Shakespeare) within the context of domestic and imperial developments in Britain and South Africa. The guiding principle of the book is the Marxist conviction that ideas are interwoven with material activity: 'the production of the ideas associated with the study of Shakespeare is thus taken to be interwoven with the material accumulation of capital and the functioning of the racist state in South Africa' (p. 6). Like Chris Baldick's 1983 book, *The Social Mission of English Criticism 1848–1932*, Johnson's book unpacks the connections between literary education and social control, and like Gauri Viswanathan's *Masks of Conquest* (1989), it shows how such connections worked in a specific colonial context. Like Viswanathan, Johnson is interested in exposing the political underpinnings of literary humanism, but he also narrows his terrain to examine how specific literary-critical moves, especially in relation to the study of Shakespeare, tie in with the imperial project. However, whereas Viswanathan mined British parliamentary and colonial debates on education to argue that English literature was central to the Raj, Johnson is far more focused on literary critics and teachers and especially on their pronouncements on Shakespeare.

Such a narrowing makes for a rich specificity: the work of well-known English cultural critics such as Matthew Arnold and Shakespeareans such as Bradley is juxtaposed with the writings of lesser known South African critics and educators. The crucial difference between the Indian and African contexts lies, of course, in the presence of European settlers in Africa, and in the case of South Africa, the political and racial divisions between Afrikaner and English settlers. Johnson patiently traces the efforts of South African educators, critics and missionaries over two hundred years to import and remodel English culture and Shakespeare according to local imperatives. Conversely, English views of the Bard's continuing power were inflected by both domestic and colonial developments. Johnson argues that the colonists were no more racist than educators in Britain; rather the flow of ideas was shaped by tensions of class, race and empire in both places. Reading critics historically, as well as 'through a theoretical lens' (p. 9), the book traces the intricately webbed relations between Shakespeare, English studies and empire.

However, these intricacies all feed into a fairly straightforward narrative of imperial and racial domination. For Johnson, Shakespeare emerges so clearly as the lynchpin securing both English studies and the Empire in South Africa that it is impossible to rescue him for alternative purposes. Thus those who attempt to construct and teach or perform an alternative Shakespeare, in the past or now, only reveal their fatal dependence upon Western structures of thought which, when imported into South Africa, deflect more radical local options. For instance, Solomon T. Plaatje (a founder member of the African Native National Congress whose novel *Mhudi*, published in 1930, was the first novel in English to be written by a black South African, and who raised his voice against colonial dispossession of Africans in vocabularies freely culled from Shakespeare, African oral forms and the Bible) displays false consciousness when he praises Shakespeare. Plaatje's love of Shakespeare is seen as a clear index of his inability to understand the real nature of imperialism, and a measure of his distance, not only from some of his own more revolutionary peers, but even from Lenin! (For Johnson, Lenin's *Imperialism, the Highest Stage of Capitalism* outlines the relationship between capitalism and empire, and defines 'the economic framework allowing Shakespeare to overrun the world' (p. 98).) Plaatje's direct descendants, according to Johnson, are contemporary critics like Martin Orkin who suggest (in books such as *Shakespeare Against Apartheid*, 1987) that an alternative Shakespeare might be of use in anti- and post-apartheid education. If Plaatje's love for Shakespeare revealed his dependence on Western humanism (and its political structures), Orkin's project to re-teach the Bard is dependent upon Western post-structuralist constructions of a radical Shakespeare. Both attempts to rescue the Bard from his place in imperial history are compromises that work to keep more radical actions at bay: in Plaatje's context, armed rebellion, and in Orkin's, the more humble choice of 'a different set of texts' to teach (p. 210).

These uncompromising views on the humanist or radical potential of Shakespeare are salutary in the context of the 'political' and 'alternative' Shakespeares that too easily mushroom within the Western academy. Often, radical academic discussions of 'race' and 'colonialism' both within Shakespearean studies and more surprisingly, within postcolonial studies, do not take note of continuing imbalances in contemporary global relations. Johnson reminds us that the legacy of imperial English studies and imperial Shakespeare cannot simply be dismantled by importing (or exporting), yet again, Western conceptions of literature and Shakespeare into classrooms the world over. In his last chapter, 'Travelling theory', he traces how critical theories acquire different political resonances as they shift from one country and academic context to another. Johnson's writing draws upon recent critiques of postcolonial studies and post-structuralism articulated by critics such as Arif Dirlik or Aijaz Ahmed and, like them, he is sceptical of radical claims made for such theory in the Western academy by 'Third World' critics.

One must, I believe, take seriously the opinion that in the 'new' South Africa, the place of English literature is itself under severe stress, and that opening education to African and other literatures so long eclipsed by Shakespeare is a far more valuable task than to continue to flog the tired Shakespearean horse and expect it to perform new tricks. However, in

Shakespeare and South Africa, this suggestion emerges via a somewhat reductive logic that is disappointing in such a densely researched book. Johnson makes it clear that in his book Shakespeare stands in as a 'representative of English studies' (p. 6). As such, Johnson is not interested in whether Shakespeare's plays participate in or militate against their imperial deployment. But in that case the extended focus on the minute details of Shakespearean criticism seems unjustified. Shakespeare's status as a metaphor for Western culture cannot be understood without some reflection on the colonial resonances of the plays themselves. Did colonial subjects attempt to appropriate Shakespeare more than they did any other canonized author (say, Milton) simply because of his exalted position, or was it because contradictions within his plays spoke to ambivalences between them? How did these different sets of contradictions resonate with each other in different circumstances? Were plays simply easier to appropriate than poetry and prose? Such questions are not asked in this book, and nowhere do we get an analysis of the human or textual 'contradictions' that made colonial subjects deploy Shakespeare for their own ends. Johnson does tell us about several such instances: not only Sol Plaatje, but even someone like Chris Hani, leader of the South African Communist Party, invoked Shakespeare to make a political point (p. 201). However, Johnson's larger framework leaves little place for understanding such moments in all their complexity because he sees little possibility that the reading of Shakespearean texts might contribute to real cultural and political struggles.

Contrary to Johnson's intentions, such a framework flattens colonized subjects: for him, their invocations of Shakespeare all flow from the master discourse, and we get no analysis of the specific ways in which colonized subjects might have drawn upon other cultural resources in order to effect their own readings of the plays. This is partly because, despite Johnson's attempt to situate the book within larger political struggles, the only protagonist who receives any real attention is 'English studies'. We hear little about the theatre, for example, and whether Shakespeare managed to break through the colonial strait-jacket in the world of performance (as was the case, for example, in India). Johnson compares Sol Plaatje's tribute to Shakespeare to a 1928 Bangalore edition of *Othello* which lavished slavish praise upon the Bard, but Plaatje might be better compared to Indian nationalists who invoked Shakespeare sporadically for their own ends. They too were no doubt shaped by their English education, but they occupied a wider and more complex political space than those who simply parroted the lessons of the English academy within the academy. The invocation of Shakespeare by nationalists might have bolstered nationalism more than it did the cultural weight of Shakespeare, or at least set up a contradiction that functioned more complexly than a simple 'betrayal' of their own cultural origins. To be sure, we may go on to critique the politics of such nationalists, but their use of Shakespeare cannot by itself function as a reliable index in this regard. The point is that despite a whole chapter devoted to him, we hear little about Plaatje himself: he is, for the most part, read as the paradigmatic 'colonial subject', just as Shakespeare is read simply as a metaphor for the 'colonial text'. Thus their encounter can be represented only in predictable ways.

Johnson engages in a remarkable exercise here. He ventriloquizes how different kinds of intellectual groups – anti-colonialists, Marxists, social historians or post-structuralists – might read the encounter between Plaatje and Shakespeare. Thus, since Fanon and Cabral 'equate the colonial subject's love of Western culture with political betrayal' (p. 96), we are to conclude that they would not approve of Plaatje, and think of him as a betrayer of his people. Similarly, although Lenin's *Imperialism* was published after Plaatje's *Native Life in South Africa*, and although the relationship of Marxism to anti-colonial struggles has been a difficult one (leading even black communists such as Aimé Césaire to pronounce: 'Marx is all right, but we need to complete Marx'), Lenin's views on imperialism are used to tell us how far Plaatje was from understanding the economic or cultural logic of imperialism. To be sure, Johnson acknowledges that Lenin's account 'sheds little light on why Plaatje pays tribute to Shakespeare and not to the London Stock Exchange; or for that matter, on the relation between Shakespeare and the London Stock Exchange' (p. 98). But he does not probe this question at any length himself, and instead uses a 'Stock Exchange logic' to analyse the role played by Western literary texts within colonialism: the chapter ends by telling us that 'the real Sol Plaatje' (or the truth about the encounter between the colonial subject and Shakespeare) is to be understood more accurately by tracing how profits from the De Beers mines directly funded research in English studies!

In Johnson's book, English studies and Shakespeare are seen as the cultural handmaidens of empire: the means of supplying labour, enforcing class divisions, and keeping racial tensions in check. I have little difficulty in believing that this was indeed to be the case, and whereas Viswanathan's account of English education in India somewhat problematically suggested that English studies had replaced colonial violence, Johnson is careful to suggest that they worked together to maintain a repressive social order. However, this history is invoked to make some rather startling pronouncements about present day academics: we are told, for example, that colonial discourse theorists are lacking because 'Unlike Fanon, who saw his critique of colonialism as directly related to the violent overthrow of oppressive regimes, these writers seek by their work to change the syllabuses in English departments at elite Western universities' (p. 106). One wonders whether the literary critics Johnson approves of, the ones who are not seduced by postcolonial theory, post-structuralism and the long shadow of the Bard, actually engage in any highly revolutionary activity!

Shakespeare and South Africa is deeply, and in my opinion justifiably, critical of postcolonial theory in the metropolitan academy, and especially its faith in the radical mimicry and hybridity of the colonial subject, states of resistance which derive from the supposed ambivalences of the master discourse itself. David Johnson makes it impossible for us to romanticize the encounter between colonized South Africans and the English literary text in this way. However, in order to do so, it homogenizes and caricatures postcolonial criticism (especially in the Plaatje chapter) and sets up reductive polarities between postcolonial Western theories and Third World pedagogy, between academic reform and revolution. In this regard it is interesting that the book analyses British and African colonialists far more than it does African nationalists or radicals. Thus we hear in remarkable detail about the imposition of colonial culture, but remarkably little about contestation, a critique that has also been levelled at *Orientalism* as well as *Masks of Conquest*. But while Said and Viswanathan make clear that their books do not explore the history of native challenges to Western discourses, Johnson comes close to suggesting that English literature in the colonies (or in the postcolony) allows no scope for struggle, only the shadow-play of false consciousness.

Jawaharlal Nehru University

Vance Adair

Jonathan Hall, *Anxious Pleasures: Shakespearean Comedy and the Nation-State* (London: Associated University Presses, 1995), 291 pp., £25.00 (hardback)

Louis Montrose, *The Purpose of Playing: Shakespeare and the Cultural Politics of the Elizabethan Theatre* (London: University of Chicago Press, 1996), xiii + 227 pp.

Patricia Parker, *Shakespeare from the Margins: Language, Culture, Context* (London: University of Chicago Press, 1996), x + 392 pp.

In her book dedicated to 'reading Shakespeare historically' Lisa Jardine signals a growing unease within Renaissance studies about the efficacy of current critical paradigms. In the light of this uncertainty, historicisms old and new may well do battle once more, thus ameliorating the stullifying complacency that, lamentably, is now a common feature of encounters between Shakespeare and 'theory'. The appealing feature of the books under review here is the way that materialism is cast as a particularly protean concept in the hands of their respective authors. Called upon to perform many feats of historical daring, which suffer only the occasional distraction by way of expeditious reference to Marxism, words like 'dialectic' appear to have lost their hitherto risible taint of idealism. A prevailing aim of all three books, accomplished with varying degrees of success, is to forge a politics of difference that returns the Shakespearean text to the volatile, unpredictable and discursively complex site of its historical emergence.

Jonathan Hall is the first to take up the cudgels with his assertion that 'we need a dialectical understanding of laughter as social production and social dynamic' (p. 9). Critical of what he sees as Freud's unhistorical account of laughter, Hall enlists Foucault to formulate a depathologizing model of the joke which argues that repression is always discursively produced. If this is something of an anomalous synthesis, Hall's avowedly ambitious *rapprochement* between Marxism and psychoanalysis finds another unlikely pair of intellectual bedfellows in the work of Bakhtin and Deleuze. Dialogism and schizophrenia constitute the fissured conditions of possibility not only for the desiring subject, but also for the theatre of emergent mercantilism which is a product of the 'contradiction between centripetal and centrifugal desires' (p.29). It is this dual pressure which Hall skilfully reads as the conduit through which Shakespeare's comedies reconfigure desire as a simultaneous narrative production of pleasure and anxiety.

Although this somewhat populous agenda smacks a little of opportunism, Hall's treatment of individual texts is almost always stimulating. The first section of the study concerns itself with the ways in which a mercantilist psychodrama of 'deterritorialization' constructs an ambivalent discourse of masculine desire. The precarious construction of identity in *The Comedy of Errors*, Hall maintains, is firmly annexed to a newly monetarized world. In an argument which also informs his reading of *The Merchant of Venice*, male erotic drives are shown to depend upon the very mobility of desire in a way that threatens to compound already prevalent anxieties about the decentring of power in these texts. Not for the first time, the figure of Shylock is read as a psychic negation of the mercantile state, yet Hall reads the text's ostensibly utopian narrative as a fractious compendium of misrecognition, displacement and disavowal which actually *produces* the narrative. Antonio's predicament is not only resonant of how 'desire has become political in a modern sense' (p.66), his melancholic disposition is read as an appropriately enigmatic vehicle of desires serviceable to capitalism. This weakening of personalized centres of authority through exchange equivalence also underlies the text's problematic relationship to the question of abstract legality. For Hall, the courtroom drama discloses the Law as 'neither abstract system nor mere hypocritical instrument of a "real" power hiding behind it. It is a discourse implicated in social history through the regulation of desires' (p. 56).

Although Hall's fastidiously symptomatic analysis yields insights of some ingenuity, his frequent Jamesonian-style detours into metacommentary can also be distracting. A discussion of irony in *The Taming of The Shrew*, for example, is only mildly illuminated by a protracted reference to the structures of 'schizophrenic communication' as it is theorized in the work of Searle, Bateson and Laing. Hall is more engaging when he returns to his main thesis which argues how the comedies' nostalgic appeals to a stabilizing centre of authority are often overthrown by dramatizing the very indeterminacy of sign production. Refreshingly, he is careful not to fetishize the floating signifier which is read, rather, as libidinally cathecting a crisis of legitimation and the psychic underpinnings of a specifically bourgeois neurosis. In the romantic comedies in particular, masculine pleasures in the rhetorical mobility of the sign are shown to be self-affirming at the same time as they threaten to divest the courtier of a stable centre of identity. In this respect Hall suggestively examines the deeply ambivalent representation of gender identity in plays such as *All's Well That Ends Well* and *Love's Labour's Lost* where, paradoxically, the female characters are called upon to rescue the patriarchal order from the male protagonist's immersion in signs. For Hall, the comedies variously rehearse the problem of the disambiguation of the sign because nothing less than the feudal myth is at stake.

The ideological lines of force in the construction of female subjectivity are brought into sharper focus in the character of Kate. In a complex deployment of identification and counter-identification she ironizes the relations of difference that provisionally secure her subjection. Again, Hall reads this indeterminacy less as a peculiarity of the all too familiar skidding signifier than as 'a dialogic response to a monologic discourse of power' (p. 158). Interiority arises precisely as an *effect* of this negated reciprocity which finds its release in the variously calibrated responses of pleasure and anxiety experienced by the audience. In the context of a play like *Much Ado About Nothing*, however, which Hall reads as a precursor to *Othello*, this traumatic overproximity of female subjectivity to the duplicitousness of signs articulates a much more violent discourse of desire. Here, the anxieties which besiege patriarchal possession involve male subjectivity in a regressive search for plenitude redolent of Lacan's mirror stage. The self-reflexive aspect of the text's theatricality returns the female to her familiar psychoanalytical role as *trompe l'oeil*, both soliciting and confounding strategies of masculine visual mastery. Only the absence of a plotter as accomplished as Iago in the manipulation of the scopic drive, according to Hall, saves the comic romance from realizing its murderous fantasies.

The final section of the study interrogates the connection between absolutism and theatricality in a way that returns Hall to his Deleuzean premises. Seeking to read the construction of the scopic drive as an agent of reterritorialization, often contradictorily aligned with the carnivalesque forces of 'vile participation' most memorably personified by Falstaff, he reserves his most pointed observations for a discussion of the monarch's 'crisis management of desire' (p. 197). Redeploying Lacan's account of the gaze as an index of insuperable loss, Hall supplements the still fashionable thesis about the visibility of power with the suitably succinct rejoinder that 'the power of capital is invisible, impersonal, and cannot in fact be put on display' (p. 266). In a timely concluding argument which reiterates the possibilities of making desire accessible to historical understanding, he proffers the wider claim that

> Shakespeare'e comedies . . . are in constant play against the commit-
> ment to global identities, to destiny made manifest, and to territorial
> order, in a way which reveals to postmodern critique the repressed
> narrative of its own history.
>
> (p. 268)

The irresistible persuasiveness of this book's historical purchase upon its subject lies precisely in Hall's acute sensitivity to their inner dialogism. What is enviable in his arguments, and those of post-structuralist Marxism more generally, is the intellectually rigorous commitment to disclosing the text not so much in relation *to* history, but as a dynamic *producer* of those relations that it subsequently attempts to negate in misrecognized form. In making this crucial transition from 'historicism' to what Zizek has recently distinguished as 'historicity' proper, Hall's study is portentous of the intellectual demands awaiting any critic seriously dedicated to reading Shakespeare historically.

In contrast, Louis Montrose strikes a reflective pose. *The Purpose of Playing* begins with an overview of the theoretical debates that have dominated Renaissance studies in the last ten years or so. Implicitly at least, he is careful to distinguish cultural politics from the 'culturalism' that has been the most frequent focus for opprobrium by critics of the so-called new historicism (the materialist credentials of which, it should be added, Montrose has long regarded with a degree of equivocation). Like Hall, Montrose eschews any uncritical engagement with the topoi of textuality as insufficiently sensitive to reading and writing practices as historically situated events. Instead, he seeks to reorientate conceptual analysis in terms of 'a mutually constitutive, recursive, and transformative process' (p. 15). Raymond Williams and Pierre Bourdieu provide a profitable point of departure for a dynamic and dialogical rendering of the slippery problem of ideology. In what has been productive of seemingly interminable transatlantic squabbling among Shakespeareans as to the proper application of Foucault's sinuous pronouncements on the relations between power and resistance, Montrose offers a mercifully brief recapitulation of the now fabled 'subversion/containment' debate to give more overtly polemical weight to this appeal for dialectical rigour. Arguing that the social, economic and political exigencies of state formation were both complex and contradictory, for Montrose it is precisely this kind of internal dissonance that both formed, and was informed by, the emergence of the Elizabethan public theatre.

As the following chapter demonstrates, however, even this most scrupulously vigilant of readers is susceptible to the occasional indulgence. Arguing that the reformation of playing was symptomatic of the transition from the ideal of civic *communitas* to a more centralized model of government, Montrose adduces a letter which, he argues somewhat ambitiously, 'concisely encompassed most of the concerns at stake for the Elizabethan regime and the Reformed episcopacy' (p. 25). For the most part, however, the analysis is conducted from less Olympian heights, particularly Montrose's account of the putatively 'marginal experience' of play-going which does not succumb to the *lingua franca* of recent scholarship. As a much needed palliative to reductive accounts of liminality, Montrose approaches the question of the semiotics of the theatre's geographical location in a way that is responsive to the 'socioeconomic, political and cultural fabric of [its] time and place' (p. 35). Of principal focus here are the ways in which the commodification of plays, and the emergence of an entertainment industry, could not fully efface the traces of its popular and religious traditions. If this sometimes allowed the theatre to occupy a contestatory relationship towards an increasingly hegemonized Elizabethan state, a reading of *Hamlet*'s complex internalization of contemporary debates on mimesis demonstrates how the theatre also had a contradictory grasp of its own institutional practices.

Taking the much disputed role of Shakespeare's *Richard II* in the Essex conspiracy as especially apposite, Montrose emphasizes how the relationship between the stage and the state was marked by a profound indeterminacy. Echoing Hall, Stephen Greenblatt's contentious account of Elizabeth's 'privileged visibility' is again singled out for censure. In an engaging analysis of what he calls the 'personation' of the monarch, a judicious sampling of the history plays is offered as evidence of the ways in which theatricality could often disrupt the ruses of mystification. As state formation inexorably brought with it a move from a metaphysical model of history to one that relied upon a social dialectic, Montrose shows how Shakespearean drama regularly alienates identity from essence through disclosing this *performative* articulation of subjectivity. Rather than too precipitately conflating it with state power, Montrose reads theatricality as a distillation of the relational and circumstantially shaped modalities of social agency so that 'in this precise and limited sense, Shakespearean drama as enacted in the Elizabethan theatre *formally* contested the dominant ideological assertions of the Elizabethan state' (p. 105).

This is an important book, and yet it is difficult to dispel the feeling that there is something oppressively familiar about it. While employing a critical method that aims to locate the Shakespearean text as a site of discontinuity, there nevertheless remains a prepossessing air of routine in the way that Montrose marshals some of his arguments. The latter part of the study, however, evinces a slightly less didactic tone with an extended discussion of *A Midsummer Night's Dream*. Beginning with a survey of homelitic discourses and marriage manuals, Montrose adroitly teases out the rhetorical and ideological tensions implicit in Elizabethan construc-tions of gender and sexuality. In a culture where women were excoriated as the most recalcitrant of subjects and at the same time venerated as pliant objects of virtue and excellence, Shakespeare's play lobs a few incendiary devices over the patriarchal barricades as 'numerous instances of dramatic contradiction and intertextual irony' (p. 121). The text's thematics of power and possession are shown to be intermittently permeable to counter-hegemonic elements, central of which is the Amazonian theme which provides the play's mythological subtext. For Montrose, if the dominant 'shaping fantasy' is that of male parthogenesis, then the matri-lineal culture implicitly evoked by this myth threatens any monological reinscription of patriarchy at the close of the text.

Elaborating a pithy account of the masculine anxieties which sub-tended a more contemporary mythological subtext, that of the putative cult of Elizabeth, Montrose argues that the cultural significance of the text depends upon the dramaturgical exclusion of the monarch. A brisk appraisal of panegyrical literature reveals a libidinal economy that struggles to cultivate the favour of the queen as a means to courtly advancement, while also anxious not to transgress the boundaries of decorum that would incur the queen's displeasure. Effectively, this fraught alliance between the domains of literary production and state power had to contend with the wide repertoire of subject positions that was available to Elizabeth. Reading the imperial votaress as a psychic negation of this problem, Montrose also shows how the text constructs a series of conflicting female subject positions in an effort both to cathect and to displace masculine fears. In the final chapter, which considers how 'social rank and social calling displace gender and generation as the play's most conspicuous markers of difference' (p. 179), the instrumental authority of the state is further undermined by a metatheatrical challenge from the imaginative authority of the public theatre. Implicating Bottom as the mediating figure of this encounter, Montrose shows how the subtle reinscription of authority by the text's close 'enacts a claim . . . for the social authority of the professional theatre' (p. 204). In an epilogue which eloquently argues for this unique social and cognitive space that was the Elizabethan public theatre, Montrose reaffirms his position as one of our foremost commentators on the ideological valencies of cultural production.

Although Montrose characterizes the 'rude mechanical' as the most propitious example of the equivocal ideological positioning of *A Midsummer Night's Dream*, in *Shakespeare From The Margins* Patricia Parker galvanizes her considerable forensic skills for an analysis of this derogatory epithet. More obviously disposed than Montrose to a scrupulously micro-political analysis, Parker literally adopts a 'bottom-up' approach to the text. Moving with equal facility through discourses as diverse as economics and orthography, her attention turns to how the ubiquitous use of joinery metaphors unsettles the text's preoccupations with shaping fantasies and 'smooth discourse', to interrogate 'the hierarchies it forges and the orders it constructs' (p. 115). Expertly botching up the already fragile project of mystification, once again the artisans are cast as unwittingly violating the text's ideological fabric.

If this last metaphor sounds a little infelicitous, consider Parker's argument that to embark upon such an analysis is 'to begin to discover a whole range of "material" wordplay in Shakespeare, including the materiality of translation itself as a transporting of words, like cloth or goods, from place to place' (p. 115). Responding to the clarion call of Catherine Belsey, Parker describes the animating principle of the entire study as the need to link 'feminist and literary criticism to a more historically grounded study of language and culture, one that takes seriously the "matter" of language as part of the "material Shakespeare"' (p. 1). Raymond Williams looms large in this study too; at one point Parker approvingly summarizes his definition of materialist analysis as that which 'takes seriously . . . the crucial importance of language and words' (p. 274). Indubitably, though, I suspect that Williams would have been a little less sanguine in recommending the conflation of 'materialism' with 'matter' that is perhaps the one major criticism of the study. Even so, a typically dazzling analysis of the vicissitudes of translation in *The Merry Wives of Windsor* allows Parker to formulate a slightly less commodious claim about word play as constituting 'the multiple breaches in the integrity of a word made by its ease of association and transportability' (p. 147). For too long exiled to the realms of political quietism, whether in the hands of the *auteurs* of textual free-play or in the purely decorative approach taken by practical criticism, Parker succeeds in elucidating how the multiple and contradictory trajectories of word-play in the Shakespearean text have a dense cultural resonance. Offering some strikingly original readings of the construction of gender in particular, Parker's prose style is exemplary of how lucidity need not impoverish the rich complexity of analysis. In *The Comedy of Errors*, for example, she traces biblical references to the site of the female body as the most conspicuous marker of deferral in a text obsessed with paradoxes of temporality. The logical confusions of retroactivity comprise a wide-ranging chapter on the preposterous, which Parker reads as the disruptive inverse of the proper and natural. Here, as elsewhere, she mobilizes a thorough knowledge both of the plays and their diffuse historical contexts to insist that seemingly marginal topoi are central to the ways in which texts continually reconstitute the very basis of their authority. Skilfully plotting the often vertiginous circuit of cultural reproduction of the *hysteron proteron* motif as it occurs in treatises on logic, politics and sumptuary laws, Parker considers its implications for the history plays to show how the ideology of linearity and succession becomes available for contestation.

In a more extended account of her seminal work on the question of 'dilation' in Shakespeare, Parker offers a slightly more reviewer-friendly anatomy of a project that she calls 'edification from the margins'. In a volume that is remarkable for its own assimilation of material in a proprioceptively tumescent way, Parker alights upon the figure of increase in Shakespeare and painstakingly reconstructs an interstitial network of cross reference between the related motifs of dilation and inflation. Revealing the interarticulation of verbal, hermeneutic and generative uses of increase in *All's Well*, Parker suggestively reads these alongside the text's metadramatic reticulation of claustrophobic anxieties about closure. This policing of the borders of its own diegetic space finds a darker echo in the text's repeated emphasis on incest and the need for carefully delineated parameters of familial identity.

An extraordinarily dexterous analysis reveals how these overdetermined relations inevitably fasten upon the woman's part as the very *non pareil* of excess (an argument which also informs an excellent chapter on epistemology and the circulation of masculine desire in *Hamlet* and *Othello*). It is around the figure of Helena that multivalent layers of socioeconomic discourse converge in a patriarchal negotiation of gender relations. Turning more specifically to the question of economic inflation as increase, compelling evidence is adduced to argue how this collocation of anxieties were endemic to a culture adapting itself to momentous historical change. Commenting on the crisis of the aristocracy, Parker is assiduously responsive to the lexical and metaphorical permutations of detail. Economic crisis, she argues,

> contributed to the larger historical phenomenon of grafting and hybridization through which this older aristocracy, tied to land and to older kinds of increase, had increasingly to supplement its deficiency through the newer forms of monetary increase, with all the stooping to the base (and base means) this involved.
>
> (p. 214)

This study is both a formidable accomplishment in scholarship and a tenacious riposte to those critics who continue to doubt the value of close reading as an indispensable tool of political criticism. In this respect at least, *Shakespeare From The Margins* is a volume that promises to be inexhaustibly edifying.

University of Stirling

Suvir Kaul

Michael H. Fisher, *The First Indian Author in English: Dean Mahomed (1759–1851) in India, Ireland, and England* (Delhi: Oxford University Press, 1996), 368 pp., Rs 485 (hardback)

Colonial rule developed in a far messier and more contingent way than our sense of the globe at the height of colonial dominance (in the late nineteenth and early twentieth centuries) allows. This means that our models of early modern European colonial conquest (and discourse) will be different from those derived from the study of later imperial rule, which tended to be more hegemonic, and to repress its connections with the cultures of the colonized. To take a single instance: while military violence, and advanced technologies of warfare (including shipbuilding and navigational methods), were essential to colonial dominance, early merchant adventurers and companies often extended their spheres of influence by offering their services to native rulers and by complementing (rather than immediately demolishing) pre-existing local structures of power and exploitation. Thus when we think of the penetration of the globe by European manpower and capital, we need to be attentive to local histories as much as to imperial mentalities – to understand, for instance, how soldiers in colonial armies were recruited and how they functioned, as well as what their officers thought and did in their efforts to consolidate colonial power.

Michael Fischer's *The First Indian Author in English: Dean Mahomed* presents us with the life and writing of one such soldier. Dean Mahomed was born in 1759, to a family that claimed, as Fisher tells us, 'traditions of service to the Mughal empire', and whose own changed allegiance to the East India Company becomes an indicator of the rising fortunes of the company, and of the expansion of the British Empire. Dean Mahomed was no different from many others who were employed in the Bengal Army of the East India Company, but very different from most in that he emigrated, at the age of 25, first to colonial Ireland and then to England, where he died in 1851. Fisher's book is a fascinating account of Dean Mahomed's professional and personal circumstances, and reprints, for the first time since 1794, Mahomed's book, entitled *The Travels of Dean Mahomed, A Native of Patna in Bengal, Through Several Parts of India, While in the Service of The Honourable East India Company Written by Himself, In a Series of Letters to a Friend.* This book, published in Cork, is the first to be written by an Indian in English. That it is a travelogue, a description of India whose generic features and narrative techniques are derived fully from the conventions of early modern European travel writing and reportage, seems historically apposite – what could such an expatriate subject do better than to try and explain, in a recognizable idiom and vocabulary, his India to its colonizers? It is of course a fine historical irony that in doing so, Dean Mahomed, colonial subject in all the most obvious ways, inaugurates a literature of expatriation whose ethnographic and ideological formulae were suggested by, and answerable to, colonialist interests.

Dean Mahomed's plan to write his account of his travels in India was, as Fisher tells us, probably influenced by Olaudah Equiano's 1791 visit to Cork to publicize his own *The Interesting Narrative of the Life of Olaudah Equiano, or Gustavus Vassa, The African, Written by Himself.* Dean Mahomed's *Travels* shares certain features of Equiano's narrative: both authenticate the experiences they report by emphasizing autobiography, and claim in such firsthand (native) knowledge a trustworthy alternative to competing colonialist accounts of places and people. Of course Equiano's text, much more than Mahomed's, was a living rebuttal to racist European attitudes that saw blacks as lacking the capacity for intellectual activity, but some of this need to humanize, to claim cultural and literary authority, is clearly a part of Mahomed's text too. But this is where the issue of authorship and discursive authority becomes murky and more interesting, for, as has also been pointed out in the case of Equiano's *Life* (and slave narratives in general), Mahomed's *Travels* is written in an idiom that is so fulsomely that of eighteenth-century British writing that it is difficult to see just how we can read, as Fisher asks us to, 'Dean Mahomed's voice as an Indian, in contrast with travel narratives by Europeans of the time' (p. 216).

This is Mahomed describing a Muslim bride and bridegroom during their marriage ceremony ('which is generally solemnized with all the external show of Oriental pageantry'): 'Beneath this temporary dome, the coy maid reclines on a soft cushion, in an easy posture, while the raptured youth, scouring through fancy's lawn, on the wings of expectation, and already anticipating the joys of connubial felicity, leans opposite his sable Dulcinea in a similar attitude' (pp. 44–5). Dean Mahomed's prose suggests a profound translation of subject and culture: its obviously literary figures are an index of acculturation, a claim of belonging to the (English) culture to which the description is addressed, rather than to the (Indian) culture described. After fifteen years in the company's Bengal Army (he joined at the age of 10) and ten years in Cork as part of an Anglo-Irish family, Mahomed reviews India through an English literary lens, and his idiom calls attention to his facility with such discourse: 'The people of India, in general, are peculiarly favoured by Providence in the possession of all that can cheer the mind and allure the eye, and tho' the situation of Eden is only traced in the Poet's creative fancy, the traveller beholds with admiration the face of this delightful country, on which he discovers tracts that resemble those so finely drawn by the animated pencil of Milton' (p. 15).

It is possible to argue that Mahomed invokes Milton here in order to lend dignity and weight to his description of people and places in India, and that this is astute rhetorical strategy, part of Mahomed's inversion of the reductive priorities of colonialist travel narratives. There is no question that he writes with a sense of rebuttal; we notice an over-compensation, an overstatement that can be credibly ascribed to the need to produce generalizations that will counter more negative representations:

> Possessed of all that is enviable in life, we are still more happy in the exercise of benevolence and goodwill to each other, devoid of every species of fraud or low cunning. In our convivial enjoyments, we are never without our neighbours; as it is usual for an individual, when he gives an entertainment, to invite all those of his own profession to partake of it. That profligacy of manners too conspicuous in other parts of the world, meets here with public indignation, and our women, though not so accomplished as those of Europe, are still very engaging for many virtues that exalt the sex.
>
> (pp. 45–6)

Perhaps this is one of those moments where, as Fisher suggests, Mahomed writes as an Indian – while his idiom is that of his English education and reading, his brief 'sketch of the manners' of his country suggests a different, and prior, allegiance.

But Mahomed's *Travels* is, in general, not concerned primarily with providing an alternative, authentic version of India or things Indian. This allows him to quote without attribution, and at length (7 per cent of the words in *Travels*), passages from John Henry Grose's *Voyage to the East Indies* (1766), and from Jemima Kindersley's *Letters from the Island of Teneriffe . . . and the East Indies* (1766). Fisher offers a close analysis of some of these sections, and suggests that Mahomed mined Grose 'for descriptions of topics that he did not know, most notably Surat and Bombay', and on occasions when Grose and Kindersley provided, 'fluently or authoritatively', the 'Anglophone' discourse that Mahomed sought to achieve. Fisher argues for a critical consciousness at work in Mahomed's borrowing, and shows that Mahomed altered errors or changed emphases in Grose, but Fisher's well-meaning claim that, in all this, 'Dean Mahomed retained his own voice, even if some of the words were those of Grose or Kindersley' (pp. 232–3) is not persuasive, if only because the entire question of 'voice' in *Travels* is too vexed to allow such easy distinctions. Fisher also reminds us that such unacknowledged borrowing and copying from earlier accounts was a feature of much eighteenth-century travel writing – 'authoritative' versions of far-away countries and cultures were generated out of such 'intertextuality' – but this reminder does not so much explain or justify Mahomed's compositorial practices as locate him firmly within the developing discourse of colonial travel.

Fisher is also right to point out that by the time Dean Mahomed began planning his narrative, he would have needed to supplement his 'memory . . . with material from the memories, diaries, or other papers of the Anglo-Irish officers then living in Cork who served with him in India' (p. 233). *The Travels* is thus a fascinating composite of firsthand observation and experience and other (more 'authoritative') accounts of India, the whole shaped by Dean Mahomed's own place as an immigrant in Cork, living within the patronage of Anglo-Irish families whose fortunes were tied up with British commercial and colonial ventures in India. *The Travels* does not provide us with a model of authentic 'Indianness', but Fisher's remarkable scholarship, which embeds the text and its author within the three contexts – India, Ireland, England – of Dean Mahomed's life, makes this book rewarding reading. Fisher reconstructs the shifting military allegiances and political relations that dictated the deployment of the Bengal Army of the East India Company, and describes the curious mix of private enterprise and company policies that made life in India profitable for the likes of Godfrey Evan Baker (the cadet to whom Dean Mahomed attached himself).

One of the ironies of Fisher's book is that it is ultimately not the story of Dean Mahomed's life in British India that turns out to be most compelling. This is because Dean Mahomed's career in London (to which he moved in 1807) and in Brighton (where he lived between 1813 and

1851) is far more extraordinary than his time in India. As an Indian immigrant in Britain, Mahomed's attempt to parley his origins into a livelihood as a practitioner of Indian medical arts, a restaurateur ('The Hindustanee Coffee House'), and purveyor of medicated baths and shampooing (author of *Shampooing, or, Benefits Resulting From the use of The Indian Medicated Vapour Bath* . . . , editions in 1822, 1826, 1838) offers us a way of imagining the making of colonial metropolitan culture. As Fisher suggests, Dean Mahomed 'marketed his Indian birth, costume, and medical methods as attractive features of his medical persona' (p. 322), and achieved a considerable reputation, including as a 'Shampooing Surgeon' to royalty. His Indian origins do not seem to have stood in the way of a long and successful marriage to Jane Daly of Cork (Mahomed had converted to Protestantism before his wedding), though Fisher's research comes up with instances in which the features of their descendants are commented upon as alien. But these descendants lived in a time of hardening colonial attitudes – as Victorian Britain consolidated its hold on the Empire, immigrant success and cultural assimilation of the kind represented by Dean Mahomed became less likely. In Fisher's telling, Dean Mahomed's Britain was more cosmopolitan than the culture of late, and full-blown, empire. This may be true, but there is something about the oddity, the singularity, of Dean Mahomed's life that resists being read as evidence of a more general racial and cultural tolerance. If Dean Mahomed's life seems truly extraordinary, it is in no small measure because of Fisher's skill in re-creating its contours and contradictions.

Stanford University

Patricia Fara

Marcia Pointon, *Strategies for Showing: Women, Possession, and Representation in English Visual Culture 1665–1800* (Oxford: Clarendon Press, 1997), xiii + 439 pp., £48.00 (hardback)

'Give me', prayed Samuel Richardson's Pamela, 'give me, good God, an increase of humility and gratitude' (quoted p. 31). Although Mr B could not furnish such divinely dispensed gifts, he did shower her with jewels, clothes and books, thus transforming this comely servant into a property owner who wielded power through her new possessions. Nevertheless, her own beauty meant that she herself became an exceptionally fine item to be displayed, discussed and evaluated by her master and his friends. As readers of Marcia Pointon's previous studies will have anticipated, her latest book exploring the complex relationships between women, possession and culture in eighteenth-century England is replete with literary as well as visual vignettes. Pointon is in the vanguard of the new wave of interdisciplinary art historians, who draw on their extensive knowledge of a broad cultural background to show how paying attention to pictures enriches our appreciation of the political, religious, gender, scientific, economic and other strands woven into our past. In *Strategies for Showing*, by focusing on women not merely as objects of possession but also as possessors of objects, Pointon moves beyond simplistic feminist analyses to expose the gendered complexities of ownership in a society hierarchically structured by material wealth.

Since Pointon repeatedly insists that portraits should be seen both as representations and as material objects in their own right, it seems appropriate to consider the appearance and structure of her own volume. Its seriousness is immediately apparent. This is no coffee table art book, but a scholarly tome produced in a conventional photocopier-friendly academic format; the text dominates the reproductions, which are, sadly, all in black and white. The geometrical harshness of the red cover is softened only by the intricate floral design of a ceiling panel in Frogmore House at Windsor. When first seen, this choice reinforces stereotypical associations of women with flowers, but appears in a very different light after reading Pointon's densely informative analyses. Botanical discourses, she shows, resonated with sexual and mythological connotations. Flower painting was as much a male as a female pursuit, yet the elaborate floral decorations at Frogmore resulted from a financial transaction between two eminent women holding influential positions. Queen Charlotte was rumoured to have paid over £900 to Mary Moser, one of the founder members of the Royal Academy, for her intricately painted room blending themes of pastoral pleasure with loyalist patriotism. Pointon's outer advertisement of female ownership and accomplishment is mirrored inside her book, since almost a quarter of its pages are devoted to reproducing eighty-nine wills signed by women between 1711 and 1760. While some left only cursory instructions, most of these wealthy testatrices revealingly quantified their emotional attachments to their property as well as to their friends and relatives by meticulously specifying to whom their possessions should be entrusted. This long appendix could perhaps have been published separately, but will provide a valuable source for future researchers.

After a brief introduction, the rest of the book is divided into six highly original thematic chapters, but regrettably lacks a conclusion that might usefully have drawn out some of the issues threaded through this exuberantly wide-ranging study. As it is, the abrupt ending unexpectedly celebrates the brilliance of Joshua Reynolds; since the first chapter opens with a biographical sketch of Robert Harley, this rich picture of women's interests is eerily framed by the achievements of two famous men. In her six studies, Pointon concentrates on the lives and representations of individual women to explore grand themes, such as consumption, marriage, work, religion and mythology. Her diverse heroines run the gamut of unusual female roles, including an aristocratic household manager, an observant travel writer, a successful portrait painter and a sexually provocative saint. Although well-known names like Emma Hamilton do appear, most of the women featured here achieve a prominence they have not enjoyed since the eighteenth century, a testament to Pointon's assiduous research. Thus we learn far more about the self-taught artist Mary Grace than the academician Angelica Kauffman, and enjoy the perceptions of the domestic tourist Dorothy Richardson rather than those now rather travel-worn anecdotes of Celia Fiennes; instead of the familiar landed ladies of Thomas Gainsborough, Pointon picks apart images of seductive Sylvias and veiled, recumbent Belindas painted by the once popular but now forgotten Matthew Peters.

From the very outset, women assume a refreshingly novel and important role as owners and distributors of property. The first chapter revolves around the domestic economy of Elizabeth Harley, and explores the affective significance of purchasing and consuming material goods: an object's economic value is not independent of its sentimental worth. Here, as throughout the book, Pointon embeds her abundant factual details within erudite analytical arguments that often helpfully review as well as explicitly challenge the secondary literature. Skilfully interpreting her anthology of wills drawn up by women who bequeathed substantial amounts of property, she provides fascinating glimpses inside the well-stocked wardrobes, kitchen cupboards and medicine cabinets of wealthy homes. Through focusing on the privileged few, Pointon gains access to the emotional rapport of women with their possessions.

Pointon effectively unsettles conventional views of women and possession by exposing the Harleys' unorthodox marital arrangements. In contrast, her study of Dorothy Richardson offers fascinating reflections on that tricky issue, the relationship between sex and gender. Benefiting from an enlightened family owning an ample library, the well-read Richardson (b. 1748) methodically described the sites she visited as she travelled around England, supplementing her own immediate impressions with learned historical and geographical accounts. In her own text, Pointon explores how this female writer traversed gender boundaries by 'lay[ing] claim to an educated process of viewing and recording that is characteristically masculine' (p. 94). Drawing on lengthy quotations from the original manuscripts, Pointon emphasizes her subject's objectivity, scholarship and knowledgeable interest in manufacturing processes – qualities generally attributed to masculine scientists. In a later chapter, she uses a portrait of Lady Worsley wearing a militaristic riding habit to address the ambiguities raised by cross-dressing. Such analyses of singular women valuably repudiate dichotomous distinctions and permit more nuanced engagement with processes of gender differentiation. But ironically, celebrating women's assertiveness entails recognizing how they contributed to their own marginalization. This is a thorny topic for modern feminists, but Pointon might have written more about how women themselves colluded in setting up the boundaries that limited their freedom. Despite Richardson's masculine scientific attitudes, before venturing into Dr Hunter's Museum she cautiously enquired whether the anatomical specimens would be on display, thus paralleling the patronizing insistence of the male curators at the British Museum that monsters and skeletons should be concealed in the basement away from sensitive female eyes. Even Maria Edgeworth, champion of education for women, restricted her sisters who manifested a scientific inclination to gentle, repetitive activities: 'Chemistry is a science well suited to the talents and situation of women . . . it demands no bodily strength; it can be pursued in retirement; it applies immediately to useful and domestic purposes . . . there is no danger of inflaming the imagination.'[1]

Pointon displays a dauntingly impressive familiarity with the literature and historiography of the eighteenth century, but is at her strongest when analysing individual pictures. Her illuminating discussions not only encourage an appreciation of paintings as beautiful objects, but also unearth for modern iconographically illiterate readers the myriad concealed meanings which would have been apparent to eighteenth-century viewers. Pointon seems equally at home with Lacanian theory, Theban harps and Hackney rate books: the bulky anthology of wills comprises merely a visible iceberg tip hinting at the wealth of research bursting out of this book. In particular, the last chapter is twice as long as the others because, in typically thorough fashion, she surveys the previously uncharted territory of religious painting before tackling her declared objective of considering 'how ideals of femininity were instrumental in the formation of national cultural identity' (p. 229). Such ambitious aims and dazzling virtuosity are somewhat overwhelming and tend to obscure the central arguments. Inspired by Michael de Certeau's challenge to integrate everyday practices within historical narratives, Pointon has provided six splendidly detailed and unusual studies that range over wide tracts of eighteenth-century England, but they remain insufficiently linked together.

In 1779, the architect George Richardson produced a newly

illustrated edition of Cesare Ripa's *Iconologia*, welcomed by Reynolds and some of the other artists discussed by Pointon. 'All the fine arts,' he declared, 'have a double purpose; they are destined both to *please* and to *instruct*.'[2] Richardson would have appreciated *Strategies for Showing*, which shares his enthusiasm for expounding allegorical symbolism and amply fulfils both his stated goals.

University of Cambridge

Notes

1 Maria Edgeworth, *Letters for Literary Ladies* (London: Everyman, 1993), p. 21.
2 George Richardson, *Iconology*, 2 vols (New York and London: Garland Publishing Inc, 1979), Vol. 1, unpaginated preface.

Tyrus Miller

Theodor W. Adorno and Walter Benjamin, *Briefwechsel, 1928–1940*, ed. Henri Lonitz (Frankfurt am Main: Suhrkamp Verlag, 1994), 501 pp., Dm 50.00 (hardback)

I

Through the influence of the Frankfurt School's most audacious writers, Walter Benjamin and Theodor Adorno, the pathos of fragmentary and interrupted forms of thought has made itself felt on the stage of present-day cultural criticism. These figures and their texts have taught us to read in the artefacts of modernity 'the incomparable language of the death's head', the expressionless grin that hovers not only over the tragic landscape of baroque theatre, but over the *Welttheater* of twentieth-century history as well. Following their lead, critics may now seek to redeem the allegorical treasure of ruined works, heaping up bits of documentation in the 'unremitting expectation of a miracle';[1] and may acknowledge the convulsive beauty occulted in the blemishes and odd fugues of an imperfect body of writing.

The twelve-year correspondence between Walter Benjamin and Theodor Adorno, one of several recent additions to their already sizeable posthumous corpus, is collected here in its entirety for the first time. The letters assembled in this volume were once scattered over two continents and several countries, and their originals have been regathered in three major collections: the Theodor W. Adorno Archiv in Frankfurt; the Literaturarchive der Akademie der Künste in Berlin, formerly in the DDR, and the Bibliothèque Nationale in Paris. Most of the originals of Adorno's letters were in the East German archives, though some key letters, containing Adorno's detailed commentary on Benjamin's *Passagenwerk* research on nineteenth-century Paris, ended up among Benjamin's working notes, which Georges Bataille, a librarian at the Bibliothèque Nationale, hid for him during the Occupation. While most of these papers were returned to Adorno immediately after the war, a few letters remained in the French collection. Another portion of the papers was lost in the Paris library and only rediscovered in 1981; this late find included more of Adorno' s letters, which offer elucidations on Benjamin's work, provide a window on to the internal conflicts within the Frankfurt School in these formative years, and fill in details of Adorno's life as a philosophy dissertant at Oxford in the mid-1930s.

Beyond their physical dispersion as artefacts, however, the letters of Benjamin and Adorno also reveal the grim literalness with which the vocabulary of brokenness and contingency came to be experienced by these German-Jewish exiles from Nazism. From letter to letter and from year to year, the unrealized projects, collapsed publishing venues, missed meetings and well-meaning schemes gone awry pile up around them, until the texts of their lives appear to have been left only 'in draft', like contextless quotes copied on to blank pages and gathered haphazardly in sheaves. This 500-page book is itself a huge fragment, its necessary incompletion casting an ironic shadow over the volume's implicit claim to present the correspondence in full.

This shadow is seen most clearly, in accordance with Benjamin's methodological insistence on a 'tender empiricism' akin to philology, not in the content of the letters, but in the damaged silhouette of their very material – those gaps in the correspondence and surrounding texts which the editor's notes regularly mention. Completeness is a fiction of the book form and is nowhere to be found in the correspondence itself, which takes its contours only from the patterns of breakage and the rhythms of beginning once again under duress. The true significance of the collection, indeed, may ultimately lie in the necessity it lends to the method Benjamin and Adorno sought to develop, both separately and collaboratively. The hermeneutics of the splinter they articulated now comes full circle, to be led back to the very ground from which it emerged: the discontinuously unfolding debates over the precepts of 'kritische Theorie', an argument conducted by post as the European catastrophe loomed.

II

In his letter of 3 September 1932, Benjamin reports to Adorno that he has been reading a history of Bolshevism, a book which has shed light for him 'on many things, including on those areas in which political fate implicates itself in private life' (p. 26). In fact, it is precisely this domain which the letters in this volume wrench into the unpitying light of historical interpretation. They document Adorno's indefatigable but largely futile efforts during the early years of the Hitler regime to get Benjamin's work published in Germany, and Benjamin's hesitations about officially registering with the Reich's Chamber of Writers, the precondition of his employment as an author. They chronicle both men's personal concerns about relatives and friends, and their endless schemes to tap sources of material support among expatriate Jews, including from the Frankfurt School's own Institut für Sozialforschung. They express a shared dismay and anger at comrades like Ernst Bloch and Hanns Eisler over shameful positions taken during the Stalinist show trials which decimated the Bolshevik old guard. And they lament the unpredictable vicissitudes of refugee politics and the increasingly desperate situation of Benjamin after the occupation of France, when as a foreigner he was legally restricted from internal movement but needful of travel to Marseilles to press his case at the American consulate.

At times, the black comedy choreographed by happenstance was worthy of Kafka's dark inventiveness. At the end of 1939, for example, Benjamin was close to obtaining a visa for a visit to the United States when news arrived of a helpful measure taken on his behalf by Miss Celia Razovsky of the National Refugee Service. She had obtained for him an affidavit of sponsorship by a Mr Milton Starr of Nashville, Tennessee. Adorno wrote to Benjamin with considerable excitement that this was a 'weighty asset' in the attempts to transport him to a safer location. Unfortunately, this well-meant intervention had precisely the opposite effect from the one intended. It cancelled all Benjamin's efforts to get the shorter-term visitor's visa, and, as he noted with terse irony, threw him back, 'without my assistance' and through nothing else than 'the sending of the affidavit' (p. 433), into the stagnant pool of applicants in the 'normal' category.

III

The first year represented in the correspondence, 1928, was a momentous one for Benjamin. His two book-length works of the 1920s, *The Origin of German Tragic Drama* and *One-Way Street*, both appeared in print. They were well received by the literary intelligentsia, and nothing at this moment of relative success could predict that very few publications, especially of this scale, would follow in the coming decade. Nevertheless, a passage from *One-Way Street* entitled 'Torso' may stand as a premonition of the politically imposed exile and wandering that would take Benjamin to Norway, Italy, Spain, Denmark and France, and that would carry Adorno from Oxford to New York to Brentwood, before his postwar *nostos* in Frankfurt. Benjamin writes:

> Only he who can view his own past as an abortion sprung from compulsion and need can use it to full advantage in the present. For what one has lived is at best comparable to a beautiful statue which has had all its limbs knocked off in transit, and now yields nothing but the precious block out of which the image of one's own future must be hewn.[2]

As this passage clearly shows, Benjamin's conception of the ruin, which captures in itself an allegorical picture of time and history, was not simply a critical category through which he approached Baroque culture. It was also an existential category through which he understood his own life and death and those of others around him.

Benjamin's application of the allegorical concept of ruin to personal life is elaborated at two key points in the correspondence with Adorno. The first comes in a letter of 4 October 1938, written from Skovsbostrand in Denmark, where Benjamin had gone to visit Brecht and to complete the composition of 'The Paris of the Second Empire in Baudelaire', an essay based on his *Passagenwerk* research. Benjamin notes a manifest change in Brecht's attitude towards him, and goes on to interpret this change as an index of Brecht's growing isolation. The communication between them has clarified itself to an unaccustomed concord, and Benjamin speculates that their seeing eye-to-eye results from the very destruction of Brecht's past ties to the world, the ruin of his once rich social life:

> I cannot completely rule out the more banal interpretation of this fact, that this isolation has reduced for him the pleasure in certain provocative ruses, to which he is inclined in conversation; it would be more authentic, however, to recognize in his growing isolation the consequences of faithfulness to that which we have in common.

(p. 360)

This isolation is thus not wholly negative in Benjamin's view, since by stripping his relation with Brecht of everything inessential, it has laid bare the true basis of the solidarity between the theologically inclined philosopher-critic and the atheistic Marxist poet.

In a letter written barely five months before his death, in which he responded to Adorno's essay on the correspondence of Stefan George and Hugo von Hofmannstahl – an intriguingly self-reflective moment in the *Briefwechsel* – Benjamin similarly employed the idea of the life as ruin, with death and loss unveiling the allegorical face of the life as *historical.* In the essay to which Benjamin addressed his remarks, Adorno had attacked the views of George and Hofmannstahl on the value of 'bearing' (*Haltung*), noting how these poets had reduced objective problems of social identification and alienation to an aesthetic ideology of choosing a proper stance. 'The necessity of estrangement is twisted into the virtue of self-sufficiency,' writes Adorno. 'The victorious individual transforms the wrongs he is compelled to do to all the others in a competitive society into moral profit through bearing.'[3]

Benjamin objects, however, to Adorno's overly voluntaristic view of bearing. Bearing, Benjamin suggests, may be unconsciously adopted, and may in this way reveal the involuntary workings of history on the individual personality. This history comes forth 'where the essential loneliness of a man enters our field of vision', a loneliness that emerges precisely at the furthest point from individual fulfilment, in 'the place of his historically conditioned emptiness' (p. 431). The vehicle by which an individual's historicity makes itself known is his bearing, which is symptomatically valuable precisely because it detaches surface appearance from any presumption of hidden substance and inner meaning. Bearing is not a symbolic expression of a deep truth, but rather the stigmata of an objective social violence in the gestures of the face and the attitude of the body.

Paradoxically, then, it might be said: the emptier the complex of gestures which constitutes the bearing, the more significant it may be for the historian. For it is precisely the estrangement that is essential to the concept of bearing, its hollow inorganicity and rigidified traits, which allows it to serve as the emblem of an individual's historical misfortune. For it is the shape in which the historical traits of the persona, bereft of individual substance, petrify, obtruding henceforth with the stark outlines of a death mask.

IV

What then are the historical traits exhibited in the bearing of this collection? As with the individual life, so too with the correspondence of two – its historicity comes to the fore where the assemblage reveals its character as a ruin. The volume itself is framed by two jagged edges at its opening and end. Adorno's half of the correspondence up to 1933 is missing; these letters were left behind in Benjamin's Berlin apartment when the Nazis came to power in March 1933 and were not recovered. The book's conclusion was also determined by the misfortunes of Benjamin's exilic flight. 'After eight years in exile, observing the rise of the enemy / Then at last, brought up against an impassable frontier,' Brecht wrote, his melancholy friend passed 'a passable one'.[4] Thus, the last missive of Benjamin's hand was not composed of pen and ink, but of multiple doses of morphine with which he 'destroyed a torturable body' on the French-Spanish border.

A written draft of this last act, left behind some hours earlier, does however appear at the end of the volume – a four-sentence note in French to Henny Gurland, with whom he had travelled to the mountain border post in the hopes of crossing into neutral Spain, dated 25 September 1940. It speaks, at its conclusion, and at the definitive realization of a life as ruin, of a correspondence which must now be interrupted for the last time:

> In a situation with no way out, I have no other choice than to end it. It is in a little village in the Pyrénées that my life will come to a close.
>
> I ask you to convey my thoughts to my friend Adorno and to explain to him the situation in which I find myself. There does not remain to me enough time to write all the letters I would have liked to write.

(p. 445)

Yale University

Notes

1 Walter Benjamin, *The Origin of German Tragic Drama*, trans John Osborne (London: NLB, 1977), p. 178.
2 Walter Benjamin, *One-Way Street and Other Writings*, trans Edmund Jephcott and Kingsley Shorter (London: NLB, 1979), p. 76.
3 Theodor W. Adorno, 'The George-Hofmannstahl correspondence, 1891–1906' in *Prisms*, trans Samuel and Shierry Weber (Cambridge, MA: MIT Press, 1967), p. 194.
4 Bertolt Brecht, 'On the suicide of the refugee W. B.' in *Poems, 1913–1956*, ed. John Willett and Ralph Manheim with Erich Fried (New York: Methuen, 1976), p. 365.

Rumina Sethi

Emma Tarlo, *Clothing Matters: Dress and Identity in India* (London: Hurst & Co, 1996), xxi + 360 pp., £19.95 (paperback)

Choosing a wardrobe, as Emma Tarlo says early on in her book, is always associated more with fashion magazines than with any intellectual gravity. Seldom do we find a serious involvement of the problem of what to wear with one's social, historical, political and cultural identities. While there exist many studies on the psychological conflicts which governed political action and thus shaped identity, there are few works on the relationship between the ruler and the ruled based so exclusively on dressing, undressing and re-dressing. Since identity-formation is linked so closely with representation, clothing becomes the inevitable, if not the ostensible issue to examine. Tarlo is concerned with the way certain kinds of clothes determine specific identities of individuals, families, caste, class, religion and nation just as, for a long time, it was the lack of clothing or nakedness that was the preoccupation of a number of European ethnologists and historians and which governed their representations. It is the author's intention to depart from similar essentialisms while venturing her defence.

It is partly for this reason that Tarlo puts forward an examination of the political dimension of British clothing habits in India along with her major concern with the adoption of European dress by Indians. The layers of European clothing worn in the excessively warm and sultry Indian climate revealed more than simply a desire to maintain British decorum and civility: it was also to insulate themselves from familiarity with those whom they governed. As a matter of fact, after the 1830s legislation preventing the East India Company officials from wearing Indian clothes, formal European dress became an even more defining characteristic of the British. This poses the significant question as to why a different dress code was advanced when British policies, in the time of Hastings in particular, sought as much as possible to rest on likeness and even friendship with the natives.

Further, while Tarlo examines the political reasons for the need to maintain a sartorial British image, her study would benefit from examining, in some detail, the 'deviant' British – those who adopted Indian sartorial manners, especially since it is her intention to break with homogeneity and stereotypes. Instead of a dismissal of the 'de-Europeanised' 'white baboos', as Lord Lytton referred to them, they can be used as prime examples of the displacement of the concepts of fixity and stereotyping which characterize the discourse of colonialism as discursive strategy. In terms of recent studies of the ambivalence of colonial discourse, it is important to scrutinize forms of both identification and difference. Despite the strict sartorial code which is crucial to its exercise of power, one can also see within colonial discourse limitless possibilities of attraction and inseparability with the 'other', what Homi Bhabha has famously called 'phobia and fetish'. Beneath the stable patterns used to schematize and govern lie the many phantasmatic images of fear and attraction, sameness and difference, and, within Edward Said's context, both manifest and latent orientalisms.

But Tarlo's aim here is an exposure of 'the dominant racist stereotype' rather than that of the views of the sympathetic few. Besides, she intends to study the Indian attitudes to European dress rather than vice versa. Here again, while the author gives us an insightful account of the partial or complete adoption of European dress by some Indian quarters and the resulting conflict between different value systems, she shows little desire to chart the psychological categories that governed the adoption of these styles. What we do get is an accurate portrayal of the social milieu through male dressing in the late nineteenth and early twentieth centuries, of a cultural dualism which kept Indian men in different public and private images. As Nayar, a high-caste man whom Tarlo cites is quoted to have said, 'When I put on my shirt to go to the office, I take off my caste, and when I come home and take off my shirt, I put on my caste.'

Tarlo then leads us through Gandhi's re-creation of Indian dress, particularly his promotion of khadi, to a different historical context where she discusses women's clothing issues. She takes contemporary Gujarati village women as her canvas, having had little access to their ideas and opinions in the colonial period. While Tarlo explains her reasons through helpful footnotes, the jump from examining identity in a male context, in a particular period of India's colonization to women's clothing in a contemporary and 'free' India is uncertain and a little contrived in an otherwise excellent study. In my view, had the author limited herself to researching the preferences of either men or women in tracing the theme of identity through clothing codes in a colonial–national–modern urban trajectory, the dysjunction between chapters 2–4 and 5–8 could be avoided. Besides, the attraction for the indigenous in the case of men and the rejection of the very same cultural mores by women in a different historical setting could be played out more thoroughly if one didn't have to tune one's mind to a changed gender situation.

However, despite this drawback, Chapter 9 is a remarkable exercise in coalescing contemporaneity and antiquity. Embarking on her fieldwork, the author found the village women in Gujarat rapidly rejecting the ancient art of embroidery which she had first undertaken to study. The question soon arose: how could she examine an art which the villagers found so uninspiring? With Westernization making inroads into the village, the women had practically abandoned the textile tradition, and embroidered clothes had made way for shiny, synthetic *salwar kameezes* not considered backward like their *ghagro-kapdus*. In such a context, what could be better than the study of a 'carefully marketed village life', the Hauz Khas village, in the heart of cosmopolitan South Delhi, which is being celebrated as an 'ethnic' shopping centre, and where 'clothes of the type worn in village Saurashtra were being converted into exclusive designer fashion garments'. What is extraordinarily 'authentic' about the Hauz Khas village is that it takes its stimulation from its creator's 'sense of foreignness'. The making of this 'Indian' village, in fact, is similar to constructions of village India by, first, the colonial administrators and second, by the nationalist intelligentsia. The Hauz Khas village, as I see it, is a combination of the orientalist and nationalist views that have together effected the idea of India as a land of villages in their efforts to approach its 'reality'. Such a village community can serve as an attractive centre of preserved culture for many romantic conservatives. But the particular paradox of Hauz Khas village lies in the destruction of the village atmosphere in the very efforts to preserve it. As it turned out, the villagers gradually metamorphosed into shrewd capitalists with the sudden influx of the urban elite, demolishing their mud and cowdung *jhuggis* to build concrete apartments, much to the horror of the commercial 'preservationists'. Yet the original inhabitants of Hauz Khas did not abandon the *ghunghat* or the veil which the fashionable socialites were quick to discard. The creation of invented authenticity also underlines an aspect of the Indian character which first seeks endorsement from the West before enacting its cultural revival. At the same time, the culture which is revived is part of 'ethnic chic' and is thus as distant from the West as it is from the village masses it chooses to imitate.

Indian clothing and one's choice of what to wear has remained a major dilemma. With its history of colonialism, it is difficult to look 'modern without appearing Western' and 'Indian without appearing traditional'; what Partha Chatterjee has called the 'liberal rationalist dilemma' of nationalist thought. Perhaps there ought to be a celebration of fluid identities rather than an assertion of the 'pure' and the 'indigenous'. The story of the birth of the nation must be accompanied by its inevitable ruptures and confusions, where the metaphor of hybridity and decomposition become more significant than any kind of authoritative orthodoxy of an older India. Emma Tarlo's answer to the issues she has raised is well summed up in the 1955 ditty, picturized famously by the film star, Raj Kapoor: '*mera juta hai Japani . . .* ' [My shoes are Japanese/These trousers are English/On my head is a Russian red cap/Yet my heart is Indian]. These lines have now found a parallel in Alisha Chinai's music video which echoes Kapoor's theme four decades later: the singer is clothed head-to-toe in Western apparel, even sporting a blonde look, but desires a loving relationship with a dhoti-clad man whose heart is 'made in India'. Such an appeal is nothing if not an invocation of cosmopolitanism even though it is dictated by the pulls of an 'Indian' heart.

Rich and picturesque in its detail, *Clothing Matters* is a pioneering study, linking an everyday concern to its sociohistorical origins. From Gandhi's loincloth to Bina Ramani's ethnic chic, Tarlo has raised important questions about ethnicity, nationalism and multiculturalism.

Wolfson College, Oxford

B. J. Wray

Marilyn R. Farwell, *Heterosexual Plots and Lesbian Narratives* (New York: New York University Press, 1996), 227 pp., £17.95 (paperback)

Julie Abraham, *Are Girls Necessary? Lesbian Writing and Modern Histories* (New York: Routledge, 1996), 213 pp., £40.00 (hardback), £13.99 (paperback)

In her Preface to *Are Girls Necessary?* Julie Abraham succinctly describes what is perhaps the most crucial, and undoubtedly the most enduring, dilemma of contemporary lesbian literary scholarship:

> Given policing by the spirits of various ages, and given the centrality of interpretation – especially interpretation as not-lesbian – to the process of policing, how might we now, in the last decade of the twentieth century, at a moment of unprecedented possibility for lesbian cultural production, criticism, and theory, identify a lesbian text or a lesbian literature?
>
> (p. xiii)

Indeed, for anyone committed to a complicated understanding of the relationship between sexualities and literary conventions, this question of textual identification(s) and the subsequent ramifications that it may hold for lesbian subjectivity in general remains a primary mode of enquiry. It seems fitting that the recent proliferation of academic studies concerned with figuring forth what a 'lesbian' text might look like, coupled with queer theory's penchant for deconstructing the stability of ontological referents, should initiate a reworking of the ways in which representations of sexuality are analysed within literary criticism. It is to this end that both Abraham and Farwell undertake their respective studies: Abraham deftly investigates the connections between lesbian writing and modern histories, while Farwell convincingly interrogates the interlining of heterosexual plots and lesbian narratives.

Each of these books attempts to negotiate the fraught and equally fruitful terrain of delineating the parameters of lesbian writing while simultaneously remaining cognizant of the very tenuous and provisional nature of lesbian identity itself. In other words, what we see played out in these two texts is an attentiveness to – at times an awkwardness with – the contradictions and paradoxes of bringing into dialogue the seemingly disparate goals of lesbian-feminist literary criticism (here I am thinking of seminal works produced by writers such as Adrienne Rich, Bonnie Zimmerman, Catherine Stimpson and Jane Rule) with what has become the new queer canon of Judith Butler, Eve Kosofsky Sedgwick, Sue-Ellen Case and Teresa deLauretis among others. Of course, marking the inherent inconsistencies and highly fictional nature of prescribed categories, whether they be literary genres or sexual identities, is precisely the struggle with which our queer academic moment appears preoccupied. But often this tension, instead of producing an expanded knowledge of the inter-relationship between movements, theories and subjectivities, functions to reveal the threshold of our thinking around conventional binary categories and unwittingly reinscribes those limiting frameworks. How to imagine beyond this threshold is the focus of the texts at hand.

Expanding on her ground-breaking essay, 'Toward a definition of the lesbian literary imagination' (*Signs* 14.1(1988):100–18), Marilyn R. Farwell opens her enquiry in *Heterosexual Plots and Lesbian Narratives* with an examination of when and how a lesbian narrative is a lesbian narrative, and whether or not certain textual strategies may be identified as specifically lesbian strategies. The contested status of both terms – 'lesbian' and 'narrative' – points to what Farwell articulates as the 'problematic question that has plagued lesbian literary criticism: where is the "lesbian" in lesbian narrative?' (p. 6). Drawing on the recent arguments of Terry Castle and Toni McNaron, Farwell strategically resolves this dilemma by fashioning a 'metaphorical lesbian subject' that 'disrupts narrative through the structural realignment of the narrative's subject positions' (p. 20). In a blatantly utopic manner, Farwell insists that this discursively constructed lesbian subject 'undermines gender opposition and hierarchy,' thereby creating a 'lesbian narrative space' (p. 23). From the outset, then, Farwell's argument is predicated on the inherently transgressive potential of this metaphorical lesbian subject (she is 'narrative's most disruptive nightmare' (p. 43), and rarely acknowledges its complicity with the well-worn tropes of lesbian alterity and radicality. Desiring to skirt the essentialist/ anti-essentialist conundrum, and subsequently to make possible the identification as lesbian texts that do not contain specific lesbian characters or themes or authors, Farwell invokes the metaphorical lesbian subject as that which 'redraws the gender boundaries in the narrative categories in which subjectivity is posited' (p. 62). She calls for a reaffirmation of gender as a category of interpretation in lesbian studies, and it is through this metaphorical lesbian subject that such a move is made possible without resorting to simplistic notions of identity constitution. In its ideal construction, Farwell's metaphorical lesbian subject moves 'between sameness and differences, utopian essentialism and deconstructive nonessentialism' (p. 68). Needless to say, this intoxicating binary blend rarely retains its dynamic mixture in Farwell's text, as the fluidity of such a combination is quickly solidified into a predictable paradigmatic imperative, wherein, not surprisingly, we come to the conclusion that 'If lesbian-feminists like Rich and Lorde have deconstructive moments, then postmodernist theorists of the lesbian subject have essentialist moments' (p. 95).

Perhaps the most laudable and rather lofty aim of *Heterosexual Plots and Lesbian Narratives* is its will to challenge existing divisions within lesbian literary studies in order to ease the 'generational conflict between the lesbian-feminists of twenty years ago and the queer theorists of today' (p. 9). Farwell dramatizes this conflict in her text with a series of oppositionally constructed definitions: 'Traditional lesbian criticism has faith in utopian narrative gestures and political and personal relevance; queer theory valorizes only the disruptive potential of postmodern techniques such as nonlinearity and performance' (p. 10). It is the imbrications of these critical camps that Farwell foregrounds in her initial chapters as a means of both deconstructing the exclusiveness wielded by each theoretical field and as a way of suggesting a more resonant method of academic inquiry: 'By comparing as well as contrasting these two theories, lesbian-feminism will appear more complex and radical than has been allowed and queer theory more conservative than it wishes to admit' (p. 87). Using an inside/out model reminiscent of Diana Fuss's discussion of the homo/ hetero binary in her introduction to *Inside/Out: Lesbian Theories, Gay Theories* (Routledge, 1991), Farwell proposes 'to uncover the potentially disruptive elements in traditional plot lines and to underscore the traditional aspects of experimental writing' (p. 14).

Ironically, but none the less predictably, Farwell's insistence on constructing a dialectical paradigm for her theorization of lesbian narratives works to undermine the force of her argument. Aside from the generalizing tendencies and defensive posturings that characterize Farwell's representations of lesbian and queer criticism – gestures that she readily acknowledges as necessary but limiting – the cumulative effect of Farwell's endless reiteration of their respective theoretical tactics is not so much a critique of dualistic thinking as it is a reinscription of these initial dichotomies and a solidification of their distinct properties. As a hybridized model of lesbian-feminist/postmodern-queer critique unfolds throughout the pages of Farwell's text, one experiences an oscillating sensation similar to that of watching an extended rally during a tennis match. Although this is not a necessarily unpleasant sensation (except for a potentially stiff neck) and can actually be quite exhilarating when the participants are equally engaged, the odds in Farwell's game are always unduly in favour of a lesbian-feminist court and tend to reveal the artificiality and forced nature of her game itself. This freighted alignment results from Farwell's opposition to 'the genderless indeterminacy that is idealized in queer theory' (p. 68), and her concomitant reliance on an anatomical grounding of social construction ('When I speak of lesbians . . . I speak of women' (p. 68)) in order to counter the invisibility of lesbians and the resurrection of a universal (gay) male subject that, according to Farwell's line of reasoning, occurs when gender is no longer a primary category of analysis. Even though I take very seriously Farwell's critique of a 'genderless' queer theory, the answer to this problematic relationship is surely not to revert to a reconstituted exclusionary matrix in which the metaphorical lesbian subject dominates the field.

While the first half of Farwell's book cogently outlines the overriding theoretical concerns of her study in terms of narrative structure and its inevitable influence on lesbian writing and lesbian subjectivity, the second half is dedicated to close readings of three prototypical narratives: the romantic lesbian narrative; the heroic lesbian narrative, and the postmodern lesbian text. Each of these readings underscores Farwell's contention that the 'Lesbian has been expanded in the twentieth century to represent the woman who exceeds discursive and narrative boundaries' (p. 17). Farwell explores the work of Adrienne Rich, Marilyn Hacker, Marion Zimmer Bradley, Gloria Naylor and Jeanette Winterson to demonstrate how her notion of a metaphorical lesbian subject functions in these texts as 'the only term that structurally realigns the gender asymmetry of the narrative system' (p. 18). Although Farwell's utopic hopes for her discursively constructed lesbian are tantalizing, I am troubled both by the recuperation of lesbian under the sign of woman via a lesbian continuum route, and by the inattentiveness Farwell displays to the discursivity of the category 'woman' itself. The textual readings within *Heterosexual Plots and Lesbian Narratives* do, however, provide a tentative framework for negotiating the ways in which restrictive and silencing narrative structures are potentially altered by a radical habitation on the part of a metaphorical lesbian subject. Farwell's book is exemplary of the rewards and pitfalls accompanying any attempt to grapple with the frequently unwieldy pairings of lesbian-feminist and queer critique, material and discursive bodies, and political and textual analysis.

Julie Abraham's *Are Girls Necessary? Lesbian Writing and Modern Histories* is less invested in binary wrangling and much more intent on teasing out the nuances of historically situated conceptions of sexuality. Abraham foregrounds the 'transaction between a writer and the spirit of the age' (p. xi) in order to examine the 'cultural policing of the representations of women's relationships' (p. xi). Indeed, the title of her book is taken from Virginia Woolf's *Orlando* as an illustration of how the tacit circulation of lesbian subjectivity in certain historical moments works both to elide and expand the possibilities of interpretation. The spirit of the age may 'set the terms under which lesbianism is understood, through setting the terms on which a text – and by extension a gesture, a relationship, a person – is understood as lesbian' (p. xii). In *Orlando*, Abraham argues that the strictures of the age are satisfied by the ways in which lesbianism is 'neutralized by their author's class, her position within imperial structures, and her marriage' (p. xii). Crucially, Abraham identifies the extent to which a politics of interpretation determines when, how and even if the lesbian will appear as a culturally intelligible subject in literary texts: ' "failures" of interpretation are a more common and effective form of social control than publicly branding and casting out offending sentences and writers' (p. xii). The historical contingency of recognizing lesbian writers and texts as lesbian becomes, in Abraham's study, the slippery ground that any analysis of lesbian narratives must traverse.

Key to Abraham's intervention into the problematics of interpretation is her separation of 'lesbian novels' from 'lesbian writing'. She categorizes lesbian novels as 'those texts written, presented, and read as representations of lesbianism by lesbian, gay, and heterosexual writers and readers' (p. xiii). On the other hand, lesbian writing is shaped by specific historical circumstances and 'has no fixed subject or form' (p. xiii). Not content with the more static identity requirements of lesbian novels, Abraham focuses her analysis on lesbian writing. The rather elastic definitional boundaries attached to 'lesbian writing' permits Abraham to examine a wide range of authors, including Willa Cather, Mary Renault, Gertrude Stein, Djuna Barnes and Virginia Woolf. These figures are linked by Abraham's contention that no distinction can be drawn between establishing the homosexual content of a text or writer and literary questions. According to Abraham,

> Literary conventions are one method through which 'the age' deter-mines where we look and what we see as 'homosexual content,' while assumptions about 'the literary' as a realm of aesthetic abstraction

obscure the role of the literary in producing both 'homosexual content' and reader expectations.

(p. xiv)

Highlighting the historical and discursive materialization of lesbian subjects enables Abraham to sidestep both the essentialist tendencies of 'lesbian novels' as well as the celebration of lesbianism as inherently subversive or unstable. Conversely, a sense of lesbian specificity is maintained by Abraham's attentiveness to literary activity itself as the site of identity production: 'Given the highly problematic relation between lesbianism and narrative, the lesbianism of the lesbian writer could be constituted, in part, through/in the very process of writing' (p. xviii). Critical of the imitative aspects of lesbian novels (Abraham refers to them as 'formula fictions based on the heterosexual plot' (p. xix), *Are Girls Necessary?* realigns the trajectory of lesbian literary criticism to consider precisely how lesbian writing of the first six decades of the twentieth century responded to heterosexual narrative hegemony.

Abraham identifies a reliance on historical narratives and a redefinition of history as the primary response of these writers to the limitations of traditional literary forms: 'History became both a subject in their writings and, like writing itself, a medium of representation' (p. xx). It is not that a recourse to 'history' solves the dilemma of lesbian representation, but rather that history as a framework for fiction allows lesbian writing to rework narrative disenfranchisement by infiltrating an already established convention. To this end, Abraham observes that 'to locate one's text in relation to the dominant cultural understanding of "history" was to gain access to the assumptions of narrativity embodied by that history' (p. 30). Through wonderfully nuanced close readings, Abraham provides a fascinating account of the ways in which these canonical writers figure forth lesbian subjectivity within a reconstituted historical frame. Unlike Farwell's dubious invocation of a metaphorical lesbian subject as the narrative disrupter *par excellence*, Abraham rejects such utopic constructions in favour of rigorous and comprehensive study of the relationship between literary forms, historical narratives and lesbian identities. Abraham's tenacious consideration of representation itself results in a book that successfully manages to negotiate the definitional (in)coherence of lesbian identities and the problematics of what qualifies as lesbian writing.

University of Calgary

Paulina Palmer

Peter Horne and Reina Lewis (eds), *Outlooks: Lesbian and Gay Sexualities and Visual Cultures* (London and New York: Routledge, 1996), 196 pp., £45.00 (hardback), £14.99 (paperback)

Outlooks: Lesbian and Gay Sexualities and Visual Cultures makes an impressive contribution to the field of gender studies, giving a fascinating insight into the strategies which artists and critics utilize to inscribe lesbian/ gay desire in the production and reception of art. The collection is divided into three sections: 'Queering art history', 'Practitioners' statements' and 'Production and consumption'. Taken together, the essays are notably comprehensive, encompassing in their scope both high art and popular culture, the art forms of the past as well as those of the present. The editors succeed, on the whole, in avoiding the danger of fragmentation and superficiality to which such a wide-ranging collection of essays can give rise, since certain themes and motifs which recur throughout the volume give it intellectual coherence and a degree of unity.

One theme to which the contributors frequently return is the dissatisfaction on the part of artists and art historians with the tenets of modernism, such as an emphasis on 'universality' as a criterion of aesthetic value and the belief that only high art is worthy of attention. In exploring the challenges which artists direct at them, the contributors foreground the importance which the inscription of personal experience assumes in their work. In the case of Francis Bacon, a tension is apparent between art and life. Emmanuel Cooper, discussing Bacon's painting and the debates it has generated, argues that, despite Bacon's unwillingness to discuss his sexual orientation and its influence on his art, his work can only be understood in terms of his homosexuality and the frequently turbulent relationships which he formed with men.

The artists who contribute to 'Practitioners' statements' likewise focus attention on the inscription of personal experience. They also discuss the strategies which they employ to interrogate and subvert traditional notions of gender and sexuality and to problematize heteropatriarchal institutions and concepts, such as the family and the unitary self. Veronica Slater comments particularly cogently on these topics. She rejects the concept of 'the pure unmediated heroic art' promoted by Gombrich and Camberwell and, looking back on her experience at art school, wryly remarks, 'I was never going to be a hero of modernism; its 'universality' did not include the questions that became the context of my work' (p.126). Reference to personal experience frequently forms the basis of her paintings. In one, she presents images of herself, her mother and grandmother, while in another she explores, as she puts it, 'the relationship between art and anatomy' (p. 128). Discussing her interest in problematizing hetero-patriarchal institutions and principles, she refers to the focus on 'the family album' in her early work. Here, she seeks to deconstruct the traditional concept of the family as stable and established, revealing 'the dysfunctional and chaotic relationships that exist within it' (p.127). The intertextual allusions which Slater introduces signal the influence of earlier examples of lesbian art and literature on her painting, while simultaneously illustrating her revision of them in the light of personal experience. In 'Soul identified as flesh' she portrays her partner standing in front of repeated copies of Gluck's *Self-portrait with a Cigarette.* The latter carries multiple associations for Slater, since, as she explains, it appeared on the cover of Radclyffe Hall's *The Well of Loneliness* and was one of the first representations of lesbianism which she saw. Her aim in introducing it into her own work is 'to create a lineage by placing Gluck's painting within a 1980s context, juxtaposing the two portraits within the one image' (p. 129).

A focus on personal experience and the revision of traditional motifs in the context of queer and postmodern perspectives on gender and sexuality also plays a part in the works of other lesbian and gay artists who contribute to *Outlooks,* such as Matthew Stradling and Sadie Lee. Lee also describes how she seeks to subvert the visual representation of woman as the object of voyeuristic scrutiny which has dogged artistic production from time immemorial. She aims to give the female figures whom she portrays a sense of confidence in their own sexuality and, in some cases, 'a challenging, threatening presence' (p.122).

Another motif which a number of the essays, particularly those in 'Practitioners' statements' foreground is 'gender as performance', a concept associated with the work of Judith Butler. The image of lesbianism which Tessa Boffin creates in *The Knight's Move* disconcerts the viewer by combining medieval conventions of masculinity with the present-day butch role.

A postmodern emphasis on the deconstruction of hetero-patriarchal institutions and the introduction of intertextual allusions, which, as is apparent from the essays in *Outlooks,* are significant features of contemporary lesbian/gay art, are also reflected in the lesbian fiction of the 1980s and 1990s, creating a link between the two cultural forms. Sarah Schulman in her recently published novel *Rat Bohemia* (Penguin, 1995) problematizes the notion of the family as a haven of warmth and security by alerting attention to the frequency with which heterosexual parents reject and ostracize their lesbian and gay offspring. Barbara Wilson in *Gaudí Afternoon* (Virago, 1991), a novel exploring transsexualism and alternative family structures, deconstructs the image of the patriarchal family unit. The lesbian protagonist, on contemplating the cathedral of Sagrada Família in Barcelona, describes the edifice as 'monumentally, phenomenally bizarre, like the Christian notion of family itself, a combination of organic and tortured form' (p. 81). Hall and her famous novel *The Well of Loneliness* play as important a role in Caeia March's *The Hide and Seek Files* (The Women's Press, 1988) as a signifier of lesbian identity as they do in the painting of Slater. Though criticizing *The Well of Loneliness* for its elitist stance and for portraying lesbians as doomed and guilt-ridden, March, like Slater, acknowledges the reading of the novel as an important *rite de passage* in the life of the woman who identifies as lesbian.

'Gender as performance' is another motif which lesbian fiction shares with lesbian/gay art; it assumes particular centrality in the crime fiction of Schulman and Mary Wings. The interaction which Wings creates between the persona of the Chandleresque sleuth and the present-day lesbian investigator in her series of thrillers focusing on the adventures of Emma Victor can be compared with Boffin's combination of medieval masculinity and the butch role in her depiction of lesbianism in *The Knight's Move*. Both representations are controversial and intellectually provocative since, as well as exploring the resemblances between lesbian and hetero-male gender constructs, they evoke the tension and clash of difference.

However, the essays in *Outlooks*, as well as being connected by the themes and motifs mentioned above, are also linked, in some cases, by features of a more worrying and problematic kind. The artists and art historians who contribute to the collection tend to adopt, on occasion, a naively uncritical approach to the works they discuss and to queer/ postmodern cultural perspectives in general. The simplistic approach to postmodernism which Peter Horne and Reina Lewis adopt in their introductory essay typifies this, marring an otherwise intelligent discussion. They unequivocally endorse postmodern cultural trends, ignoring the problems relating to loss of agency and political emphasis in which they can result (p. 3). They also ignore the gendered aspect of postmodernism, making no attempt to distinguish between the implications which its perspectives and conventions hold for women and those they hold for men. They appear strangely unaware of the fact that the relationship between postmodernism and lesbianism / feminism is acknowledged by theorists and critics to be both ambiguous and controversial. Some reference to the debates surrounding the issue and to existing commentaries on it, such as the perceptive discussions by Robin Wiegman and Judith Roof in *The Lesbian Postmodern* (ed. Laura Doan, Columbia University Press, 1994), would have improved the essay and made its treatment of the postmodern more convincing.

There are also other important issues which the contributors to *Outlooks* tend to ignore. Oppressive aspects of the contemporary lesbian and gay scene and the art-forms relating to it, such as the obsessive preoccupation with youth and the ageism which it both reflects and promotes, and the notion that 'pleasure' and the sexualization of the body are necessarily politically liberating, the latter recalling the more immature and sexist aspects of the 1960s sexual revolution, receive no consideration or critique. Little attempt is made to discuss the connection between 'pleasure' and 'politics'. In fact, the terms 'politics' and 'political' are frequently used extremely loosely, with the result that, at times, their meanings strike the reader as contradictory and confused.

Another limitation which the collection manifests, one again exemplified by Horne's and Lewis's introductory essay, is the lack of interest which the majority of the contributors reveal in linking queer cultural perspectives to the cultural and political movements of the recent past. As is often the case in studies of queer topics, they are so eager to celebrate the brave new world of queer perspectives and to appear fashionably avant-garde that they ignore the connections which these perspectives reveal with the political and cultural formations of the previous decades. They ignore the fact that performativity and a critique of hetero-patriarchal institutions and principles are not unique to queer culture but assumed prominence in the cultural forms and practices produced by the political movements of the 1970s, such as Gay Liberation an the Women's Movement. Illustrations of this are to be found in, among other publications, Lisa Power's *No Bath But Bubbles: An Oral History of the Gay Liberation Front 1970–73* (Cassell, 1995).

The failure of contributors to refer to the issue of ageism or to discuss the connection between pleasure and politics, combined with the other problematic aspects of *Outlooks* mentioned above, in my view limit its value. However, a number of the essays are unaffected by these limitations and are intellectually excellent. The essays in the opening section 'Queering art history' are particularly illuminating in illustrating the variety of different approaches currently available to critics and art-historians. The essays it contains vary considerably in style. They include the descriptive, as exemplified by Richard A. Kaye's account of the changing representations and interpretations of the figure of Saint Sebastian; the analytic, illustrated by Thais E. Morgan's discussion of the ambiguities of the term 'perverse' in the art and life of the 1860s and 1870s as reflected in the unequal friendship between Simeon Solomon and Algernon Charles Swinburne and the art which it produced; and the polemical, represented by Wendy Leeks's interpretation of Ingres's painting of the classical story of Antiochus and Stratonice in the light of Freud's case study 'Dora' and feminist readings of Freud's essay. In addition to interpreting Ingres's painting afresh, Leeks utilizes her reading of it as the starting point for an original theorization of the encoding of the marginalized female / lesbian gaze in painting, thus creating a space for a female / lesbian point of view.

These three essays illustrate, in addition, the range of intellectual stances which *Outlooks* reflects. The essays of Morgan and Leeks are more ambitious in scope than Kaye's. Kaye's discussion of Saint Sebastian is well researched and competently carried out. Treating the motif chronologically, he gives a comprehensive account of the different meanings projected on to the figure of the saint in different periods. These include, he observes, 'camp token, political comrade', and, in the present era of the AIDS crisis, 'patron saint offering comfort against a new plague' (p.101). However, apart from a short paragraph commenting on the inappropriateness of the figure of the saint to the Gay Liberation era of the 1970s, Kaye makes little attempt to explore the ideological and political resonances of the motif. In contrast to Kaye, Morgan and Leeks tease out and comment on the ideological implications of the topics which they address. Unlike Kay, they are not content merely to describe but also aim to construct an argument. Morgan's discussion of the friendship between Solomon and Swinburne and the art which it produced furnishes the springboard for a perceptive discussion of nineteenth-century cultural and sexual issues. The friendship between the two men, as Morgan illustrates, generated some of the most stylistically innovative and ideologically challenging work of the period. The friendship, along with the art relating to it, has the effect of interrogating the boundary between the homosexual and the homosocial, as defined by Eve Sedgwick, and problematizing the line of demarcation between the two. In addition, it gives a glimpse of the different perspectives on same-sex desire and the representations of the male body in literature and art operating in the period. It highlights, in particular, the contradictions existing between art and life, and illustrates some of the pitfalls awaiting the artist who sought to inscribe homosexual desire and to discuss issues relating to sexuality in his work.

The uncertainty on the part of homosexual artists as to what degree of sexual openness was acceptable is reflected in Solomon's paintings. They give a fascinating insight into the strategies available to the artists of the period to encode homosexual desire, while simultaneously masking its immediacy and preventing it from being too obvious to the viewer. Strategies of the latter kind include the introduction of a classical or religious context and the utilization of period costume. These have (or are intended to have) the effect of distancing the painting's homoerotic content and giving it a veneer of cultural respectability.

The story of Solomon's and Swinburne's friendship gains additional interest from the differences in social standing and artistic reputation between the two men. Whereas Solomon was a relatively obscure Jew from a middle-class background, Swinburne was a well-known writer with aristocratic connections. In its focus on male homoerotic bonding and friendship betrayed, and the vivid glimpse it gives of the contradictions and hypocrisies of Victorian life, the story has the human interest and dramatic tension of an exciting piece of theatre. It would make an excellent topic for a Gay Sweatshop performance or a television documentary or play.

Equally interesting, in a different way, is Leeks's reading of Ingres's painting of Antiochus and Stratonice in the context of psychoanalytic and feminist theory, and the concept of the female / lesbian gaze which she goes on to develop from it. A feature of Ingres's painting is the figure of the maid, who stands in the doorway on the edge of the work. This figure is, in fact, the focus of Leeks's particular interest, since she bases her reading on Freud's references to the maid in his case study of Dora and on Dora's dream of contemplating Raphael's Sistine Madonna in the Dresden Art Gallery. Interpreting the maid as an image of femininity, Leeks describes her as signifying, in accord with the interpretation of Hélène Cixous, the point of intersection between the bourgeois family unit and the public world. The maid, while necessary to the survival and status of the family, simultaneously acts as a disruptive presence within it, on account of her gender and working-class status. Leeks's argument culminates in the proposal that the maid, far from being a subsidiary figure of little importance, furnishes a viewing position for the female / lesbian spectator. Her interpretation of the painting, and her suggestion that the figure of the maid furnishes a female / lesbian viewing position, make inventive use of psychoanalytic / feminist theory. However, the contrast she draws between the lack of power assigned to the male characters and the power which the females enjoy, on which she bases her theorization of the female / lesbian gaze, is, in my opinion, questionable. It appears to have little foundation in fact. The maid stands alone on the margins of the painting and, as Leeks admits, there is no indication of her giving any reaction to the events that she is viewing (p.56). Leeks's comment that her presence in the picture emphasizes the guilty nature of the secret being revealed and introduces a judgemental aspect into the scene is, in my view, unconvincing. The maid seems to me to be portrayed more as a part of the domestic furniture than as a figure of any significance in her own right. Nor, despite the literary references to her role as Stratonice's confidante to which Leeks draws our attention, is there any indication, in Ingres's delineation of her, of any connection existing between the two women. On the contrary, they strike the viewers as separated from one another, both spatially and by the different social roles of maid and mistress which they occupy. Leeks's observation that 'In this scenario the two females retain their power and together escape the cycle of male control' (p.57) thus appears to be an example of wishful thinking. The maid, in this particular instance, gives no indication of the disruptive potential which theorists such as Cixous assign to her. She is too distanced from her social superiors for us to envisage her having any relationship with them, apart from menial. None the less, despite my criticisms, Leeks's essay is a significant achievement. The ideas she puts forward are important in initiating a lesbian reading of the male-dominated art of the past and in taking a step towards the theorization of the female / lesbian gaze.

In contrast to the first two sections of *Outlooks*, in both of which the essays are well chosen, the concluding section 'Production and consumption' is more problematic, regarding both the choice of essays and, in some cases, their content. Simon Watney's 'The waves of dying friends: *gay men, AIDS and multiple loss*' is, in my view, an unsuitable choice. Watney's indictment of heterosexual society for its lack of concern about the AIDS crisis and the account which he gives of the 'coping mechanisms' utilized by the bereaved are certainly important. However, his essay makes little reference to the production and consumption of lesbian / gay art. When, in the concluding pages, he does move on to discussing the topic of cultural representation, as illustrated by the memorials to victims of AIDS in the USA and London, his choice of examples is limited and his comments a little predictable.

Lewis's and Katrina Rolley's discussion of photographic representation in women's magazines in 'A(ddressing) the dyke: *lesbian looks and lesbians looking*' is another essay which is problematic. Lewis and Rolley fail to substantiate the argument, which forms the core of their essay, that the photographs of women in mainstream magazines such as *Elle* and *Marie Claire* have the effect of creating 'a paradigmatically lesbian viewing position in which women are induced to exercise a gaze that desires the represented woman, not just one that identifies with her' (p.181). The attempt they make to equate the pictures of women playfully assuming a butch appearance in present-day magazines with the adoption of a butch role by lesbians in the 1950s, as discussed by Joan Nestle, is equally unconvincing. Lewis and Rolley ignore the fact that the historical and social context of the two incidents is totally different. Whereas the butch image adopted by the models in women's magazines exemplifies the readiness of mainstream, heterosexual publications to appropriate and cash in on lesbian style, the butch image assumed by 1950s lesbians, as Nestle points out, had explicit political significance, since it acted as a signifier of lesbian identification in a hostile environment. In my view, Lewis's and Rolley's attempt to equate these two different examples of 'butch' is insulting to the lesbians living in the 1950s to whom Nestle refers; it trivializes the courage they showed in challenging accepted images of femininity in a homophobic era.

The two most successful essays in the concluding section are, in fact, the shortest and the least ambitious. Carl F. Stychin in 'Promoting a sexuality: *law and lesbian and gay visual culture in America*' gives a clear, unpretentious account of the relationship between lesbian and gay cultural representation and the state funding of culture in North America. An interesting feature of Stychin's essay is his discussion of the arguments relating to the visual materials utilized to promote safe sex education and the ideological contradictions which they can involve. The homophobic assertion that 'The promotion of homosexuality leads to the spread of AIDS' can result, as he points out, in the conclusion that 'safe sex cannot be gay sex, for the gay man is constructed as disease carrier' (p. 155).

Another essay in this section which merits comment is Sunil Gupta's informative and lively 'Culture wars: race and queer art'. Gupta explores the relationship between the Black Arts Movement and developments which have recently occurred in black and gay politics. She also describes the immense difficulties which black artists encounter in coming out and exploring their lesbian / homosexual identification in their work; she cites as an example the pressure imposed on them by heterosexual peers to support the institution of the black family. Artists whose work she considers include Mumtaz Karimjee, Rotimi Fani-Kayode and Ingrid Pollard.

Outlooks is well presented and includes a number of aptly chosen plates illustrating the works of art under discussion. A problem with these, however, is that they vary considerably in clarity. It is unfortunate that, considering the key role it plays in Leek's reinterpretation of the work and the use she makes of it in the argument she constructs about the lesbian / female viewing position, that the reproduction of Ingres's painting of Stratonice and Antiochus is one of the more blurred. This is due partly to the fact that it is so small. In this case, a larger reproduction would have been preferable.

Outlooks is both visually and intellectually stimulating – and makes a valuable contribution to our understanding of the production and reception of lesbian and gay art. The essays it contains, though varying in perception and cogency of argument, perform a significant service in illustrating the vitality of lesbian / gay art and the critical response to it at the present time.

University of Warwick

Lorelee Kippen

Catherine Waldby, *AIDS and the Body Politic: Biomedicine and Sexual Difference* (London and New York: Routledge, 1996), 192 pp., £12.99 (paperback)

In *AIDS and the Body Politic* Catherine Waldby condenses nearly two decades of writing on AIDS and the body into a study of how biomedicine constructs itself as a master discourse, able to speak for the health of the body politic because it alone can 'visualize' and thus potentially eradicate the disease. This ambitious and timely study documents the ways in which biomedical discourse and its various technologies operate as regulatory mechanisms in the maintenance of a phallocentric status quo, one in which the white, heterosexual 'male' body, despite its actual risk status, serves as the model for the 'healthy' body politic. Building upon Mary Douglas's work in *Purity and Danger*, Waldby argues that where bio-medicine is concerned the ideal body is 'an immunologically perfect body without orifices, whose individuality cannot be compromised, the body which neither takes nor gives infection' (p. 13). Biomedicine's continual, if implicit, reference to this phallic ideal in its construction of 'the normal' and 'the pathological' effectively works to exclude certain bodies from medical representation and thus to seriously impact future directions in AIDS research. To make this point, Waldby rehearses many of the crucial arguments made by AIDS theorists and cultural critics over the last fifteen years or so, as a means of illustrating the persistence of this imaginary phallicized body in the biomedical imagination, and its normativizing force as a metaphor for the ideal social order, one which contains itself against the threat of polluting forces through strategies of medical governance.

Many of the arguments that Waldby elaborates and advances in her study will be familiar to those working not only in AIDS research, but in related fields in the social sciences and humanities. If there is one critical influence that directs Waldby's study more than anything else, it is Judith Butler's work on performativity, and especially this question which she poses in *Gender Trouble*: '[What are] the political stakes in designating as *origin* and *cause* those identity categories that are in fact the effects of institutions, practices, and discourses' (p. xi; emphasis in original, cited in Waldby, p. 143). In *AIDS and the Body Politic*, however, Waldby does not so much expand this theoretical territory as fill it out, using the sophisticated analyses of various critics to illustrate how biomedicine performatively constitutes, transforms and then regulates the bodies that it seeks to heal. It is paradoxically through biomedicine's use of figurative language that the scientific claim of being able to transparently represent the 'real' of the disease and the 'truth' of sex achieves the status of a hegemonic discourse. Waldby explains that '[v]iruses are an ontological threat because they challenge the status of the human, because viral infection involves the colonisation of human genetic identity with viral genetic identity' (p. 1). In her account, this means that the confusion between the two 'identities' renders the metaphorical 'war on AIDS' equivalent to a war on sex and aberrant sexuality, making it increasingly difficult, ontologically and epistemologically, to separate the two.

Despite the fact that critics have long recognized that disease and sexual identity become indissociable in AIDS discourse, the task of analysing and deconstructing the binary oppositions, metaphors and analogies through which biomedicine bases its claim to knowledge and scientific supremacy is potentially infinite in its scope, because, as Waldby notes, 'there really is no end to the metaphoricity of biomedical discourse' (p. 5). Part of the difficulty in attempting such a project arises from the fact that it is necessary to engage with the oppositions, metaphors of sexual difference and identity categories that biomedical discourse sets up, in order to dismantle them. Waldby's analysis does not, in my view, successfully trouble such oppositions and sexual metaphors, even though she acknowledges the problem and in the last chapter gestures towards the possibility of 'queering' the body politic, thus making 'queer' a revisionist category that can undo all categories – especially the 'cleansed' category of the heterosexual male.

Because the sheer scope of Waldby's study prevents her from problematizing identity categories such as 'woman', other subcategories (such as 'lesbian') and other crucial components of individual identity, such as race, class, ethnicity, nationality and gender, are also necessarily subsumed by the research parameters. Further, by largely adhering to the categories that biomedicine uses to produce its imaginary anatomies and morphologies, a certain amount of theoretical sophistication is sacrificed for the more immediate goals of political efficacy and field coverage. Waldby's decision to forgo a detailed analysis of identity categories can be partially attributed to the fact that '[f]or purposes of establishing HIV transmission all women are deemed to be heterosexual, irrespective of their self-identification' (p. 137). Yet, despite Waldby's excellent discussion of the ways in which the classification of sexuality is carried out by the technology of the HIV test, whereby certain categories of sexual difference are subsumed by other categories that are considered to be more coherent in terms of judging risk, this still does not explain why those problematic categories are, for the most part, left intact. This omission or decision, as it were, seems to be more a function of the theory itself than a failing on the part of the author. The notion of democratic futurity which haunts the present project and leads to an evacuation of the social content in those identity categories discussed, negatively works, in this case, to erase the specificity of bodies, sexual practice and their identifications within a larger national economy whose impulse is to annex difference by promoting a sense of the body politic as '*not* community' (Cindy Patton, *Fatal Advice*, p. 19). It is perhaps for this reason alone that Waldby's invocation of 'queer' at the end of the book seems the least convincing of her many astute arguments, at least in terms of how it may be possible to politically short-circuit the performative circle that biomedicine both engenders and sustains.

Waldby's decision not to pursue, in great detail, the issue of categorical 'cleanliness' or 'purity' in biomedical discourse does not in any way detract from the important contribution this book makes to the understanding of biomedicine as a powerful force in the era of an AIDS epidemic. Especially crucial, I think, are the ways in which *AIDS and the Body Politic* enables an understanding of the means by which bodies are themselves to be conceived as the movement of boundary, in much the same way that Judith Butler noted with some exasperation in *Bodies That Matter*. As Waldby trenchantly observes, biomedicine's metaphorical production of sexual difference and historically specific notions of HIV/ AIDS takes place through a range of scale, from the micro-anatomic level of virology and genetic identity to the macro-anatomical level of epidemiology and the body politic. Analysing the discursive mechanisms by which the metaphysics of disease and sexual identity become laminated or projected on to each other in a phenomenological register created by the latest visualizing technologies, Waldby identifies how biomedicine introjects (incorporates and then projects) 'outside' norms and ideals on to the interior of the body, and vice versa. Waldby also shows how contagion and abjection come to interline each other within a discursive matrix that perpetually (con)fuses the two concepts, whereby the obliteration of the disease equates to the erasure of the abject bodies it associates with the disease. The scope of the study works well, in this sense, to trace the outlines of micro- and macro-scoping modalities of representation used in biomedical discourse and to discern the wider practices that enable biomedicine to create what Waldby calls the 'primal scene of immunology'. As Waldby succinctly sums it up in her chapter by the same name,

> it [biomedicine] first miniaturises the social scene it wishes to examine, and so maps itself onto the interpretative strategies of the laboratory, which read cultural practices into the behavior of microbial life. It then moves in quick succession through the clinical gaze,

which concerns itself with the relationship between the patient's symptoms and their invisible bodily interior, to the epidemiological gaze, which pictures the 'act of transmission' for 'biomedicine'.

(p. 80)

In this manner, the 'act of transmission' – homosexual anal sex – is conceived as the primal scene of immunology and AIDS. Given this breathtaking analysis, it seems less than generous to have wanted one thing more: an examination of the ways in which this 'primal scene' also works to suture over biomedicine's own conceptual historicity and the historicity of 'other' sexually transmitted diseases. I would be interested in knowing, moreover, whether, in this process of introjection that constitutes bio-medicine's 'primal scene', such a thing as 'immunological memory' still exists. This 'queer' form of memory which was elaborated during the 1960s may just provide the missing link to understanding how these various bodies function as screen memories that biomedicine alone is able to produce and to sustain.

University of Calgary

Martin McQuillan

Andrew Gibson, *Towards a Postmodern Theory of Narrative* (Edinburgh: Edinburgh University Press, 1996), viii + 301 pp., £15.95 (paperback)

Judith Roof, *Come As You Are: Sexuality and Narrative* (New York: Columbia University Press, 1996), xxxvi + 211 pp., £13.50 (paperback)

Hans Kellner has said that narrative, 'for the post-structuralist, [is] guilty until proven innocent.'[1] These two books hold different opinions with regard to narrative's guilt. For Roof, narrative is far from innocent, while for Gibson (if a monograph produced in Edinburgh can be forgiven a small Scottishism), the case against narrative is 'not-proven'. Both of these timely works are a response to the neo-structuralist narratology of the 1980s. After Barthes's call for a thinking about 'structuration' rather than structure in *S/Z*, a second generation of revisionist narratologists (from Peter Brooks and Mieke Bal to Ross Chambers and Seymour Chatman) sought to move beyond the allegiance to formalism which had character-ized the study of narrative. This work combined the model of narrative production inherited from structuralism with the insights afforded by the theoretical diaspora of the 1970s and 1980s, perhaps most successfully combining narratology's interest in the construction of subjectivity with the concerns of psychoanalysis and/or feminist theory. One might think here of texts such as Leo Bersani's *A Future for Astyanax*, Peter Brooks's *Reading for the Plot*, Teresa de Lauretis's essay 'Desire in narrative', or Mary Ann Doane's *The Desire to Desire*. Inventive and insightful as this work was, it did little to question the actual model of narrative which came from the texts of the mid-1960s. Post-narratology has made advances but has failed to adequately rewrite a model of narrative which, to quote Barbara Herrnstein Smith's appeal in 1981, is:

> [N]ot only empirically questionable and logically frail but also methodologically distracting, preventing us from formulating the problems of narrative theory in ways that would permit us to explore them more fruitfully in connection with whatever else we know about language, behaviour and culture.[2]

In other words, post-narratology could be said to be not 'post' enough.

Andrew Gibson's *Towards a Postmodern Theory of Narrative* is a long awaited response to Smith. It proposes a model of narrative constructed in light of all that is known about postmodern culture. Gibson offers a rigorous critique of the existing field of narrative theory by examining the metaphorical content of narrative tropologies. Following Bachelard in *The Psychoanalysis of Fire*, Gibson asks whether, 'for all the subtleties of our various poststructuralisms, we have yet thought quite hard enough about the critical imaginary, particularly in the case of narratology' (p.3). He suggests that the 'narratological imaginary has been haunted . . . by dreams of the geometric' (p.3).

This reading of narrative theory as a methodology determined by metaphors for the centre is soundly argued and promises much. However, the problem for post-narratology has always been: where does one go from here? How is narrative to be released from its description? Gibson suggests the geometric inscription of narrative means that 'our thought about narrative has never escaped from metaphysics' (p.20). Therefore, a postmodern theory of narrative must attempt to think narrative beyond the constraints of the metaphysical because the transgressions of postmodernism reject the metaphysics of 'unitary space' (p.30). As a consequence of postmodernism, argues Gibson, 'we are ceasing to inhabit that space, and it can no longer be that of our thought' (p.30). This is encouraging. Just as Cixous imagines 'another thinking as yet not thinkable', and Derrida looks towards 'a science of science which would no longer have the form of logic', and Foucault hoped for 'a politics not yet in existence', so we must imagine a narrative that would no longer have the form of narrative. Herein lies the problem. As Ricoeur's monumental, but seldom read *Time and Narrative* demonstrates, 'time becomes human time to the extent that it is organised after the manner of a narrative; narrative, in turn, is meaningful to the extent that it portrays the features of temporal experience.'[3] In other words, Ricoeur argues, 'there can be no thought about time without narrated time.' Conversely, there can be no thought about narrative without time and, as Derrida says in 'Ousia et Gramme':

> The concept of time belongs entirely to metaphysics and it designates the domination of presence.
> . . . if something connected with time but which is not itself time needs to be thought of outside the determination of Being as presence, we are no longer dealing with anything which could be called *time*.[4]

This means that a narrative thought of from outside the forms of narrative production would no longer be a narrative. Furthermore, the work that these forms do is metaphysical. For example, one might think of the figure of closure as an attempt to determine presence. The fact that closure is strictly impossible is because presence is merely an illusion of the self-identifying subject.

This situation presents Gibson's theory of transgressive postmodern narrative with conceptual difficulties which he finds hard to negotiate satisfactorily. On the one hand, he offers a series of wide-eyed readings of postmodern texts (from Godard to Greenaway and Kerouac to Kubric) which attempt to demonstrate the multiple spaces imagined by postmodernism. On the other hand, Gibson's application of postmodern theory adopts an *à la carte* strategy in an attempt to convince the reader of postmodernism's pluralist credentials. A chapter on deconstruction is followed by one on dialogics. A discussion of postmodern monstrosity is followed by an unconvincing reading of interactive-virtual fictions. This diversity can be suggestive but more often seems like a reproduction of postmodern eclecticism. As such, Gibson's argument does not wriggle free of metaphysics but rather demonstrates how, at every turn, the metaphysical reinscribes itself within a larger system of narrative thought. *Towards a Postmodern Theory of Narrative* is essential reading for anyone working within the discipline of narrative theory. It asks all the correct questions and is informed by detailed scholarship. However, anyone awaiting the return of narrative theory, from the last outpost of structuralism to an active participant in the understanding of the world provided by critical theory, will be left wanting.

Judith Roof's *Come As You Are: Sexuality and Narrative* is a less ambitious book. Indeed, it could even be said to be a somewhat old-fashioned book. It has more in common with the craving for narrative desire, which characterized narrative theory in the 1980s, than it does with Gibson's innovatory redefinition of narrative. However, Roof arguably fulfils Gibson's project of analysing the white mythologies of narrative theory in a more lucid and coherent way. Roof wishes to investigate how ideas of narrative and sexuality inform one another and suggests that 'narrative and sexuality somehow jointly engender and reproduce a hetero-sexual ideology' (p. xiv). The narratological imaginary, suggests Roof, is informed by dreams of heterosexism: 'our very understanding of narrative as a primary means to sense and satisfaction depends upon a metaphori-cally heterosexual dynamic within a reproductive aegis' (p. xxii). This inescapable inscription leads Roof to the startling aporia, 'to have sexuality is to have narrative; to have narrative is to have sexuality' (p. xxiv). Roof asks, if thinking outside of the whole system of Western logomachy is impossible (or at least defining narrative without narrative, or determining narrative's ideologies without reiterating them is impossible), then what does narrative inscription mean for homosexuality?

On the one hand, this book can be read as another account of the construction of lesbian identity. Roof examines the narrative paradigm of beginning, middle and end to suggest that the middle is 'the realm where the perverse and the normal intermingle and where the lesbian becomes visible' (p. xxxiv), the point being that the beginning and the end reclaim the transgressive into a normative order. On the other hand, this queer turn in narrative theory offers a challenge to the assumptions of narratology which disturbs, illuminates and transforms. Roof's readings of texts such as *Roseanne, Star Trek: The Next Generation*, Djuna Barnes's *Nightwood* and Colette's 'The secret woman' are thorough and informative if unsurprising. However, Roof's invaluable contribution to the debate (whither narra-tology?) comes in her outstanding analysis of Todorov, Greimas and Barthes in Chapter 2. She argues that 'structuralist analyses of narrative bring to light how covert metaphors of (re)production dependent upon binaries inflect our understanding of narrative' (p. 59). In many respects Roof's conclusion is a side issue. Rather, it is the sensitivity of her reading of previously untouchable texts which is arresting. Her discussion uncovers the long forgotten ontological status of key theoretical conceptions which have become mere operators and techniques within textual analysis. Roof offers a critique of such alleged post-structuralisms as the tropes of economy, transfer, exchange, supplement and contract. Gibson attempts to open up the debate by introducing new voices to narrative theory (his argument appropriates Alain Badiou, Michel Serres, Nathalie Sarraute, Gianni Vattimo and Clément Rosset) without necessarily advancing the argument. Roof's meticulous rereading, on the other hand, encourages the reader in the belief that post-narratology has made a too quick dismissal of these structuralist texts. This may not have been Roof's design but by the logic of her own argument a certain return to structuralism may be a necessary way forward: 'by defining what we seem to take for granted, we might find a way to begin to think in a radically different way' (p. 187).

However, Roof's argument – subtle and flexible though it may be – contains a problem. Her reading of structuralism would seem to imply that the heterosexual metaphor of the binary is characteristic of any available theory of language. She suggests that 'to combat heteroideology would mean thinking outside the system altogether, changing conceptions of time, cause and effect, and knowledge' (p. 186). If her reading of the heterosexual imaginary of narrative theory is just another name for binary logocentrism, then this is not just a problem of heterosexuality. It is a problem for heterosexuality as well and Roof seems to be in danger of tripping over her metaphors as her argument chases after something that we know already and have known at least since structuralism. This is not to suggest that Roof is unaware of this (the continual punning through-out the book suggests a playful self-knowledge as a means of confronting this aporia). Rather, the text seems to be a prisoner of its own argument as it ultimately finds itself recontained by the system it attempted to subvert in the first instance.

While *Come As You Are* questions narrative theory, it is also an application of narrative tropologies to queer theory. In truth, narrative has been free of narrative theory for some time. Questions of narrative can be identified as performing a crucial role in key aspects of theoretical production: for example, in Foucauldian discourse analysis, the decon-structive readings of Paul de Man and J Hillis Miller, the construction of identity in postcolonial discourse, and as a locus within the work of Lyotard and Jameson. Perhaps the challenge, which both these texts in their different ways point towards, is not the writing of a post-structuralist narratology but rather the writing of a narrative theory that does not throw up a prohibition between advancement and the structuralist heritage which informs it. As Ruqaiya Hasan comments:

> As in the past, so in the present, at issue is the identity of structuralism; as in the past, so in the present, the 'post-ness' of post-structuralism is but an affix to structuralism, almost as if the very structure of the word iconically announced the impossibility of a clear break.[5]

The problem may be that narrative theory will be better served when it realizes that a break with the past is not the stake for a more cognitively powerful model of narrative. Rather, that the episteme of narrative is a philosophical concept connected to a problem which can only be isolated and understood as a solution emerges. Narrative is the name given to a problem which is larger than its theoretical operation allows it to describe.

As long as this problem continues to be understood as narrative there can be no question of moving beyond narrative; 'post-ness' is not the issue. The current model of narrative may be both metaphysically and hetero-sexually inscribed but this is because its problems are the problems of the signifier. Narrative is suggestive in its absence. As Roof says, 'its metonymical slide through other signifiers points to a lack it stands in for and never fills' (p. 48). This is the logic of the aporia; it is also the logic of narrative. Narrative is, to quote Roof, 'the logic that can never be found but can always be narrated' (p. 48).

Staffordshire University

Notes

1 Hans Kellner, 'Narrativity in history: post-structuralism and since', *History and Theory* 26 (1987), p. 9.
2 Barbara Herrnstein Smith, 'Narrative versions, narrative theories', in W. J. T. Mitchell (ed.) *On Narrative* (Chicago: Chicago University Press, 1981), p. 227.
3 Paul Ricoeur, *Time and Narrative* (vols 1, 2, 3), trans K. McLaughlin and D. Pellauer (London: University of Chicago Press, 1984, 1985, 1988). This quote is from Vol. 1, p. 3, following quote Vol. 3, p. 241.
4 Jacques Derrida, '*Ousia* et *Gramme*: note sur une note de *Sein Und Zeit*', quoted in David Wood, *The Deconstruction of Time* (New Jersey: Humanities Press International, 1989), p. 2.
5 Ruqaiya Hasan, 'Directions from structuralism', in Nigel Fabb *et al.* (eds) *The Linguistics of Writing: Arguments Between Language and Literature* (Manchester: Manchester University Press, 1987), p. 104.

Stefan Herbrechter

D ésormais . . . à demeure, or 'radical' hospitality

. . . l'impossibilité de demeurer dans l'indécidable . . .

Jacques Derrida, 'Demeure: fiction et témoignage', in *Passions de la littérature: Avec Jacques Derrida* sous la direction de Michel Lisse (Paris: Galilée) (Philosophie en effet), 1996), FF 210.

Jacques Derrida, *Adieu: à Emmanuel Lévinas* (Paris: Galilée) (INCISES), 1996), FF 168.

Jacques Derrida, *Cosmopolites de tous les pays, encore un effort!* (Paris: Galilée) (INCISES), 1997), FF 66.

D ésormais . . . à demeure – the untranslatability of this title begs translation, for it is always the untranslatable that calls for translation the most urgently. The importance, however, lies between this 'untranslatable' and its (impossible) translation, within this temporary space of interlinear 'trans*lation*' – but would this still be translation or already something else, other than, or the other *of* translation? – that calls for translation before any 'original'. In this sense, Jacques Derrida's entire work is an elaboration of a certain concept of translation, of translation as an ethical imperative or an unconditional law. And it is also in this sense that Derrida's work has, in its more recent aspects, (re)joined the writings of Emmanuel Lévinas.

It would be unjust to say that Lévinas's recent death alone has produced this intensified interest in his writings. Derrida has always been a very careful *and* 'sympathetic' reader of Lévinas.[1] *Adieu*, however, is at once the most comprehensive and critical reading of Lévinas's entire work. Its two parts – 'Adieu', a twenty-five-page long oration pronounced at Lévinas's funeral (27 December 1995)[2] and 'Le Mot d'accueil', a seminar held during a two-day conference (*Hommage à Emmanuel Lévinas*) at the Sorbonne in December 1996 – contain some of the most beautiful and moving passages ever written by Derrida. The prevalent tone is one of grave sincerity and friendship: 'Depuis longtemps, si longtemps, je redoutais d'avoir à dire *Adieu* à Emmanuel Lévinas' (*Adieu*, 11/1). But this *adieu*, or rather '*à-dieu*' in Lévinas's terms, is not so much the end of being or a finality, but – and this is the central theme of all three of Derrida's writings reviewed here – the condition for any hospitality and hence an ethics of alterity. 'The *à-dieu* greets [*salue*] the other beyond [*au-delà*] being' (*Adieu*, 27/10).

The question of dwelling (*demeure*) and of receiving the other is asked most urgently in Lévinas's *Totality and Infinity* which is being reread by Derrida as an 'immense treatise on hospitality' (*Adieu*, 49). The problematic that preoccupies Derrida's texts is the inevitable violence involved in dwelling and thus also in hospitality. The French text here benefits from another untranslatable near homonymy: '*la violence de l'hôte* [host and guest] / l'autre.'[3] To receive the other '*chez soi*' in one's home – what is usually referred to as hospitality – is based on the usurpation of a place on which also any notion of ipseity (identity), propriety and politics must rely. Lévinas instead proposes to think hospitality not as a secondary element that follows from any territorial claim but as an 'opening' that occurs before any dwelling takes place or indeed only comes to 'justify' dwelling as the possibility to receive – a radical notion of hospitality (*hospitalité/accueil*), or the hospitality *of* the other as host.

However, here also lies an immense problem which arises out of the relation between an 'ethics of (radical) hospitality' (or indeed ethics *as* hospitality) and the jurisdiction and politics of hospitality. Derrida refers to Kant's idea of 'cosmopolitan right' in view of universal and eternal peace which he discusses in more detail in his *Cosmopolites de tous les pays, encore un effort!* The practicability of such a radical ethics of/as hospitality in the current (European) political context is the central concern of this pamphlet-like, very short and openly political piece of writing, which represents a speech read (in absence) at the first convention of the *'villes-refuges'* (towns of asylum) (initiated by the International Parliament of Writers, of which Derrida is a vice-president which was held at the Council of Europe in Strasbourg in March 1996.

In *Cosmopolites...* Derrida argues for a new status of the town with regard to international law, by reinventing the ancient and medieval institution of the *'ville franche'* as a town of asylum which would serve as an implementation of the radical hospitality discussed above:

> Whether it be the stranger in general, the immigrant, the exile, the refugee, the deportee, the stateless, the displaced person (all categories to be carefully distinguished), we invite these new towns of asylum to bend the politics of the State, to transform and refound the modalities of the city's belonging to the State, for example within a Europe that is in the making or within the structures of international law which are still dominated by the rule of the sovereign State, a rule which is intangible or supposed to be so, but also a rule which is becoming increasingly precarious and problematic.
>
> (*Cosmopolites*, p. 14)

The suggested new 'cosmopolitics' (*cosmopolitique*) of the other town – or the town of the other – could not come at a better time, namely when the 'new' Europe, while opening its 'internal' frontiers, increasingly resembles not necessarily an economic but a sociopolitical fortress, and is careful to restrict 'non-European' (im)migration by law. It also comes at a time when hospitality becomes a 'crime'[4] and the immigrant the prime scapegoat for the current economic crisis.[5]

The ethics of (*archi-*)hospitality on which a new cosmopolitics relies reveals a struggle between the absolute and unconditional law of hospitality before any being – which alone makes any being as dwelling possible – and its slow and painful, political and juridical implementation through international law, which can only ever be a limitation of the Law. This singular 'universalism' of the always preceding other experienced in the face-to-face with the other (human), which is at the root of the ethics of alterity as hospitality, must be seen as an attempt to resist another universalism, a neocolonial, neo-imperial process described by Derrida as *'mondialatinisation'*.[6]

There is no alternative to hospitality, the other always preceding, as manifested in the face-to-face. In this sense even hostility towards the other has already to be seen within the context of a hospitality. This always pre-ceding, radical and absolute hospitality is the condition for an 'interruption of (one)self' (*interruption de soi*): 'hospitality, is this not an interruption of (one)self (*soi*)?' (*Adieu*, 6). The subject is a hostage (*(h)ôtage*) of this dwelling/remaining without dwelling (*demeurer sans demeure*), in which 'the home (*le chez-soi*) of the dwelling place (*demeure*) does not signify the closure but the place of Desire towards the transcendence of the Other' (*Adieu*, 63).

This dwelling place is and has been, for Lévinas and Derrida, language, and French in particular.[7] But this language is 'inhabited' by the other: 'My language, the only one I hear myself speak in (*m'entende parler*) and in which I know how to speak (*m'entende à parler*), it is the language of the other.'[8] The irreducible monolingualism of the other is nothing else than this original law of radical hospitality, or 'the Law as Language', of the language that is never one's own. The Heideggerian 'house of language' (*Haus der Sprache*) is an impossible dwelling place, and this impossible is not a dwelling place. What remains is testimony, testimony of this impossibility to dwell, and of its 'passion' (*pathos* in all its meanings).

This question of testifying is also the question of the 'third' (*tiers*) and the question of the question, that is the precondition of any philosophy or thinking. Derrida's opening essay to *Passions de la littérature*, 'Demeure: fiction et témoignage', investigates the relation between the testimony as an always autobiographical and 'miraculous' appeal towards belief, and literature as passion, or the passion *of* literature. Instead of rekindling the old dispute between those who claim Derrida as a 'philosopher' and those who see him as a 'literary critic', 'Demeure' should make clear that literature functions as the place (*demeure*) of the third, of testimony, and thus speaks of the possibility of justice. It is the interruption of the face-to-face by the third which gives rise to language and which constitutes the 'birth of the question' (*Adieu*, 63). Testifying to the im/possibility of dwelling remains henceforth (*desormais*) the horizon of hospitality, from now on and 'permanently' (*à demeure*). Lévinasian ethics has thus been decisively 'supplemented' by a deconstructive twist of (cosmo)politics:

> The accomplishment of an effective possibility of ethics, is this already a politics? Which politics?
>
> (*Adieu*, 183)

University of Wales, College of Cardiff

Notes

1 Cf. in particular 'Violence and metaphysics: an essay on the thought of Emmanuel Lévinas', in *Writing and Difference*, trans. Alan Bass (Chicago: University of Chicago Press, 1978); and 'At this very moment in this work here I am', in *Re-Reading Levinas*, ed. Robert Bernasconi and Simon Critchley (London: Routledge, 1990).

2 Translated as 'Adieu' by Pascale-Anne Brault and Michael Naas in *Critical Inquiry* 23 (Autumn 1996): 1–10 (in the following, the first page number given in the text refers to the texts in French, while the second, wherever appropriate, refers to this translation; other translations are all mine).

3 Cf. Émile Benveniste on the etymology and meaning of 'hospitality' in *Le Vocabulaire des institutions indo-européennes*, Vol. I (Paris: Minuit, 1969), pp. 87–101.

4 Derrida refers to the '*délit d'hospitalité*', a law project (*loi Toubon*) aimed at stiffening the '*loi Pasqua*', and which makes granting hospitality to 'illegal' immigrants a criminal offence. Cf. also the recently introduced, controversial '*loi Debré*'.

5 For a historical analysis of the decline of (French) hospitality in a specific Franco-Maghrebine context see Tahar Ben Jelloun, *Hospitalité française* (Paris: Seuil (L'Histoire immédiate), 1984).

6 Cf. 'Foi et savoir: les deux sources de la "religion" aux limites de la simple raison', in *La Religion: Séminaire de Capri sous la direction de Jacques Derrida et Gianni Vattimo* (Paris: Seuil, 1996). See in particular pp. 21 and 58: 'the mondialatinisation (this strange alliance between Christianity as experience of the death of God and tele-techno-scientific capitalism) . . . which becomes henceforth (*desormais*) Europeo-Anglo-American in its idiom.'

7 'I am monolingual. My monolingualism remains (*demeure*) and I call it my dwelling place (*demeure*) . . . I remain in it and I inhabit it. It inhabits me.' Derrida, *Le Monolinguisme de l'autre* (Paris: Galilée (ICISES), 1996), p. 13; see also my forthcoming review '(N)ever at home in language' (*OLR*, autumn 1997).

8 Ibid., p. 47

Abstracts and keywords

Vincent Quinn and Mary Peace
Luxurious Sexualities

This article traces the evolution of modern histories of eighteenth-century theories of luxury and of sexuality; it argues that although these fields are crucially related, few commentators have linked them in an effective manner. It gives brief accounts of work by John Sekora and Christopher Berry, both of whom explore luxury in terms of socio-economic theories derived partly from J. G. A. Pocock. The article argues that these economic theories pay insufficient attention to the sexualized nature of eighteenth-century writings on luxury – in particular, they shy away from analysis of effeminacy even though this term is frequently encountered in enlightenment attacks on excessive economic consumption. Then there is an outline of recent work about gender and sexuality in the eighteenth century; this mentions Alan Bray, G. S. Rousseau, Randolph Trumbach, and others. This section traces the contributions that these writers have made to histories of effeminacy and homosexuality, but notes that they are less interested than they might be in luxury and the body politic. The article also argues that historians of luxury and sexuality tend to ignore visual aspects of eighteenth-century culture, although recent texts by Terry Castle and Kristina Straub use theories of the gaze to explore enlightenment constructions of gender. The article then describes a series of papers from *Luxurious Sexualities: Effeminacy, Consumption and the Body Politic in Eighteenth-Century Representation*, a multi-disciplinary conference featuring scholars working on luxury, masculinity, the body, sexuality, and economic discourse in the eighteenth-century. The writers discussed are: Cath Sharrock (writing on masturbation and sodomy), Philip Carter (on effeminacy and economic theories of luxury), Miles Ogborn (on visual aspects of Macaroni culture in Vauxhall Gardens), Robert Jones (on

Textual Practice 11(3), 1997, 597–601   © 1997 Routledge 0950–236X

effeminacy and military encampments), Sue Wiseman (on representations of the breast as both luxurious and virtuous), Marcia Pointon (on jewellery in representations of Queen Charlotte), and Brian Young (on Gibbon and sex).

Keywords
luxury; effeminacy; consumption; the body politic; eighteenth century

Philip Carter
An 'effeminate' or 'efficient' nation? Masculinity and eighteenth-century social documentary

This article examines the theme of masculinity within eighteenth-century 'documentaries' on national character. It is well known that civic writers believed luxury was undermining the social fabric while more 'progressive' commentators questioned this jeremiad assessment. Typically, this debate has been considered in relation to eighteenth-century political or social theory. Rather less has been said about the centrality of gender, and in particular masculinity, in discussions on the national condition. Attention is paid, first, to pessimistic commentaries which described the rise of the 'effeminate' nation. Effeminacy emerges as a complex phenomenon with meanings beyond those suggested by a recent, often sexually reductionist, historiography. Effeminacy was a subject of equal interest to progressive writers who, while not denying its existence, redefined its status from an absolute state to a state of mind. This debate had implications for conceptions of the antithesis of effeminacy, masculinity, which the article moves on to examine. Within social documentary and conduct literature, civic and enlightened writers promoted two competing, though ideally compatible, discourses of 'classical' and 'refined' manliness. The article concludes with some thoughts on the validity of masculinity as a subject for historical enquiry. Traditionally, the enlightenment is said to have witnessed the establishment of incommensurate categories of male and female, the latter being defined in gendered terms. The legacy of this division is apparent in modern studies which treat 'gender' as synonymous with 'women', and the resistance, in some quarters, to the study of masculinity in past societies. However, an examination of social documentary reveals that writers were aware of the notion of male as gendered, not least in terms of their appreciation of the vulnerability of male identities and their relative proximity to the state of effeminacy.

Keywords

masculinity; effeminacy; luxury; enlightenment; Brown, John 'Estimate'; Hume, David

Miles Ogborn
Locating the Macaroni: luxury, sexuality and vision in Vauxhall Gardens

This article interprets the connections and tensions between luxurious consumption, masculinity and the visual in the 1770s. It does so by providing a reading of a fracas in London's Vauxhall Gardens involving a parson, an actress and three fashionable men – subsequently identified as 'Macaronis' – who had stared at her and fought with him. The interpretation provided here adds to previous interpretations of this incident by understanding the problems of men looking at women through two contexts, or locations, which reveal the importance of commodity consumption to these relationships between sexuality and vision. The first context shows the Macaronis – flamboyantly fashionable and heavily satirized men – to be figures which operated within 'the world of goods' as signs of luxurious consumption and its dangers. The second context, that of Vauxhall Gardens itself, shows this landscape – the site of the affray - to have been structured by the conjoint forces of commodification and illusion. Within this wonderland of consumption the attractions were visual ones, and they often offered the pleasures of deceived vision. The Macaronis disrupted the pleasurable conventions of these gazes and, in the process, showed themselves to be dangerous illusions and illegitimate narcissists who revealed the tensions upon which the Gardens and the wider landscape of commodified consumption were based.

Keywords

commodification; luxury; Macaroni; masculinity; Vauxhall Gardens; vision

Robert W. Jones
Notes on *The Camp*: women, effeminacy and the military in late eighteenth-century literature

During the eighteenth century the army was often derided as effeminate or luxuriant. The motivation for this charge frequently came from within the discourse of civic humanism whose adherents regarded the existence of a standing army as the sign of a degenerate and corrupt culture. The unseemly potential of the military went, however, far beyond the political claims of those imbued with civic discourse. The army could also appear suspect when considered with reference to the relationship between male display and masculine propriety envisioned by the splendid uniforms and luxurious lifestyles enjoyed by many officers. For many commentators the officer class seemed obsessed with the trappings of their profession and more concerned with the extent of their appeal to the ladies than with the rigors of campaigning. Indeed one of the most common attacks on the eighteenth-century military was the assertion that officers had debased the dignity of their regimentals in order to solicit the attentions of women. The apparent transformation of the army into a spectacle to be enjoyed by an inquisitive and sexually curious female gaze further enforced the sense in which the army could be condemned as dissolute or corrupt. This concern was often underlined by a sense that the army was the antithesis of the well-ordered family. Notoriously, these camps were transformed into fashionable destinations for society ladies. The presence of these women at military bases served to enforce the idea that the army of late Georgian England was sunk into a vain effeminacy, and was therefore unable to rouse itself at the hour of the kingdom's need. This article seeks to explore these connections through an examination of the literature which represented military encampments during the invasion scare of 1778–79. Richard Brinsley Sheridan's afterpiece *The Camp* and the anonymous novel *The Coxheath Camp* provide the main focus for this investigation.

Keywords
effeminacy; luxury; military camps; gender identity; femininity; sensibility

Sue Wiseman
From the luxurious breast to the virtuous breast: the body politic transformed

This article argues that the pleasure of the enlightenment symbol of the breast as an icon of political liberty internalized an earlier set of relations in which the breast was associated with luxury and pleasure. It traces the genealogy of this transformation and, in doing so, argues that although some critics (Nancy Armstrong) have heavily emphasized the importance of the domestic in late eighteenth-century fictions there is also a strong case for recognizing a shifting place of femininity in political iconography. Critics, including Mary Jacobus, Ruth Perry, Felicity Nussbaum and Marina Warner, have written illuminatingly on the place of the breast in the seventeenth and eighteenth centuries, and this article examines more specifically the breast's associations with luxury and virtue in political iconography.

Marcia Pointon
Intriguing jewellery: royal bodies and luxurious consumption

Jewels worn about the body have traditionally constituted the most spectacular way of displaying extraordinary wealth while simultaneously disguising capital as artistry. Confronted with someone wearing a diamond *parure*, notions of aesthetic value fuse with speculations of financial worth. Jewellery signifies, however, in much more complex ways than this simple equation might suggest. Jewels raise issues of the Law, for court societies in Europe have, since earliest times, depended upon gifts of valuable jewellery as the medium of national and international diplomacy. Whereas money passing hands is understood to be a tithe, a levy, or a bribe, jewellery made up of precious stones and metals compresses into one object that can be displayed upon an individual body, marks of wealth, of esteem and of symbolic possession. This article explores the significance of jewellery as worn by Queen Charlotte and examines the rhetorical formations that permitted the boundaries between excess and legitimate ostentation, and between femininity and sexuality, to be negotiated. The period of the 1780s, marked by the diamond necklace affair at the court of Marie Antoinette, was ostensibly one of wholesome familial calm at the English court. This paper explores the ways in which Queen Charlotte indulged her love of precious stones and jewellery, while avoiding the fate of her French counterpart.

Brian W. Young
Gibbon and sex

This article analyses the question of sex as this informs the argument of Gibbon's *The Decline and Fall of the Roman Empire*. It deliberately eschews the possibility of drawing an inferential approach regarding any putative reading of Gibbon's own sexuality from a study of this text. The intimate connection between luxury and sexuality in the work is examined, and the major theme of pagan virtue activating a creative luxury which is overwhelmed by the sterilities of Christian virtue is followed through in an examination of the opening volumes.

Although himself a childless bachelor, Gibbon berated celibacy and other 'monkish virtues'. Sex provided a healthy dynamic to societies which the pursuit of celibacy denied, and this was a means of attack which

Gibbon took up when writing about the early Church. His critique of asceticism derived from an ambivalence towards luxury, and from an obvious distaste for Christian conceptions of virtue. Alongside his critique of the Church is a strongly developed denunciation of the 'effeminate luxury of Oriental despotism'. He laments the rise of the eunuchs and their insidious influence on the life of the court. Allied to this is an interesting discussion of silk, the negative impact of which is traced through the political geography of which Gibbon was a supreme master.

Gibbon's interest in sexuality went well beyond the usual remit of his contemporaries in investigating history, and this places him at an interesting distance from the exponents of the supremely masculinist assumptions of 'civic humanism'. Gibbon was not a conventional moralist and, in discussing issues that were usually unexplored, he found a means of undermining the pieties of specifically Christian notions of the past. This was something of which later readers of *The Decline and Fall*, such as Thomas Bowdler and Macaulay, were well aware.

Keywords
Gibbon; historiography; sexuality; luxury; Orientalism; Augustanism

Notes for contributors

Authors should submit two complete copies of their paper, in English, to Alan Sinfield, *Textual Practice*, Arts Building, University of Sussex, Falmer, Brighton BN1 9QN. It will be assumed that authors will keep a copy. Submission of a paper to *Textual Practice* will be taken to imply that it presents original, unpublished work not under consideration for publication elsewhere. In order to ensure both the widest possible distribution and the most secure protection for the articles in *TP*, contributors will be asked to assign copyright to the journal. This will not restrict contributors' republication of their own work, after twelve months have elapsed.

The manuscript

Submissions should be typed in double spacing on one side only of the paper, preferably A4 size, with a 4cm margin on the left-hand side. Articles should normally be of between 7000 and 8000 words in length. Tables should not be inserted in the pages of the manuscript but should be on separate sheets. The desired position in the text for each table should be indicated in the margin of the manuscript.

Photographs

Photographs should be in high-contrast black-and-white glossy prints. Permission to reproduce them must be obtained by authors before submission, and any acknowledgements should be included in the captions.

References

These should be numbered consecutively in the text, thus: 'According to a recent theory,[4] . . .', and collected at the end of the paper in the following styles, for journals and books respectively:
John Hartley and John Fiske, 'Myth-representations: a cultural reading of *News at Ten*', *Communication Studies Bulletin*, 4 (1977), pp. 12–33.
Christopher Norris, *The Deconstructive Turn* (London and New York: Methuen, 1983).

Proofs

Page proofs will be sent for correction to the first-named author, unless otherwise requested. The difficulty and expense involved in making amendments at the page proof stage make it essential for authors to prepare their typescripts carefully: any alterations to the original text are strongly discouraged. Our aim is rapid publication: this will be helped if authors provide good copy, following the above instructions, and return their page proofs as quickly as possible.

Offprints

Twenty-five offprints will be supplied free of charge.

Index

Volume 11

Articles

Reviews

For Product Safety Concerns and Information please contact our EU
representative GPSR@taylorandfrancis.com
Taylor & Francis Verlag GmbH, Kaufingerstraße 24, 80331 München, Germany

www.ingramcontent.com/pod-product-compliance
Lightning Source LLC
Chambersburg PA
CBHW071408100726
47908CB00004B/1098